TOKYO SEVEN ROSES

VOLUME I

Anthem Press
An imprint of Wimbledon Publishing Company
www.anthempress.com

This edition first published in UK and USA 2013
by ANTHEM PRESS
75–76 Blackfriars Road, London SE1 8HA, UK
or PO Box 9779, London SW19 7ZG, UK
and
244 Madison Ave. #116, New York, NY 10016, USA

Original title: Tokyo sebun rozu
Copyright © Hisashi Inoue 2002
Originally published in Japan by Bungei Shunju Ltd., Tokyo
English translation copyright © Jeffrey Hunter 2013

A CIP record for this book is available from the British Library.

ISBN-13: 978 0 85728 043 5 (Hbk)
ISBN-10: 0 85728 043 0 (Hbk)

This title is also available as an eBook.

This book has been selected by the Japanese Literature Publishing Project (JLPP),
an initiative of the Agency for Cultural Affairs of Japan.

TOKYO SEVEN ROSES

VOLUME I

Hisashi Inoue

Translated by Jeffrey Hunter

ANTHEM PRESS
LONDON · NEW YORK · DELHI

1945

April 25

Early this morning my older brother, who lives in the corner house down the street, carried our betrothal gifts over to the Furusawa family residence in Senju. I had handed him 500 yen in cash and a bolt of cloth for hakama trousers, for which I bartered two hundred and fifty fans to take to them. This is a very large outlay for us since, with the shortage of materials these last years, we haven't made any fans for some time now, and quite honestly it's the most we can afford, given how things are these days.

When my brother came back, he said, "It seems that when the Furusawa boy met Kinuko for the first time at the restaurant the other day, he was so shy he never looked up and saw only her hands. So the morning of the day after tomorrow, the 27th, they're going to send him over here. Mrs. Furusawa says to make sure that Tadao gets a good look at the girl who's going to be his bride."

Kinuko blushed, and Fumiko and Takeko teased their older sister that she probably didn't see Tadao's face, either.

My wife and I talked it over and decided that Kinuko and Tadao should go together to the Shinbashi Embujo Theater, which just happens to be the opening day for Kikugoro VI. If we let them go on their own, they're sure to at least see each other's face.

The double cherries in front of the Takahashi house are in bloom. People walking by on the street are stopping to point at them.

April 26

I got up early today to repair my three-wheeled truck, but just couldn't get it going. I've taken a job with Furusawa Enterprises delivering fertilizer and tools to farmers in Katsushika, so I was desperate to get the truck up and running, but no luck. I listened to Masao Sasaki on the radio at noon performing "The Watchman's

Rounds" on the mandolin. That picked me up a little, and I decided to take the truck into town to have it looked at; with me pulling the truck with a rope, Fumiko steering and my wife pushing from behind, we managed to get it to Daihatsu Motors in Nihonbashi Hon-cho.

The mechanic looked it over and told me the truck was completely worn down. "If we had the parts, we could probably get it running again," he said, "but we don't have anything in stock. There's nothing we can do." So we ended up dragging the miserable piece of scrap through the burned-out wasteland back home to Nezu. I wanted to cry. I called Furusawa Enterprises on the phone, told them the situation and apologized. Then I went to my brother's house.

"I was hoping to get a little business delivering stuff around town, but with the truck kaput, it's all over. I'll start making the rounds again tomorrow for supplies for fans. You went to a lot of trouble to introduce me to the Furusawas. I'm sorry I let you down," I said, bowing to him.

"You know, I know this saké brewer in Toride," my brother said. "Remember—I think it was about five years ago—he ordered two thousand fans with his company logo to be printed on them? That order that I got for you, remember? Anyway, the other day I went to get some saké from him, and he said he had a three-wheeled truck he didn't need anymore, and asked if I knew anybody who'd be interested. He wanted 7,000 yen, with a down payment of 1,000 yen, the rest in installments. Why don't you go see him on Monday? Or if you prefer, I could buy it and rent it out to you."

My brother reached into his cash box and took out five 200 yen notes recently printed by the Bank of Japan. The paper and printing of the 100 yen notes these days are really cheap and crappy, but these brand-new 200 yen bills have the crisp sound of genuine money. I thought how nice it would be to drive through the countryside in the spring, instead of slogging through the dust and ashes of Tokyo. I accepted the crisp bills and headed for home.

I know it's not really fair to call my truck a piece of junk. After all, I bought it eight years ago, in the spring of 1937, when business at our Yamanaka Fan Shop was booming. We'd gotten the exclusive commission to produce the commemorative fans that the *Asahi*

Shimbun was giving to all their readers to celebrate the achievement of a new world record, when the paper's airplane *Kamikaze* broke the Asia-to-Europe record on a goodwill flight, making the journey from Tokyo to London in 94 hours, 17 minutes and 56 seconds. We had twelve or thirteen employees then. When the Korakuen Baseball Stadium opened in September that year, we made the commemorative fans for that, too. That little three-wheeler certainly more than paid its dues. By all rights, I shouldn't badmouth it.

And the reason I even thought of starting a delivery service was because we already had that three-wheeler, which of course led to us getting to know Furusawa Enterprises, and now to Kinuko marrying into the Furusawa family. That little truck wasn't such a troublemaker at all—in fact, it was more like some beneficent deity who descended from heaven to grant our every wish.

When I was walking by the Takahashi house next door, I suddenly heard the roar of a B-29. A single plane. That was odd. I quickly looked up into the night sky; there hadn't been even a cautionary alert siren, not to mention an air-raid siren. Maybe this was just reconnaissance. But reconnaissance flights came during the day. Then, what really scared me, after the sound of the engine strangely faded, there was the roar of a whole formation.

"Ah, Mr. Yamanaka is out wandering the streets," called out Shoichi. He's in his first year at Azabu Middle School. He was sticking his head out of the second-floor window of the house, laughing. "You're the fifth person to fall for it. It's just a record." Shoichi's head disappeared inside for a moment, and the sound of a formation of B-29s stopped a few moments after.

"Nitchiku just put out this record of B-29s exploding," Shoichi said, back at the window and waving a pamphlet. "See—'Death-defying Recording Finally Completed!'"

"What a stupid thing to put out at a time like this. To say nothing about the kind of people who would buy it," I said, glaring up at him.

"Don't be unpatriotic," Shoichi jeered. "This was produced by the Fortification Department. And it's recommended by the General Defense Headquarters and the Ministry of War."

Shoichi can be a troublemaker, but he's a good boy at heart and he's generally pleasant and cheerful. In fact, sometimes I like him better than Kiyoshi, even though Kiyoshi's my own son. Kiyoshi studies hard, but there's something dark about that kid. I waved goodbye to Shoichi and headed on my way.

When I got home, my wife, Kazue, was sewing Kinuko's kimono. Lately she's been up until dawn sewing away, preparing Kinuko's trousseau, which includes a set of futon and three kimonos. It's a big job for one person.

"Don't overdo it. You need to take a break. If you push yourself too hard, you're going to collapse in a heap before the wedding takes place," I told her.

"If an air-raid siren goes off," she replied, "I'm going to tie everything in Kinuko's trousseau in a big bundle, and I want you to carry it to the air-raid dugout in Ueno Park. If these are destroyed in a raid, I'll kill myself."

I pulled my low desk over next to my wife to write in my diary.

April 27
I woke up early this morning and went to Ueno Station to stand in line for a train ticket. It was a sunny day, with just a couple fluffy white clouds drifting from east to west. More than two weeks have passed since the last air raid; the station, no longer thronged with air-raid refugees leaving the city, was back to its normal routine.

When the train crossed the Arakawa Canal, after Kita Senju, the scenery changed. The yellowish-brown, charred city blocks were gone, replaced by green fields of barley, with little swaths of yellow and pink—mustard flowers and cherry blossoms. In the area around Kanamachi there are rows of willows, the fresh spring leaves on their weeping branches act as a kind of wall that reflects the light so brightly it can be hard to see.

I arrived at the Yamamoto Saké Brewery at exactly 10 A.M. The proprietor wasn't there—he'd been drafted to work at the army's woolen cloth factory in Kashiwa—so I tried to explain my business to his retired father, but I couldn't seem to make any headway.

"I can't say anything about the truck unless I ask my son," the old man said. "Who are you, anyway?"

"I'm Yamanaka, from Nezu. A few years ago you placed a large order for fans with your company's logo on them."

We repeated this exchange several times, until finally the old man yelled at the top of his lungs: "*We don't want any fans!*" He kept shouting angrily, "No fans! No fans!" I couldn't get another word out of him.

Eventually, the missus of the house came out and told me that a big steel drum that was tossed out of a B-29 had fallen a few yards from her father-in-law, and he'd never been the same since then. "On top of that," she went on, "he's been in a bad mood the last few days. He loves broiled eel, so when the government decided to turn all the eel ponds around here into rice paddies, and I happened to say that from now on there wasn't going to be any more broiled eel over rice, he started sulking. When they reach this age, they're just like children."

I had seen the government decision in the *Asahi Shimbun* this morning while I was waiting in line at Ueno Station. The headline read: "Say Goodbye to Broiled Eel." According to the article, Minami Shonai Village, a model farming village at Lake Hamana in Shizuoka, where the famous Hamana eels come from, is going to convert sixty-three hectares of eel ponds into paddies that can be double-cropped with rice. This year they are going to convert the first forty hectares, with the goal of producing two thousand additional bales of rice and increasing their delivery to the government by one thousand bales over last year's harvest. Apparently, eel-cultivation ponds are being converted into rice paddies all over the country.

Now, nothing could make me happier than having more rice, but I also like broiled eel. I don't know whether to feel sad or happy. That's all right; from now on I'll have broiled eel in my dreams. That's one of my talents—to be able to dream about my favorite foods. When I get into bed, I might say to myself, "Tonight I'm going to dream about tuna sashimi and all the rice I can eat," and then without fail, that's the dream I have. Tonight I'll order up dreamland broiled eel.

Mrs. Yamamoto said that she'd tell her husband about my coming about the truck and assured me that he'd be willing to sell it, which is a relief, and I handed her the five 200 yen bills as a down payment. After that good news, I asked if she would sell me some food. I bought five *sho* of soybeans, three *kamme* of potatoes and two large bunches of mitsuba greens for 10 yen. For someone like me from

Tokyo, to get all that for 10 yen was like committing highway robbery. Mrs. Yamamoto also told me about some other farm families in the area who might have food for sale, and I went to two places. I got one *sho* of rice, another *sho* of soybeans, two bunches of onions and two *kamme* of wheat flower, all for 45 yen. In the past ten days I've been able to buy, one way or another, a dozen packets of ajinomoto, five packs of high-quality seaweed, five hundred *momme* of sugar, a large bottle of Yamasa soy sauce, five hundred *momme* of salt cod and a bottle of ketchup and Bull-Dog sauce—and on top of that, everything I bought today. We'll be able to send Kinuko off to her new home with quite a feast. There should even be enough left over for the party when she comes back for her home visit after the wedding. If only we had a little fish or meat, it would be perfect. But I'm not complaining.

It was nearly five in the evening when I got back home. When my wife saw what I brought back she squealed like a little girl. She really looked happy. Then Kinuko came home. She had rendezvoused with Tadao at Keisei Ueno Station.

"Didn't he see you home?" I asked.

Kinuko replied that he'd have walked her home but was too embarrassed to come in. "And," she continued, "along the way we ran into Shoichi, who said to Tadao, 'You're a lucky man. You're marrying the beauty queen of Nezu Miyanaga-cho,' which made Tadao blush to the gills and dash off."

Takeko, pushing up her sleeves, said, "That Sho-*chan*! I'll give him what he deserves the next time I see him! Don't worry, Kinuko, I'll take care of him! I'm the one that got him into Azabu Middle School. I helped him study, which is why he passed the exams. He acts humble and polite in front of me, but I won't let him get away with this!"

"He's at that age," said Fumiko, putting her chopsticks down. "He thinks he's clever. Do you know what he said to me this morning? 'Congratulations on becoming the new beauty queen of Miyanaga-cho.' He was just dying to say it, I could tell. Boys that age are hopeless."

"The new beauty queen of Miyanaga-cho? That's a compliment. He was trying to be nice," said Takeko.

That was when Kiyoshi slapped his chopsticks down on the table and went upstairs. The atmosphere was growing oddly tense, so I changed the subject and asked Kinuko how the performance at the Shinbashi Enbujo was.

"The curtain was delayed. We had to wait a very long time for it to start."

"It's always like that on the first day of a run."

"When *Tied to a Pole* was over, Kikugoro came out in his costume as Tarokaja and spoke to the audience. Everyone loved it. But then he said that eighteen of his fellow actors, including Koisaburo and Gennosuke, have gone missing in the air raids, along with countless other victims. Omezo is the only one in their entire troupe who hasn't lost someone in the attacks. The same was true of the musicians, and the majority of them have gone off somewhere, so that the only shamisen player left is Wasaburo. He said most of their costumes, sets and props had gone up in flames, and what we were seeing was their best attempt to make do. 'All we have left is our art,' he said. 'Our art is not just makeshift, or something we've managed to rescue from the flames; we've worked to polish it all our lives, and we're confident it's worth your while.'"

"That's just the kind of thing you'd expect from Kikugoro VI."

"And he went on, 'I'm born and raised in Edo. Our family has lived here for generations, and we've enjoyed your patronage for many long years. If we can offer you some entertainment and cheer, if we can encourage the warriors of industry who are working so hard to increase our nation's fighting power, we'll have made our small contribution to the war effort, and we're determined to remain here in the Imperial capital to the bitter end.' Then he said how, due to paper shortages, newspaper space has been restricted and they aren't able to advertise, so he was afraid many people don't know they're still here performing and doing their best to keep up people's spirits. So he said to please tell all our friends and neighbors that they're still performing at the Shinbashi Enbujo. And that we all needed to do our best to remain steadfast and brave until we triumph in our sacred struggle. That," continued Kinuko, "was the message that Kikugoro VI delivered to us. But he is so thin. When I saw him last fall with you, Father, he was almost fat. In this last half-year, he's become little more than skin and bones."

"It's the same with everyone."

"During the intermission we ate our bento box lunches. Tadao's had a beef cutlet in it. It was delicious."

"How were your seats?" my wife asked.

"First class. In the orchestra, seats 11 and 12 in Row T."

"That's great!"

"They cost 15 yen 50 sen each. Tadao paid for mine."

"You should have gotten second- or third-class seats and saved the difference. But I guess it can't be helped; it was a special occasion, after all. When you're a member of the Furusawa family, though, you have to try to save as much money as you can."

"Did you have a chance to talk to Tadao?" asked Fumiko.

"He talked a lot about the family business. Tadao is only twenty-four, but he's already taken over from his father and is working hard. He says he has a license to drive a truck, and the business makes about a million yen a month."

I suspected that much myself. The top priorities of the government are increasing the production of food and weapons. Businesses involved with these things are booming. Furusawa Enterprises sells fertilizer and tools to farmers—indispensable for increasing agricultural production—so the government would never choose to put a halt to them. They are sitting pretty, as long as they have the goods to sell, since no matter what they charge they could always find buyers. And because the farmers want fertilizer and tools so badly, they are eager to slip soybeans and rice to Furusawa Enterprises under the table, which the Furusawas then sell on the black market. They would have to be feeble-minded not to be making money hand over fist.

"They're building a retirement home for Tadao's grandmother in Shimoyagiri, Matsudo. And Tadao's sister Tokiko is going with her grandmother to Shimoyagiri, to take care of her. It's a kind of evacuation, really."

"So you won't have a sister-in-law looking over your shoulder," said Takeko. "That must make you happy."

"Not really. In fact, it makes things harder."

"Huh? Why?"

"Tokiko is a hard worker. Her mother died when she was only fourteen."

"Then who is the lady who's there now?"

"Her stepmother."

"Yes, they say she was a geisha from Kameido," said my wife.

When my brother first brought the marriage proposal to us, he warned me that sooner or later we were going to find out Mrs. Furusawa is a former geisha. He didn't know about her relationship with Tadao, but he said she didn't get along with Tokiko. "Make sure to include that in your considerations," he said.

It seemed like my wife was trying to get across the full implications of this situation to Kinuko. "She can't cook and she's no use in the business, either. She and Tokiko are always at each other's throat because of that. Her only talent is her smart mouth, they say. Though she's just a stepmother, she acts like she's Tokiko's real mother and she's constantly scolding her, asking how dare Tokiko treat her that way. She'll probably be a handful for you, too, Kinuko."

"All Tadao said to me was 'Try to get along with my mother.'"

"Well, what do you expect? No one tells you all the family secrets from the start."

"Anyway, after her mother died, Tokiko quit high school and took over the household. They have five employees, and she has to cook for them all. But in spite of that, she's shouldered the entire thing and is also helping in the business. She got her truck driver's license, too, and works as hard as Tadao. There are only three women from Ueno to Senju who have a truck driver's license. And now Tokiko's going to Shimoyagiri with her grandmother. I know I'm not up to replacing her. That's why I said it makes things harder that she's going."

"No matter how hard Tokiko works, she can't be Tadao's wife. Just remember that, and don't worry," my wife said.

I'm sure she meant to comfort Kinuko, but it was a pretty lukewarm effort. I got up and turned on the radio. The seven o'clock evening broadcast announced that two-thirds of Berlin has been occupied by the Red Army. After the news, the entire family listened to Information Bureau Director-General Hiroshi Shimomura present a program called "Winning the Battle for Okinawa." While admitting that we have lost many soldiers in the fighting up to now, he said that the enemy forces have lost exponentially more planes and warships. He added that there is no longer any distinction between the frontlines and the home front, and that the entire population of One Hundred Million Japanese must unite into one flaming ball of patriotic fire and rally every last ounce of strength for the battle of Okinawa, responding alongside the Imperial heroes of the Special Attack Forces, as well as the courageous fighting of the islands' residents. He concluded by saying that since all One Hundred Million are prepared to give their lives for the Emperor, the divine realm is indestructible and the Greater East Asia War will be brought to a successful conclusion. In Berlin, he added, a growing number of German housewives are joining the German soldiers in their struggle, tossing hand grenades from their windows at the Red Army tanks rolling through the city streets. These Berlin housewives, he said, are models for the Imperial home front.

I write today's entry while listening to the fifth installment of Yaozo Ichikawa's serialized program "Yamaoka Tesshu."

April 28

There haven't been any bombing raids here in central Tokyo since the 19th, and we're enjoying a period of good, relaxing spring weather. Actually, every day several B-29s do appear over the city, one at a time, leaving their white plumes of exhaust in the sky. They must be checking out their next bombing target. This always happens before a major air raid. It's so quiet that there's nothing to talk about. A shiver runs down my spine when I think of the next air raid, but there's no use spending your days worrying about the future. There's one secret to surviving life in the Imperial capital—all that matters is the present, and the only thing to do is to be grateful for the quiet we're enjoying now. Anyway, at last I can sleep peacefully, now that we're not subject to nightly air raids. That's what I appreciate most. I just pray that the air raids hold off until Kinuko gets married and makes her return visit home.

I believe that the peace we're enjoying here is, without a doubt, a gift from the heroes of the Special Attack Forces. The enemy is closing in on Okinawa, and the brave pilots of the Special Attack Forces are courageously launching themselves at our foes. As

Information Bureau Director-General Shimomura said in his radio address last night, the Special Attack Forces pilots are inflicting serious damage on enemy warships. If the Americans want to win in Okinawa, they'll be concentrating on the air bases the Special Attack Forces pilots are departing from in Kyushu instead of attacking the Imperial capital of Tokyo. And that's what's behind the major movement of enemy B-29 squadrons to Kyushu right now. Naturally, they don't have the manpower to make aerial attacks on the capital at the same time. There was an article in this morning's *Asahi Shimbun* that supports this. "Before dawn on April 27, some 150 B-29s attacked various bases in southern Kyushu for the second day in succession." I can only thank from the bottom of my heart the heroic pilots who have brought this calm and peace to us.

Speaking of the newspaper, this morning Mr. Tokuyama from the newspaper distribution office came by and said, "Mr. Yamanaka, you're taking both the *Asahi* and the *Yomiuri,* right?"

"Up to last year I was taking all three—the *Asahi,* the *Yomiuri* and the *Mainichi*—but in January you said I had to drop one, so I quit the *Mainichi.* Why, is something the matter?"

"Tomorrow, all of the newspapers are going to carry an announcement that says that from May you can only take one paper. I don't care which you keep, but you'll have to drop one."

I was stunned to hear this. Because I can't make fans anymore and every day is so filled with problems, the time I spend poring over the newspapers or listening to the radio is my escape. The *Asahi* and the *Yomiuri,* along with the radio, are my last little pleasures. It is painful to contemplate losing one of them, and presents me with an extremely difficult choice.

"The newspapers sent out notices like this to us," said Mr. Tokuyama, pulling out a piece of paper to show me. Hoping to delay making a decision as long as possible, I asked Mr. Tokuyama to allow me to copy it:

From May 1, customers subscribing to two newspapers are requested to reduce their subscriptions to a single newspaper. We ask for the cooperation of all our readers as we fulfill our mission as journalists during this time of war in response to the severe shortage of newsprint. We are instructing our distributors to implement this measure, and respectfully request your understanding in this matter.

Asahi Shimbun
Tokyo Shimbun
Nihon Sangyo Shimbun
Mainichi Shimbun
Yomiuri Shimbun

As I was copying it I thought, eight years ago I received work from both the *Asahi* and *Yomiuri*. The *Asahi* order was for twenty thousand fans, the *Yomiuri* order was for three thousand. I was glad for both orders, but seventeen thousand times gladder for the *Asahi* order. I knew I'd just have to bite the bullet and quit the *Yomiuri*. So I said to Mr. Tokuyama, in a voice not much above a whisper: "I'll stick with the *Asahi*."

April 29
Today is the Emperor's birthday.

Today, April 29th, is the felicitous forty-fourth birthday of his Imperial majesty. With the most reverent wishes for the excellent health of his august personage, I wish to express my deepest concern and appreciation for his tireless, laudatory and honorable efforts day and night to direct our sacred nation as both our supreme military leader and head of state during these most challenging of times.

It's Sunday, there's no sign of any air raids, and on a day like this I would have preferred to stay in bed and catch up on my sleep, but that's not the way it works. I have to bring the very last remnants of my inventory, two thousand flat fans and four hundred folding fans that were in storage at Ensoji Temple in Yanaka, to my uncle's house in Tsunohashi, Shinjuku. My plan is to entrust these fans, which are my family's last hope for earning our rice in the future, to my uncle, who's evacuating with his family to Yamanashi, in the hope that I can keep them from going up in flames. The head priest at Ensoji is also evacuating to the countryside. You'd think that the Imperial capital, with all the dead and homeless from the air raids, is where a

Buddhist priest should be, but the end must be near, because they're fleeing the city in droves, like rats leaving a sinking ship.

I borrowed a cart from my brother. Not only is he lending money, but he has carts and lots of other stuff behind the house that he rents out. No doubt he got them from someone who owed him money—another example of his shrewdness. Apparently he plans to stay in Tokyo to the bitter end, buying up everything he can from those fleeing, bargaining them down to the last yen. Kiyoshi was glued to his desk, studying, wearing a headband with the slogan "Navy Accounting School or Bust!" So I asked Shoichi Takahashi to help push the cart from behind while I pulled from the front.

"I'll give you a yen for helping me get it to Shinjuku and back," I said, offering him an unusually high fee. He didn't seem very pleased, so I added, "Fumiko and Takeko will also be pushing," and he immediately brightened up.

After we made our way through the charred ruins of Hongo Ward, we came upon a crowd of people. Shoichi, maybe tired of pushing the cart and a good deal of the novelty of being alongside Fumiko and Takeko having worn off (actually, probably a combination of the two), asked if we could rest for a minute.

If he deserted me here, I'd have a tough time getting the cart to Shinjuku, so I agreed to a short break and went with him to see what was going on. A little space had been cleared of tin sheets and roof tiles. About twenty people were seated on chairs, next to a stick with a placard that read: "Outdoor Discussion Group Sponsored by the Patriotic Industrial Associations Movement: People Living Underground Discuss Their New Lifestyle."

A man about thirty-two or thirty-three, wearing a brand new national civilian uniform, appeared to be the moderator. "All of you here today are courageously living in underground shelters after having been burned out of your homes. Though all of the buildings of our sacred empire might be reduced to ashes, we must fight to the very end from wherever we are, until we have attained victory over the American and English devils. In other words, though all One Hundred Million Japanese might end up living in underground shelters, the battle will go on. You have all already experienced a month of life underground. You are pioneering models for the rest of the population and are actually leading your lives in a way appropriate for the glorious moment when all One Hundred Million Japanese will offer their lives for their country. Your experiences are a precious manual for all Imperial subjects. We will be publishing the results of this discussion meeting in a pamphlet and distributing it throughout the country, so please speak freely and share your thoughts and ideas."

These seemed like opening remarks, which meant that the meeting was just starting. The participants spoke up and offered various advantages of living underground.

"Sometimes I look up at the entrance hole and see a stray dog looking down at me. That was a first me for, seeing a dog from that angle. It was a very interesting feeling."

"You don't need any furnishings when you're living in a hole in the ground, and it made me realize how few of the things that I once thought were indispensable for daily life are actually necessary. That really gave me something to think about."

"Living in a hole underground made me appreciate the truth of all the slogans about extravagance and waste, like 'I Don't Need It until after We Win the War' and 'Extravagance Is the Enemy,' because I'm really putting them into practice in daily life."

"When you live in an underground shelter, you don't have to worry about air-raid sirens, because you're already underground."

"If you feel like it, you could dig your hole a little bigger every day. It's really the only kind of house that you can keep expanding as long as you have the energy to do it."

"Yeah, I agree. And you find all sorts of things while you're digging, which is fun. Just the other day I dug up a pot for cooking. It's still perfectly usable, which is great."

"It's very peaceful underground. You don't have to worry about the neighbors. No one can snoop on you."

Up to now, the mood was upbeat. But it seemed there were also complaints.

"It's so hot underground."

"We need electric power."

"The government should give us candles."

"We need to know the city's street construction plans as soon as possible. We don't know where it's safe to dig our underground shelters without that information."

"We'd like the distribution of rice and miso to take place at our underground shelters. Right now we have to travel a distance to pick up our rations. It's really inconvenient. New underground distribution stations should be constructed."

"Do we need the permission of the landowners to plant vegetables on their property? Most of them have already evacuated, and there's no way to get in touch with them. It's a big problem."

"Newspapers should be delivered to underground shelters, too."

The sunny, upbeat atmosphere dissipated, and the comments gradually started to sound desperate. It was shifting from a discussion to something more like the germ of a protest. Just then an elderly gent who had been sitting in the corner listening with a smile, dressed in the kind of fresh white shirt and tie you rarely saw any more these days, stood up and said: "My name is Kyosuke Yamazaki, and I'm a professor in the engineering department of Tokyo Imperial University. The university has strong and enduring ties to the Hongo District, and I've been listening to your comments because I want to offer the university's services to residents. We in the engineering department can assist you with construction, and the law school can help with any legal questions. The medical school is there to come to your aid, too. Tomorrow I'll organize a student volunteer group, a kind of Subterranean Life Monitoring and Support Group if you will, and have them visit you. Just talk your problems over with them. I want to thank you for the valuable accounts of your experiences you've shared with us today."

I have to say that I was grateful to them, too. Sooner or later Nezu is bound to be burned to the ground like most of the rest of the city, and we'll have to live in a tunnel dug into the side of Ueno hill. If I could remember what I'd heard today, it is bound to come in handy. It is clear we'd need candles—I'll start stockpiling them.

"What a crummy meeting," said Shoichi, walking back to the cart where Fumiko and Takeko were waiting. "It's all men, that's why it's no good. Bad planning."

"So there's a rule that a meeting isn't interesting unless there are women in it?

15

"If women had been there, they would have brought up interesting things, like the fact that it's impossible to keep yourself clean when you're living underground. One of my friends is the son of a director at Meidensha Electric Company, and he told me about something that took place in the women workers' dormitory."

Apparently, according to Shoichi, the Meiho Dormitory, which was for female employees and members of the Girls Volunteer Corps, didn't have any bathing facilities, so they went to the local Kusatsu Ogon Bath. But because it was so crowded, like all public baths, they stopped going regularly. They started to come down with foot diseases, which finally resulted in an epidemic of fungus infections.

"Meidensha has another dormitory for male workers. But even though their personal hygiene is worse than the women, not a single man came down with a fungus infection. That means that women are more susceptible to things like that. That's why if there were some women at the meeting, they would have talked about how hard it is to stay clean when you're living underground, and I think that would've been interesting."

"Oh, so that's all you meant."

"But that's important. I saw this movie *Girls on the Base*, starring Mitsuko Mito, at the Asakusa Shochiku, and in spite of the fact that Mito and the other girls never had a bath in their dormitory, their faces, necks and hands were always sparkling clean. That's strange, isn't it? They're always talking about how important it is to be scientific, but these movie people completely ignore science and logic…"

"Sho, I never realized you were such an expert on the ladies," I said with a chuckle. "I had you pegged as the more serious type."

"I am! I'm going to the Naval Academy at Etajima."

"Father, what are you laughing about?" asked Takeko. "Shoichi, what are you two talking about?"

"Man talk," said Shoichi gruffly, going back to the rear of the cart.

The cart was light going home after we'd dropped off our load in Shinjuku, so we sent Fumiko and Takeko back by train and Shoichi and I took turns pulling the empty cart back. On the way, he explained how the proprietor of the Kusatsu Ogon Bath chivalrously ended the epidemic of fungus infections by making the bath available exclusively to the girls eight times a month, from seven to eight in the evening. With regular baths, the girls soon recovered.

When I got home, a pot of rice porridge was sitting on the table, so we all sat down to eat. But there was something odd about Kinuko. Tears were rolling down her cheeks into her bowl.

"What happened?" I asked.

"I scolded her," replied my wife. "She messed up sewing a kimono simply because she doesn't pay attention to anything I say. It goes in one ear and out the other. It would be bad enough if it were someone else's kimono, but it's her own! She needs to be more careful or she's going to make a fool of herself at the Furusawas. They won't take her seriously. And as her mother, I'm the one they'll blame. That's why I let her have it..."

As my wife spoke, she got more and more excited. It's one of her worst faults. Sometimes she just gets carried away and ends in a tizzy. We've been married for twenty-four years, so there's not much that I'm not used to by now, but this particular trait of hers still drives me crazy.

"Kinuko isn't our daughter anymore!" I shouted before I even realized what I was saying. "As far as you're concerned, she's a Furusawa now. You have no right to scold her."

"Have a little more," my wife said, filling my bowl with another helping of rice porridge.

I'm not usually that easily mollified, but I ate it, because I was hungry from pulling that cart to Shinjuku and back.

April 30
This morning there was a sudden announcement on the radio: "Fleets of several enemy planes are moving from the south toward Honshu. All Imperial subjects should be on the alert." I loaded Kinuko's trousseau into the cart that I hadn't returned to my brother yet. I'm always loading it with food and daily necessities, but today was different. Just when I was done and ready to pull the cart to Ueno to a dugout shelter there, I heard the Neighborhood Association leader making an announcement over a megaphone:

"Only people over sixty and pregnant women may evacuate to the dugout shelters. Everyone else remain in the neighborhood. Only the residents of Miyanaga-cho can defend Miyanaga-cho. Nezu remains completely intact from the air raids, and we need to keep it that way. You've all seen the pitiful state that people whose houses are burned are reduced to. If you don't want that to happen to you, you need to stay here and defend Nezu. It's your duty to protect the neighborhood. If you see any able-bodied individual fleeing when they should be here defending our homes, write a letter to the Neighborhood Association and report them. We will immediately contact the police, and they will be punished. The time to retreat is when Miyanaga-cho has become a sea of flames, not before."

After that "plea" for all residents to stay put, there was no way I could pull the cart to Ueno. I lined up ten buckets of water in front of the house, put a ladder up to the roof, and stood there with a rope flame-beater in hand. Eventually the air-raid siren began to blast. The radio announced: "Fighters are attacking the western Keihin region. There are no planes above the Imperial capital." It was hard to just stand there waiting, so I went into the back yard and split some kindling. The all-clear was sounded at 11:30 in the morning, so I unloaded Kinuko's trousseau and ate some boiled potatoes for lunch. It turns out that the attack was focused on the area from the western Keihin area to Tachikawa and Tokorozawa. It suddenly came to me that the target was the air bases there.

Kinuko had been planning to go that morning to her office at Mitsubishi Corporation and officially hand in her resignation, but when the air-raid siren went off, she decided to wait. In the middle of lunch, however, she suddenly stood up and said that she wanted to get it done that day. She said it very softly, like a puff of air that escapes from the faucet that's been shut off at the main when you turn it on. Having worked at the company for three years and a month, she seems to have been having mixed feelings about quitting.

Late this afternoon I got some good news: the daily cigarette ration, which had been reduced to three a day, will be restored to five per day starting May 1st. Not only that, but the forty-five cigarettes allotted us up to May 9th will all be made available today. I really enjoy smoking, and though I try to scrimp, I smoke seven a day. Whatever isn't included in the rations, I buy from my brother down the street—fake cigarettes, at 2 yen for ten, called "coffee cigarettes."

You can see lines of tiny Japanese and English print on the papers they're rolled in, so they must be made from paper recycled from Japanese-English dictionaries. They're a mix of wormwood and tobacco, sprinkled with coffee grounds, I guess to make them taste better. My brother has Hikari brand cigarettes, but a pack with ten cigarettes is 11 yen 50 sen. There's no way I can afford a cigarette that goes for 1 yen 15 sen, so I smoke the coffee cigarettes. Once Mrs. Takahashi, the wife of the head of the block group, gave me a Hikari, and I immediately went outside and lit up. It was terrific—the first real cigarette I'd smoked in a week. I got a little buzz, as the nicotine spread through my system and my fingertips tingled.

"Hey, Mr. Yamanaka, you want to sell me a cigarette?"

It was Shoichi, poking his head out from the second-story window.

"Will you sell me one, please?" he repeated.

"What are you saying? You're a middle-school student. I'm going to tell your mother."

"So you don't want to sell me one. That's good, Mr. Yamanaka. That's how it should be. Japanese shouldn't get involved in the black market. Otherwise we couldn't smash our planes into the enemy battleships. We're willing to give our lives to protect good people. But no one wants to give up his precious life for people who are selling things on the black market."

With that, Shoichi pulled his head inside.

May 1

My wife took Kinuko to Mitsukoshi, that institution of a department store, where we have decided to hold the wedding ceremony. We received a notice this morning from the store: "Please choose the pattern of the long-sleeved kimono you'll be wearing for the ceremony on the 4th. We would also like to do a wig fitting." Mitsukoshi rents everything needed for the ceremony. It's the only wedding hall that's so convenient. Kimono fabric is subject to rationing restrictions, and to get a kimono you have to use your clothing coupons. It would mean the whole family would have to donate their coupons just to purchase the wedding kimono, and no one would be able to get any other clothes. Of course I want Kinuko to have a long-sleeved kimono to wear for her wedding, but if that means that the rest of the family has to go without new clothes for a year, people would talk, which would upset Kinuko more than anyone. That left us the choice between buying one on the black market and having her get married in everyday clothes. We don't have the money for a black-market kimono. If Kiyoshi found out he'd probably be angry, but the fact is we're surviving by slowly selling the fans I made two years ago, before we ran out of materials, on the black market, and there aren't many fans left to sell. At the same time, getting married in an everyday dress—well, I know we can't afford luxuries, but I would feel bad for Kinuko. Tadao kindly offered to have his family supply the wedding kimono, but my wife refused out of hand. The Yamanaka family may be poor fan makers down on their luck, but we have our pride. There is no way we could just sit back with a smile while the bridegroom's family takes care of everything.

Fortunately, my wife heard that Mitsukoshi rented wedding kimonos and the problem was solved. We've since found out that the Mitsukoshi wedding hall was so popular that on average twelve couples get married there every day. It isn't surprising, then, that the first wedding starts at seven o'clock in the morning, and the last at seven o'clock at night. Sometimes the last two couples of the day have held their reception before they actually get married. Often they are already a bit tipsy, and I heard that recently someone started dancing during the invocation by the Shinto priest. The couples draw straws for their slot in the day's wedding schedule. When my wife went there the other day, she drew number two, so Kinuko is getting married at eight o'clock on the morning of May 4th.

Just when our worries about a wedding kimono for Kinuko were taken care of, it seems that the war in Okinawa has taken a turn for the better. Roosevelt, the leader of our enemy, who suddenly died on April 12th and fell into the burning pit of hell where he belongs, had declared that the Americans would take Okinawa by April 25th. His replacement, Truman, said that the complete submission of Okinawa by April 25th was the president's last wish, and he was going to see that it came true.

But look, April 25th is long gone; it's already May and Truman wasn't able to keep his promise. Not only that, but the valiant fighting of the Navy Special Attack Forces and all the Imperial forces have weakened the enemy considerably. All that's needed is one last push. One more thrust and the enemy will be nothing but flotsam and jetsam drifting on the waves off Okinawa.

All the same, when you look at the western front of the war, it appears that our allies the Germans have been defeated and Berlin will fall in a few days. This is just my opinion, but I think that the defeat of the Germans may, in the end, be a stroke of luck, a divine intervention, leading our Empire eventually to glorious victory. The main victors of the battle in Europe are the U.S., England and the Soviet Union. They've managed to stay on good terms with each other because they've had a common enemy in Germany, but what will happen now that they've vanquished their foe? Will they still get along? Not likely, not at all. All three of them are, by nature, little more than thieves. Their true character will surface as they fight over the spoils, and their alliance will fall apart. It'll probably end up a fight between the Soviet Union on one side and the U.S. and England on the other. That's the moment our Empire should join forces with the Soviet Union. As we all know, just before the Greater East Asian War, our Empire and the Soviet Union were like honeymooners. We just need to revive that relationship and join together to bring down America and England. Then we can work out who's on top with the Soviet Union. And that's why there's no reason to feel bad about the defeat of Germany.

I was thinking about all this when Mr. Takahashi came over with a mimeograph set, a stylus and stencil paper, clutching them to his chest like a precious treasure. He's the chief of the photography department at a newspaper as well as the head of our block group and a director of the Miyanaga-cho Neighborhood Association.

"Everyone says your calligraphy is beautiful," he began, "so I'm here to ask you a favor. A notice has come down from Air Defense Headquarters." Takahashi pulled a mimeographed sheet out from the breast of his national civilian uniform. In the upper right was written "For All War Refugees."

"Eventually, Nezu is going to be bombed and the whole area will be burned to the ground. This pamphlet explains in detail what to do when your home is burned. I think that everyone living here in

Nezu should read it. I want to mimeograph it and distribute a copy to every family."

"I see. And you want me to make the stencil."

"I'll take the stencil to the Nezu National Primary School tomorrow morning and start making copies. By evening everyone in Nezu will be reading your calligraphy. I can offer you two candles for doing the job."

"There's no need for that. This is public service, after all. Still, the candles will be appreciated."

"Where did you learn your skill as a copyist?"

"Daiichi Toko Company, on Suzuran Street in Kanda." In the world of printing and copying, Daiichi Toko is the equivalent of Tokyo Imperial University in the world of law, so that made me feel pretty important.

"All the printers' type has been requisitioned by the government. The type's being melted down for bullets. So I thought about mimeographing instead," said Takahashi.

"I've mainly worked with printing the names or logos of businesses on fans, and when you can't use type for that, you need to make a mimeograph stencil. So I learned all the calligraphic techniques and mimeograph styles when I was at Daiichi Toko. Really, I was more an apprentice than anything else."

"That must have been quite difficult."

"Not really. I've always liked calligraphy. If I didn't, I would have given up my business of printed fans when the printers all went out of business. It was because I enjoy calligraphy that I came up with the idea of mimeographing names on my fans. It only lasted for a short time, but our mimeographed fans earned a pretty good reputation."

I told him that the idea of mimeographing on fans came to me one day while I was watching my wife sewing. I tested it out by putting a photo of Setsuko Hara on top of several sheets of newspaper, then laying a wax stencil on top of that, and tracing the outlines of Setsuko Hara's face with little strokes of the needle. When I tried printing it, the result wasn't bad. My next experiment was a photograph of Mieko Takamine wearing a light summer kimono. I printed that on paper for flat fans. I wanted to use this new method to fill an order for one thousand fans from Asakusa Shochiku. That must have been the summer of 1937. I used blue ink, but I thought it lacked something, so I made the lips red with a little dab of paint. Those fans were a big hit.

"I had one of them myself," said Takahashi. "In fact, I gave one to each of my neighbors. Now we use it in the kitchen, and poor Mieko Takamine has gotten all covered with grease."

"Eventually, we ran out of paper for making fans, and we couldn't keep the business going... Anyway, that's pretty much the story of my experience with mimeographs."

Assuring Takahashi that I'd finish the job by morning, I got right to work. The grating on the backing board was clogged with wax, so I took a new brush and cleaned it thoroughly. As I was reading the notice, I came across these instructions: "Homeless air-raid victims who wish to use trolleys, the National Railways, or long-distance trains immediately following a major attack may ride free of charge, even without proper identification. In addition, in cases of major attacks only, those evacuating to relatives in the countryside are to be given free passage on the National Railways for several days following the attack (individual stations may issue free passes in some cases)."

I couldn't help but question "immediately following a major attack" and "in cases of major attacks only." I've often seen air-raid victims arguing with station employees about this, and there's nothing more pitiful. The distinction between a major and a minor attack is lost on someone whose home has been destroyed. Having your home burned to the ground is a major disaster, any way you look at it. That needs to be taken into account, and I believe that if the authorities show that kind of concern, the people will respond in kind. The spirit of the self-sacrifice in the hearts of the One Hundred Million citizens of our nation is built on just that kind of mutual trust. So I intentionally miscopied those two passages, replacing them with "whether or not immediately following a major attack" and "in all cases of attacks, whether major or not." If the people of Nezu were burned out of their homes, they could hand this notice to the train station staff and argue, "I don't care what you say, look at this notice from the Air Defense Headquarters." Of course, if Takahashi notices the change, I'll have to correct it, but...

My wife and Kinuko got back home at five o'clock.

May 2

Mr. Takahashi came over in the pouring rain to pick up the wax mimeograph stencil. He held it up to the light and nodded in approval. "Great job. I'll have to ask you to do all the stencil copying from now on."

"That's fine with me. It's not like I have a lot to do these days."

"Good. I'll leave the backing board and the stylus with you, then."

He didn't notice the miscopied passages.

Today we were supposed to deliver Kinuko's trousseau to the Furusawas, but the heavy rain made it impossible. I decided to postpone until tomorrow and go instead to the Komagome Post Office. I left with my wife, who was off to her family home in Shimotsuma to pick up our kimonos for the wedding. We'd taken all our good clothes to her parents' house. After seeing her off, I stopped to see my brother down the street.

As I slid open the door to his house, my sister-in-law Otae was in the kitchen, her eyes red from crying, and Sen-*chan* from the Mimatsuya was sitting in the living room, her back up very obviously over something, exhaling expensive tobacco smoke through her nostrils. My brother was on his knees between the two, picking up the pieces of a broken teacup. He seemed relieved when I arrived and came to greet me, stepping down into the entryway, which is very grand, at least four *tsubo* in area, with a concrete floor and a sofa and a table. It's where he meets his customers. When I told him I decided to deliver Kinuko's stuff to the Furusawas tomorrow, he said to me, "Shinsuke, you really don't know anything, do you? Tomorrow is no good. It's the day of the monkey. If you deliver the dowry goods on the day of the monkey, the couple will end up divorced. You know how the word for monkey and getting divorced are pronounced the same. Bad luck. But there's a nice vase in a wooden box in her trousseau, right? I'll deliver that to the Furusawas today. If one thing is delivered today, it means that her entire trousseau was delivered today."

"Is that how it works?"

"Yes, that's how it works," he said, pushing me toward the door with the end of his umbrella. "I have some business with Furusawa today anyway. Two birds with one stone."

As soon as we got out the door, lowering his voice, he asked, "Shinsuke, you going anywhere in particular?"

I told him I was headed for the Komagome Post Office to withdraw money from my time-deposit account to buy things for the wedding.

"Where have you been? The Komagome Post Office was destroyed on April 13th. There's a temporary post office in Asaka-cho where you can go. By the way, you noticed what was going on here, didn't you?"

"What do you mean?"

"The trouble between my old lady and Sen-*chan*."

"Yeah, of course I noticed."

"My old lady is Sen-*chan*'s aunt. That means that Sen-*chan* is her niece."

"That's what that means, of course."

"So they're like family, right? But they're constantly at each other. Women are really inflexible."

My brother kept strolling along with me, though he was supposed to be delivering that vase to the Furusawas. I realized he wanted to ask a favor. We had arrived at a burned-out section of the city. Though it was usually very dusty and charred-smelling, today, with the rain, there was neither dust nor odor. Here and there people were busy baling water out of their tunnels.

"Compared to most families, things are going pretty smoothly at your house, I think," I said. The population of Nezu had tripled since the air raids began. Every air-raid refugee who had a relative living in Nezu had moved in with them. For the first ten days or so, things went okay, but after a month every house had turned into a zoo. Fights were breaking out over food, clothes, anything. "I've heard of a few really crazy situations right here in Miyanaga-cho— where the husband starts something up with a woman who's moved in with the family."

"Sometimes they start having an affair," my brother said.

"Yeah. What a recipe for disaster."

"Well, that's what's happening to me," he said lightly, then paused before continuing. "I had a plan. As you know, Sen-*chan* lost her only son in the war, and the restaurant she was running with her husband in Asakusa was destroyed in an air raid, which also killed her husband. She's all alone. That means the only place left for her to live, until her dying day, is with her last surviving relative, my old lady—with me. Since she's the old lady's blood relation, I thought Sen-*chan* would be okay with that; you know, not feel like she was a burden. But after all, she's no relation to me, so I worried that she'd probably feel uncomfortable living off of my charity, and I didn't want that. And the old lady would feel bad about it too, since she was putting me in the position that I had to take in her niece. So that's when I decided the solution was to sleep with Sen-*chan*. If I was her lover, she could hold her head up and not feel beholden to anyone, and at the same time the old lady would also be off the hook. She wouldn't have to feel bad about giving me an extra mouth to feed, because now I had a relationship with Sen-*chan*. Since they were aunt and niece, okay, it might be a little uncomfortable at first, but eventually they'd work it out.

"That's what I thought, anyway. But ten days have gone by and they're still at each other's throats. So this is where you come in, Shinsuke. Once Kinuko goes to live in the Furusawa house, you'll have an extra room, right? I'd like to have you put Sen-*chan* up there. How about it? Think it over, will you?"

It's all well and good to ask someone to think it over, but a lot harder when you're the one who has to do the thinking. I could think it over for a hundred years and not come up with a good answer.

Off my brother went, deftly hopping over the puddles, back to Miyanaga-cho.

The temporary post office at Asaka-cho was like a battlefield. It took me half a day to make withdrawals from two time-deposit accounts. The postal clerks kept giving priority to any refugee who needed to make emergency withdrawals, so I couldn't complain, even when they cut in line. I suppose this can't be helped. One of the reasons the place was so crowded is that most of the refugees brought along a guarantor. This is because a new regulation has made it possible for refugees who have lost all their papers—savings account passbooks, time-deposit receipts, limited-term deposit receipts, fixed deferred savings account receipts, government bonds certificates, stock certificates—to withdraw a maximum of 5,000 yen at a time, on the spot, if they bring along their refugee identification cards and a guarantor. I wonder how many people were cheating. For example, it would be very easy to make an advance arrangement with a guarantor and, even if you only had, say, 2,000 yen in your account, you could claim you had 5,000 yen and the guarantor would back you up. The Komagome post office has been destroyed in a fire, which means they don't have any records either and can't know if you were lying, so they'll just pay out. I'm sure this must happen. What's going to happen to the country's finances? And what if this practice spreads and we become a nation of One Hundred Million crooks? The sacred Greater East Asia War would degenerate into a mud-slinging match between the Anglo-American demons and a nation of cheap crooks. Thinking about this in the post office, I suddenly felt a terrible rage, to a degree I'd never experienced before, about the enemy air raids and squadrons of B-29s.

I was exhausted when I got back home. When Kinuko saw me, she said, "There's a spot of blood on your jacket!" She dabbed at a stain of red on my right elbow with a damp cloth. Looking more carefully, I saw it wasn't blood but ink. And I remembered: there was a sign at the post office wall: "Those Who Have Lost Their Registered Seals May Use Their Fingerprints." One of the refugees must have brushed up against me with a thumb daubed with red ink.

May 3
Today I pulled the cart with Kinuko's trousseau to Senju under cloudy skies. Kiyoshi helped me, pushing from behind. He made quite a fuss, accusing me of being a heartless father for taking him out of school for something as stupid as this, asking why I couldn't get someone else to do it, but in the end he did his part. On the way, as we were crossing a razed section of the city, we saw a paper carp streamer flying in the sky, like a symbol of the invincible Japanese spirit.

The entire Furusawa family came out to welcome us. The clerks promptly unloaded the cart. Mr. Furusawa said warmly: "Lunch is being served in the guest house." Kiyoshi had already taken hold of the handle to the cart. "I'm Kinuko's brother, Kiyoshi," he said. "Please take good care of my sister," and with that he turned and headed back the way we'd come. Tadao's sister Tokiko followed after him calling out, "You must be hungry. I made breaded pork cutlets over rice. Please, come in and eat with us." But Kiyoshi was off and running. Tokiko made her way back to the house. "I've been snubbed," she said with a smile.

"I'm sorry he's such a rude kid."

"I don't give up so easily. I'll catch up with him on my bicycle."

"What?"

"I'll make some rice balls and go after him on the bicycle. There's just one road Kiyoshji can take, the Dokan Sando. I'll catch up with him in a flash. Please, come in, relax and enjoy yourself." Kicking her wooden sandals off in the entryway, she leaped up into the kitchen.

I liked her instantly.

Tadao said he had a delivery to make to Ohanajaya, just before Aoto, and the grandmother said she'd be taking a nap. In the end, it was just me and Mr. Furusawa who settled ourselves down in the guesthouse. His wife soon brought a bottle of beer. As she poured for us, I found myself trembling in pleasant anticipation.

"I never thought I'd see beer again," I said. I drank it down in a single chug. I felt a delightful shock, and little sparks began to go off in my head. "I can die peacefully now," I sighed.

"Why don't we put another bottle on ice?" said Mrs. Furusawa, transporting me into heaven, and she left us to do so.

"We plan to hold the reception here tomorrow, and from the day after that, this'll be where Tadao and Kinuko live. That's why we replaced the tatami," Mr. Furusawa said.

The tatami were fresh and green, smelling of dried grass. The tatami in our house were so old and soft that it felt like you were sitting on water, but these tatami underneath my knees had a pleasant firmness.

"Please, have the pork cutlet. This pork is nothing special, but tomorrow's beef will be really good."

"No, this pork is delicious."

"Not half as good as the beef we'll have tomorrow," Mr. Furusawa continued in a slightly peeved tone. "I sent one of my clerks to Yonezawa, in Yamagata Prefecture. He's supposed to arrive at Ueno Station on the first train tomorrow morning. Nothing can beat Yonezawa beef."

"It's amazing he was able to get a train ticket."

"With train tickets, if you think you can't get one, you never will, but if you think you can, they just materialize. That's how it is."

He sounded like a Zen monk.

"We'll be having fish, too. I sent another one of our clerks to Choshi."

I was beginning to feel a little sorry for myself, and changed the subject. "Did you hear the seven o'clock radio broadcast last night? Hitler was killed in an explosion, and Mussolini was executed by his adversaries."

"Yes, that's right. But the really bad news I got was about the konnyaku noodles."

"What?"

"I was hoping to serve the Yonezawa beef as sukiyaki, but I just can't seem to get ahold of any konnyaku noodles."

"Ah, that's what you mean. But I guess we don't have to have sukiyaki. After all, think of the times we're living in. Just having a platter of beef is more than enough. You can braise it in some tempura oil, and we can eat it with Yamasa soy sauce. That'll be more than anyone's expecting, I'm sure. It'll be a great treat for everyone there."

"Don't you think Kikkoman soy sauce is better?"

"Don't get me wrong—I'm not picky. Kikkoman will be fine."

"I really want to have sukiyaki, though. We've always served sukiyaki on festive occasions in the Furusawa family, you see."

"Ah yes, I see."

"I'm thinking that maybe we can make do by slicing some konnyaku very thin, so they are almost like noodles."

This old guy might really take a liking to Kinuko, I thought. She loves to cook, and she's a master with a kitchen knife. Watching her julienne a daikon is watching an artist at work. She's faster on the chopping block than an earthquake shaking the handles on a chest of drawers. She gives a locomotive racing *chugga-chugga-chugga-chugga* at full steam a run for its money. She's going to have this old man eating out of her hands in no time.

"We're going to have Hikari cigarettes. I've got a thousand. And a hundred bottles of beer. But the things I'm proudest of are the wedding favors for the guests: light bulbs."

"Light bulbs?"

"Light bulbs are good, but by themselves, just a little… ordinary, don't you think?"

"Are they?"

"Two light bulbs and… a package of dried squid. What do you say to that?"

"Incredible."

"There's more. A bag of dried sweet potatoes."

"…"

"And the capper, a string of bars of laundry soap, six bars to a string. Big as oranges."

These might be appropriate favors at the extravagant wedding of a serene royal princess and the young heir to a noble family that has demonstrated its martial prowess in the Meiji Restoration, but it doesn't seem right for the heir to a business selling farm implements in Senju and the daughter of an out-of-work fan maker in Nezu. When you think about the Imperial soldiers giving their lives to defend Okinawa and the refugees living in shelters dug into the earth beneath their burned-out homes, two light bulbs is more than generous, but adding a package of dried squid is just ostentatious. And then, on top of that, to throw in laundry soap, which costs 20 yen a bar on the black market! A copy of *Weekly Asahi* sells for 20 sen. A *tsubo* of land in front of Kokubunji Station on the Chuo Line is 10 yen. A bottle of ephedrine cough medicine is 50 sen, which everyone says was expensive—and here he is talking about laundry soap at 20 yen a bar. I wish this guy would take Kinuko's feelings into consideration a little. When she sees these extravagant wedding favors and realizes that her own parents hadn't contributed a single sen for them, she is bound to feel pretty embarrassed.

"You don't look well. Is something the matter?" asked Mr. Furusawa. "You're shaking."

I said that I'd just remembered something important I had to take care of, made my excuses and fled. I ran into Mrs. Furusawa in the yard.

"The beer is finally cold," she said.

"I'll wait until tomorrow," I replied, and rushed out the gate.

At five o'clock my wife returned from Shimotsuma with my father-in-law. He's a very cheerful guy, normally, but today he seemed unnaturally quiet. I went up to my wife, who was preparing dumpling soup, and asked, "What's the matter with your father? Another argument with his daughter?"

"No. He's been like that since the train went over the Arakawa Canal. I guess it's because of how much things have changed since his last visit to the city…"

"Oh yes, the last time he came was in October last year, wasn't it?"

"That's right. Remember? He brought us those chestnuts."

"And the air raids started in late November. That's why. Of course he's shocked."

"He listens to the radio and reads the papers, so he knew that things were pretty bad here in Tokyo, but when he saw it with his own eyes, he actually wept. 'I never dreamed it would come to this,' he said."

Dumpling soup is a top-rated favorite in our house. Even Kiyoshi puts on a smile when he hears we're having dumpling soup. And tonight he actually became talkative. He told us how Tokiko had come after him on her bicycle and given him three rice balls wrapped in nori. And how he looked at his watch, to time himself to see how fast he could eat them. After he'd finished, only three minutes had passed. He knew that no matter how quickly he shoved them down, he couldn't eat three rice balls in three minutes, so he checked his watch and discovered it had stopped while he was eating. So in the end, he had no idea how long it had taken him to eat the three rice balls. Anyway, he talked up a storm. For a second there I thought someone had secretly exchanged him with Shoichi next door.

"I may have lost a sister with Kinuko getting married, but I gained a new one with Tokiko. That's a fair trade. Actually, I think I got the better end of the bargain."

"Don't be smart," said Kinuko as she placed a dumpling in Kiyoshi's bowl. "That's your punishment."

"You should make friends with Tokiko," said Kiyoshi. "I think she's the kind of person you can rely on. Do what you need to get along with Tadao, but make sure you get Tokiko on your side."

"I can't do that. Tadao's going to be my husband, you know. Here, you get another punishment."

My father-in-law ate a mouthful of the soup, put his chopsticks down and went out onto the veranda. He seemed to be looking at the peonies while listening with one ear to the exchange between Kiyoshi and Kinuko. I took a teapot out to the veranda and poured a cup of tea for him.

"Shinsuke," he said, "why don't you come to Shimotsuma."

"You mean, evacuate from this place?"

"Yes, I guess so."

"But you're already taking care of Kikue and her family. You don't have room for us." Kikue is my wife's sister. Her husband was killed in battle on Java. She has three children, all very young, and it wouldn't be right for us to crowd them.

"You can live in the storehouse. If that's not good enough for you, I'll ask one of my friends to put you up."

"I would have no problem living in the storehouse."

"So you'll come, then?"

"But I like living here in Miyanaga-cho. That makes it hard to decide. If it was my older brother, well, he'd go anywhere. Instead of carrying on the family business, he left it all on me and went off to Taiwan, to Manchuria—and then just showed up here again in Miyanaga-cho. He's so casual about everything; sometimes I envy him. Me, on the other hand—I've never lived anywhere else. And if I went to Shimotsuma, I wouldn't have work."

"Work?"

"I'm thinking of starting up as a delivery service here. Though this thing is no good…" I stepped down into the yard, took four steps, and rapped my knuckles on the wall of the shed I kept the three-wheeler in. "It finally bit the dust. But I found someone willing to sell me a secondhand one."

"What're you going to do for gasoline?"

"I've hidden thirty gallons in a hole in the ground beneath the shed, along with six *sho* of Mobil oil, two gallons of gear oil, and three kilos of grease."

"And when that gasoline runs out?"

"Kinuko's new in-laws have promised to hire me to deliver some of their stuff, so I'll be able to get gas. Places selling agricultural equipment get a special gas ration."

"I see."

"And somehow I don't think that Nezu will be destroyed. I don't have any basis for that, it's just a feeling…"

"I don't agree with you there, I'm afraid. I think this is a pretty dangerous spot. I mean, you're right next to the Imperial university."

"Yes, at first everyone says that. Single B-29s are flying over the area every day on surveillance runs, so people think that the university is the next target. But so far they haven't dropped a single incendiary bomb here. They know that it remains untouched, but they haven't bombed us. Why?"

"Why do you think?"

"Because they don't want to."

"Humph. You're starting to sound like a Zen monk, son," and with a skeptical expression, he went back into the living room.

I recalled muttering to myself over lunch that Mr. Furusawa was sounding like a Zen monk, and I stood where I was for a while, considering whether I was starting to sound like him. Maybe I am. You have to think that you've attained some kind of enlightenment to survive in the Imperial capital. If you really thought about things logically, you wouldn't last a single day. I'm like Furusawa in that I've chosen to believe that I'm enlightened. And I have to believe that with all my heart—I believe in myself, believe in Miyanaga-cho, believe in the nation, believe that we'll all survive. It's a quiet night. I'll believe that the quiet will continue for one more day. Tomorrow is Kinuko's wedding day.

May 4

The wedding ceremony of Tadao Furusawa and Kinuko Yamanaka was held with solemn dignity at nine o'clock in the morning at Mitsukoshi in Nihonbashi. The ceremony was supposed to start an hour earlier, but when we arrived at Mitsukoshi at seven-thirty, and were awaiting our turn, a fierce argument broke out between the middle-aged woman in charge of the Mitsukoshi wedding hall and an unpleasant, overbearing, middle-aged man wearing a national civilian uniform, which resulted in a one-hour delay in our ceremony. As I listened to them going back and forth at each other, I gradually grasped the situation. The man, apparently from the Central Material Deployment Association, had come to requisition formal wedding wigs. His mission, as he explained with irritating officiousness, was to supply the wigs to a troupe of traveling actors who would be departing at noon on a tour to entertain the "warriors of industry" working in factories producing military supplies in the north Kanto region. The actors were putting on a play entitled *Bride on a Special Attack Forces Volunteer Base*, and the play couldn't be performed properly without a formal bridal wig. Furthermore, he continued, plays with brides were extremely popular, so the traveling troupe had decided to insert a bride wearing a formal bridal wig in all their plays from now on, and because of that, they didn't have enough wigs, so the Central Material Deployment Association was requisitioning Mitsukoshi's entire stock. This information, he added, had been communicated yesterday to the head of the store, who had approved the request.

The woman working at the wedding hall insisted that it was unfair that the first couple to get married that day should have the use of a rented wig when none of the other couples on the same day would. She pleaded that if today's brides were allowed to use the wig, Mitsukoshi, major department store that it was, would somehow be able to assemble as many as five or six wigs to offer to the Central Material Deployment Association tomorrow, holding firm to her insistence that she have a day's advance notice.

I listened to this argument with a very strange feeling. The Central Material Deployment Association seems to have a reserved space in the lower left corner of every newspaper, and I'm so accustomed to the announcement they ran there that I have it memorized. There is always the headline in big letters: "The War Situation Is Grave; We Need Your Aluminum Change," followed by the words:

You all know how critical 10 sen, 5 sen, or even 1 sen coins are in manufacturing new aircraft. Your each and every aluminum coin can become a part of an aircraft's wing or motor, contributing to the valiant fight of our Special Attack Forces volunteers. All Imperial subjects must unite as one and contribute their aluminum coins to the effort to crush our arrogant foes. Please bring your coins to any bank, trust company, insurance company, municipal credit union, farm bureau, credit association or mutual finance corporation...

Because of this announcement, the connection in my mind between the Central Material Deployment Association and aluminum coins was as automatic and inseparable as that between Mitsukoshi and department store, Teikoku Theater and play, heart palpitations and Kyushin Heart Pills, cuts and Hariba Ointment, middle-aged women and Teikoku Hormone Manufacturing Company's Ovahormone Elixir. It's never occurred to me that, as well as our aluminum coins, the Central Material Deployment Association might also want formal wedding wigs.

As anyone would have guessed, the Mitsukoshi woman lost in the end. It's not that I didn't want Kinuko to be able to wear a fancy wig on her wedding day, but after all, we are in the middle of a war. After the argument was settled, it took some time to get the wigs and hand them over, so the actual ceremony started an hour late. Kinuko was beautiful in the formal wedding kimono, wig or no wig. She looked so splendid and regal that it was hard to believe she was my own daughter. Tadao wore a brand-new national civilian uniform. If only he were two or three inches taller and not wearing those spectacles with lenses thick as pancakes, he would have seemed a perfect match for Kinuko. On the other hand, if his height and vision were normal, he'd have been drafted long ago and we wouldn't have been celebrating a wedding today. When I thought of that, he suddenly looked just fine. As the couple stood in front of the Shinto altar, the Shinto priest entered carrying a low wooden stand with a cloth resting on it. There was a rust-colored stain about the size of a small lozenge on the cloth. The priest placed the tray in front of Kinuko and said: "Before we begin the ceremony, I'd like to receive some blood from the bride-to-be, while she is still a pure and unsullied virgin."

Apparently this was news to Kinuko, and she raised her demurely lowered head and looked over at Tadao.

"At this wedding hall, before drinking the ceremonial saké to commemorate the marriage, we receive a drop of blood from each loyal bride of the Empire, which we use to make headbands with the rising sun of the Imperial flag in blood."

The priest picked up something from the wooden tray. "Please prick the tip of your ring finger and squeeze out a drop of your blood onto this cloth."

What I had over-hastily taken for a stain was, in fact, a drop of blood from the bride of the previous newlyweds—or more precisely, since it was given before they were technically wives, the girls' last drop of blood as an unmarried virgin.

"As you are well aware, with the sudden demise of Hitler and Mussolini, the leaders of our two allied nations, and the dramatic changes in the war situation in Europe, it cannot be denied that the influence of the Axis powers has been greatly diminished. Regardless of the fate of our former allies in Germany and Italy, however, the path of our sacred Empire remains unchanged. The last of the three great nations who rose up and joined together to create a new world order in both East and West to remain standing, we will continue to advance valiantly with the bright torch of the Imperial Declaration of War borne proudly aloft, undaunted by the darkness on all sides. Steadfastly determined to defend this Land of the Gods against the Anglo-American demons, fiendish partners in an alliance to threaten our Empire and menace our survival with unjust and draconian economic sanctions, our staunchly unyielding spirit will not waver in the slightest to the very end of the Greater East Asia War."

Everyone in the hall seemed to be powerfully uplifted by this stirring, if unexpected, oration from the Shinto priest, and we all leaned in toward him, as if drawn by a magnetic field. Only Kinuko was pulling back from the priest's gesticulating right hand. It was the hand that was still holding the needle.

"What, indeed, is the purpose of this holy war?" the priest went on. "To preserve the peace of our Empire. To liberate Asia. And, furthermore, to establish a foundation of human justice, in the form of building a new order of mutual prosperity and coexistence for Asia and the world, grounded on the highest moral principle. As such, as long as we steadfastly uphold this conviction as a people, whatever changes that occur in the war in the West are meaningless to us. If we press indomitably onward, inflamed with the same fiery courage on the home front and on the battlefront, filled with spirit and hope, determined to defend our country to the last man, the Empire is indestructible. Members of the Furusawa and Yamanaka families, I just said 'filled with spirit and hope, determined to defend our country to the last man,' and the spirit of which I speak is the spirit of our Special Attack Forces volunteers. Now, at this very moment, at bases of the Special Attack Forces volunteers, one after another of those proud young eagles prepared to martyr themselves for their lofty ideals and brimming with the determination to destroy the enemy by turning their bodies into living balls of fire, are taking off into the skies, heading for the seas off Okinawa with only enough fuel to carry them to their final destination. This cloth will be delivered to one of those bases, where it will be presented to one of those young eagles by his commanding officer just before he takes flight. Yes, that's right—before Kinuko Yamanaka becomes the wife of Tadao Furusawa, she'll be the wife of one of those brave young eagles. And so the home front and the front lines of battle will be mystically united, and through that union, the spirit of that young eagle, that 'spirit and hope to defend our country to the last man,' will be conferred upon Kinuko Yamanaka. It goes without saying that it will also be transmitted to her husband, Tadao Furusawa, and the spirit of the Special Attack Forces volunteers will fill the home front—"

Just at that moment, a siren wailed on the ground floor above us. A cautionary alert siren. The priest looked up and spun around where he stood, dropped the needle on the tray, and rushed over to the side of the woman from Mitsukoshi, who had been waiting in a corner of the hall.

"Don't worry," she reassured him, "this is below ground, and as sturdy as a bomb shelter. An incendiary bomb could fall right on top of us and nothing in the room would budge." She spoke in such a loud and ringing tone that I'm sure she was trying to reassure us as well. "It's bound to be just a surveillance mission. They never bomb in the middle of the day. Anyway, other couples are waiting. Please continue."

This seemed to be as much a first for the priest as for us. When he returned to the altar, Kinuko was squeezing out a drop of blood from her finger.

After the ceremony we went to another room to have a photograph taken. My wife had tears in her eyes.

"Wipe your eyes," I whispered.

"Wipe your own," she said.

The photographer made a stern face and turned to us. "Please don't talk or move. One photographic plate per couple. There's no reshoot."

Just before he pressed the shutter, a warning siren sounded. I hope that photo turns out to be a good one and none of us is frowning.

In a room next to the one in which the photograph was taken, two rows of narrow tables had been set up. On the table were servings of red-bean rice, in portions about the size of an Athena inkbottle from Maruzen Stationers, and fruit juice. I ate the rice, savoring each grain as if it were the last, as I introduced my family members. The Furusawas devoured their red-bean rice in a flash, like horses munching on a carrot; we Yamanakas took the tiniest possible bites, like silkworms chewing on a heaping pile of mulberry leaves that never seems to diminish in size. The gap between our daily diets was on clear display. Finally the woman from Mitsukoshi brought in a dozen bottles of beer.

"The difference between today's ceremony and tomorrow's is going to be as dramatic as night and day. You're very lucky. Congratulations," she said and bowed.

The Foodstuffs Division of the Municipal Economic Agency is in charge of food distribution in the Imperial capital. Just yesterday, the agency announced a change in the special liquor allowance for those joining the army and going off to the front, or for civil ceremonies such as marriages and funerals, declaring that from May 5th the ration will be cut in half. Soldiers who are drafted or demobilized are now allotted two *sho* of blended saké or one case of beer; from tomorrow that will be halved. Likewise, the one *sho* of blended saké and six bottles of beer allotted for weddings will also be reduced by half.

"Here's the full one dozen bottles of beer that has been allotted to the two families together," the Mitsukoshi woman went on. "I'm sorry about the wig, but couples getting married from tomorrow on will have to go without a wig and also have only half the liquor. Please bear that in mind and continue to give Mitsukoshi your patronage."

"We'd be happy to, but you don't have anything to sell," said Mr. Furusawa tauntingly. "Every floor is empty. The only things for sale are items made from wood—chopping boards, wooden rice paddles, and wooden sandals."

"Yes, but we still have more to sell than Takashimaya. The only thing on sale there are military swords."

And with this successful rebuttal by the redoubtable woman from Mitsukoshi, the ceremony ended.

We said our farewells to Tadao and Kinuko and the entire Furusawa family and returned to Nezu. At noon my wife and I went to the reception at Furusawa Enterprises near Ohashi, Senju. At the reception there were platters of sashimi, bubbling pots of sukiyaki with Yonezawa beef, trays heaped with peanuts, large bowls of mountain vegetables—it seemed as if the clock had been turned back to 1937 or 1938, it was such an incredible spread. There was as much saké and beer as you could drink, and cigarettes were on the house. I couldn't but be astonished anew at the prosperity of the Furusawas.

My brother, who had been the go-between, sidled up to me and said in an irritatingly patronizing tone: "Hey, Shinsuke, do you know how much all this cost? Aside from the wedding favors, it comes to 130 yen a head. Kinuko's caught the goose that laid the golden egg." He stood there smoking a Hikari cigarette. But he had a method to the way he did it. He'd take two cigarettes from the tray. One he put in his mouth, and when he stuck his hand into his pocket to pull out a match, the other cigarette disappeared. I knew very well what he was doing, but since he was one of Furusawa's suppliers of all the black-market contraband they dealt in it seemed unnecessary to pull this kind of trick. "I have no intention of using my daughter to get my hands on someone's black-market leftovers," I said. But my brother wasn't the only one filching cigarettes. When I looked around, everyone at the reception seemed to be no less wondrously dexterous. One, a real master of his craft, could toss peanuts into his mouth and his breast pocket at the same time. I started to feel like I was at a magician's convention. Suddenly I heard the sound of the "Rising Sun March" on the shamisen and a woman's voice singing as she danced.

> The Rising Sun Flag that I waved in my little hand,
> that day, tied to my mother's back—
> It's a faded memory now, but
> the patriotism burning in my heart back then
> still runs hotly through my veins.

"Isn't that Sen-*chan*?" I asked my brother in surprise. "Where's your wife? She was at the ceremony at Mitsukoshi."

"The old lady attended the wedding ceremony and Sen-*chan* is here at the reception. I had them take turns."

He looked happily at Sen-*chan* and began to wiggle his hips to the rhythm of the shamisen. "As you know, before Sen-*chan* got married and went to work at the Mimatsuya Restaurant in Asakusa, she was a very popular geisha in the entertainment district behind Kannon-sama. Putting her experience to use as an entertainer is a great idea, don't you think? Just imagine if the old lady was here instead with her hair and teeth falling out. She'd destroy the mood. In other words, the right person for the right place."

And then he floated away to Sen-*chan*'s side and began to dance with her. Tadao's stepmother was playing the shamisen. She was a former geisha, too, from the Kameido entertainment district, and apparently hadn't forgotten what she'd learned there.

As we helped ourselves to the sukiyaki, I found myself next to a man who had fought together with Mr. Furusawa in the navy. His name was Fujikawa, and he was employed as a receiver at the city hall in Kamagaya, Chiba. During the Great Kanto earthquake, he told me, he had stood on the deck of the flagship of the Kure Naval

District Fleet that had rushed to the scene, and together he and Furusawa watched the smoke rising from the burning city.

"You know, the commander-in-chief of the Kure Naval Base at that time was none other than our Prime Minister Kantaro Suzuki. He was worried about the Imperial palace, so he felt compelled to order the fleet to sail immediately from Kure to Shinagawa Bay. All Japanese revere his Imperial Majesty, of course, but no one as much as Prime Minister Suzuki."

"He's the grand chamberlain, too, isn't he?"

"Yes, he's His Imperial Majesty's right-hand man."

"Which means…"

"It's completely different from the Tojo cabinet or the Koiso cabinet. The Emperor is personally in charge. For the first time, His Imperial Majesty's honorable wishes will come to the fore in the government."

"It looks like the time's coming when all One Hundred Million subjects, superiors and inferiors, will unite to fight for the homeland."

"Well, I don't know about that," said Fujikawa, sticking one Hikari between his lips and another into his pocket as he lit a match. "I do believe, however, that His Imperial Majesty will start… taking control… of the war situation now…"

"Taking control?"

"Bring an end to the fighting, I mean."

"Hey, hey, you're not supposed to be talking about the war." It was my brother, back clutching a large bottle of saké. "Don't come crying to me if you get dragged away by the military police. And what's the point of thinking about tomorrow? If we can just enjoy today, what more can we ask for? Sen-*chan*'s here and I have plenty to drink. This is paradise." He took a swig of saké directly from the bottle.

The wedding favors were distributed at six o'clock. With the blackout, you can't exactly keep the lights lit and go on partying through the night. The favors included, just as Furusawa had told me the other day, two light bulbs, a package of dried squid, a package of dried sweet potatoes, and a rope of laundry soap. I don't know how many hundreds or thousands of couples got married across the country today, but the Furusawas had without a doubt thrown the most lavish celebration of them all. As we were about to leave, Kinuko gave us a small package wrapped in newspaper.

"It's some leftover Yonezawa beef. Give it to Kiyoshi and the others."

No matter how you look at it, I think it's too early for Kinuko to be acting like the lady of the house and handing out gifts to her family. But I accepted it, gratefully. When I stepped out the door, something black brushed by my head. It seems that the swallows have returned from the south.

May 5

I stayed home today with the intention of writing down what happened yesterday, but at 10:35 A.M. there was a cautionary alert siren, which was called off at 11:20. In that period, three planes flew overhead, one at a time. Thinking that it was just more surveillance, I ignored the warning. In the evening, Kiichiro Aoyama, the head of the Miyanaga-cho Neighborhood Association, dropped by to complain: "You're qualified to be on the fire-defense brigade, but when the sirens sounded this morning you just stayed inside your house and didn't make any preparations. Only the residents of Miyanaga-cho can defend the neighborhood from firebombs. If one member of the fire-defense brigade shirks his duty, he puts Miyanaga-cho at risk. That's completely irresponsible. If it happens again, I'll report you to the police, so be forewarned."

I wonder how the Neighborhood Association chief knew that I had stayed inside and didn't bother to strap on my leggings during an alert. Maybe he can see through walls.

I listened to songs by Yumeji Tsukioka and Masako Kawada on the radio and went to bed early. I was awakened at 11:30 by a cautionary alert siren. At 11:40 the air-raid siren sounded. Nighttime alerts are often the real thing, so, thinking at last we were really going to be bombed, I strapped on my leggings and put on my fire cap. Since I didn't have to worry any longer about Kinuko's wedding trousseau, it was somehow less tense than before. Searchlight beams moved back and forth, caressing the clouds hanging in the sky. When they faded, stars were visible through breaks in the clouds. I was on the alert, but in the end nothing happened. At 12:30 the air-raid warning was canceled and at 12:50 the cautionary alert was called off.

May 6

This morning, the seven o'clock radio news said that a squadron of twenty planes had dropped torpedoes in the Inland Sea. I wondered if control of our air space had fallen into enemy hands. It was the start of a chilly, anxious day.

My father-in-law returned to Shimotsuma on the early morning train.

At eight-thirty in the morning, Kinuko came for her visit home, bringing Tadao with her. It seems that Furusawa Enterprises is closed on Sundays. They left as soon as they finished breakfast. In just two days, Kinuko has been transformed into a different person. Up until the day before yesterday, you'd have to describe her as rather sharp—though not in a bad way. She had a straight nose, a firm mouth, and her narrow eyes were clear and cool. Her neck was as long and thin as a crane's. In middle school she was the vice-captain of the table tennis team and her body was taut; when she crossed a room, she always walked in a straight line, taking the fewest steps possible to get to where she was going. "She's a real beauty," my brother used to say, "but if she's not careful she's going to turn into a beautiful young boy." But Kinuko this morning? She was all round and soft, like a sponge wrapped in a jellyfish. Her eyes looked like wet velvet, with a rich glow. In short, she was suddenly sensual and warm. Maybe the food at the Furusawas was that much better. Or maybe this happens to all girls when they get married. They brought gifts for us: cloth for a suit for my brother, salted salmon and three bottles of beer for me, 500 *momme* of sugar for my wife, and beautiful new paulownia wood sandals for Takeko, Fumiko and Kiyoshi. The three kids actually were more excited about the sugar than the sandals.

My wife immediately set about simmering the salted cod we'd purchased for the occasion. We were hoping to have a nice lunch of a stew made of the cod, potatoes, and onions, with a side dish of salted salmon, but the B-29s had other plans. At nine o'clock a cautionary alert siren sounded, so we extinguished the charcoal burner and prepared to evacuate the house. The cautionary alert was canceled twenty-five minutes later, but stews shouldn't have the heat turned off halfway through, apparently; we were left with some very unpleasant tasting "cod-potatoes." At 11:25, we had broiled the salmon and I was trying to drink a beer with Tadao with the salmon for a snack when the cautionary alert sounded again. I put on my leggings and went outside, and as if they'd been waiting for me, they sounded the all-clear. By this time the salmon was cold and the beer was flat. At noon, just as we had all sat down to eat some freshly cooked rice, the cautionary alert siren sounded for the third time. It was canceled again at 12:25. In other words, from 11:25 in the morning, Tadao and I spent an hour going in and out of the house smelling the salmon, beer, and freshly cooked rice and then heading outdoors again. I'm happy to eat whatever's on the table, but I hate letting food get cold.

After lunch, Kinuko and Tadao took Takeko and the others to Asakusa to see a movie starring Denjiro Okochi at the Asakusa Shochiku Theater. It was *Legends of Valiant Swordsmen of Japan*. As I helped my wife clean up, she said: "The Furusawas have already spent 10,000 yen on Kinuko and Tadao. With betrothal gifts, the new tatami, the reception and then today's gifts, this is adding up. Apparently, every so often someone in the neighborhood throws a stone in the Furusawas' window, angry at how much money they're making from the black market. Kinuko said that she thinks there's something unsavory about the family."

"What does Tadao think about this?"

"About what?"

"What does he think about the splashy way his family throws their money around?"

"He probably doesn't think anything at all about it."

I thought that if Tadao stopped by the house on his way back I'd tell him the story of the great banker Zenjiro Yasuda. No matter how important the visitor was, the only thing Yasuda ever served was plain, cold soba noodles. Once his wife suggested that at least he offer the cold noodles on a the traditional woven bamboo sieve, with a sprinkling of chopped seaweed, but he refused, saying that he didn't want his money flowing away like water through a sieve. Without that kind of thrift, Yasuda would never have become the great banker he was. Of course, this was originally the punch line of a comic routine by Musei Tokugawa, so it's not very likely to be true.

Takeko and the kids got back at 4:30. Tadao and Kinuko had said goodbye to them on the west side of Azumabashi in Asakusa, and were going to take the trolley to the last stop at the Minami Senju Train Depot and then walk the rest of the way. When they were leaving, Tadao gave each of them a little gift of 10 yen. He's never going to be a great banker, that's obvious.

May 7

I can't help thinking that the B-29s have gotten more efficient. Recently their surveillance flights over the city seem to be getting longer and longer. They used to fly off after fifteen, maybe thirty minutes, but this morning one spent an entire hour circling overhead. The problem is, as long as they're up there, the cautionary alert remains in effect. In the last few days, in particular, with water restrictions, we can only get water for two-and-a-half hours, from 10 A.M. to 12:30 P.M. The B-29 appeared as if it had coordinated itself with our time slot, and flew around for an hour, which means we couldn't fill one bucket full with water. As always, the tap dribbles out like an old man's piss, and it takes fifteen or twenty minutes to fill a single bucket. Sometimes the water stops altogether, and we're lucky if we can fill five or six buckets in our allotted two-and-a-half hours. That's not enough to give yourself a sponge bath before bed. In fact, it's not enough for cooking and washing dishes. That's why it's such a bother to have a single B-29 looping around for as long as it likes. But I wonder why the B-29s seem to be able to do as they please lately. It's disturbing.

We had a regular meeting of our block group in the workshop. The women were in the back room. They'd covered the windows with blackout cloths and were making bandages for the soldiers. There aren't enough for the men at the front, and we also need to stockpile bandages for the air raids and the invasion of the Homeland. The Great Japan National Women's Association has started a bandage drive. Our block group had been assigned the task of making one thousand bandages. Of course no one had any white cotton, so they gathered together every piece of used cloth they could find—old sheets, old curtains, old bathrobes—and were taking out the seams and tearing and cutting them up into bandages. Families that didn't have enough old cloth brought bundles of still quite useable clothes, though they were none too happy about it. Sometimes, where we men were gathered, we could hear the sound of cloth ripping in the back room. It was heartrending, almost like a person crying.

"This year the citizens of Tokyo have been told that they need to save 11 billion yen. Last year it was 9.5 billion yen, so that's, let's see, an increase of sixteen percent." We couldn't see who was speaking in the darkened workshop where we were meeting, but we all knew it was the voice of Takahashi, our block group leader. Working at a newspaper as he did, he always had the facts at his fingertips—though he was actually a photographer, not a reporter.

"According to our company's research, the present population of Tokyo is 2.2 million."

Someone gasped in the darkness. It wasn't me, but I was startled by the figure, too. In the ad hoc census held in February of last year, the population had been nearly 7.5 million. Naturally, a large part of the population had evacuated since then, and many had died in the bombings. But I had thought that at least four million people were still here, so the figure of 2.2 million was shocking! In the fifteen months since last February, seven-tenths of the city's population had disappeared. What is going on?

"Dividing 11 billion yen by 2.2 million, each person needs to come up with 5,000 yen."

This time we all gasped.

"That's right. Now in my case, my monthly pay is 200 yen. That means, over a year, with everything thrown in, I might or might not make about 3,000 yen. In other words, if I saved my entire income, I couldn't even come up with the amount that's being assigned to one individual. And there are five people in my family, which means I'm supposed to save 25,000 yen, but as I've said, I can't even come up with one person's share, so that goal of 11 billion yen is a complete fantasy. The government knows this, of course. If they know it, why do they put it out there and assign it to us? The only thing that I can think of is that these government officials want to make an impression on somebody that they're doing their job, so they come up with these crazy figures…" Takahashi suddenly swallowed his words. "But I'm not here to criticize the authorities. Anyway, the metropolitan government seems to have decided to requisition 9.5 billion of the 11 billion yen needed from the postal savings accounts of residents, and has said that it's our duty as citizens to raise the remaining 1.5 billion yen through additional contributions to savings accounts to be used by the government…"

"I don't like being bullied like this," said Gen the tailor. He was the best off in our neighborhood association. He brought two bags of dried sweet potatoes to the meeting (I brought one piece of dried squid). When the Wartime Simplified Clothing Ordinance went into effect in June two years ago, long-sleeved kimono and double-breasted Western suits were outlawed. Since then he's had two years of incredible business turning double-breasted suits into single-breasted suits. The hardest thing for him has been finding enough thread, and he's taken to saying, "I run out of money when I run out of thread."

"If you knew from the start that our portion was going to be 1.5 billion yen, why didn't you just say so, instead of trying to scare us?"

"Well, 1.5 billion yen is still a lot you know. For example, in my case, it means…" And Takahashi laid out his family budget:

Regional Association dues1	5 yen
Neighborhood Association dues	25 yen
Professional Union dues	20 yen
Women's Association dues	5 yen
Middle School tuition (Shoichi)	2 yen
Public Elementary School (Kazuko, Jiro)	1 yen each
Total:	68 yen

"From my salary of 200 yen, it's my duty as a citizen to put this much aside every month. Then there's taxes—30 yen. That means, of my 200 yen salary, we have only 100 yen a month left to live on. I'm not complaining, but that's tough. Anyway, from next month, let's try to come up with 40 or 50 yen, including the wives' portions.

Outside Shoichi and Kiyoshi were talking. No one inside said anything, so we could all hear them clearly.

"I think the German's surrender was part of their strategy. After all, they say that the entire Nazi Party has gone underground.

The members of the Nazi propaganda ministry, and the party organization, the heads of the Gestapo and the Schutztaffel—they've all disappeared. Kiyoshi, that's very strange. They're pretending to be defeated, but soon they'll start an underground resistance campaign against the Americans and the British. That's got to be what's going on."

"I guess that's the kind of simplistic reasoning you'd expect from a first-year middle school student. As a second-year student, I have a better grasp of things. I've thought the whole thing over carefully. The war is over in Europe. The Allies have nothing left to do in Europe, so they have time on their hands. Now they're going to redirect all the forces in Europe over to Asia."

"I've never heard anything so stupid."

"Just listen, Sho. England, in particular, is raring to go. It has a lot of colonies in Asia. They don't want to be outshone by the Americans, because that'll give the Americans a big say, and they're going to take the Brits' colonies away from them. That's what's going to make the British our most dangerous enemy. They're going to come at us with everything they've got. England is the most racist country in the world. I was talking about it today with the school janitor, and he said that the British don't even consider you a human being unless you speak their language. Everyone else is subhuman to them, he said. The Americans speak English, too, but the Brits even look down on them as inferior. They see themselves at the top, the Americans far, far down the ladder, and everyone else—just barnyard animals. That's the way they are, he said. As proof, they have vicious nicknames for every other nationality. They call the Italians 'wops,' which means something like affected sissies; they call the French 'frogs'; the Germans are 'squareheads'; the Chinese, 'chinks,' because of their slanted eyes."

"This guy sure seems to know a lot for just being a janitor."

"Before that, he was an English instructor there."

"I see, that's why he knows all this. And what do the Brits call us?"

"'Yellow bellies,' which means cowards. They say that our skin is yellow, and when you add 'belly,' he said it means a coward."

"I really hate those English bastards. Once I graduate from the naval academy at Etajima, the first thing I'm going to do is kill one of them. But Kiyoshi, do you think the Russians will come over to our side? We had a neutrality treaty with them. It would just be another step to become allies."

"I doubt it. I mean, way before the neutrality treaty, we had the Protocol concluded by Italy, Germany and Japan. The Germans called it the Anti-Comintern Pact, right? It said that all three of us would fight together against any threat from the communists. And that led to the Tripartite Pact, and then the Tripartite Declaration of War, and the Axis Military Alliance. The Japanese-Soviet Neutrality Treaty came after those, so the Russians probably resented us. And since then the Russians have declared that they have no intention of extending the neutrality pact. It's still good for a year, but they might announce that they're abandoning it at any minute. Anyway, Sho, why do we need to team up with the Soviets? After we win the Greater East Asian War, we're just going to have to fight them anyway."

"Yes, I suppose you're right."

"The only thing is we want to Soviets to keep out of it while we're fighting the Americans and British. We just have to pray that the Russians don't attack us before we finish them off."

"The other day Foreign Minister Togo said the same thing. There was a major foreign policy statement in the papers this morning, and it just kept repeating that our only enemies are the Americans and the British."

"Are you just going to let them go on mouthing off like that?" asked Gen the tailor. "It's dangerous to discuss the war in public. You never know when the military police might be listening."

"I wouldn't worry about it, unless they were saying something a lot worse than that." It was the first time Dr. Igarashi, our local dentist, had spoken. I think he'd actually been napping up to then. "They're not going to be carting off the precious young men the Empire needs to fight its battles. All right, I'm off now. Got to study, got to study."

The women's bandage-making session seemed to have come to an end, too, and Mrs. Igarashi emerged from the back room. "My husband's going to become a medical doctor, on top of being a dentist. With the shortage of doctors, the Ministry of Health has decided to allow dentists to get their medical licenses by just taking a paper test."

"And that's what I have to study for."

"Really? And when's the test?" asked Gen the tailor.

"At the end of September."

"You're starting pretty late, then. Sounds kind of scary to me. I'm the first to say that you're the best dentist in Nezu, but starting out as a doctor at your age? That's not right."

"Don't worry," said Dr. Igarashi with self-assurance. "People today don't have very complicated medical problems. Most of them have been wounded in air raids, or have some kind of skin disease. If you know how to treat wounds and the names of the proper lotions to rub on people's skin, you can do just fine as a doctor. I'm sure the Ministry of Health doesn't expect much more."

The wind is blowing tonight, but so far no cautionary air-raid alerts. I hope I sleep soundly.

May 8

The cautionary alert sounded at 11:30 this morning. According to the radio, a dozen or so large planes were approaching the coast; the announcer immediately corrected himself, saying a hundred small planes. Suddenly the air raid sirens sounded. I certainly didn't appreciate the idea of celebrating the monthly anniversary of the Imperial Declaration of War to the accompaniment of machine-gun fire. The clouds were low in the sky and it was dark, and from time to time a strange wind blew. There was definitely something ominous about the whole thing.

Just as I was saying to my wife, "I don't care if I get in trouble with the Neighborhood Association leader, let's take shelter in one of the dugouts in Ueno Hill," a mailman from the Hongo Post Office delivered a special delivery postcard. From this month, both the telegraph and the post offices have eliminated all holidays, and in places that have been targeted by aerial attacks, they will be open twenty-four hours a day, so they still deliver mail even when a cautionary alert had been sounded. I took the postcard and offered the deliveryman a dried sweet potato. The postcard was from the Yamamoto Saké Brewery in Toride, and it read:

Thank you for coming all the way up here to inquire about the three-wheeled truck. I'm sorry I couldn't meet you in person. If you're still interested, I'm prepared to sell it. I'm not interested in installment payments, however. I want 7,000 yen in cash. This is my condition. I'm afraid it's not negotiable. I'll be back at home from the woolen cloth factory in Kashiwa on the weekend. If you can't make it on the weekend, you can work it out with my wife. I've explained the matter to her in detail.

The postcard had been mailed from the Toride post office on April 28th. It had taken eleven days to get from Toride to Nezu. Given that mail trucks were often bombed and all their letters and packages reduced to ashes, I was glad it had arrived at all. About ten small planes continued to buzz through the skies over Nezu without doing anything until a little after noon (12:25, to be precise), and then the air-raid alert was lifted. I learned later that about one hundred small P-51s, with an advance guard of two or three B-29s, had come in low over Chiba and, in squadrons of fifteen to thirty planes, had attacked air fields and military supply factories with machinegun fire.

Throwing my backpack over my shoulder, I went to my brother's house. He was in the process of dividing the living room in two with a rusty sheet of corrugated tin roofing.

"I took Sen-*chan* to Kinuko's wedding reception, right? Since then the old lady's been up in arms." He made the gesture of a demon's horns over his head.

"She says she never wants to set eyes on Sen-*chan* again. But at the same time, I can't send Sen-*chan* away, either. I'm putting up this barrier as a last resort. It seems that the old lady is especially upset about not getting to eat any of the sukiyaki. Can you believe it? Her nose is out of joint about the food."

I showed my brother the postcard from the Yamamoto Brewery owner and asked if I could borrow another 6,000 yen, in addition to the 1,000 he'd loaned me on the 26th. I added that I'd put up the 2,000 flat fans and the 400 folding fans that we'd stored in Yamanashi as collateral. And I said that if I could get started in the delivery

business, money would be coming in and I could pay him back at
the rate of 10 yen a day.

"How about I just buy the fans from you? With summer coming
up, I know I'll be able to sell them at a good price. It's not a bad deal
for either of us." He began to count crisp 200 yen bills from his cash
box. "7,000 yen is not expensive for that three-wheeled truck, but
let's try to get them down to 5,000." He took three strings of laundry
soap down from the ceiling and stuffed them into my knapsack.

"You wait for the right moment, and then you give his wife one
string of soap bars."

Apparently as a black marketer, you have to have a good grasp of
human psychology.

"Don't offer her the soap right off the bat. She'll only think that
you're desperate to have the truck. The secret is to just take out
the soap real casually, when the negotiations seem to be hitting a
bit of a sticking point, and say, "Oh, by the way, I brought you a
little present." If things go smoothly, there's no reason even to bring
out the soap, and it'll be yours to keep. And you know, soap can
be converted into rice, into potatoes—into just about anything you
please."

By the time I left my brother's house, the cautionary alert siren
was called off. Under the regulations in effect now, Toride counts
as a mid-range destination, which means you have to line up at the
window to buy a ticket. So I put a little trick I learned from my
brother to use, and bought a ticket to Matsudo. Matsudo is a close-
range destination. At the ticket office I saw the following notice,
which I copied out:

Some passengers seem to be under the impression that
they're allowed to purchase round-trip tickets to close-range
destinations, and they walk up to the window and demand a
round-trip to such-and-such station. This shows a complete
absence of patriotism and the spirit of self-sacrifice. Our Special
Attack Forces pilots take off from their airstrips with just enough
fuel to carry them to their destination, where they are prepared
to give up their precious lives and become corpses floating on
the sea. That's why the Special Attack Forces are known as

"the one-way ticket to death." In accord with this spirit of self-sacrifice, we are no longer selling round-trip tickets.

I went all the way to Toride on my Matsudo ticket and then paid the extra fare of 4 yen 20 sen. This is the way my brother always travels to mid-range destinations on close-range tickets. Since it was Tuesday, the brewery owner wasn't at home, so I negotiated with his wife. She served me salted boiled beans and rice balls with miso, but she refused to budge on the price, saying, "My husband told me not to take so much as a one sen off the asking price of 7,000 yen." But, just as my brother suspected, she was no match for the laundry soap. When I took out one string of bars, she began to waver. "When I tell my husband I agreed on 6,500 yen, he's going to smack me for sure. But I'm used to that…" When I placed the second string of soap bars in front of her, she said with a laugh, "If he smacks me, I'll smack him right back. Lately I've taken to doing that, too." And with that, we had a deal—actually slapping hands on it—at 6,500 yen. I didn't bring out the third string of soap bars. We decided that I'd pick up the three-wheeled truck on Saturday afternoon, when her husband was home again, and I gave her 5,000 yen, with the balance to come on Saturday. She in turn gave me a present of two light bulbs, two *go* of cooking oil, three carrots, six *momme* of miso and four *go* of saké. I was so happy that I gave her the third string of soap bars. I guess I'm not cut out to be a black marketer. The old man I met last time hadn't made an appearance the entire time I was there, so I asked after him.

Tears suddenly came to her eyes as she explained: "He finally went off his rocker. The slightest sound of a plane and he'd run out into the road screaming, 'A drum can's exploding, a drum can's exploding!' He'd dance around like a crazy person and ended up foaming at the mouth and collapsing. The day before yesterday my husband admitted him to a hospital in Ichikawa." Her wet eyes were crinkled into little half-moons.

"There are a lot of people in Tokyo who've been driven crazy by the bombings, too. There were several dozen at Ueno Station. They dance around in the station like madmen until some of the staff chase them out with sticks. They don't seem to have any family or anyone taking care of them. Your father is so much more fortunate than they are. He has someone like your husband to look after him, and someone like you to cry for him…"

With that attempt to console her, I said goodbye, wondering if I had really offered her any comfort at all.

When I tried to buy a ticket for Tokyo at Toride Station, the "Sold out" sign was up. I asked the woman at the ticket window, who was wearing a military cap, if I could purchase a ticket to Matsudo, and she told me, "At this time of day, we don't sell tickets going in the direction of Tokyo. So we have very few available to Matsudo."

"But I can buy a ticket going in the other direction?" I asked.

"Yes, as many as you like," she replied.

From evening, trains had been heading slowly north over the flat Kanto plain like cattle plodding to their barns. They were made up of three cars and absolutely packed, with people even hanging off the front of the engine. I found a foothold on the deck and tried as much as I could to stick my head into the car to keep myself from getting knocked out by the telephone poles along the tracks. Naturally I couldn't see any scenery—or much of anything else. With nothing else to occupy me, I began to consider why the railway would restrict people from traveling to Tokyo in the evening. I suppose the first reason is the shortage of supplies in the city. Maybe the second reason is that they're afraid of having trains bombed and destroyed by nighttime air raids on the city, so they prohibit trains from coming into Tokyo night. And the third reason… well, I really couldn't think of one. And as I searched unsuccessfully for that third reason, the train pulled into Shimotsuma Station. It was pitch black by now. I gave my wife's cousin, who works at a bank, the two *go* of cooking oil and asked him to get me a ticket going back to Tokyo the next day. Then I went to my wife's parents' house and gave my father-in-law the saké. He was sitting next to the hibachi and quietly listening to "Sanshiro the Bailiff" on the radio. Though it was still evening, Kikue (my wife's younger sister) and her three children were already asleep, and the house was very quiet—except for the mellifluous voice of Musei Tokugawa coming from the radio. I ate some pickles and rice and am preparing to go to bed. It's nine o'clock.

May 9

My wife had mentioned to me at one point that there was really great salmon trout fishing in Sanuma Pond in Shimotsuma from late spring through early summer. I happened to remember her remark and asked my father-in-law about it. He replied, "Why don't you see for yourself? I'll go along with you."

After breakfast I packed up a set of fishing gear, tied it to a bicycle and went to Sanuma with my father-in-law. He seems to know the best fishing spots, and he made a beeline for the east bank, behind the Hachiman Shrine. It's a very big pond, connected to Kinugawa River—in fact, big enough to be a lake, really. Though there were a lot of clouds in the sky it was still a surprisingly bright day, and somewhere in the distance I heard a lark calling. The bank we were on was covered with greenery, and on the opposite shore were fields of wheat. As the wind blew from our direction out across the water's surface, it gradually reached the golden fields of wheat on the other side. The stalks nodded in gracefully rippling waves, shimmering like a gold-leaf screen. I think I've gone back with my wife to her home about a dozen times since we were married, but every time someone suggested we go see Sanuma, I'd always begged off, muttering to myself, "For someone like me, from Nezu, Shinobazu Pond in Ueno is all the water I need to see." I always spent my time there just lying around the house and had never seen Sanuma once. Standing there on the bank, I felt that it had definitely been my loss.

My father-in-law started swishing a long-handled net along the bank. As I watched him, thinking that I had no idea you fished for salmon trout with a net, I realized he was actually catching the little freshwater shrimp that would be our bait. Following his lead, I put a shrimp on my hook and dangled my line in the water. The white bobber stood straight up. A dragonfly landed on top of it. Up to this point, I had done everything my father-in-law had, but from this moment on our paths parted. Just as I was watching the dragonfly take flight from my father-in-law's bobber, the tip of his fishing pole flipped up and the shrimp on his hook had been transformed into a three-inch fish. It had a scarlet sheen along its sides, as if it had been daubed with a red paintbrush from head to tail. It was a really beautiful fish.

After he'd pulled in about a dozen fish, my father-in-law left. He's a cabinetmaker, and he has several chests and desks he's made on display in a corner of the house; apparently a customer was coming from Tsuchiura to look at a desk that morning. As he left, he said: "If you evacuate to Shimotsuma, I guarantee your fishing will improve."

"Yes, I'm sure it would," I said. "But like I told you last night, I've bought this three-wheeled truck, so I think we'll stay in Tokyo a little longer."

Apparently the salmon trout can tell the difference between a pro and an amateur, because I didn't catch a single one. They obviously don't think much of us amateurs; they won't give us the time of day. Eventually I heard a siren softly in the distance. It was a cautionary alert. Here in the country, they used temple bells and lookout-tower gongs to pass on the air-raid warning. The lark and the frogs sang along, and the effect was quite bucolic and totally unlike a cautionary alert in the city. Though I've been through hundreds of them and should be used to them by now, still, every time one goes off, it gives me a start. It feels like a giant's hand is squeezing my heart and I tremble from the depths of my being. But my only reaction upon hearing the siren there on the banks of Sanuma Pond was to yawn. I felt sleepy.

Suddenly there was a roar in the eastern sky. I saw a squadron of several heavy bombers flying toward me at a very low altitude. Their gleaming silver sides carried a bright red rising sun mark as they approached; no doubt they had taken off from Tsuchiura. They were flying somewhere to escape an enemy raid. I waved at them, thinking they must be eager for the main event, the battle for the Homeland to begin, and hoping they'd find a safe place to hide until then. The squadron flew to the west, their bodies casting a reflection on the pond's surface.

Immediately afterward there was an air-raid siren. I went into the Hachiman Shrine and drifted off. When I awoke, it was 11:30. I went out to the bank of the pond again and smoked a hand-rolled cigarette. Four or five people were standing there quietly, fishing. Tobacco smoke rose from the fishermen's lips. Apparently the air raid and the air-raid alert had both been lifted. The saying "paradise is where you find it" suddenly came to mind. That's right. Any place where the cigarettes are good and a leisurely smoke can give you a feeling of peace and serenity is paradise; today I spent a half-day there myself. Unfortunately, there's no paradise to be had in Tokyo these days. There, we smoke our cigarettes anxiously, to calm our nerves. For just a minute, I considered giving up my plan to buy the three-wheeled truck, and moving here to the banks of Sanuma.

I left Shimotsuma on the one o'clock train and got back home to Nezu at five. When my wife saw me she shouted: "Tachibanaya—Ichimura Uzaemon—died at Tanaka Hot Springs in Shinshu. He went just after noon three days ago. A heart attack. I was glad we saw him in Moritsuna at the Shinbashi Enbujo in February."

I expected her to be worried about her husband, who had disappeared for two days, but she surprised me.

May 10

I spent the entire day in the shed. The only time I left it was when there was a cautionary alert siren at noon. I've been carefully taking apart the old bike. Though it doesn't run and is of no use to me as transportation, it's another thing when it's dismantled into parts. Most are still usable, and can even be sold at a good price, but the way things are these days, even a half-burned bike standing outside a charred home is taken apart and carried away in just a few hours. My bike was never burned, so its parts are all "first rate."

Kiyoshi, after returning home from school at four, even helped me. He said that yesterday, when I was in Shimotsuma, was a strange day. For starters, there was not a single air-raid warning siren anywhere in Tokyo. The first time since May 2nd, apparently. "The first real air-raid alert was November 1st of last year," he said authoritatively. "There was the Doolittle raid three years ago, but that was nothing compared to the air raids that started last year. Anyway, we won't count those. From November 1st to yesterday was a total of 190 days. Of those 190 days, there were no cautionary alerts on sixty-three days. In other words, there are alerts on an average of two out of every three days. If we just count March, April and May, the rate is a lot higher. Of the seventy days from March 1st to yesterday, there were only fifteen days without air-raid alerts. That means that there were alerts five out of every six days."

Kiyoshi really does belong at the Naval Accounting School.

"The weather yesterday was strange, too," he went on. "It rained in the morning, then suddenly became clear, and then there were clouds in the afternoon. The breeze quickly turned chilly, and then it poured. There was thunder. Just before you got home in the evening, the sun came out through the rain, and it was too bright to see. And that's how it was."

"Yes, that is strange."

"Germany finally surrendered unconditionally, right? Leaving us fighting all alone. The heavens must have sympathized with us so much they wept. Some say the rain that fell yesterday was heaven's tears, and the thunder, which is so rare in May, was the heavens sobbing."

"Who said that?"

"Sho."

"Well, I wouldn't put too much stock in it, then."

"Some say it's a harbinger of big changes. In other words, the divine winds."

"I suppose that was Sho-*chan*, too."

"No, that was the explanation of the school principal at the morning assembly. He seemed pretty certain of it."

"Well, then, maybe it's right."

May 11

Heavy rain clouds covered the city from the morning, and it was a gloomy day. Though it looked like it might start pouring at any minute, not a drop fell. It was incredibly frustrating. If it was going to rain, let it rain; if it was going to clear, let it clear—I just wished it would make up its mind. The clouds felt like a heavy weight pressing down making my headache. Dismantling the old three-wheeled truck took until the afternoon. There were two cautionary alert sirens in that period, at 8:30 and 10:25. Each time a single B-29 flew slowly through the skies and then left. What were they planning? Were they getting a good look, so they can come back and destroy parts of the city still standing?

My brother dropped by and asked if I wanted him to sell the three-wheeled truck parts for me. Up to yesterday, that was my plan, but this morning I changed my mind. I figure that the three-wheeled truck I'm buying from the owner of the Yamamoto Brewery in Toride must also have plenty of years on it. Eventually, it'll start breaking down, and the day will come when the parts from my old truck will come in handy. So I turned down my brother's offer. I collected some of the sheets of newspaper that were spread under the tatami mats and carefully wrapped each truck part in it. It would be stupid to store them in the shed. Of course, you have to worry about thieves, but an air raid would be worse. How about under the manhole just outside the house? If I do it during the day, people will see. I'll get up at four in the morning and take care of it. I think I still have some of that special heavy waxed paper in the closet. If I wrap the parts a second time in waxed paper and put them in a barrel, they'll be protected from the dampness down there. At that point I thought to myself, my mind is pretty sharp in spite of the oppression of the weather, and I gave myself a little mental pat on the back.

In the afternoon I made a mimeograph. Takahashi, the block group leader, has brought over another notice from Air Defense Headquarters, like the last one. This one had the title "What You Need to Know about P-51s":

Since the enemy has taken Iwojima, there have been repeated attacks by planes from enemy bases. The most nefarious of these planes is the P-51. Attacks by P-51s are certain to increase. So it's important to have an awareness of the attack strategy of the P-51. Through repeated attacks, we have already learned to defend ourselves from the B-series, and we must now do likewise for the P-series. Never underestimate the enemy, weak and incompetent as they may be. By employing their strategies to our own advantage, we are certain to be able to attain final victory.

The P-51s, flying from Iwojima, have had to attach extra fuel tanks to make the long flight, but even with additional fuel tanks, they can only maintain flight patterns over the mainland for 15–20 minutes. Though armed, the weight of the extra fuel means they can't carry large bombs. They will attack mainly with guns and cannons. Their machine guns are 50-caliber and are mounted in four places.

The P-51's cannons and machine guns are mounted stationary, so the greatest danger is to those in the direction of the line of flight. They are able to dive very sharply to low altitudes, and in this attack pattern always hit their targets. It's dangerous to watch them approach. Compared to bombs, the aim of their guns is quite accurate, so extra care should be taken.

P-51s mainly attack air bases and factories, but recently they have also been targeting trains, ships, cars and other vehicles. Locomotives have become a favorite target. It's a great mistake to think that trains are safe because they're moving. Compared to the speed of a plane, a train is for all practical purposes a stationary target. In Burma and the Philippines, P-51s relentlessly targeted automobiles, repeatedly dive-bombing them until they were incinerated. Railway authorities should take all necessary precautions in evacuating their passengers. Once passengers have detrained, they should immediately seek cover, making use of the local terrain and keeping as low to the ground as possible. The lower you are the more successfully you remove yourself from machine-gun range and maximize your safety.

It is erroneous to think that cannons do not cause fires. During the May 8 attack in Chiba, several fires broke out. Approximately one in five P-51 cannons contains incendiary materials. These will ignite. Both evacuation and fire-prevention measures are called for during attacks by P-51s. In other words, the best defense against air attacks is evacuation and firefighting.

During P-51 attacks on Manila, many of the victims were wearing white. As summer approaches, avoid wearing white clothing outdoors. Use your white clothing and light-colored summer kimonos to make bandages for soldiers at the front.

—Air Defense Headquarters

Just over the last few words, Mr. Takahashi had written in pencil: "Please use bold lettering for this and write it larger than the rest." I cut this stencil exactly as written. Like last time, he gave me two candles for my work.

May 12

"Mr. Yamanaka, my wife is making rice with red beans and tempura. This truck has been a big help in our business for a long time, and she says we have to give it a proper send-off before we hand it over to you. I hope you'll join us in our little thank-you party," said the proprietor of Yamamoto Brewery in Toride. The three-wheeled truck was parked next to the verandah. A little table had been set up in front of it, and a bottle of saké and a dish of rice and red beans were on the table.

"I got back from the woolen cloth factory in Kashiwa yesterday evening, and I stayed up half the night checking the truck out and getting it ready for you. Of course I washed it, too," Mr. Yamamoto said, pouring me a cup of saké. "I drove it out along the Rikuzenhama Highway to Ushikunuma, and it ran in top condition. As far as I can tell, it's in perfect shape."

It had been pouring rain in the morning in Tokyo, but here in Toride at noon the sun was casting its golden rays everywhere. I gave Mr. Yamamoto the balance of 500 yen and, as a gift, a half of a salted salmon and 200 *momme* of sugar. As I drank my cup of saké, I walked around the truck, looking it over. A five-gallon can of gasoline, five *sho* of Mobil oil, a gallon of gear oil and a kilo of grease were packed into the truck bed.

Seeing my eyes wide with astonishment, Mr. Yamamoto said: "Just a little discount and a little thank you. The fact is the front light is broken."

"That's fine with me. I don't plan to drive it at night anyway. But why should you thank me?"

"Those three strings of laundry soap bars really are great to have."

Mrs. Yamamoto came out carrying a large plate of tempura. If they're so happy about the soap, I'll try to drop by again soon and bring them some more, I thought as I ate the tempura and the rice with red beans. Clearly Furusawa Enterprises has a black-market source for soap; if I ask, they should be able to supply me with ten or twenty strings. Come to think of it, the Yamamoto Brewery must still have quite a supply of saké, and I'm sure the Furusawas would be interested in trading soap for saké. As the go-between, I'd take a small fee, just a minimal charge. All three parties would benefit... When I got to this point, I gasped. This would make me a black marketer.

But was it really fair to lump people who distributed goods because they enjoyed bringing a smile to people's faces together with people who did it for profit, calling them both black marketers and making them guilty of the same crime? Maybe the former should be called "white marketers." That's what was going through my head as I sat there talking with the Yamamotos.

At one, I straddled my new three-wheeled truck and kicked the starter backward with my left foot. It snapped back with tremendous force, and hit my heel painfully. But I didn't want to make a grimace in front of the Yamamotos, who were watching, so I put on a broad smile and slowly circled the yard next to their verandah five times, giving them plenty of time to say goodbye. Their children followed me out the gate waving little Japanese flags. I responded by squeezing the rubber bulb of the horn a dozen times.

I crossed the bridge over Tonegawa River, drove through Abiko, Kashiwa, and finally left the Mito Highway at Matsudo heading south until I reached Ichikawa. By that time I was completely used to the truck. It was a very straightforward machine, the only idiosyncrasy being that powerful back-kick of the starter. I was wondering what I'd do if a P-51 dive- bombed me on the way home, but with nary a "P" in sight, the long drive with the spring breeze at my back was very pleasant. I was enjoying myself.

By the time I reached Tokyo, it was sunny there, too. I was having so much fun that I turned right after crossing Kuramaebashi Bridge and took Kiyosugi Street north to Senju.

"It's a great three-wheeled truck. Cheap at 8,000 yen," Mr. Furusawa said, praising my purchase. My brother must have told him it cost that much, so I couldn't very well say, "No, it was only 6,500 yen..." Instead I explained that the gasoline, Mobil oil, gear oil, and the rest of it had been included in the price.

"What a deal," exclaimed Furusawa. "How about selling it to me for 10,000 yen." He already had his wallet out.

I guess to be successful in the black market, you needed to be ready to take advantage of every opportunity. I was impressed. I also refused.

Hearing my voice, Kinuko stuck her head out of the house.

"I'm making chicken and eggs over rice tonight. Why don't you eat with us?"

Tokiko also urged me to stay. I went inside and had a beer with Furusawa. Soon after that the food was served. I thought it would be just for the family, but no. All five of their employees got the same thing. It is very admirable that the family didn't get special treatment. My opinion of Furusawa improved somewhat. Of course, he can afford to serve chicken and eggs over rice to everyone because he makes money during the day selling farm implements and at night as a black marketer.

As I was carefully chewing the tough chicken, a police officer came in from the kitchen and said to Mrs. Furusawa in a low voice: "I'll take six bottles today." She lifted up the trap door in the kitchen floor and took out six empty beer bottles from the storage space below. The police officer wrapped them up in a cloth. "I'll be back tomorrow," he said, "probably after dark." And he disappeared just as he had come.

"Doing business with the police is expensive," Furusawa said. Then seeing my puzzled expression, he explained, "They charge 15 yen for a bottle of beer, but I buy it without a peep. It's very convenient having the local police officer as your partner in crime, you might say."

"So the police, who are supposed to be policing the black market, are part of it?"

"Of course. What did you think? His monthly salary is 60 yen. Can he eat on that?"

No, no one could. Rice is 20 yen a *sho* these days.

"There's a steel helmet factory near here. The monthly pay is 68 yen. It goes without saying that the 'warriors of industry' there can't survive on that. So they're secretly making pots and pans."

"I see. Well, they look a lot like helmets, I guess."

"That's right. From a distance, it looks like they're making steel helmets. But the military police inspectors know the difference between helmets and pots. So when the military police are scheduled to come around, the local policeman lets the factory know in advance. For his trouble, he gets ten or twenty pots. They help each other out. There's one fire truck in the Senju Fire Station. One night, there's an air raid. The fire truck sounds its siren and runs out to put out a fire. But that's not what's really going on. The truck, siren wailing, is driving in the opposite direction of the fire. It crosses Senju Ohashi Bridge and heads straight for Soka. The fire truck is packed solid with pots and pans. On the way home, it's full of rice and vegetables."

"Oh, I see. They're all in on it, to put a little frosting on the cake. So that's how it works."

"As the saying goes, Soka and Koshigaya are just a hop, skip, and a jump from Senju. Sometimes they'll take a load as far as Koshigaya, but if a fire truck from Senju is seen driving along the roads of Saitama like they owned the place, there's always the risk of being reported. That's why most of the deals take place in Soka. It's actually more complicated, but anyway, they're all in it together, helping each other out. You could say that all of Minami Senju is one giant black-market family. People are just trying to make up for their miserly wages. And they're all working incredibly hard to do it. I mean, they all have two jobs, really. But it's because of that giant black-market family that everyone can survive. And after all—and this is the point, right?—they need to stay strong and healthy for the final battle for the Homeland."

"I see. So it all ties into that."

"Some of the country's top leaders try to tell us that true and faithful Imperial subjects shouldn't have anything to do with the black market. But where would we be if that leaves them so malnourished and weak that, when the battle for the Homeland starts, they have to hobble up to the enemy, leaning on their bamboo spears like canes? People should use the black market to stay fit and strong. That's real patriotism, if you ask me."

It made sense in its way. I was completely taken in and just sat there drinking my tea.

"Shinsuke, there isn't any shortage of goods in the city and the surrounding areas. If you know how to look, there's quite a lot. You'd be surprised what people have. You could say that the city and the surrounding area is like one giant bathtub sitting over a fire."

Furusawa seemed partial to the word "giant."

"The upper part is hot, but it's still cold at the bottom. What's needed is a paddle to mix the water up. Black-market trading is the mixing paddle. And what's the essence of the black market? The movement of goods. You've just bought a fine device for moving goods around, a three-wheeled truck. You have a very important duty to perform."

When I was about to leave for home, Tokiko gave me ten dried persimmons cooked in syrup and said, "These are for Kiyoshi." I got back to Nezu at 6:30. Fumiko and the others ate the rice and red beans I'd brought home from the Yamamotos. I asked the wife to bring two sweet, dried persimmons over to the Takahashis, and I'm sucking on one myself as I write this.

May 13

The sun was out this morning. As I was washing down the three-wheeled truck, Fumiko and Takeko, on their way to the Naval Technical Institute, came over and said it was a nice machine and it looked like it was very fast. Fumiko was enrolled in the Shukutoku Home Economics Girls High School in Koishikawa Omote-cho, but from autumn of last year the school had sent her to the Naval Technical Institute instead. Apparently they are instructed not to talk about what was going on there, so she never speaks about her job. It seems she is working as a kind of assistant draftsman. Her notebooks are filled with her careful writing, as clear and sharp as those of a mimeograph-stencil copyist. That must have attracted the attention of her teachers. Takeko was a student at the Girls High School in Komagome Nishikatamachi. Up until recently she'd been working at the Oki Electric Factory as part of the mandatory student labor program, but with an introduction from Fumiko, in mid-April she switched to the Naval Institute. She seems to be an assistant-assistant draftsman; all this conjecture and "seeming" is rather pathetic, I admit, but I simply don't know what's going on as far as her education is concerned or what it might have to do with military matters.

To be honest, I don't understand the point of the Outline of Educational Policies for Victory in the War that was announced this March. The authorities decided to cancel all higher elementary school, middle school, high school and university classes. Only primary schools are still operating. The sole exception to the new policy is medical schools, which were declared "a link in the policy for victory in response to the attack on the Homeland." I don't want to say anything unpatriotic, but if we close down the entire educational system, we're at risk of falling behind the British and the Americans. Kiyoshi is doing excavation work at the military weapons storehouse in Koishikawa instead of attending classes. I guess the plan is to build a completely underground weapons storehouse. He says that they're also going to construct an underground shelter big enough to hold ten thousand people. A couple weeks ago I happened to say, "It's too bad you can't keep up your education, after you just managed to get accepted into a prefectural school."

Kiyoshi looked at me with an angry glare. "I hate grown-ups who don't know anything but say things like canceling all classes is going to put us behind the British and Americans. Listen, Dad, the Empire is taking all the necessary steps to make sure that never happens."

According to Kiyoshi, "special science classes" have been established at Tokyo Higher Normal School, Kanazawa Higher Normal School, Hiroshima School of Secondary Education and Tokyo Women's Higher Normal School. "At Tokyo Higher Normal School, there are five special classes," he said, "fourth, fifth and sixth years of elementary school, and then first and second years of middle school. The classes are limited to fifteen students."

"So, the cream of the crop."

"Yup. The idea is to hold special, small classes for the gifted. A fourth-year elementary school student who was on the 'Science for Children' radio program at the start of March was amazing."

The boy calculated the surface area of Sumidagawa River from Shirahigebashi Bridge to Eitaibashi Bridge using a map of a scale of 1:20,000. First he attached the map to a large board. Then he inserted rows of pins on both banks of the river as well as at the two bridges. In this way, he surrounded the entire area of the river he wanted to calculate with a wall of pins. Then he filled the walled-in area with BB-gun pellets. Before doing this, he'd calculated how many BB pellets it took to fill one acre of land, according to the map's scale. So by counting the number of pellets needed to fill in the river, he could calculate its area.

"The idea of converting the river into BB pellets was brilliant. And he's still just a fourth-year student."

"I wonder what he'd do if he didn't have all those BBs."

"Dad, that's exactly why I hate getting into a discussion with you. A student at my school, Tokyo Prefectural Daigo Middle School, was selected to enter the second-year middle school class at Tokyo Higher Normal School."

"So they take students from other schools, too?"

"That's right. The first criterion is a perfect grade-point average. Then they check the genetic background of the parents and relatives— emphasizing the father, they say. The father of the boy selected from my school was a professor at Tokyo Imperial University. So we can leave the studying up to the students in these special classes, and I'm sure they'll come up with something important for us all. The Empire hasn't canceled all classes, you see."

The fact that I can remember something Kiyoshi said so long ago must mean that today was an uneventful day. There was a cautionary alert siren at 11:40 in the morning. A single B-29 appeared in the sky. There was no air-raid attack siren after it. Gen the tailor said that the Air Defense Headquarters and the Eastern Military Operations Headquarters had adopted a new policy of not sounding air-raid attack sirens when they decided that an enemy plane was on surveillance and not a bombing mission. The air-raid attack sirens consume a lot of electricity.

May 14

"I've got your first delivery job for you," said my brother as he came by the house at seven in the morning.

I was in the middle of rubbing myself down with a towel.

He explained that Maeyama Paper Company in Ikenohata Shichiken-cho wanted me to pick up some blackout paper at the Taihei Paper Mill in Ukima-cho, Oji. "You know what blackout paper is, don't you? That black-flocked stuff you put over your windows to keep the light from being seen from outside."

"Of course I know what it is."

"There are 12,000 sheets, about twice the size of a newspaper. I don't think you can do it all in one trip. You should probably make two."

"Okay."

I put on the more worn of my two national civilian uniforms. "I'm surprised that there's still that much blackout paper to be found."

"The authorities are more lenient when it comes to materials related to air defense. They'll pay you 250 yen to make the delivery. I collected it in advance," my brother said, slapping a stack of 10 yen bills down in front of me as I was tying up my leggings.

"You can pile up all the money in the world, but that's not good enough. I arranged to have them provide you with gasoline, too. They're going to send over two cans of gas by evening."

I just stood there, taking it all in for a second. Two round trips to Oji—it would only take half a day. And there I was, about to make the same amount of money in half a day that a mid-level executive in a first-rate company earned in a month.

"Are you sure you didn't ask for too much?"

"Look, a small truck to Karuizawa is 5,000 yen. A large truck is 10,000 yen. That's what things cost these days. That's the market rate."

"Yeah, but we're doing this illegally."

"You should take a lesson from Nippon Express. They're not supposed to be delivering anything but military supplies. Yet their trucks are driving around in the middle of the day doing moving jobs. When it comes to moving jobs, Nippon Express is no more legal than this. You should just follow their lead and do your job without worrying about whether you're illegal or not. Your rate may be high, but your client's still making a profit. If he wasn't, he wouldn't hire you."

Counting out 10 yen notes, my brother lifted them off the pile. "I'm taking twenty percent as commission. That's the market rate, too."

He fanned his face with the bills.

I drove to Shichiken-cho and picked up the proprietor of the Maeyama Paper Store. With him in the truck bed, I drove on to the Taihei Paper Mill. A cautionary alert siren sounded on the way, but I ignored it and kept on driving. All of the trees along the road were as black as if dipped in an inkpot. None of them had any leaves. They'd been burned off in the fire bombings. Driving along, I felt as if I were in some strange land made of black wire, where black was the only color. Not an auspicious way to begin my new career.

But in fact, it could hardly have been more auspicious. On my second trip, the security guard at the paper mill stopped me and said: "The personnel director has something he wants to talk to you about. Will you go look for him in the office?" When I went to the office, the personnel director said: "Would you make a trip for me to Sekiyado, just past Noda?"

It was a job for me. Fifteen Taihei Paper Mill workers were living in the company dormitory, and the personnel director was having trouble finding enough food for them. While he was searching for provisions, he'd managed to locate 1,200 salt-cured herring. He wanted me to go pick them up.

"Sekiyado—that's where the Tonegawa River, flowing just south of Koga, splits in two. The main branch stays the Tonegawa River and goes out to Choshi and the smaller branch becomes the Edogawa River and runs through Noda, Nagareyama, Matsudo, and from Ichikawa through Gyotoku and out into Tokyo Bay..."

"Yes, that's it."

"But this is the first time I've ever heard of catching herring in the Tonegawa."

"Yes, well, be that as it may... We'll supply the gasoline, and how about one hundred of those salt-cured herring as your fee?"

It was an offer I couldn't refuse. With the blackout paper for the Maeyama Paper Store, a letter to the Sekiyado district chief of the National Patriotic Agricultural Association, and seventeen reams of paper, I headed back to Nezu. My plan was to deliver the blackout paper and finish my first job, then leave Tokyo at about three in the afternoon. The personnel director said that all I had to do was bring the seventeen reams of paper and the letter addressed to the district chief to the Sekiyado warehouse. When I said, "It seems pretty strange to me that there would be herring in an agricultural warehouse. Next thing you know you're going to tell me we're growing rice in the ocean," the personnel director just laughed and said, "Well, yes, be that as it may... just do as I ask."

I gradually came to understand what was going on. Taihei Paper Mill had for a long time supplied the Tokyo Bureau of Telecommunications with the paper they used for various kinds of money orders. "Nobody could beat us at supplying the absolutely lowest grade of paper that would still hold up," explained the personnel director. But in March of this year the Tokyo Bureau of Telecommunications suddenly sent a brusque message thanking them for their years of service and informing them that they wouldn't be needing any more paper.

The Tokyo Bureau of Telecommunications had been trying to stop handling any telegraphic or other kind of money orders. Come to think of it, before the Komagome Post Office burned down I remember seeing a notice on the wall saying, "We will no longer handle any telegraphic or standard money orders until the end of the war. We will continue to process postal money orders for the time being. However, they will be limited to two per individual."

"Now we're making materials for drum cans and buckets," said the personnel director. He gestured with his chin toward a pile of cardboard stacked up against the wall behind him. "It looks like cardboard, doesn't it? But it's much stronger. When it's attached to a bamboo frame, it can be used to make buckets or drum cans."

"But it doesn't leak?"

"It'll last for about thirty minutes. We're getting help from the army's Air Defense Technical Institute. But we're having a hard time. This kind of expensive, high-quality paper is not really up our alley. "

"And the blackout paper?"

"I have to make sure that fifteen employees get fed. The authorities look the other way."

I asked why it was the job of the personnel director to make arrangements for the salt-cured herring.

"When it comes down to it, managing personnel is managing their food supply."

Very wise, I thought to myself. And having written this much, I see the clock in the living room says three o'clock. Time to put my fountain pen down and head out to Sekiyado.

May 15

I arrived at the National Patriotic Agricultural Association warehouse in Sekiyado at six o'clock last evening. The night watchmen unloaded the paper and then loaded the herring, in wood crates, into the bed of my three-wheeler. But there was no way I could drive back at night with the headlight broken. It would be too dangerous. I decided to get up at 4 A.M. and head back then. The night watchman agreed to let me sleep on the floor in a corner of his room.

"Dawn is dangerous, too. You'll need to keep a close watch on the road ahead," he said. He was about my age and had a red nose.

"That's when all the farmers working in the fields are coming home."

"Coming home? Don't you mean going to work?"

"Yes, that's how you'd think it'd be. But this year, it's just the opposite," the watchman said, sipping from a 2 *go* bottle of blended saké. "Here in the rice paddies in Higashi Katsushika, the farmers go out into their paddies at seven in the evening and come back home at about three or four in the morning. Under instruction by the Agricultural Association."

"Because of air raids?"

"That's right. Especially by P-51s. They seem to enjoy picking off farmers in the fields. Sixteen killed so far."

"There's nowhere to hide out there. Once they spot you, your number's up, I guess."

"The authorities have issued all sorts of instructions. 'Build foxholes in the sides of the raised dikes separating agricultural fields.' 'In order to keep agriculture running smoothly at this time, each village must appoint messengers and promptly deliver notifications to farmers by suitable means conveying pertinent information and air-raid alerts.' 'Carrying out agricultural labor successfully in a timely manner is the most important factor in increasing food production, so farmers must rouse their patriotic determination to defend the Empire and sacrifice themselves unstintingly for the Emperor, continuing to work in their fields according to their prearranged schedules even during air raids as long as the enemy remains out of visual and aural range.'"

"You've really got them memorized," I said.

"That's our job, memorizing government notices. We have to be able to spout them off without a hitch. If we dug evacuation holes and appointed messengers for each village, people wouldn't panic when a siren sounded. That's the truth. But we don't have anybody to dig holes. And we don't have anybody we can spare to be messengers. So whenever a sirens sounds, everyone runs for their life."

"So that's why you've reversed day and night."

"Yup. We've taken it a step farther, instructed each farmer to carry rice straw baling at all times. When they hear the P-51s coming, they can wrap themselves with the baling and just lay out in the field, looking like a bale of rice."

Everywhere I go the main themes of conversation are food shortages and air raids. Everyone is wracking their brains to come up with the best ways to survive the attacks of the B-29s and P-51s. Someone wrote a letter to the editor in the *Asahi Shimbun* that went like this:

Transportation systems are always a mess the day after an enemy bombing raid. Though the government knows that this contributes to a loss of productivity, they have not established any policy to combat this problem. Our top priority should be to see that those who are actually contributing to productivity can get to work, but commuters working in the Marunouchi area of central Tokyo are greatly inconveniencing everyone else. Government officials and company employees working in central Tokyo only go to work to put up a good front. They spend the first two or three hours of the day after an attack sitting around the water cooler chatting about the raid. Then they bustle off home without having done anything of any value. According to my personal observations, this is the case with almost everyone working in Marunouchi. Nothing could be less productive. Government officials and company employees who only commute to work the day after a bombing raid to shoot the breeze around the water cooler are parasites harming our national interest. On days following a bombing raid, only those who are working in manufacturing should be allowed to commute to work, and all other commuters should be banned from using the trains and required to do voluntary labor in their local community instead. I hope the government will take resolute action against deleterious and unproductive waste of our transportation system for such frivolous commuting.

I agree about ninety-nine percent with the letter writer. But on one point, I have a difference of opinion. I think the letter writer mustn't forget the fact that an atmosphere of camaraderie is created anywhere in Japan when people start talking about B-29s and P-51s. Two topics—air raids and the black market—are keeping all One Hundred Million Japanese going. They're the glue that binds One Hundred Million hearts together. The reason that after only five minutes complete strangers can be conversing like friends who have known each other for a long time is because of their shared hatred for the bombings. The reason two people can sleep together under a single coverlet in the corner of a night watchman's room is because the black market plays such a critical part in both their lives.

I found out that the reason the Agricultural Association warehouse was acquiring paper was to buy farm implements and fertilizer next spring. Herring, no matter how well cured they are, won't last until spring. So they decided to exchange the herring for paper that they can store until spring. I mentioned that my oldest daughter has just married into a family that ran a company selling farm implements and fertilizer, and said they should feel free to contact me next spring. When you think about it, the only reason the night watchman of the Agricultural Association warehouse could feel comfortable sharing the association's secrets with a first-time visitor is because we have the air raids and the black market as common ground. As he was falling to sleep, he said, "Isn't it strange? These days white paper with nothing printed on it is as valuable as money, and every day paper money is becoming more worthless."

The warehouse is on the banks of the Edogawa River. The sound of the river lapping against the banks kept me awake. I got to thinking it was very strange that the National Patriotic Agricultural Association should be worried about next spring. When the war reaches the Homeland, farmers will automatically become "soldier-farmers," and under the military authorities, they will have to fight to the last man. This is inevitable and inescapable, since farmers are the mainstay of the National Volunteer Force. And another thing—everyone is always talking about it, so I can't imagine there's anything wrong with writing it here—when the enemy attacks Tokyo, they'll advance from three directions. The first force will land at Kujukurihama Beach and advance due west. The second force will land at Kashimanada

Bay and proceed southwest. The third force will land on the coast near Mito and cut off the Joban Line, the Mito Line and the Tohoku Main Line, and move south. When that happens, Shimotsuma is going to be in danger. The reason that I just can't make the final decision to evacuate to my father-in-law's house in Shimotsuma is because somewhere in the back on my head I'm worrying about that third line of attack. Whether I die in Shimotsuma or Tokyo, I'm loyal to the Emperor and patriotically serving my country. It's all the same loyalty and patriotism, wherever it happens. So it seems pointless to evacuate.

But putting that aside for the moment, I have the feeling that all three lines of attack—right, left and center—are going to march right through Sekiyado. Next spring the farmers around here are going to be holding bamboo spears, not hoes. But I guess that in spite of everything, farmers just can't help worrying about fertilizer for the coming spring. And then there is what the watchman said before he fell asleep. As I thought about these things, I found myself wide awake. After tossing and turning, I finally fell asleep at about eleven o'clock.

I was awakened by the sound of something breaking and a man shouting. It was dark outside. I lit a match and looked up at the clock. It was 2:30.

"A tango! Isn't that enemy music?" somebody was saying.

Once more there was the sound of something breaking, like a roof tile. The Edogawa River was on the right of us and an open field on the left. The noise was coming from beyond that open field, where three roads met. The high walls of the warehouse and the open space in front of it acted like the body of a cello, and the sound carried amazingly well. Worried about my three-wheeled truck, I went outside. There was a police box at the crossroads, a red nightlight hanging like a huge round fishing bobber in the front. The light from inside the police box illuminated the darkness with a phosphorescent glow. I was relieved to see that my three-wheeled truck was safe, and I walked up to edge of the open field. A young man and a policeman were facing off over a cart that was between them.

"It's the 'Continental Tango,'" said the young man, bowing, but in a very determined voice. "It's German. It's not enemy music.

German tangos are not outlawed." He had a slight accent. "These records come from a trustworthy source. They are a gift to the Sashima Youth Group from the director of the Iwama Hospital in front of Hokkekyoji Temple in Shimousa Nakayama." Sashima was close to Shimotsuma, just a few miles east across Tonegawa River. "I left Iwama Hospital at noon yesterday. If you don't believe me, you can check. The phone number of the hospital is—"

"Don't you know that the Tripartite Axis Alliance is over and done with? Germany is no longer our ally or anything else to us. In fact, they're cowards and weaklings who surrendered unconditionally. How can there be anything good about their music?"

"How can we know if it's good or bad without listening to it? There are also records by Mieko Takamine and Ichiro Fujiyama. And Masako Kawada and Hamako Watanabe, too... Everyone's waiting to hear them. We're all exhausted—day after day of working in the wheat fields, planting potatoes and sweet potatoes, irrigating. We just wanted a little R and R, and we found out from the local government office that someone offered to donate two hundred records to us."

"You've got some nerve talking about R and R when everyone else in the Empire is busting their hump day and night. And what are you doing here instead of at the front? You look perfectly healthy to me. Coward!"

"My feet are bad. The fields are the front for me."

"You've got an answer for everything, don't you? A smart ass. Well, we're going to end your little R and R right now. Do you think anyone has time for R and R when we're at war? You're going to break every one of these records with your own hands. There's nothing wrong with your hands, is there?"

"Precisely because we're at war, the aim of the Commissioner of Rural Police is to bring a little rest and recreation to rural areas."

Before I knew what was happening, I found myself standing in front of the policeman and speaking up. "That's what they said on the radio the other day. Things may be a little different in Tokyo than here in Kanjuku, but they're not the opposite, I'm pretty sure. The restriction of one theater per district was abolished, and right away, the number of movie theaters in Tokyo increased. Twenty-two theaters reopened the next day, so anyone can see a movie if they want. In the manufacturing district in Oji, some theaters are even showing movies in the middle of the night. The idea is, by providing entertainment to the working people, they're revitalizing their fighting spirit. If that's happening in Tokyo, I think that people in Sashima should have a little entertainment, too. Play hard and fight hard. That's what the Commissioner of Rural Police said."

"And who do you think you are?" said the policeman sharply as he gripped the handle of his saber. "I haven't seen you around here before. Who are you?"

"I'm delivering—" I blurted out, stopping before incriminating myself.

"He's with the National Patriotic Agricultural Association," came a voice behind me. It was the night watchman. "He's new. Here, this is for your wife," he said casually, waving two salt-cured herring like a pendulum and walking into the police box. He was a real lifesaver.

"They're good simmered. The salt broth is healthy, too. Hard-working guys like you have to make sure to get enough salt."

"One joker after another," said the policeman, shrugging and following the night watchman into the police box.

After watching the young man with the records get away, I went back to the warehouse. I left Kanjuku at 3:30, and arrived at the Taihei Paper Mill in Oji at a little after 7 P.M. Then I went home and took a nap. After I got up, I started writing in this diary.

On the morning of May 14th, approximately four hundred B-29s attacked Nagoya and dropped firebombs over the entire city. Everyone says that the city has been demolished. The gold sculpture of a male dolphin on the north side of Nagoya Castle was destroyed; the statue of the female dolphin on the south side had already been removed, so it was safe. Such large-scale, daytime firebombing of a city is new. It doesn't bode well. Nagoya was the center of fan production in Japan. If I remember correctly, seventy percent of Japanese fans were produced there. When I was young, I apprenticed there for a short time, just three months, at the Takemoto Ryofusha company near Atsuta Shrine, so I have a connection to the city. I can picture the faces of many of my old friends. I hope that the proprietor of the Ryofusha is all right; he's the same age as me. But I know perfectly well that lately my prayers along those lines are useless.

May 19

I know that extravagance is our greatest foe, but this morning I treated myself to half a salt-cured herring. My wife and I shared it for breakfast, and just as I was lighting a cigarette, the radio announced, "A squadron of seventy to ninety B-29s has passed over Hachijojima." A cautionary alert siren was sounded at 9:55, and soon after a plane arrived from the south and flew in slow circles over Nezu before disappearing into the dense clouds to the east. Clearly it was on a surveillance mission, which probably meant that the main force was on the way. I suddenly remembered how the other day Mr. Ito in the Publications Department of Shinchosha said that Mondays and weekends are dangerous, and I tied my air-raid hood so tightly around my neck that it hurt. Today was Saturday. Maybe a major air raid is on the way.

Eventually, a sound like thunder came from the east and the southwest—the familiar sound of bombs being dropped and exploding. My brother had decided that if we had an air raid during which we could hear bombs exploding, the job he had lined up for me would be postponed. So the explosions I heard meant that my job for the day will be put off at least until tomorrow, and at least as far as today is concerned, I still don't have those sumo tickets in hand. The B-29s carrying six-pound incendiary bombs or electronic bombs depart from the U.S. bases in the Marianas, they say. I read it in the newspaper, so it must be true. Major General Curtis LeMay is the head honcho at that air base. In the late 1930s, he was a young first lieutenant and stunt pilot looking to make a name for himself. He succeeded, and when the U.S. started bombing Germany, he was promoted to major general and given command of the Eighth Air Force. This was all printed in *Aviation Asahi*, a reliable source, but it makes you wonder about the U.S. Air Force's promotion policies when a daredevil first lieutenant becomes a major general in such a short time. LeMay led the force of more than two thousand U.S. planes that carried out the five-day carpet-bombing attack on Hamburg, which completely destroyed the city, earning him the reputation of a merciless barbarian. I can't help but think it's very strange that LeMay should be the one deciding my work schedule and daily activities. In fact, I think it's fair to say that my life is entirely in his hands. I wish I could fly straight to the Marianas and shout, "Tell this lousy stunt pilot to stop messing around with my work!" but unfortunately, I don't have wings. It drives me crazy.

As I was thinking this, standing in front of the house holding my flame swatter, I heard people walking by shouting things like "Incendiary bombs are raining down on Nihonzutsumi," "Mukojima has been hit," "A bomb fell on Sumidagawa Station near the Arakawa River." It looks like the old folks who seem to enjoy checking out the air raids on their way to the shelters in Ueno were at it again. The shelter in Ueno Hill is the designated evacuation spot for the residents of Nezu, so when the time comes, I'll be taking my wife by the hand and going there myself, but I have no wish to go near the top part of the hill, near the statue of Saigo. Toward the end of March, I heard from "Demon" Yosaburo, the head of the Nezu chapter of the yakuza's Musashi Volunteer Squad, that more than two hundred thousand people killed in the predawn air raid of March 10th were cremated in a temporary crematorium hastily thrown up next to Saigo's statue. It took five days to incinerate them all, he said. Come to think of it, from around March 13th the police had the stairs at that entrance to the park cordoned off. Anyway, since hearing that from him, when I go to Ueno Station I walk along the west bank of Shinobazu Pond from Ikenohata Naka-cho out to Ueno Hirokoji. It's really a long detour, but somehow I feel that Ueno Hill is filled with the spirits of the dead. At that time, "Demon" Yosaburo also said: "Shin-*chan*, do you know how many crematoriums there are around Tokyo? There are twelve: the Mizue Municipal Crematorium in Harue-cho, Edogawa Ward; Kirigaya Hakuzensha in Nishi Osaki, Shinagawa Ward; Ochiai Hakuzensha in Kami Ochiai, Yodobashi Ward; the Yoyohata Hakuzensha in Nishihara, Yoyogi, Shibuya Ward; Sunamachi Hakuzensha in Kita Sunamachi, Joto Ward; Yotsugi Hakuzensha in Aoto, Katsushika Ward; Nippori Hakuzensha in Machiya-cho, Arakawa Ward, Horinouchi Nisshin Kigyosha in

Koenji, Suginami Ward; Tama Reiansha in Tama Village, Tokyo Metropolitan District; the Mizonokuchi Municipal Crematorium in Kawasaki City; the Toda Crematorium Incorporated, in Saitama Prefecture; and Tanizuka Seitensha in Kita Adachi County, also in Saitama. And, do you have any idea, Shin-*chan*, how many bodies these twelve crematoriums can incinerate, working full time, in a single day?"

Of course I don't have any idea about such a grisly subject, nor do I want to, I told him. (The reason he calls me Shin-*chan* is that we were in the same class in our primary school behind Nezu Gongen Shrine.)

"Just 1,500 bodies. To be precise, 1,518. There's no way they could cremate more than 100,000 bodies. That's why the Parks Division of the City Planning Department instructed the members of the Nezu Volunteer Chapter to burn the bodies on Ueno Hill."

"The Parks Division?"

"That's right. Cremating the bodies of air-raid victims is the job of the Parks Division. Don't ask me why. In fact, I don't think the officials of the Parks Division, who should know if anyone did, have a clue either. The bureaucrats had estimated that no matter how fierce the air raids, they'd never have to cremate more than 1,500 in a single day. Then in a single night, several hundred times that number were killed. They were completely off base. We wouldn't tolerate that kind of sloppiness when we calculate the potential deaths in one of our gang wars."

I think the Parks Division was assigned the task of taking care of the bodies of the air-raid victims because of what happened during the Kanto earthquake. That just suddenly occurred to me. They cremated a large number of victims in the parks then, too, and even buried them there. As I was remembering that I heard someone shout: "A lot of bombs fell on Senju, too."

I wondered if Furusawa Enterprises and Kinuko were okay. My heart skipped several beats and seemed to strike against my breastbone. Each second feeling like a thousand years, I waited for the all-clear, which finally sounded at 11:40. I managed to get on a Keisei Line train at exactly noon. It would have been faster to take the three-wheeled truck, but gasoline was my lifeline, the next most precious thing after life itself, so no matter how desperate the emergency, I can't use the three-wheeled truck for anything except work.

The Keisei train was horribly crowded. You couldn't even get into a car unless you leaped from the platform, throwing yourself into the wall of bodies. Of course there were no seats, no straps to hang or poles to hold onto. The passengers were packed in so tightly we held each other up without any extra support. As the train lurched on, we all swayed forward and backward. The reason no one toppled over was that the car was packed to the gills; there wasn't room to fall down.

"What terrible driving." "What do you expect from a girl driver?" Two middle-aged men to my right and left were talking over my head. The man on the right wore a national civilian uniform cap and the one on the left a military cap. They didn't seem acquainted, but they both smelled strongly of sweat and were wearing dark glasses. Dark glasses are very popular lately. I thought it might have to do with people getting pinkeye at the start of spring, but now it was early summer, and the dark glasses hadn't gone away. If anything there seemed to be more people wearing them. Igarashi, the dentist in our block group, offered the explanation that a lot of people were having eye trouble from the smoke and ash produced by the air raids, so they had taken to wearing dark glasses.

"Senju is going to wind up completely burned out. Kokusan Precision Machine Tools is there, and Sekiya Iron and Steel Company. With the student laborers and drafted laborers at Kokusan, there must be at least thirty thousand workers. I work at a vegetable stand in the Kawaharamachi bazaar, so I know," said the one in the military cap.

"Yes, and there's Kanegafuchi Textiles on the east bank of the Arakawa River and Dainippon Textiles on the left bank. On the north side of Dainippon Textiles is Sumidagawa Station. There's no way the B-29s are going to overlook those."

"At Sumidagawa Station, all the wrestlers from the Futabayama Stable are loading barges, they say. I came to see that. I left home real early in the morning, but because of that cautionary alert a little while ago, I wasted half the day in the dugout shelters in Ueno," said the one wearing the national civilian uniform cap, grabbing my right arm.

The train suddenly slowed down. I didn't like being grabbed, but since he was another sumo fan, I decided to forgive him. In other words, I just ignored it.

"There's no way I'll be able to see the sumo tournament starting on the 23rd, so I was hoping to at least get a glimpse of Futabayama from a distance."

"If you're looking for tickets, I can help you out," said the one in the military cap, lowering his voice a little. "Tickets for opening day and the last day are 20 yen, and from the second through the sixth days, 15 yen. Let me know if you want one."

"Traitors!" shouted a woman standing in front of us, twisting her neck around. "Talking about industrial secrets and personnel distribution, and on top of that, trying to arrange a black market deal right here in public. Where's your patriotism?" She was wearing a dress refashioned from a kimono and—dark glasses.

I got off the train at Senju Ohashi and asked the woman at the ticket-taking gate, "I came because I heard that some bombs fell in the area. Do you know where?"

"On the gas company in Minami Senju," she replied. The gas company was on the south side of Sumidagawa Station, considerably southwest of Furusawa Enterprises, near Senju Ohashi, at least 12 or 1,300 meters away. Feeling relieved, I slumped onto the bench in the station waiting room, where I rested for about ten minutes. Then I crossed Senju Ohashi Bridge and looked over at Furusawa Enterprises beyond the street the train ran along. A small delivery car was parked out in front. Tokiko, Kinuko's sister-in-law, was briskly giving instructions to an employee who was loading bags of fertilizer into the car. Kinuko came out from the back carrying a tray. There was tea and a steamed sweet potato on it. Kinuko gave the tray to the man in the driver's seat, then walked over to Tokiko and said something. I could see from the bounce in her step that she was fine. I went back to the Keisei Line station. If I had let them see me, Mr. Furusawa and Tadao would insist on inviting me in, and then they'd want me to stay for supper. They'd be having something like beef sukiyaki or pork cutlets over rice or chicken and eggs over rice, something far better than what I'm used to eating, and then they'd give me a string of soap or a big bottle of soy sauce as a present to take home. That's the way it always is. It would be like I used Kinuko and the air raid as an excuse for a good meal and a handout. If a bomb had fallen a hundred meters from them, there'd be an excuse for coming to visit, but the bomb had fallen on the gas company a safe distance away.

When I returned home my wife sad: "You're back so quickly. I guess Furusawa Enterprises was safe."

I nodded. "I just made sure they were all right and came back without being seen. Kinuko seems to be doing just fine." I walked over to my desk, where this diary was sitting.

"Yes, if you go there too often it just looks like you want something, doesn't it, and that won't do."

She made me some tea. I felt like she was commending me for being a decent person, and it made me happy.

That evening dark gray rain fell from the cloudy sky, and Fumiko, Takeko and Kiyoshi made their way home through it at about the same time. We had salt-cured herring for dinner; that's the end of the salt-cured herring. The rain kept up into the night, and it was cold. It was strangely quiet, making for a rather sad, melancholy evening. My wife and I had a strong cup of our best tea, which we kept for special occasions. Now that's gone, too. The whistle of a train far away in the distance sounded for a moment like a cautionary alert siren. It gave me a start. The sound of the bamboo flute of a traveling masseur drew close, then faded. I hadn't heard one of those in a long time. Five or six years ago there was a boy masseur who used to walk through the neighborhood playing his flute and calling out, "Massage, upper and lower body, 50 sen." Nowadays a complete massage is 5 yen. The cost of a massage has gone up along with everything else. Speaking of massages, the other day the missus at the Yamamoto Saké Brewery in Toride told me that a large number of wounded soldiers who had become masseurs had evacuated to Toride. She said they charged 3 yen for a full massage and all seemed to be making a good living. Maybe the masseur who passed through the neighborhood just now was also a wounded soldier. Thinking that if that was the case, I'd be happy to pay 5 yen for a massage, I went outside to call him in. But there was no trace of anyone on the street. Just the fine rain that continued to fall silently.

May 20

This was a supremely unpleasant day. For starters, a mist-like rain fell all day, and I felt just as gloomy as the weather. Next, the job that my brother got for me turned out to be a very dirty business, casting me as little more than a looter's accomplice, or a thief stealing a neighbor's possessions as their house burned down. I even hesitate to write about it in this diary. But intentionally leaving it out would be like lying to myself, and I don't want to do that, either. I've decided to take the middle way and just record it as briefly as I can.

The person who rented me and my truck for a day is a guy named Otsuka, who has recently made a fortune manufacturing military goods. Otsuka gave my brother a piece of paper and these instructions for me: "Have him go to these addresses, pick up the furniture, and bring it back to our warehouse in Matsudo Mabashi." There were five addresses in Nakano Ward on the list. So I made five round trips between Nakano and Matsudo Mabashi. From the first address I brought back two paulownia wood chests. From the second, a dozen or so chairs of various sizes. From the third, five office desks; from the fourth, several bookshelves; and from the fifth and last, four tea boxes that seemed to contain dishes, bowls, and medicine.

I realized what it was I was actually hired to do on the first trip, when I passed Nakano Station on the road to the south carrying the two paulownia chests. An army tank was demolishing a house. Another house nearby was being dismantled by men wearing light yellow uniforms. The roof had already been removed, and they had tied a heavy rope around the beams, pulling away in unison and singing a song in voices as thick and rough as the rope they were heaving:

> Be a man, be a man,
> Spread your wings and soar.
> Hit hard and explode into fragments
> Like fragrant cherry blossoms of Kudan.
> Be a man, give it your all.

The light yellow uniforms must mean that they were prisoners. This was Nakano; the Toyotama Prison was nearby. I suddenly realized that these houses were being demolished by government order to create fire lanes. In the major predawn air raid of March 10th, they say that forty percent of Tokyo was burned down, and the next day the city's Defense Department issued its sixth order to demolish buildings for fire lanes. I think I read about that in the paper at the end of March. Each family notified that their home would be torn down was allowed to take thirty objects with them. But as everyone knew, there weren't enough rental vehicles to allow them to move even that small amount. After spending three or four days at the local ward office to get the necessary relocation papers, families returned to their houses and tore up the boards from the floors and walls to make boxes for their possessions. They used the rush-mat surfacing of their tatami flooring to wrap and carry belongings, which they tied up with rope they received as a special ration from the government. When they'd finished packing up all their worldly goods, they applied to have them shipped out from the proper train station. Those evacuating to the Tokaido area applied to have their possessions sent from Shiodome or Shinagawa; those going to Tohoku applied for delivery from Akihabara or Sumidagawa; those going out along the Central Line, from Iidabashi or Shinjuku. But to make this application, they had to wait in long lines at the stationmaster's office. People camped out overnight, sometimes two nights, before their turn finally came. When at last they reached the front of the line, they asked: "When should we bring our things here? Tomorrow? The day after?" The answer was almost always the same: "A month from now." Naturally, everyone complained that they were being forcibly evacuated and having their home demolished by order of the government, and that they couldn't possibly wait a month.

The newspaper article reported the railroad's answer to this:

We are determined to overcome every obstacle to carrying out national policy with regard to evacuation of the general population, evacuation of mothers and infants, transportation of air-raid victims and forced evacuations. The staff of every station is working full time, without breaks to eat or use the restroom. We are doing the best we can

—*Asahi Shimbun*, March 23

This "Reply from the Railway Authorities" became the subject of conversation even here in Nezu, where not many were evacuating. Shoichi saw right through the flimsy logic of it. "If they don't have time to eat, they have no reason to use the toilet. And if they have no time to use the toilet, it means that they want to go but don't have the time, which means they must be eating. This makes no sense at all." I should add that the neighborhood consensus is that the reason there have been no forced demolitions in Nezu is that the area is so far away from National Railway lines. There are no main roads here, either.

So what can you do when you're told that you have to wait a month to ship your household goods? Do you unpack everything you've already boxed up? Do you sit in a house without floorboards, walls or tatami mats, waiting for the day when they agree to let you ship your few remaining worldly possessions? The majority of the evacuees sells their belongings and just take the bare necessities (only clothing and bedding are allowed as hand-carried luggage on the trains) when they leave the city. And even if you were lucky enough to have the railway staff say, "Bring your belongings to Sumidagawa Station tomorrow," you're in an impossible bind. Where are you going to find a rental truck? Even if you could find one, how will you pay for it? There's even a shortage of pull carts and flatbed carts. Aside from a few very wealthy people, the majority of evacuees just unpacks their belongings and sell them. And there are people who take advantage of their misfortune and force them to dispose of the lot for almost nothing. I heard this from the security guard at the warehouse in Matsudo Mabashi, after I'd delivered my last load and received my payment and the sumo tickets, but apparently this Otsuka who had hired me once beat the price of an ebony wood desk worth at least 2,000 yen down to 20 yen. He bought a fine office desk with two side leaves for only 5 yen. And the even more devious thing is that, since he might draw unwanted attention to his racket if he had the booty delivered directly to his warehouse, he will wait a suitable amount of time, storing it here or there (and probably paying a storage fee), only taking it into his warehouse after the dust settled, and always using some third-party delivery service—like me—to carry his plunder back to his lair. I can't describe how painful it was to find myself the factotum, however unwitting at the start, of such a crook. It made me sick to my stomach. And he apparently also sells things like desks, chairs, and bookshelves for almost nothing to important officials and high-ranking military men relocating because their offices have been bombed. In this way he curries favor with the authorities, as insurance. He is as underhanded as they come.

When I got home the National Chorus was singing "Song of the Young Eagles" on the radio. The seven o'clock news followed. I had my wife fill up the washbowl halfway, cleaned myself up, and sat down to eat. Naturally, I put the sumo tickets up on the Shinto altar. Picking up my chopsticks, I was about to put a wheat dumpling in my mouth when the announcer began to speak in a grave voice. "His August Majesty Prince Kotohito Kan'in, who had been recovering from an illness under the care of his wife Princess Chieko and their daughter-in-law Princess Naoko at his mansion in Odawara, passed away peacefully at 4:10 today, May 20th. He was eighty-one years old."

I spit out the wheat dumpling in my mouth and sat up on my knees in formal position.

"Imperial Chamberlain Nagaakira Okabe was immediately dispatched as the Imperial envoy to convey the Emperor's august condolences to the prince's main residence in Kojimachi, Tokyo, and due to the death of Prince Kotohito, the Imperial palace will observe official mourning. We have an additional announcement from the Information Ministry: 'There will also be a state funeral for Prince Kotohito Kan'in, former Chief of the Imperial Japanese Army General Staff and bearer of the Grand Order of Merit, Order of the Golden Kite (1st Class), and the Collar of the Supreme Order of the Chrysanthemum.'"

I was doubly saddened by this news. It was very unfortunate to have Prince Kan'in, former chief of the Imperial Japanese Army General Staff and the most senior member of the Imperial family, who had so nobly served our nation through the three Imperial reigns of Emperor Meiji, Emperor Taisho and the present emperor, pass on while we are still at war. I don't believe any member of the Imperial family was as beloved as Prince Kotohito. The other reason I was sad is that I knew that the start of the sumo tournament scheduled to begin on May 23rd was almost certain to be delayed—at least one day. And just as I suspected, the announcer said, "Out of respect for the stirring leadership on the home front that former chief of the Imperial Japanese Army General Staff Prince Kan'in exercised in the Greater East Asia War, the All-Japan Sumo Association has decided to postpone the start of the sumo tournament at Meiji Shrine from May 23rd to May 25th. The program for the first day of the tournament is as follows, after the intermission:

> Shinshuzan versus Aichiyama
> Wakaminato versus Komatsuyama
> Hajimayama versus Shachinosato
> Surugaumi versus Midorishima
> Hirosegawa versus Kusunishiki
> Jintozan versus Kuganishiki
> Yakatayama versus Onoumi
> Kyushuzan versus Tsurugamine
> Oonomori versus Wakashio
> Kasagiyama versus Kotonishiki
> Hishuzan versus Tatsutano
> Kashimanada versus Takatsuyama
> Kiyomigawa versus Fudoiwa
> Wakasegawa versus Futamiyama
> Masuiyama versus Kashiwado
> Sakuranishiki versus Futasegawa
> Itsutsuumi versus Tokachiiwa
> Shionoumi versus Nayoroiwa
> Azumafuji versus Saganohana
> Maedayama versus Mitsuneyama
> Akinoumi versus Terunobori
> Bishuyama versus Haguroyama
> Terukuni versus Kaizan

and for the final match of the day,

> Sagamigawa versus Futabayama.

The announcer repeated the program, so I was just able to record it all in my diary. As I look at it, I can envision what the opening day will be like. And in the tournament taking place in my head, it's entirely up to me whether Futabayama wins or the gold star goes to Sagamigawa.

After I'd finished the wheat dumplings, Shoichi came by, playing that block group song, "Knock, knock, knock on your neighbor's door, the door opens on a familiar face," with lyrics by Ippei Okamato and music by Nobuo Iida, on his harmonica, to pass around the circulating clipboard with the latest Neighborhood Association notices. There were three notices on the clipboard.

- Notice of the Formation of the Miyanaga-cho Unit of the National Citizens Volunteer Battle Corps

  Our neighborhood will be the first in the nation among all forty-three prefectures, two urban prefectures, one circuit and one metropolis of the Japanese Empire to form a special attack squad. The Imperial Japanese Army Headquarters and the Cabinet Information Agency have extended their support. Let us establish a corps here in our neighborhood that will be an inspiring model for neighborhood associations in the rest of the country. The inaugural ceremony for the corps will be held at nine in the morning on May 27 (Sunday) in front of Nezu Gongen Shrine. All members of the Neighborhood Association are requested to attend.

- Induction Notice

  Architectural ornaments artisan Saitaro Hinata of Block Group No. 3 has been honored with induction into the Imperial army. A prayer ceremony will be held for him at Nezu Gongen Shrine at 9 A.M. on May 22. A glorious departure ceremony will take place at his home 5 A.M. on May 23. Please be there to see him off.

- Apology for Delay in Collecting Night Soil from Toilets

  Neighborhood Association members in charge of contacting the farmers whom we have contracted for removal of our night soil are doing their best, but we wish to apologize for the repeated delays in the collection of night soil from the toilets in the neighborhood. We are continuing to negotiate with the farmers in Shibamata 2-chome, Katsushika and Kanamachi 2-chome, Katsushika, so we ask for your continued patience. The able-bodied men of the farming families in those areas have been inducted into the army, and though the farmers are eager to collect our night soil, they have no one to do the pick up. Moreover, their horses and oxen have been requisitioned, so they have no means of transporting it. The farmers are very distressed by this situation and are not simply ignoring our agreement, so we ask for your understanding. Furthermore, the fee up to now of 50 sen per barrel may increase to 78 sen per barrel. At any rate, we ask that all families in the neighborhood, given the war situation, try to reduce their amount of bodily waste as much as possible.

Shoichi was talking to Kiyoshi about this last item, blaming it on the Keisei Electric Railway. "Shibamata 2-chome is right along the path of the Keisei Electric Railway. At Takasago Station the lines split to the right and the left. The line going to the right crosses Edogawa River and heads toward Ichikawa, but the first station on the line going to the left is Shibamata 2-chome, where the farmers who've contracted to pick up our night soil live. They can transport the night soil by train. And the very next station on the line is Kanamachi. It's the last station on the line. Kanamachi 2-chome is practically next door. The problem could be solved by transporting the night soil by train. It's the perfect solution."

Kiyoshi agreed, pointing out that Seibu Railroad—now officially the Seibu Agricultural Railroad—has been delivering the night soil from the Shinjuku area on west to the farmers along the line. They've instituted a special night delivery schedule, after the last passenger run of the day, and employing only their most skilled drivers, to keep their load from sloshing around and soiling the cars. He suggested they write a letter to the president of Keisei, proposing that he follow the lead of Seibu.

"Yeah, that's a good idea," agreed Shoichi. "And let's write one to the head of the Neighborhood Association, too. I mean, we can cut down on water and electricity, but I don't see how we can cut down on 'bodily wastes.' Though I have to admit, I've found a way."

Shoichi explained that he tried to spend as much of his free time as possible at friends' houses, where he used their toilets. You can tell their parents don't like it, he added, but they can't refuse. They don't have this problem in Kojimachi, Aoyama, Azabu or the other well-off areas. The joke going around school was that the night soil in those neighborhoods was richer, because the residents there eat better, and farmers will do anything to get their hands on it.

Up to this point, I had been looking at the newspaper and listening to them talk when suddenly—though I don't think it had anything to do with the topic of their conversation—I felt the need to use the toilet. Looking down at the cistern under the light of the bare six-watt bulb, I saw the waste heaped up like Mount Fuji. If I lowered my rear as close to the ground as Mitsuneyama does when he's getting ready to charge his opponent, my ass would be a paper's width away from it. I should get a stick and flatten it out, I thought, but I was afraid the smell would kill me. Normally you'd cut up garlic and throw it in, but in these hard times, that would be throwing precious food to the maggots. While I contemplated whether to pee or not to pee in my squat position, I got a cramp in my legs and had to shuffle off on my hands and knees out of the room—the final unpleasant event of a thoroughly unpleasant day.

I forgot to mention that at noon, while the rain was misting, a cautionary alert siren sounded. The all clear was given at 12:39. The fact that there was no air-raid siren was the only good thing to happen all day.

May 21
A cautionary alert siren sounded at 12:05 midday. It was called off at 12:45. The rain stopped, but the skies never cleared, and a single B-29 appeared overhead, flying from Kanda toward Tokyo Imperial University, then on toward Shinjuku, and finally in the direction of Shibuya. We don't have cautionary alert sirens for just a single plane anymore. Both the enemy and our side are getting thick-skinned Today's B-29 dropped "paper bombs" before it disappeared. I've

never actually held one in my hand, but I've heard they're printed in Japanese calligraphy on very good paper and say things like: "Americans have 'American spirit'"; "People of Japan: Evacuate Tokyo Immediately"; "Americans are kind"; "B-29s are impregnable flying fortresses."

On May 7th, planes dropped a half-million yen in counterfeit 200 yen and 10 yen bills on Saitama and Tachikawa. There's nothing special about 10 yen bills, but 200 yen bills are another matter. The genuine 200 yen bills have only begun to circulate in April, and they're such a large denomination that we've barely caught a glimpse of them ourselves, so how on earth did the enemy get a hold of them? And the quality of the counterfeiting is really astounding. The portrait of Fujiwara no Kamatari and the image of Tanzan Shrine are perfect, of course, but I've heard that even the details of the paulownia-blossom decoration and the watermark are exact replicas. I've also heard that a dishonest warrior of industry working at a military factory in Saitama picked up some of these notes and tried to deposit them in his postal savings account, but he was caught by the clerk. It turns out that the printing of the counterfeit notes is higher in quality than the genuine notes printed by the Bank of Japan, which was how the postal clerk noticed it. Aside from the counterfeit bills, most of the other paper the Americans drop is only printed on one side, with a note saying something like: "We intentionally haven't printed on the back of this paper, so that students may use it as note paper or Neighborhood Association officials may use it for notices." I wouldn't want to say it loud enough for anyone to hear, but once you get over the outrage, you have to be impressed.

Right after the cautionary alert was rescinded, Fumiko and Takeko came home. Both of them had been assigned by their schools to work as some kind of assistant draftsmen at the Naval Technical Research Institute in Meguro Ward. Up to now they had never gotten home from work before the six o'clock broadcast of *Citizens' Hour*.

"Did something happen?" I asked.

They replied in unison, "Did it ever!"

Their words tumbled out in overlapping sentences, but this is the gist of the story: When they entered the grounds of the Research

Institute as always, at 8:20 this morning, teachers from Shukutoku Home Economics Girls High School (Fumiko's school) and the Girls High School that Takeko attends were there waiting for them. At the guardhouse by the entrance, the teachers began by saying that a decision had been reached after careful discussion with the head of the First Division of the Naval Technical Research Institute, and that Fumiko and Takeko were no longer needed there. As far as Fumiko was concerned, she had worked very diligently at the First Division these last eight months, and she knew that the engineering officers had valued her efforts. She also knew, without any favoritism, that her sister had been a better worker than most. She asked their teachers to tell them why they were being let go, refusing to leave until she received an explanation.

Her teacher responded: "It's a military secret, and we weren't told the precise reason ourselves, but it seems that the important research has been completed, and the scale of the operations is going to be downsized. We were simply informed that all the schoolgirls working here were going to be returned to their schools. It's not due to any dissatisfaction with your performance."

Comforted, Fumiko and Takeko went to say goodbye to the engineering officer who had been their boss. He was talking to someone on the phone, but when he saw them he suddenly nodded vigorously toward them and said into the mouthpiece, "By the way, Amano, I have two very hardworking, bright girls here with me. I was wondering if you might want them? They're sisters. Fumiko and Takeko Yamanaka. Fumiko, the older sister, is a very lively young woman, and her sister is very easygoing. I can vouch for them both—you won't regret it... Okay, I'll take care of the permission from their schools."

"So, Father, which Mr. Amano do you think our boss was talking to?" asked Fumiko.

"There are a lot of Amanos. I haven't any idea. The only Amano that comes to mind is the honorable merchant Amano Rihei in *The Treasury of the Forty-Seven Loyal Retainers*.

"Don't be silly, Father. Who's the most famous Mr. Amano in Tokyo right now?"

Before I could say anything, Takeko chimed in impatiently, "The stationmaster of Tokyo Station!"

"Mr. Amano went to middle and high school with our boss," continued Fumiko.

"So that means—"

"Yes! From tomorrow we're on the staff at Tokyo Station! We're being transferred from the Naval Technical Research Institute to the Personnel Department of the General Affairs Office of the Tokyo Railway Bureau. Our applications are already completed. Because of our boss's introduction, it all went unbelievably smoothly. Both Takeko and I are working in the Passenger Transport Division of the Business Department. We're National Railways girls now!"

Their boss's recommendation is probably not the only reason it all went so smoothly, I thought. Tokyo Station—and indeed all nine of the Railway Bureaus—are desperate for workers. In fall of the year before last, the government instituted a "Labor Policy for Victory in the War" that declared that "it is forbidden to employ men as ticket takers or conductors at any railroad stations throughout the nation." Most of the male employees of the National Railways who had received solid training by the railroad were drafted and sent to the front or dispatched as special employees to the railways in Manchuria or Java. Young women were being hired to bridge the gap, but since there was no time to train them before they started working, operational efficiency dropped dramatically. With reduced efficiency, it has become necessary to hire more workers... That vicious cycle probably played a big part in my daughters' new jobs as National Railways employees. But not wanting to hurt their feelings, I just said, "That's wonderful!"

Nevertheless, I couldn't help adding ruefully, "It's a shame that you'll have to drop out of school, though."

"We're not dropping out of school. We're just transferring, Father," said Fumiko, looking at Takeko and laughing.

"I'm transferring from Shukutoku, and Takeko is transferring from her school, to Tokyo Station High School for Girls."

"It's officially accredited by the Ministry of Education. We were surprised at first, too. Weren't we, Fumiko?"

"We were floored."

No one was more floored than me, but according to what they told me, there are 213 girl students working at Tokyo Station (and there will be two more tomorrow), divided into two teams. Each team starts work at eight in the morning, does night duty, and then returns home again at eight the next morning. The next team takes over for the following twenty-four hours, which the first team has off.

This spring, some of the girls expressed the desire to study—not just one or two, but more than 180 said they wished they had the opportunity to continue their education. As everyone knows, from April all schools with the exception of primary schools and medical schools have been canceled. In other words, officially speaking, the only schools for the general public still operating in Japan are primary schools. But the girls working at Tokyo Station proposed studying in the morning following their overnight stay, after they had completed all their duties. They had asked only to be able to have time to study on their own, offering to give up their sleep to do so, and pleading to be allowed to read school texts and other books.

This plea reached the ears of three people who were impressed by the girls' seriousness. One was Stationmaster Amano, who offered the girls a room on the third floor as their study hall. The second was Principal Kuramochi of Kaedegawa High School for Girls in Nihonbashi, who said that there was only so far the girls could go with independent study, so he would arrange to send instructors to offer them daily classes: Japanese and Chinese on Mondays; geometry on Tuesdays; mathematics on Wednesdays; history on Thursdays; physics and chemistry on Fridays; and sewing on Saturdays. He told the girls to feel free to ask these instructors to assist them with their studies, and since his own subject was moral education, he will come to the study hall whenever he had free time and deliver morally uplifting talks to them. The third person to be impressed was a high-ranking official in the Ministry of Education. He has permitted the students to hang a sign at the entrance to their study hall with the words "Tokyo Station Branch of the Kaedegawa High School for Girls," and he has promised to provide certificates to those who had graduated from elementary school after two years of study and Special Course Certificates of Accomplishment to high school graduates after one year of study.

"So the girls in each team will have one hour of official classes from eight in the morning every other day. Takeko and I will undergo a special week-long training course eight hours a day starting tomorrow, and we'll become full-fledged employees starting May 29th."

"But we get our uniforms tomorrow. They're great—dark navy blue tunics with white collars, pants and black sneakers."

"You should try to find some red beans so I can make red beans and rice to celebrate," my wife said from the kitchen. "For tonight, you'll have to be satisfied with steamed sweet potatoes. But keep an eye out for red beans, dear."

I'm really impressed, and I know I'm not alone in that feeling. Today's young people are truly outstanding. National Daiichi Higher School students arrive at school these days at six thirty in the morning, so they can take classes from seven to eight. Adults may have decided to cancel all school beyond primary school, but they can't eradicate the desire of young people to learn and improve themselves. When National Daiichi Higher School students finish their class at eight, they hurry off to their jobs as student laborers, arriving at the factory twenty minutes later. In ten minutes, they're in place and ready to go, and then they work from eight thirty to five. Those on the night shift work until five in the morning, and then rush to school. The Municipal Middle School that Kiyoshi attends is the same. As of last week, there is one hour of classes in the morning. When class is over, he goes to the Army Munitions Warehouse to excavate air-raid shelters. I can't help but resent the recent educational policy that refuses to take into account young people's passionate desire to learn. They're not asking for spending money, for food or to go see a movie; all they're asking for is a chance to read, even if it's only a page a day; a chance to do some math, even if it's only a problem a day. We should let them read, let them study math. Why can't we at least give them their mornings to fulfill their passion for learning?

The same is true when you look at the battlefield. Mr. Takahashi, who has been in Kyushu reporting on the Special Attack Forces soldiers, showed me a photograph of a brave young man about to board his Special Attack Force plane. He had the face of a boy, but was on his way to die. When I saw what he was holding, I choked up completely. He had an old doll—maybe something his sister or his sweetheart had given to him—and he was about to climb in his plane with it. "This kid is too young for immortality," I muttered to myself. And Mr. Takahashi, said in a low voice, "The night before this photo was taken, this boy sharpened a brand new pencil down to a stub, then took another one and did the same thing. He must have sharpened thirty pencils into shavings, without sleeping all night. We weren't allowed to use this photo."

Isn't there a better way to do things? Compared to me, someone who makes his living by aiding and abetting some crook who's practically stealing the last worldly goods from people who are losing their homes, someone who gets all worked up about whether he's going to see a sumo match or not, today's young people are really outstanding.

"By the way, what kind of research were you two assisting with at the Naval Technical Research Institute?" I asked Fumiko.

She replied without a moment's hesitation, cutting me off completely. "Our boss made us promise that we wouldn't talk about it, even to our parents and siblings. I'll die before I say anything."

Takeko added, "Anyway, it was very advanced, and we really couldn't understand what it was about."

My daughters are really something.

May 22

"Last night someone tossed an anonymous letter into the Neighborhood Association offices, and I wanted to talk to you about it." It was the Neighborhood Association leader who'd dropped by as I was smoking a cigarette after breakfast.

"But first, I need to thank you for the mimeograph work you did for us. It was a fine job. The person at the Information Bureau said it was easier to read than the work of their in-house copyist. If he could, he said, he'd fire him and hire you instead." He opened the ceramic button on the pocket of his national civilian uniform and took out several nib pens—rare commodities these days—and lined them up on the table. There were six in all. "These are for Kiyoshi. And this is for you." Then from his left pocket he took out a pack of Asahi cigarettes. The cigarettes we occasionally get as part of our rations are a brand called Kinshi; the tobacco is mixed with knotweed and by no stretch of the imagination can it be said to taste good. When you smoke Asahi, though, the nicotine slowly spreads to the tips of your fingers and your whole body feels pleasantly buoyant. That's real tobacco. There is a way to get a hold of Asahi cigarettes. You take an empty pack and stuff it full of white rice, then stand in front of a tobacco store, wait for a moment when no one else is around, and hand the pack to the proprietor. And like magic, the rice is instantly transformed into Asahi cigarettes! With this method, you don't need any tobacco coupons. White rice is a rare commodity, so not many people do this. I wonder how the Neighborhood Association leader got a hold of these. While acting a little puzzled, I bowed and accepted the cigarettes.

"Now, let's see. Here's the letter that was tossed into the office." He took a piece of paper folded into quarters out of his right pocket and placed it on the table. At the same time he drew a Kinshi cigarette out of his lower left pocket, opened a matchbox that had "Complete Victory in Our Sacred War/Carrying Out the Nation's Policies" printed on it, and lit his cigarette. He must be some kind of magician, I thought, the way he kept pulling things out of his pockets. And lighting a cigarette with a fresh match each time was a real luxury. You need a ration coupon to get matches, and then people are limited to six matches per day.

"I think that the author of this anonymous letter is your Kiyoshi. Anyway, I'd like you to read it."

The sheet of paper was ripped out of a notebook, and written on it was this childish poem modeled after a Chinese ode:

A Denunciation of the Neighborhood Association Leader's Call for a Reduction in Bodily Wastes

A pleasant dump or a liberating piss is one of life's great pleasures,
The gold of the honey bucket enriches the nation
High and low alike must empty their bowels and bladders

And the sage uses his time on the pot to ponder the deepest measures.

The smell of shit, the familiar odor of our sacred realm,
A glorious summit of night soil rising in the toilet's cistern,
No one can withstand the sweet desire to take a dump
Nor urge to take a leak can, as all mankind knows, overwhelm.

Noble as my resolve to put a stop to my shit itch is,
My eyes crossed in pain, I fold in agony,
I can endure no more, and my bowels explode.
My dear mother weeps, wasting her precious laundry soap washing my soiled britches.

Striving with all my might to damn the natural flow of pee,
I faint in mid-day, shaming myself in public,
My pants dripping like a filthy wash cloth—
How bitter! Precious garments reduced to rags of penury.

The petty thoughts of the moron
Only result in the waste of precious goods.
Only a fool presses his inhumane ideas on others
As if he has forgotten there's a war on.

Ah! The Neighborhood Association leader's plan violates the Way of Heaven!
O! This inane policy goes against all human reason!
How sad! The community notice clipboard rushing around
Solely for the purpose of self-glorification's inflating leaven.
—Anonymous

I knew immediately that this was Shoichi's handwriting. The night before last, when I went upstairs, Kiyoshi and Shoichi were working quietly on something together. No doubt they had put their heads together to compose this silly poem, and then Shoichi wrote it out. His handwriting was exactly the opposite of the "fat, wormy squiggles" he accused me of making; they looked like the tracks of a sparrow dancing across the page, so I recognized his hand immediately.

"The rhymes are completely forced, and there's no meter, so it's obviously an amateur production. But on the other hand, some of the Chinese characters are pretty difficult. I don't see how a first- or second-year middle school student could have written this." I'd decided to play dumb. In a contest between that unintentionally sidesplitting clipboard notice and this anonymous poem, it seemed to me the poem was the winner. For one thing, it made some sense. For another, it had a human touch. I had to protect the two boys, who, after all, were perfectly in the right.

"I happen to have some indisputable proof, so don't expect me to be put off that easily. Take a look at this watermark at the corner of the page."

I did as he asked. The paper was smooth, heavy and of high quality, the kind that snapped crisply at the flip of the fingers, and it bore the watermark of the brand name Kokuyo.

"Paper these days doesn't have a watermark, now does it?"

No, it most certainly does not. Most of it is absolute junk, recycled newsprint that's folded and stitched together into the shape of a notebook before being sandwiched between some low-quality heavier sheets that could almost pass for a cover. When you erase it, it peels off, and if you erase again, it tears. That's the sad state of notebooks these days. Not that it's entirely the fault of the notebooks. The erasers are also to blame. You can hardly tell if they're made from rubber or clay.

"The president of Kokuyo is an old school friend, you see, and when I went to view the plum blossoms in Kameido in February last year, I stopped by his house on the way home. He gave me ten high-quality paper notebooks as a present at the time, and I handed out some to acquaintances. I gave Kiyoshi the last two notebooks as his middle school graduation present."

"Yes, we really appreciated that. Kiyoshi treasures those notebooks, and he still has one that remains untouched..." As I was thanking him I realized what I'd just said and the blood drained from my face. If those kids were going to toss an anonymous poem into the Neighborhood Association office, why hadn't they used paper from one of their cheap notebooks? Okay, they were proud of what they did—it was their masterpiece. That must have been why.

"Seems like a perfect case of 'You catch the thief red-handed, and it turns out to be your own son,'" the Neighborhood Association leader said, exhaling a big puff of cigarette smoke.

"I guess so. I should have kept a closer eye on him. I'll read him the riot act when he gets home," I said, gracefully waving the white flag and bowing low. "I should have noticed what was going on. I take responsibility as his parent. Please accept my apology."

"I have to say, I can't understand what young people today are thinking, using a fine notebook for something like... this. That was my first reaction, anyway. But when I thought about it a little more, this poem hits the nail on the head. I agree. My request that people try to restrict their toilet use really does go against human nature."

This was odd. Something was up. I waited, expecting the worst.

"I was trying to keep a lid on a stinky situation, but when your toilet cistern stinks, the only solution is to vacuum the shit out from the bottom up. In other words, we need to clean out the toilet cisterns of every family so that they can use them freely and continue to fight this Greater East Asian War without holding anything back. That's how it should be. I learned my lesson. On the way over here, I met with the staff in charge of toilet maintenance for the Neighborhood Association and gave them a good scolding, but what was the point of that? There's nothing they can do... The farmers in Shibamata and Kanamachi want our night soil. The residents of Miyanaga-cho want the night soil carted away. The farmers want what we have, and we want to give it to them, but there's no way to bring the two sides together. The waste management staff can't do anything, no matter how much I push them. It's like a marriage proposal. A man wants a wife; a woman wants a husband. But there's no go-between to set things up, so they remain single. Yamanaka, will you be our go-between?"

After his usual long song and dance, he'd finally come to the punch line.

"You have a three-wheeled truck, Mr. Yamanaka. You're a delivery service. You're the perfect go-between for this problem.

Ten buckets lent to us by the farmers are sitting empty behind the Neighborhood Association office. Will you make six or seven round trips to the Edogawa area with five of those buckets loaded in your truck? The waste management staff will empty the cisterns. By the time you get back, the buckets will be waiting for you. You just have to transport them. The farmers will unload them, so you won't have to get your hands dirty at either end. And guess what—we can start with the Neighborhood Association office. After all, it's a public facility, for the entire neighborhood, and in cases like this we have to put the public's needs first and private needs second. If I may say so, as far as I'm concerned this comes under the third priority outlined in Official Notice No. 153, issued based on the Army Control Ordinance. I think I've said enough, but just let me add that the Neighborhood Association will take care of the gas. And on top of that, we'll pay you 30 sen per bucket."

After having finished his oration, the Neighborhood Association leader left in a cheery mood. I wasn't angry. If anything, I couldn't help being impressed by how skillfully he'd used the boys' poem to his own advantage. And his mention of Notice No. 153 was a very effective threat. I took it out to look at it again, and it was clear that he had me by the short hairs. The gist of the notice was a list of all the things that can and cannot be transported. What cannot be transported:

1.   Anything to be transported a distance over fifty kilometers
2.   Goods from department stores or other retailers as a service to their customers
3.   Garden stones, marble or artificial stone
4.   Trees, bonsai, pots or wreaths
5.   Cameras, domestic animals, sports or entertainment equipment

What can be transported:

1.   Military goods and materials
2.   Goods needed in case of natural disasters
3.   Rice, grain and fresh foods
4.   Mineral ore, coal and charcoal
5.   Daily necessities

The items were listed in order of priority. The Neighborhood Association leader had apparently decided that human waste fell under the third item, since, though it's the end product of "rice, grain, and fresh foods," it's still undeniably "rice, grain and fresh foods." And his assertion that the Neighborhood Association office toilets should be emptied first because it's a public facility was very clever. After all, the Neighborhood Association office is his own house. It's the luxury Eiwa Apartments that he owns and operates. Basically, the Neighborhood Association leader used the boys' poem and the authority of Notice No. 153 to get his own toilet cleaned out.

Kiyoshi came home in the evening, but I didn't say anything to him. By that time, I'd become very fond of his little ditty.

May 23
In the morning, while I was lining the bed of the three-wheeled truck with old rush mats, my brother came by. He wanted me to go to Furusawa Enterprises to pick up some things and deliver them. It seems he'd arranged for the whole of Furusawa Enterprises to stay in an inn located in Shinanomachi, Yotsuya Ward, behind Keio Hospital, from tonight through May 25th. The inn is the Shinanoya; though it's not large, it's very well-appointed, the gardens are immaculately cared for, and on top of that, it's very quiet. It's one of the finest inns in the whole capital; the only drawback might be the slight odor of disinfectant that wafts from the hospital when the wind is blowing in the wrong direction. The Shinanoya is also quite exclusive. In recent years, it's been a favorite of the military. The instructors from the Military Academy in Ichigaya, as well as the officers of the Azabu Regiment Headquarters and the Imperial Guards hold private meetings there, they sometimes hire geishas from Araki-cho to entertain them, and they generally monopolize the inn. But since Sunday morning, when Prince Kan'in died, it has been vacant.

"In other words, since the Prince gave up the ghost, the inn is quiet as a grave," my brother said.

I ignored this disrespectful levity.

"Prince Kan'in was the chief of the Imperial Japanese Army

General Staff, the head of the Army, so all army officers are banned from entertainment, including fooling around with geishas, and they have to be on their best behavior through tomorrow. That's how I was able to reserve the place for the Furusawas."

He'd thought of this inn because he had some dealings with its proprietor, and because it's close to Meiji Shrine, where the sumo tournament is going to start on the morning of May 25th. The tournament will be held to the east of the Japan Youth Hall, which is just five or six blocks away. Furusawa had managed somehow to come by ten tickets for the opening day of the tournament.

"Since lining up from the night before has been prohibited, and the tournament hall opens at 7 A.M., hordes of people are going to pour in on the first morning train and the lines are going to stretch halfway across town. This is the first sumo tournament I have a chance to go to since November last year, and I don't want to watch opening day from way in the back. Furusawa was saying something about the family getting up at 3:30 in the morning and setting out from Senju half an hour later. That made me think of the empty inn in Shinanomachi, so I decided to make some arrangements."

As he explained, my brother hauled over a *to* of white rice for the proprietor of the Shinanoya Inn. "Think of this as a down payment," he told him, "and if we can work everything out, I'll bring you another three *to*. I'm prepared to sell it to you for an amazing bargain—just a little higher than the official government price. But in exchange, I want to reserve the entire inn for Furusawa Enterprises from May 23rd through May 25th. I'll throw in five *sho* of saké to sweeten the pot." Any inn owner who would pass up a deal this good had to be either a teetotaler or a madman. They struck a deal on the spot, and my brother wanted to deliver the rice and saké now. In addition, all the fish, meat, and vegetables that the Furusawas would eat at the inn over the next two nights and three days, as well as Kirin beer and saké, had to be delivered to the inn by noon.

"Aren't you worried about the extravagance?"

"I'll get what's coming to me, don't worry about that," he said.

There are two outbuildings and three formal guest rooms at the Shinanoya Inn, said my brother. He's having a geisha come from Araki-cho to entertain an important official at the Daily Commodities

Bureau of the Agriculture and Commerce Ministry in one of the outbuildings. (I chose not to ask what will be going on between the two of them.) Another guest room will be occupied by five employees of Furusawa Enterprises, where they'll have a chance to enjoy some rest and relaxation. The second guest room would be for Mr. Furusawa and his wife. The third would be occupied by himself and me, he said.

"I wanted to bring Sen-*chan* but I guess this time it's my wife's turn. So you bring your wife. Don't stand on ceremony. There are three baths. You'll think you died and went to heaven. And remember, it's close to the sumo."

"So you're taking care of four things at once—an outing for the employees, a family get together, entertaining a business connection and sumo."

"Actually, it's five in one. The other outbuilding will be for Tadao and Kinuko. Sort of a belated honeymoon. In view of the situation, if we did each of these separately. It would be unfair to our soldiers and warriors of industry. That's why we're doing them all at once."

I told my brother that I had a previous engagement and I couldn't bring the truck to Furusawa Enterprises that day. He persisted, saying that I should take care of it as quickly as I could and then go to the Furusawas in the afternoon or evening. I pointed to the rush matting spread out on the truck bed. "I'm delivering the night soil from neighborhood toilets to Katsushika. The mats are to keep the shit from splattering all over the truck. You don't want me carrying rice and saké in the same truck bed, do you?

"And I'll pass on the Shinanoya Inn for tonight. But it's okay, I'll come over tomorrow night. I want to see Terunobori up close if I can."

"Yes, by all means, come by." He hurried off, no doubt in search of someone else to deliver his goods for him. "Kinuko is looking forward to it, so make sure you come. But before you do, go to the public bath and get the stink off you. I know Terunobori has been your favorite for a long time," he added, then turned the corner and disappearing from sight.

I like Komusubi Terunobori because he's very skillful and he's got class. He didn't take part in the autumn tournament at the Korakuen in Koishikawa, having just been discharged from the army and in poor physical condition, so we haven't seen him wrestle for a long time. But I'm really looking forward to watching him show what he's made of in the ring for the next several days running. I gave the truck's starter a healthy kick backward and the engine kicked in. My next-favorite wrestler after Terunobori is Ayanobori, but he's been drafted and is at the front. Along with Dewaminato, and Tamanoumi… I was thinking about the three wrestlers still fighting at the front as I arrived at the Neighborhood Association office.

I made nine round trips; it took until seven in the evening. All in all I delivered forty-five buckets of waste to the fields on the west bank of Edogawa River. On my first trip, a misty rain was drizzling, and I was feeling as gloomy as the sky. As I made my second and third trips, though, my spirits brightened. The reason was simple. When I stopped my truck in front of the communal night soil cistern at Shibamata 2-chome and Kanamachi 2-chome, the farmers waiting there applauded and thanked me profusely. As I prepared to leave, they gave me some of the famous miso with scallions they make there and grilled Edogawa River fish; they treated me like an honored guest. Each time I arrived back in Miyanaga-cho, the Neighborhood Association leader put an Asahi cigarette in my mouth, and when we'd finished the Neighborhood Association office and started emptying the cisterns of the neighboring house, the old man who lived there gave me a piece of Japanese paper with the light verse:

> How grateful I am
> for this Kasai boat
> departing from Nezu.

The meaning, he explained, is something like this: In the Edo period, boats from all the outlying areas would moor along the riverbanks of the capital to pick up the city's night soil. Boats from the Kasai domain located in the low area between Arakawa River and Edogawa River had been coming to the city to pick up night soil longer than those from any other region, so all the night soil boats came to be known as "Kasai boats." But now a "Kasai night soil truck" was driving from Nezu to Kasai— just the opposite of how things went during the Edo period. "And what a wondrous development that was!" he exclaimed. It was remarkable how much information could be packed into just seventeen syllables.

Everyone, both the farmers and my neighbors, was delighted and grateful to see me. Anyone would be happy to be received with such appreciation. As if my feelings were somehow communicated to the weather, from afternoon the skies cleared and the sun shone brightly. And on top of that, there wasn't a single cautionary alert siren. In the end I even began singing to myself, not something I do very often.

After my last, ninth load of night soil had been emptied into the communal night soil cistern at Kanamachi 2-chome and I had been rewarded with two *sho* of soybeans, I drove to the west bank of Edogawa River and headed my "Kasai truck" slowly in the downstream direction. To my left was the clear, blue Edogawa River. Flowing slowly and steadily, the broad band of water looked like a giant bolt of azure cloth. On the opposite shore is Matsudo, and true to its name, "pine doorway," there are stands of pine trees. As I drove along, the ruins of Satomi Castle, thickly shrouded in groves of pines, came into view. The site of the former castle is slightly elevated, and as a result the thick, deep green pine grove looks like an island—to me, as I drove, even more so because I was looking at it across the broad expanse of the river. To my right, the farmers' fields glimmered green in the soft light of dusk. Here and there were little patches of the scarlet of late-blooming clover and the brown of tiled roofs. Taishakuten Forest was like a green knob.

I learned from the people here that they plant clover as green manure, and that roof tiles are a famous product of the area. I saw a pear grove at the foot of the raised bank. Flocks of birds were flying above the new leaves. This was peace. But in the world as it is today, especially for eyes accustomed to Tokyo, with its piles of rubble and destruction, this peace, the belt of green, was almost too lovely and, because of that, slightly menacing. Looking up, I saw the dark figure of Mount Fuji looming. With the sun behind it, it was black. I used to think that Mount Fuji had a divine beauty. But lately, I have begun to think it a traitor, a friend of the B-29s. If traitor is too harsh, then double agent at the least. Acting as a guidepost for the B-29s, B-24s and P-51s, Fuji has become a despicable doublecrosser. I looked to the left again to where a path leads down the elevated bank. A little boat had crossed the river to this bank, and two farmers carrying spades hopped off. I drove down the pathway, stopped and began to fill the buckets I had on board with water from the river. If I splashed twenty buckets on the truck bed, I thought, the "Kasai" would be all washed away and my old three-wheeled truck would be back.

"What a smelly truck," someone said. It was a young boy who seemed to be in about the second year of primary school, and who had an exceptionally rectangular face, the precise shape of a wooden clog. A little girl with bobbed hair was tied in a bundle on his back. She looked about two years old and was very cute, with a broad forehead.

"That's why I'm washing it."

"Are you a parent?"

"What do you mean by that?"

"Do you have kids?"

"I do."

"Do you ever buy them presents?"

"Sometimes."

"That's nice."

"You're a strange kid, handing out parenting advice to grown-ups. How about you? Does your father buy you presents?"

"I don't have one. He disappeared somewhere."

"You have a mother?"

"In Osaka."

"Then who takes care of you?"

"My sister and me live with our uncle. So, mister, here's the deal: I have a bag of dried sweet potatoes. Will you buy some as a present for your kids? My uncle grew them for us, and they're different from everyday dried sweet potatoes. They're thick and soft and sweet, as if sugar is seeping out from the inside. Delicious! I'll sell you five slices for 2 yen—normally, that's my asking price, but for you, 1 yen 50 sen. It's a steal! Buy them before I change my mind."

He sure had his patter down for such a little tyke. His round eyes were constantly shifting back and forth, but there was something sweet about him, and you couldn't dislike him. I offered to buy his sweet potatoes.

"Did you save these from your afternoon snacks?"

"If I told you I'd pinched them from a store, you wouldn't buy them, would you? So let's just say I saved up my snacks. Hey, you want me to wash your truck? Would 5 sen per bucket be too high?"

"Five sen is fine, but why are you so eager to make money?"

"Train fare to Osaka. I want to take a trip out there on my summer vacation." He undid the sash holding the baby and turned his back to me, as if telling me to hold the baby while he washed the truck. As I took the little girl off his back, I said: "These are not the kind of times when you can just take a trip to Osaka because you want to."

He dipped the bucket vigorously into the river. "I'm sure I'll get there somehow. After all, there's nothing separating Katsushika and Osaka but the distance, right?" He seemed quite strong. "Mister, if she cries, just say, 'Sakura, I'm going to have the Head Priest of Daikyoji eat you up.' That'll make her stop crying right away. That's how I trained her."

I dropped the boy and his sister in front of Daikyoji Temple in Shibamata and took the Rikuzenhama Highway toward Nakagawabashi, with the ringing of the temple bells behind me. The day before yesterday I wrote how outstanding today's young people are. Even little children these days are incredibly strong and independent. As long as one boy as resilient and brave as this one is alive, the Empire has a bright future ahead of it, no matter what adversity we face in the coming days.

May 24

I woke up to my wife saying that a cautionary alert siren had sounded. I turned on the radio. The announcer's voice was different than usual; he was speaking very quickly. "Squadrons of enemy planes are flying north, and those in the lead have already passed over Hachijojima. Intense caution is advised. They are scheduled to reach the mainland by about 12:30 A.M. All members of the army, government officials and citizens alike should prepare fully for an air attack and be ready for a fight to the death." I fell asleep last night at ten after writing in my diary. Since my wife woke me up at 12:05, I had only slept about two hours, but my mind was surprisingly clear. The enemy was coming to clean up the sections of the city they had left undestroyed; the bastards were almost certainly going to carpet Nezu with incendiary bombs. As I said that to myself, I tied on my air-raid hood. My wife had groped her way to the kitchen and seemed to be making some rice balls.

Fumiko and Takeko were talking as they came downstairs. "I wonder if we could run all the way to Tokyo Station in thirty minutes," said Fumiko.

"I can't do it," said Takeko. "I'm not as fast as you are. But I think I could make it in less than an hour."

I placed my hands on their shoulders from behind. "You're still in training. Having you rushing about the station will only be a hindrance to the others. Tonight you're going to take refuge in the shelter in Ueno."

Kiyoshi was stuffing books into his book bag. "Dad, I'm sorry," he said. "You had to make nine round trips to Katsushika because of that poem Shoichi and I wrote. We just did it as a joke." It's unpleasant to have someone apologize to you at a time like that. It's too much like a last farewell.

"I can't wait until your next one. He deserved every word. Next time, count me in, too," I said as I dashed out the door. Without gasoline, the truck wasn't going anywhere. I decided to transfer the thirty-five gallons of gasoline I had stored in the hole underneath the floor of the shed to beneath the manhole cover in the street out front. It was too dangerous to leave it in the shed. I called for Kiyoshi to help me, and we lined up the cans of gasoline in front of the manhole. I also brought out the one *to* one *sho* of mobile oil, three gallons of gear oil and four kilograms of grease. After it was all outside, I took a minute to catch my breath. A huge full moon hung in the western sky, like a painted stage backdrop. For the briefest moment it occurred to me that this whole thing might be a play, or was taking place in a dream.

"What's the matter, Dad?"

Kiyoshi's voice brought me back to myself. I started to lift the manhole cover, but maybe because I had been daydreaming, or perhaps because I wasn't really as awake as I thought I was, or maybe because I was so tense, I let the partially lifted cover slip, and it dropped on the middle finger and ring finger of my left hand. With a groan of effort, Kiyoshi lifted the cover. Blood was pouring out of my smashed fingers. Squeezing the veins at the base of the fingers, I said, half-deliriously, "Kiyoshi, you've got to put the gasoline in the manhole. Don't forget to put the cover back on. And be careful; don't do something stupid like this." Then I ran into the house. Of course, it was pitch dark. "I've hurt myself!" I shouted to my wife. "Where are the candles?" I shouted.

"Have the bombs already started falling? I didn't hear anything," my wife said from the kitchen, as if she hadn't heard a word I'd said.

Fumiko lit a candle. The tips of my fingers were completely smashed. We painted them with mercurochrome from Takeko's first-aid kit and wrapped them in gauze, and I rushed over to Igarashi, the dentist studying to be a doctor.

His diagnosis was that it would take a month for them to heal, and even then the fingernails would be deformed. He advised me to see a surgeon tomorrow. A year ago there were three surgical clinics in Nezu, but now not one remained. Two of the doctors were ordered to report for duty at the National Hospital, and the third went off to the front. "I'll try to go to Keio Hospital tomorrow. I have an appointment in the neighborhood anyway..." I said. "If Keio Hospital is full up," replied Igarashi, "try going to the Kanto Haiden Hospital nearby. I have a friend who works at the pharmacy there. I'll write you a letter of introduction." As he headed for his desk, there was the sound of anti-aircraft gunfire, which rattled the shelf of medicines.

I was so pumped with adrenalin that in spite of having been fairly badly injured I wasn't feeling any pain. I thought, how strange this is. Going outside, I saw that the sky to the southwest was glowing red. Maybe my suspicions are wrong, I thought, even as I was preparing for the worst. I could hear someone yelling, "A hit!" in between the anti-aircraft fire and the sound of the bombs exploding. People were clapping. In the sky, a B-29 erupted in flames over the Sumidagawa River, breaking into three or four giant balls of fire as the plane exploded. The balls of fire seemed to shoot off to the far side of Ueno Hill where they disappeared from sight. "Another hit!" someone shouted, followed again by applause, louder this time. Was it coming from Yodobashi? The fires on the ground illuminated the sky brightly, making the belly of the B-29 shine. Flames were shooting out of its four engines as it began to circle overhead. "He's trying to come down over here!" "Fall in Tokyo Harbor!" "Go, get away from here!"

I walked in the direction of the voices. The roof of the Eiwa Apartments was packed with people watching the attack. "He went down in the bay. Great! Thank you!" Gen the tailor called out, beating a pot. "Hey, should someone who is qualified for firefighting duty be up there making music?" I shouted to him. "It looks like Nezu has been spared tonight. I don't think they're coming here," someone shouted back. "I hope not, but I feel sorry for the places that are getting hit." "The anti-aircraft gunners are making them pay tonight. But you never know where the planes are going to fall." "I wonder how things are in Yotsuya and Gaien. They're not burning, are they?" "It looks like Kamata, Ebara, Tamagawa, Omori, Oi, Osaki—around there. And in the west, Yodobashi, Nogata..."

At that moment, the sky to the southwest flared up brilliantly. Incendiary bombs were falling fairly close by. "That was Kojimachi!" "Are you sure? Not Shinanomachi?" "No, definitely Kojimachi." The roof of Eiwa Apartments showed no signs of emptying out. The air was filled with the sounds of bombs dropping, explosions, anti-aircraft fire and the hissing of incendiary bombs near and far. Competing against the uproar, I'd shouted myself hoarse. I decided to go home, but the enemy planes just kept coming, with no end in sight. They arrived in one, two and threes, in an endless succession, from the west. The searchlights and anti-aircraft fire couldn't keep up with their numbers. Just when one plane was picked up by the searchlights, another plane emerged from the shadows of the smoke filling the heavens, and the process repeated itself. But compared to the predawn air raids on March 10th and April 13th and 14th, this one was nothing—and just as I said that to myself, there came the terrifying sound of a bomb approaching with incredible velocity and Sendagi Hayashi-cho, right next to Nezu Gongen Shrine, went up in flames. I immediately hit the ground, but three of the people up on the apartment roof watching the attack were injured. Taken by surprise, they jumped down without thinking, injuring themselves badly. Gen the tailor, fortunately, fainted, so he didn't break anything. Eventually the dawn began to appear in the east, and as if this were a previously agreed-upon signal, the air raid ended. When it all seemed to be over and I was able look up again, I saw little shreds of paper falling everywhere—on roofs, on the ground, on people's heads and shoulders, covering every surface. They were different shades, ranging from reddish brown to black. It must have been the direction of the wind, but such a quantity of paper ash fell in Shinobazu Pond that if it would have filled more than a hundred bags if it could have been collected.

It's six in the morning. My middle and ring finger of my left hand are in incredible pain. I've taken all the painkillers I received from Dr. Igarashi, but they only work for about two hours. I regard this as an indication of just how terrifying the air raid was. Though it may have seemed that I was being entertained by watching the balls of fire bursting above me, the sound of those bombs falling was so frightening that I didn't feel the excruciating pain that I feel now. I can't write any more. The movement of my right hand pushing my Yamato glass-tipped pen seems to reverberate in my left hand. I'm going to rest for a while and then go to the hospital—though in the pain I'm in now, I doubt I'll be able to sleep.

May 25

Yesterday I was awakened at ten in the morning by my wife saying softly, "During the air raids last night, both Shinanomachi and Samon-cho in Yotsuya Ward burned. Keio Hospital and Kanto Haiden Hospital were destroyed." She was weeping.

The Chuo Line and the Sobu Line were still running, and the Keihin Tohoku Line was operating between Tamachi and Omiya. I got off at Shinanomachi. At the ticket gate a civilian air-raid warden announced hoarsely: "All roads to Samon-cho and Shinanomachi are blocked. The side streets are most dangerous. The ground is still burning in some areas." When I explained that my daughter was staying at an inn behind Keio Hospital, he said: "If you're talking about the Shinanoya Inn, it took a direct hit from the incendiary bombs. They fell at about one bomb per *tsubo*. Almost nothing was spared."

I remember pushing my way past the air-raid warden and running ahead, but after that my memory is like a corrugated tin roof strafed by a machine gun, perforated with holes. The smoke smarted in my eyes and my nose was assaulted by an acrid smell. People were walking around looking at the corpses lying everywhere, searching for family members and loved ones. There was a huge truck with a mountain of what appeared to be charred mannequins, piled so high that they might fall off at any minute. Firemen wearing their square hats were shoveling more blackened things on to the heap. There was a water basin like a giant chopstick holder; the "chopsticks" sticking out of it were blackened human legs. A woman black on one side of her body and white on the other... A man with napalm covering his right eye was chanting *Namu Amida Butsu, Namu Amida Butsu,* frothing at the mouth like a crab and revolving around one spot. After walking around him once, I shouted, "Tadao!"

May 26

At noon, I returned from Furusawa Enterprises in Minami Senju to Nezu Miyanaga-cho. The day before yesterday, I had taken Tadao directly back home from where I found him in Shinanomachi. As soon I got him home, I collapsed, and I spent the rest of the day in bed at the Furusawas. An eye doctor stayed with Tadao the whole time. He kept washing the napalm off his eye until finally he was able to open it, just at about six, when the wake and funeral were held. There were no remains. It was a very sad funeral, with just five memorial tablets lined up on the Buddhist altar. My wife, my daughters and Tadao's sister Tokiko were weeping helplessly. The elder Mr. Furusawa and his wife, who had lost their son, daughter-in-law and their grandson's wife in a single blow, took care of everything.

"We're living in terrible times. People lose their entire family in one day all the time, as if it were nothing out of the ordinary. We have to be grateful for the fact that at least four members of our family are still alive." With a frozen smile, old Mr. Furusawa repeated this line to every teary face. Just as automatically, his wife added, "If only it could have been us instead of them." There was only one moment when old Mr. Furusawa looked really stricken. A particularly heartless mourner said: "This is what they get for raking it in on the black market and acting like big shots."

Sen-*chan*, who had lost both her new "husband" and her aunt, was there, too, briskly helping the old couple with the funeral. She seemed delighted by this sudden turn of events, which after all had liberated her from a hellish situation as the mistress forced to cohabitate with the wife. At 10:30 P.M. there was another cautionary alert siren and the funeral guests, saké bottles in hand, rushed out to the shelter in the back yard. I stayed in the house. I was perfectly happy to be barbecued by an incendiary bomb in front of Kinuko's memorial tablet. Sen-*chan* stayed, too. Reeking of saké, she said to me: "Shinsuke, I plan to take over your brother's house on the corner. I'm going to stay there."

"I don't care," I replied. "Tonight's going to be the end for Nezu, anyway."

The electricity went off together with the cautionary alert siren, and partly because of that, the sky from Ueno Hill to the south seemed brighter than it had at dusk. The sound of bombs dropping and exploding went on continuously, as loud as a packed train rumbling along the tracks. After the air raid last evening, at night the fires burning on the ground light up the sky dimly and during the day the smoke filters out the sun's rays, so it's as if the city of Tokyo has been placed into an enormous, dimly lit cave. The best way to describe it is to say that the whole thing seems like a dream.

"Nezu will be all right. It's protected on the east and west by Ueno and Tokyo Imperial University, so they won't dare burn it down," said Sen-*chan* decisively, pulling the saké bottle toward her again. She seemed to really believe the rumor that had been passing around Nezu lately. This is the gist of it: The enemy thinks they've already won the war, so they don't want to burn down precious, irreplaceable treasures that they can confiscate later. Where are such treasures to be found here in Tokyo? First, Tokyo Imperial University. The university library and the libraries and archives in the literature department are the greatest storehouse of precious books in the Empire. Tokyo University's Red Gate is also an architectural treasure. And in Ueno, there are the Imperial Museum and the Imperial Art School Museum of Art. Plus the pagoda at Kan'eiji Temple and the tombs of the shoguns. So Ueno Hill is also a mountain of treasures and the enemy won't firebomb it. Because of that, Nezu, which is sandwiched right in between these two, is one of the safest places in the entire country. People are saying you'd have to be a real idiot to leave Nezu.

It's true that Nezu wasn't bombed last night. But the Imperial Palace was bombed and the Main Palace was destroyed. Thirty-four members of the Police Fire Brigade, the Imperial Guard and the Palace Guard died fighting the fires. The Yomiuri Shimbun and Mainichi Shimbun buildings also burned down. That there was no morning newspaper testifies to the fact that the Asahi Shimbun building must have also suffered major damage. According to Mr. Tokuyama at the newspaper delivery office, the papers are all out of business for a while. From tomorrow morning, there's going to be one joint special edition printed and edited by the *Mainichi* combining the *Asahi, Tokyo, Nihon Sangyo Keizai, Mainichi* and *Yomiuri* newspapers. And someone said that of the seventy-seven air-raid alarm stations in Tokyo, only one had survived—the Koiwa Station. The electricity is still cut off and the radio is silent. We have no way of knowing the enemy's movements. And yet in spite of all this, Nezu remains safe. With ash and scraps of burned paper falling from the rest of the burned-out city, this little belt—Nezu, Yanaka Shimizu-cho, Hanazono-cho, Sakamachi and Sakuragi-cho in next-door Shitaya Ward—remains quiet and untouched. Maybe the rumor that Nezu won't be attacked is true after all. If it is, then I was an idiot to let Kinuko get married and leave Nezu. I am the biggest fool possible.

May 27

Tadao is a little better, so I was able to ask him about what happened on the night of the 24th in more detail. He had already told us a little of what had happened, but whenever he reached the crucial moments of his story, he would fall silent or start coughing and it was hard to make out the chain of events.

Tadao and Kinuko had arrived at the Shinanoya Inn after nine on the evening of May 23rd. They were late because they'd been to see *The Living Chair*, which was being advertised as "Daiei's Big Spring Hit," starring Tsumasaburo Bando and Mieko Takamine at the White Chain Shinjuku Toho Cinema. The Furusawas and my brother and his wife had arrived before 5 P.M., and were drinking beer and eating sukiyaki in the second outbuilding. When Kinuko and Tadao started eating, the two section chiefs from the Daily Commodities Bureau of the Agriculture and Commerce Ministry, who'd been invited to stay in the first outbuilding, showed up. "We've already had two successful rounds with geishas from Araki-cho since this evening, so let's skip that. Instead, why don't we spend the night playing mah-jongg?" they suggested. In other words, they were hoping to be allowed to earn a little extra spending money in a friendly game. The Shinanoya Inn generally catered to army staffers, and they kept a table and mah-jongg set on hand for the officers of the Military Academy in Aoyama, who were diehard players. Both Mr. Furusawa and my brother were pretty much wiped out from all the beer they'd been drinking, so Tadao interrupted his meal and went to the first outbuilding. One of the geishas was an expert mah-jongg player, so they were able to put together enough people for a game.

Of the five remaining in the second outbuilding, the two men drifted off to sleep. The women—in other words, Tadao's stepmother, my sister-in-law and Kinuko—seemed to have spent their time gossiping, but Tadao, of course, was uncertain of this. This was the conclusion he'd come to from the few things that the maid who showed up periodically to serve them passed on. Tadao was having great luck at mah-jongg that night and was having a hard time losing to his guests. When the air-raid siren sounded, he had Big Three Dragons—three white, three green and three red dragons. Once he got one more good tile, he'd be set up for a huge win. Knowing there was no way he could successfully lose the hand, and as an excuse to shuffle the tiles, he suggested, "Shall we go into the shelter?"—when suddenly a hissing sound, like an unexpected shower at dusk, seemed to zero in on them, he found himself bounced up in the air and the iron tea kettle on the floor went flying. An excruciating pain stabbed his ears, as if he was being yanked upward by them. The sound of the explosion was so loud that he seemed to hear nothing, almost as if he had earplugs. The expression "thunderous silence" flashed into his mind, he said. When he came to his senses, hundreds of red snakes were climbing up the door. Looking more closely, he saw they were flames. He kicked his way through the paper door on the other side of the room and dashed outside.

The next thing he remembered was grasping a strip of cloth like an emergency lifeline and being lead onto the grounds of Keio Hospital. Ahead of and behind him were patients. He saw the back of a nurse at the front of the cloth strip. They were temporarily evacuated to the concrete annex of the hospital, and when the all-clear was sounded, he received treatment for a burn on his left shoulder in the Kitasato Memorial Medical Library on the hospital grounds. The person who treated him was wearing a doctor's robe with a cloth tag reading "Keio University Hospital Defense Squad, Assistant Squad Vice Leader Keinosuke Shizume" sewn on his breast. A student volunteer gave him a hard biscuit to soothe his hunger. From about six o'clock the next morning he began wandering around the site where the Shinanoya Inn had been.

Listening to Tadao, I thought about the Fukushimas, fan makers like me. He was the proprietor of Hosendo in the Asakusa shopping district. Since fleeing the air raids on the night of April 13th with his daughter, he'd disappeared. The family still treated him as missing. Hosendo specialized in dancer's fans and had a very high reputation among geishas and professional entertainers nationwide. His daughter had already received her professional dancer's license and was exceptionally good looking, known as the reigning beauty of the Asakusa shopping district. Of course there was no proof that Fukushima and his daughter had been incinerated in the air raid. No one had seen or identified their bodies. So naturally the family and all their relatives were scouring the city for any trace of them. Several of them did so to the point of collapsing in exhaustion, while others went funny in the head. Were we better off, compared to the misfortune of the family at Hosendo?

The sliding door on which Tadao saw red serpents of flame climbing faced the second outbuilding. In other words, the second outbuilding must have taken a direct hit. The air raid shelter was also hit with several six-pound incendiary bombs, and all that remained of it was a bowl-shaped crater. Kinuko and the others were in one of those two places. From the fact that they didn't call out to Tadao, they must have still been in the second outbuilding. I mentioned this to my wife.

"It would be far better if they were just missing," she said, her face as gray and lusterless as a piece of old newsprint. "At least then there'd still be hope."

She had a point.

Up to just several years ago, there were 250 fan makers in Tokyo. Now there are only three—Ibasen in Nihonbashi, Otaya in Nezu and me. And none of us is making any fans. The same can be said of everything in Tokyo. Everything has disappeared. At the beginning of the year, former Prime Minister Koiso said in a radio broadcast, "No matter how fiercely the enemy attacks, it will take at least three years to reduce the capital to ashes, but in those three years we will drive the demons completely out of Greater East Asia, which means that it is absolutely impossible that the Imperial capital will be destroyed." But now, in just four nighttime air raids, the area from Ikenohata Shichiken-cho all the way to Hatagaya, beyond Tsunohazu in Shinjuku, is nothing more than a wasteland. What on earth is going on?

May 28

Oh, Kinuko.

At last the radio came on again, just before seven o'clock this evening. According to the news, this morning the Imperial emissary was dispatched to the mansion of Prince Kan'in in Odawara, and the Imperial funeral oration was declaimed. Following the example of his Imperial highness, I would like to recite an oration before your remains.

The Imperial funeral oration read:

As robust as a mighty fortress, he became a soldier by choice, loyally exerting himself in the line of duty. He contributed nobly to society, and exercised his office with lofty consideration and stalwart rigor. He served honorably in two campaigns, earning the highest accolades for his courage in deed and brilliance in strategy. For many years, as an eminent officer of the Supreme Command of the Imperial Army, he tendered his wise counsel to Military Headquarters.

He always spoke frankly to his sovereign without concealing

his heart, and he strived tirelessly to promote peace and harmony with others.

While masterfully shouldering these weighty responsibilities, he also humbly dedicated himself to the prosperity of the subjects of our sacred realm, promoting their material and spiritual advancement and proffering his sage guidance and prudent direction based on a profound spirit of humanity and compassion.

Truly, he was an august and virtuous elder of the Imperial family and a pillar of the realm.

How can we refrain from lamenting upon hearing of the sudden passing of so worthy a figure? We have sent our Imperial envoy to confer the appropriate benefaction in money and goods and express our sympathy.

It was in the bothersome Chinese-style writing that you'd expect. Rare for someone in my trade, I pursued a specialized course of study at university, but in those days nobody thought university study was worth much of anything. What good, anyway, would scholarship be for the son of a fan maker? Sitting in the workshop and learning how to mix paste to the right consistency was much more important. And because I actually enjoyed making fans, even attending a business course in middle school would really be an inexcusable waste of time. As I began to realize that, I became less motivated in my studies and I skipped my classes and spent most of my days at home in the workshop. I dropped out after just one year.

So, Kinuko, composing a lofty funeral oration for you in Chinese is beyond your father's abilities. It will just end up as a simple eulogy, or a remembrance, or something in between. I ask you to bear with me and listen anyway. I don't suppose it's proper for ordinary subjects like us to imitate the Imperial family or the princely houses and deliver funeral orations to our loved ones. But I don't care. The Main Palace has burned down. The Omiya Palace has too. So have the palaces of Prince Chichibu, Prince Mikasa, Prince Higashikuni, Prince Fushimi, Prince Kan'in, Prince Yamashina and Prince Nashimoto. That's how it should be. Now the shared sufferings and glories of all One Hundred Million Japanese can become an unyielding pillar at the heart of the Empire. All of us have to face the enemy's air attacks as fellow Japanese, each like all the rest. I'm not the only one who feels this way. Since the air raids on May 24th and May 25th, everyone is saying the same thing. How, then, could anyone fault me for reciting an oration before the tomb of my daughter?

Kinuko, you were music. When a new popular song played on the radio, you only had to hear it once or twice to have it memorized and then I'd hear you singing it in your room upstairs. There was nothing I loved more than to listen to you singing while I made fans in the workroom below. You also had a remarkable musical sense. You knew which songs would be hits and which wouldn't. Do you remember the 10 sen bet you made with me when you were in third or fourth grade of primary school? Nitto Records put out that song "Russian Girl," by Yoshiko Kawaji, whom I liked so much. I remember, the lyrics went, "Russian girl, you're so cute / I hold out my hand, and invite you to go for a stroll / You smile right away, and give me your arm / *Aaooshin harashode / Harashode ronron.*" The second verse went: "Russian girl, you're so sweet / In the morning you go to milk the cow in your bare feet / The coffee you make has the flavor of love / *Aaooshin harashode / Harashode ronron.*" I especially liked the music to the song; I used to sing it at all the time. Then one day you said to me: "Papa, stop singing that song, it's never going to be a hit." And then we went back and forth about whether it would be a hit or not. It was about to escalate into a full-fledged argument when my apprentice Tominosuke intervened.

"Why don't you make this into a bet? If Gen the tailor is humming this song in his workshop within a month from today, you win, Mr. Yamanaka. If not, Kinuko wins." Gen always hummed the latest hits as he worked. So we let his habit be our referee and made our bet. I lost. A month later Gen was humming "Dance, dance the Tokyo song…" That Tominosuke was a funny kid, wasn't he? Soon after he started working here, I asked him to go to a paper dealer in Yotsuya. He said to me: "Master, when you send your apprentice out on an errand, you should do it early in the morning, before breakfast. That way he'll take care of the errand quickly and hurry back for his breakfast. That's the way to make sure he doesn't loiter." Just like he was the master and I was the servant. I wonder what happened to him? A few years back I heard that he became a navy civilian employee and was sent to some island in the South Pacific. Maybe you've already met him up there in heaven.

But after you started at middle school, you didn't sing popular songs the way you had before. Instead, you put your energies into table tennis and the abacus. That was November 10, 1940, ten years ago, during the All Tokyo Girls Commercial Schools Abacus Meet commemorating the 2,600th year of the founding of the Empire of Japan, when you came in sixth place in the singles competition. Your mother and I were so proud of you. That was a wonderful experience. And we went to all the celebrations—the lantern parade in front of the Imperial Palace, the flag parade, the marching bands, the portable Shinto shrine parades. We all received special rations of sticky rice to make red-bean rice. It was the happiest time in my life.

Then you found a job in the Metals Department of Mitsubishi Corporation. It was the first time anyone in Nezu Miyanaga-cho had been picked up by a major company like that, and we received celebratory saké from Nezu Gongen Shrine. I felt like we had really come up in the world, all because of you.

After you started working at Mitsubishi, you began to take lessons in Japanese music, and I remember how you used to sing "The Iris Bathing Gown" as you dusted the furniture. I can still see you cleaning the house in time to the song's rhythm. To me, your speaking voice and your laughter were music.

You always used to say that you didn't want to marry a company employee, that you wanted to be the wife of someone who ran a big shop or his own business. That's why when the Furusawas approached me, I thought it was a good idea, though now I'm not so sure. It seemed that a business with special designation from the Ministry of Agriculture, selling fertilizer, shovels, hoes and scythes to the farmers of Katsushika was a perfect fit for you, a master of the abacus, but I can't help thinking that it turned out to your detriment instead. When trade is good, the business flourishes. People flock to a flourishing business. A flourishing business is a draw for the black market. Just about the only thing you can't buy on the black market is an Order of

the Golden Kite medal; everything else is for sale. And that's how ten
tickets for the summer sumo tournament found their way to Furusawa
Enterprises. Those tickets robbed you of your life. If I had known this
would happen, I would have married you off to Gen the tailor.

You probably don't know this, but Gen always had a thing for
you. He told me he was fond of you from before you even went to
primary school. He was twenty-eight or twenty-nine at the time.
I just found out about his feelings for you last summer. When we
were talking at the regular meeting of the block group, I happened
to say: "The trains in the city are so crowded that Kinuko's coat is all
worn out. People are packed in like sardines. They tumble together
so tightly that that they rub the nap off each other's coats."

Several days later Gen brought over a man's overcoat that he'd made
into a woman's coat. "I work at home, so I rarely get out. In the old
days, I used to make coats out of fine cloth, but this was just sitting in
the mothballs in my chest of drawers, so I reworked it for Kinuko."

Since he hadn't taken any measurements, I asked how he knew it
would fit you. He replied: "It'll fit. I see Kinuko every day from my
workshop. I know how tall she is and what her measurements are.
If I've got this wrong, I'll cut my eyes out with my sewing shears."
I felt a chill run down my spine at that moment. And though I
thought it was probably cruel, I said: "Gen, you're in your mid-
forties. You're twice the age of Kinuko. Don't embarrass yourself. It's
disgusting. Please take the coat back. Why don't you exchange it for
some rice? It'll bring two *to*, I'll bet." I figured straight talk was the
best. He didn't give up right away. He hung around, saying how he'd
liked you since you were a little girl and that you used his workshop
as your playroom and stopped by there every day, and how happy
it made him. Finally he looked at me pleadingly and said: "Please
don't tell Kinuko about this. If you do, I'll have to move out of the
neighborhood." And he rushed out the door. Since I promised him,
I never mentioned his feelings to you. But maybe I made a mistake.
If you'd married Gen, you'd probably still be alive. And I could still
be comforted and cheered by your musical voice.

But Kinuko, maybe it wouldn't have made any difference in the
end. When the final invasion of the Homeland takes place, we're all

going to die anyway. I may look like I'm still alive, but this is just a temporary reprieve, until the final battle. It may sound strange, but we're all half-dead. The place where you are now and Nezu are actually very close to each other. They talk about the border between the land of the dead and the land of the living, but right now, they're as close to each other as two sides of a coin. If that weren't the case, how could so many people be dying every day?

I don't know when the final battle for the Homeland will take place. It probably depends on how long Okinawa holds out. But rumor has it that that won't be much longer. If the enemy was so occupied with Okinawa, they say, they wouldn't have been able to launch the air raids on Tokyo on the 24th and 25th. I agree. Which probably means that the final battle will be sometime this fall. Or maybe the spring of next year? At the very latest, by the Obon holiday next summer, I'll be with you.

Your mother just grumbled from the bedroom, "Don't you think it's time you put that diary down?" I guess the scratching of the glass-tipped pen on the paper is keeping her awake. I'm sorry, but I'll stop here tonight. Just as I expected, this has turned out to be a very strange funeral oration. But I have to admit I feel better for writing it. My heart is as clear as an autumn sky, and just as melancholy. I'll be seeing you soon.

May 29

I was awakened at five in the morning by the Neighborhood Association leader banging on our sliding glass door. "Two liaison officers from the Police Force Transportation Department are waiting for you at the Neighborhood Association office. Please come right away," he shouted, and banged on the door once more for good measure. Ah, at last the Police Force Transportation Department has caught up with me, I thought. There are twenty-four trucking companies in the thirty-five wards of Tokyo. They're all large companies, with several trucks and more than a dozen three-wheeled trucks. All of these companies have pledged their cooperation to the Police Force Transportation Department in emergency relief efforts following air raids. The fact is if they don't make that pledge, the Police Force Transportation Department doesn't allow the companies to remain in operation. The "emergency relief trucks" carrying food, necessities and medical teams around the city after an air raid are all donated by these big trucking companies. Everyone in the city knows this. What most people don't know about are the liaison officers, who all belong to the Police Force Transportation Department. Whenever an air raid all-clear is sounded, they go out in teams of two and walk through the burning city. Their beats take them from nearby Kojimachi and Tsukiji to as far as Arakawa, Sunamachi and Kamata. They're always on foot, and they force their way through the still-raging fires to reach their destinations, the trucking companies. I heard from the owner of a certain small trucking firm in Ueno that at first the liaison officers had a fleet of fifty Miyata Gear-M bicycles, the idea being that they could get in touch with the large trucking firms more quickly if they had bicycles. But during the air raids on March 10th, thirty of the bicycles were ruined. Immediately after an all-clear it might look like the ground isn't burning, but it's still very hot below the surface. The subterranean heat melted the tires and warped the spokes of the bikes, and since then the liaison officers have traveled on foot.

I heard something else from that trucker in Ueno. "With the large trucking companies taken out by the air raids, there aren't enough trucks or three-wheelers around. That means that the liaison officers are going to come looking for us, the small firms. In fact, they say that there's already a notice up on the wall at the Police Force Transportation Department for 'Small Truckers in the Metropolitan Region.' Someone I know saw it, so I'm sure it's the truth. People like us just have a single truck or three-wheeler, and it's our sole means of support. If that one precious truck is confiscated by the police, we're left high and dry. So nowadays when an air-raid siren sounds, what I do is head out to Saitama or Chiba. I wait a good half-day out there after the all-clear is sounded, and then make my way home. For a trucker, no one is scarier than the Police Force Transportation Department. They're powerful enough to silence a crying baby or make a bald man grow hair. But almighty though they might be, they can't confiscate a truck that's not there. And besides, sometimes you even pick up a job or two out there in the countryside while you're cooling your heels. When the air-raid siren sounded on the morning of April 30th, I rushed off to Soka. Someone there wanted me to deliver a bunch of empty soy sauce barrels to Noda way up the Edogawa River, and I made five *sho* of gasoline and three *sho* of soy sauce on the deal. Of course if you get caught, you'll be in big trouble, but I'll deal with that when the time comes. And don't blab this around. I can't stand to see you doing this in such an amateurish way, so I'm telling you this out of the goodness of my heart."

I had a different take on things myself. There's a big trucking company, Ryogoku Freight, out in Ryogoku. It's got to be the biggest trucker in the downtown area. As long as it's still up and running, I don't think they'll be chasing after us small fry. Even liaison officers don't want to waste their time. When they think of the downtown area, the first thing that comes to mind is Ryogoku Freight. They'd have no reason to concern themselves with the little guys in Ueno and Nezu. That's how I saw it. I was more afraid of the Foodstuffs Division of the Municipal Economic Agency myself. They were always requisitioning the vehicles of small truckers in order to keep the delivery of food flowing as smoothly as possible. But recently they'd acquired a powerful new ally—the city's sanitation trucks had started making foodstuff deliveries. The Sanitation Department had given up on emptying toilets, so now they had all those trucks just sitting around. So that's why I thought my little three-wheeled truck would be safe from confiscation for the time being, but the appearance of these communications officers might mean that Ryogoku Freight was hit. My truck was going to be requisitioned. I was prepared for this when I went to the Neighborhood Association's office.

"Was there an air raid last night?" I asked timidly.

I addressed the two liaison officers, greedily chowing down on the breakfast of dried mackerel and white rice provided to them by the Neighborhood Association leader, in a deferential tone: "I'm sorry, but I was sleeping and I didn't know. For the last day or two, there haven't been any sirens. We used to be able to hear five sirens here in Nezu—the one on the roof of the Tokyo Museum of Nature and Science, the one at Sendagi National Primary School in Komagome, I forget where the third and the fourth are, and then the fifth, at Horin National Primary School in Kanda Kanazawa-cho. But none of them work anymore, so…"

"Please, sit down," said the Neighborhood Association leader, speaking for the two liaison officers, who were too busy stuffing food in their mouths to say anything. "They've explained what they need to me, so please listen carefully." We left them to their breakfast and went out to the entryway. "They're not here to requisition any trucks for emergency relief. They're looking for volunteers to assist the National Defense Health Corps."

This was the gist of what the Neighborhood Association leader told me: Tokyo was hit very hard during the air raids on the nights of May 24th and 25th, but this triggered an outpouring of warm fellow feeling from neighboring prefectures, a real example of a misfortune turned into a blessing. On the morning of May 26th, police stations in Kanagawa Prefecture mobilized volunteer food relief teams, and with ninety-seven bales of the prefecture's emergency rice supplies, they prepared 36,000 rice balls, which they immediately delivered to the city in trucks from their Prefectural Freight Delivery Battle Corps. Some thirty physicians, nurses and pharmacists from the Kanagawa National Defense Health Corps, divided into three teams, also immediately left for Tokyo as volunteers to tend the air-raid victims. Various organizations in Chiba Prefecture demonstrated an even warmer neighborliness. On May 26th, 27th and 28th, the Patriotic Food Preparation Corps of the four cities of Chiba, Funabashi, Ichikawa and Matsudo sent thirty thousand rice balls to Tokyo, as well as donating two hundred *kan* of foodstuffs such as Chiba's famous peanuts, seaweed, tsukudani, pickles and dried mackerel. On top of that, Chiba University of Medicine and the Physician's Associations of the three cities of Chiba, Funabashi and Ichikawa also sent six medical teams to treat the citizens of Tokyo. "And isn't it wonderful news? Today the National Defense Health Corps of the Ichikawa Physician's Association will be arriving in Tokyo. You know the Municipal Community Center between the bronze statue of Saigo in Ueno and the Gakushuin Academy? If you're standing with your back to Seiyoken Restaurant, it's in front of you, to your left. Well, they're going to set up an emergency treatment station there and provide medical assistance to residents. That's wonderful, isn't it? When push comes to shove, a good neighbor is worth his weight in gold."

What a windbag. I couldn't take it any longer, so I asked point blank: "They want me to transport the doctors from Ichikawa, right?"

"Yes, that's it."

"The Sobu Line is running, isn't it?"

"But they've got medicines and equipment to bring along, too. And when they're done, you'll need to take them back again."

"All right. This being what it is, I'm not asking for any payment. But where am I going to find the gasoline?"

"It seems to me like you don't fully understand the meaning of 'volunteer,'" said the liaison officer sucking on the bones of the mackerel. "If we were going to supply the gasoline, we wouldn't bother to ask for your cooperation, we'd just order you to go to Chiba and bring them back. Since we're not offering you anything, we're asking politely."

I crossed Ichikawa Bridge and entered the city of Ichikawa a little after 6 A.M. The directions I received from the liaison officer said: "Cross Ichikawa Bridge and keep going on the Chiba Road. Ichikawa Police Station will be on your left about six hundred meters ahead. Go another hundred meters and Ichikawa Station is on the right. Keep going another hundred meters and, again on your right, you'll see Yoshida Clinic. The head of the May 29th National Defense Health Corps is the director of Yoshida Clinic. He's also the vice-president of the Ichikawa City Physicians Association."

Dr. Yoshida loaded two orange crates into the back of my truck and said: "The two nurses and the other doctor are taking the train. Okay, let's go." He seemed like a very efficient, no-nonsense doctor.

"Oh, right, I forgot. The Mabashi Branch of the Matsudo City Food Production Corps wants to send three hundred rice balls and twenty *kan* of peanuts in the shell to the people in Tokyo. After you drop me off at Ueno Park, I want you to go back to Mabashi. I think the wounded will be glad to have them."

Actually, the more direct route would be to stop by Mabashi first and then go to Ueno, which would avoid the trouble of a double trip, but twenty *kan* of peanuts is very bulky, and I decided that I couldn't carry both the peanuts and Dr. Yoshida at the same time. After all, the back of the truck is only the size of a single tatami mat.

"I don't mind making the second trip, doctor, but can you find me some gasoline?"

"The medical staff and supplies are to be provided by the twenty members of the Ichikawa City Physicians Association and the rest is supposed to be provided by Tokyo. That was the agreement."

I explained that I was "volunteering" my services without pay and as Dr. Yoshida listened with his head cocked skeptically to one side, I also told him about the Tokyo Rationing National Volunteer Corps.

Given the times in which we're living, no one would complain about working for free, but using up the tiny ration of gasoline we received was something to be avoided at all costs. I explained my plight in dead earnest.

I don't know how it works in Chiba, but in Tokyo everything is organized in a military system. For example, a tofu maker is an infantryman belonging to the Processed Foods Battalion. The old guy who repairs pots and pans and the shoe repairman are senior soldiers in the Daily Necessities Battalion. Geishas are female soldiers in the Mess Battalion, and the fuel deliveryman is a member of the Fuel Battalion.

On top of all these battalions is the Central Headquarters. The head of the Central Headquarters is the head of the Tokyo Metropolitan Economic Agency. There are six vice-heads in the Tokyo Metropolitan Economic Agency: the heads of the General Affairs Department, the Foodstuffs Department, the Forestry Department, the Resources Department, the Department of Wartime Relief in the Civil Affairs Bureau, the head of the Economic Affairs Police Bureau of the Metropolitan Police Department and various leading citizens.

And together with these "battalions" there are also distribution battalions on the ward level. I say "together with," but some say that's not really right. They say that the various battalions are on top and the ward distribution battalions are below them in the chain of command. But if that were true, then the pot and pan repairman would rank higher than the rice distribution center, which is why I say "together with." Anyway, no one understands how they all fit together.

You often see announcements in the newspaper that say something like: "The government has decided to distribute appropriate rice rations, 76,000 boxes of hard biscuits, 3,000 boxes of emergency rations of canned salmon, herring and sardines, tsukudani, bottled goods, miso and soy sauce, to victims of the air raids of the night of such-and-such…" This is something that Central Headquarters has decided and ordered the various battalions under it to carry out. But the actual ward distribution battalions or companies in the area hit by the air raid never see any of the stuff reported in the newspaper actually being distributed. You can ask anyone. For starters, the members of the ward distribution battalions and companies are themselves air-raid victims, and there's no way they could be distributing these supplies. I have no idea why or how this kind of organization came into being. What we residents actually see is rice balls being handed out to lines of air-raid victims from emergency relief trucks. Sometimes the victims also get a little packet of tsukudani, which they're told is emergency relief from the city. The next most familiar sight for us is air-raid victims huddled in the auditorium of some national primary school and, having received a hard biscuit and a blanket, looking relieved to be alive. Or maybe members of the Mess Corps cooking up food in some burned-out spot outdoors.

So it seems that the orders of the Central Headquarters are carried out—a little. But the strange thing is, a few days after an air raid, even here in the shopping streets of Nezu, suddenly, somehow or other, a few cans of salmon or herring are offered for sale—at the eye-popping price of 50 yen a can! I guess even in a can, they're still fish, and somehow they jumped into the vast ocean of the black market and just swam away.

"Come to think of it, after every major air raid, emergency supplies from Tokyo appear out here," said Dr. Yoshida with interest. "When there's an air raid, the city Sanitation Bureau sends emergency medical supplies to the ward offices of the areas that have been hit. Alcohol, zinc oxide, anti-tetanus serum, eye drops, disinfectant, absorbent cotton, gauze, bandages, oil paper, abdominal bandages, slings, sucrose drips… These basic emergency medical and sanitation supplies are always packed up and ready to go, so they can be sent at a moment's notice to areas that have been hit. But somehow or other they end up getting across the Edogawa River from Tokyo and heading our way instead. Then if I happen to mutter to myself while walking through the clinic's waiting room, "I wish we had some gauze," within that day some unknown person appears at the clinic's rear door. "I just happened to get a hold of some gauze today," he'll say. "Would you by any chance be needing any?" I don't know what's going on, but it seems like a big chunk of the world has become a black market. Now I'm not saying that everything that goes by the name of the black market is bad. I just ate black-market eggs over rice for breakfast this morning, and I'm all for the black market when it's a matter of mutual benefit, of two people helping each other out. If our Empire's leaders are saying that kind of neighborly black market is a bad thing, the least they can do is supply us with food of sufficient quality and quantity."

"I agree completely."

"Just compare the number of tuberculosis patients in Ichikawa today and four days ago. You won't believe it. They've nearly doubled. As far as I can see, the reason for about half of them is the so-called ration distribution system. People need to buy food on the black market just to avoid getting sick. That's why I can accept the neighborly black market. But to have a perfectly healthy man come by my door selling medicines and medical supplies... Anyone that healthy should be at the front or working in a war goods factory. The only other place you'll find such strong, healthy men is—"

"Government offices and the police, right?"

"People like that, who take advantage of their position to do black marketing, are completely different from those who do it to help each other out. In fact, that shouldn't even be called the black market. It's an insult to the black marketing we do just to get by. So I said to the man selling the gauze, 'Do you need any medical treatment? If you do, I'll take a look. I'll treat you. And I'll accept the appropriate payment in gauze.' That's the only kind of black market that our clinic is willing to participate in."

I was grateful that I'd been assigned to pick up a doctor like this. Mr. Furukawa had had a unique philosophy about the black market, too. "The black market," he said, "is the movement of goods. Think of Tokyo and the surrounding area as a giant bathtub. The top layer of water is so hot that it's burning, but the bottom layer is still cold. In other words, things are not mixed properly. You need a paddle to stir up the water and mix the hot and the cold. The black market is that paddle." He'd seemed almost proud of what he was doing, like he was making a patriotic contribution to the war effort, which rubbed me the wrong way, but the doctor's explanation of the black market as neighbor's helping each other get by hit home with me. We have to survive another hundred or so days in this world, and his words seemed to offer a valuable lesson for the brief time that remained ahead.

"But why are we talking about the black market? Oh, right. You brought up the subject of gasoline."

"We small-time truckers also get notices of fuel rations. We dash to the Fuel Battalion. The Fuel Battalion is the Tokyo Unified Fuel Distribution Association, but they always say, 'What a shame! You're too late.' They send an official of the association out to let the big truckers know in person when fuel's available, but they send a postcard to us. These days a regular special delivery takes five or six days to arrive. The deadline for picking up your fuel ration is expired by the time you get the card…"

"You should protest."

"No, that won't do any good. In fact, it would do you in. Sometimes they do say that if you have a complaint you should take it up with the Tokyo Bureau of Communications. Well, anyway, for a small trucker like me, running out of gasoline is the same as going out of business. Nothing would make the big freight firms happier than if all us little guys were destroyed. Nippon Express, Ryogoku Freight, Shinagawa Freight—they all have their eyes on our trucks and three-wheelers."

Dr. Yoshida took four or five clamshells and a cardboard box about the size of a lunchbox out of the orange crates and said: "Stop for a minute outside the police station. I have some business with the station chief. Don't be surprised. The chief and I do a little neighborly black-market business to help each other out. I think these will get us a *sho* of gasoline." On the clamshells were labels reading "Boric Acid Ointment," and the label on the box read "Lactose."

A long line of air-raid victims snaked under the leafed-out cherry trees of Ueno beneath cloudy skies. Those who had decided to leave the city were exchanging their air-raid victim identity papers for a number to receive the free train ticket out of the city provided to all evacuees. Girls wearing armbands saying "Asakusa Ward Office" were walking along the line handing out hard biscuits to each person. A paper banner with the words "Tire Repair" stood in front of Seiyoken Restaurant. Other banners reading "Free for Air-Raid Victims," "At Cost for Ordinary Citizens," "National Defense Bicycle Battalion Tsukiji No. 12 Company," and various other messages flapped smartly in the wind, which was decidedly cold for the end of May. Aside from the flapping of the banners, the scene was eerily, disturbingly quiet, in spite of the large number of people gathered. From time to time a child cried. None of them sounded very strong. It was more like they were chanting to the Buddha than crying like a real baby.

The other doctor and the two nurses from Ichikawa were already there. One of the nurses rushed over and, pulling on Dr. Yoshida's examination coat, said, "Doctor, you're late, you're late!" I followed them, carrying the orange crates. The middle and ring fingers on my left hand, which I'd smashed with the manhole cover during the air raid on the night of May 24th, started to ache again.

Dr. Yoshida began treating patients. The first in line was a man who looked to be about my age with a hole burned into the right shoulder of his national civilian uniform.

"When did this happen?"

"During the air raid on the night of May 25th. More than a hundred incendiary bombs fell on the plant. The type and the printing machines were all destroyed."

"So you were doing your part at a printing plant."

"Kyodo Printing Company in Tomisaka. The manuscript for next month's *Aviation Asahi* was also destroyed."

"So I guess I won't get next month's issue."

"No, I guess not."

"I was looking forward to it. I read it every month."

"That means you've been reading the type I set."

"I guess so. I feel like we know each other. Where will you go?"

"Kubota Village in Yonezawa City. My in-laws live there. I'll be joining the rest of my family. I promise to grow a lot of rice while I'm there, Doc."

"You do that."

"Yanagiya Kingoro is living just four houses away, they say, though he doesn't have any relatives there."

"The famous storyteller?"

"He's going by his real name, Keitaro Yamashita, so at first no one knew it was Kingoro. Then later someone noticed that he looked familiar, and the whole village was buzzing. In the end, he gave a performance in the gym of the local national primary school. The local military association asked him to do it, so he couldn't refuse."

"Well, with Kingoro in the neighborhood, you shouldn't be bored."

"According to what my wife has written to me, he's normally a pretty gloomy character. She says no one has heard him laugh even once since he got there."

"The shoemaker's son goes barefoot and the doctor's health is a mess, I guess."

"And the comedian never cracks a smile."

"All right then. Here's a month's supply of boric acid ointment. By the time this runs out, you'll be wading through the rice paddies."

"Thank you. I won't be sleeping with the soles of my feet aimed at Ichikawa for a long time, I guess."

"Take care of yourself."

During all this back and forth, Dr. Yoshida's hands never stopped moving. He treated the man briskly and efficiently while never dropping the conversational ball. By the time he was done, it was as if he and his patient were old friends. I walked back to my three-wheeled truck deeply impressed.

It was 9:30 A.M. when, having loaded up the peanuts and the rice balls, I left from Mabashi. Someone told me that there had just been an air-raid siren and that the radio had announced that B-29s accompanied by P-51s were heading north from Ogasawara and the Izu Peninsula, but I just kicked the starter on the truck and set off.

The medical team from Ichikawa was there in Ueno waiting for my peanuts and rice balls. The longer it took me to deliver them the more air-raid victims would miss their free handouts. I was in a hurry. The stuff in the back of my truck was a farewell present to the air-raid victims who were leaving Tokyo. It was a little send-off from the citizens of Ichikawa and Matsudo. I couldn't afford a minute's delay. And I was familiar with the Rikuzenhama Highway leading out to Yagiri. I knew that there were lots of chestnut and pine trees along it, and if I had to, I could drive my three-wheeled truck into one of those natural hiding places.

The wide road from Shimoyagiri through Konodai to the eastern edge of Ichikawabashi, though, was different. To the right, along the Edogawa River, was the barracks of a mounted rifle battalion. A large shelter had been excavated into the side of the cliff along the bank of the river, atop which stood the ruins of Satomi Castle. When I delivered the night soil from the toilets of Miyanaga-cho to the communal night soil cisterns of the farmers across the river in Shibamata and Kanamachi, some of them were saying that an underground war room armed with some kind of new electronic weapons was being built in the tunnel. On the left side of the road was an Army Training Camp, a rifle range, the Third Independent Anti-aircraft Gun Battalion and a Field Heavy Artillery Battalion— in other words, a sort of "Army Main Street," which might be the target of the B-29s and P-51s flying north. If I wasn't careful as I drove through that area, I could easily get mixed up in the fighting. And if worse came to worst and I needed to ask someone on the side of the road to take me in, if they weren't farmers but the Imperial Army, I couldn't expect a warm welcome.

While I was turning this over in my mind, and was just coming up to the Joban Train Line tracks, suddenly a huge dark shadow appeared in front of me. A pointed nose, a rounded belly and the outline of the wings, sticking out straight, as sharp and clear as if cut out with a pair of scissors. Toward the back of the body was a big star. A North American P-51 Mustang, exactly like the pictures in the newspaper. Just as I recognized it, I felt the air pressure of an explosion at my back. It was like being caught in a sandstorm. While it was a sound, it had an actual physical substance. I immediately turned the wheel to the left. The P-51 came at me from the right, so I half-instinctively turned left to avoid it. I was lucky that there, in the middle of nowhere, was a little crossroads with a road going off to the left. If I had to stay on the straight path, I would have plunged into the wheat fields. I kept driving. Maybe I could have turned around at the crossroads and headed back for Matsudo, but I was afraid to go in the direction that the P-51s were coming from. Another P-51 might come after me. And turning right at the crossroads was more dangerous. The Joban Train Line tracks were there, and beyond that were open fields. Beyond the fields was the Edogawa River. There was no place in that direction to hide, and on top of that, it was a dead end. How about fleeing back to Mabashi? I was almost to Matsudo, and going back to where I started meant I'd have to retrace my route later, which would be a waste of gas. And that would also be as if I was chasing after the P-51 that had just appeared. I didn't want the P-51 pilot to get any ideas, like, "Who does that little three-wheeled truck think he is, chasing after me, a jet fighter plane? I'll show him…" He'd fill my truck so full of bullets that it'd look like the mouth of a sprinkling can. This was not a time to call attention to myself.

I drove about one hundred meters straight ahead, and at last the real reason I had suddenly turned left dawned on me. I saw a pine forest spreading out like a border along the horizon. When I was driving along the Rikuzenhama Highway, I kept catching glimpses of that long green belt to my left. I hadn't registered it consciously, but some corner of my mind that was enjoying itself without the permission of the master, me, had noticed it. At that decisive moment, the playful part of my brain took over and said to the boss, "Turn left."

I sensed the sound of an engine behind me. I stopped the truck and stuck my head out the left window to look back. I saw an amorphous shape floating in the heavy, leaden-gray clouds over the Edogawa. The shape suddenly flashed and began to descend, grew dramatically in size, and came directly at me. It had wings. I leaped into the wheat field. I was prepared for machine-gun fire, but the P-51 skimmed right over my head, raining down exploding bombs like an evening shower, and left. As I was watching it leave, it picked up altitude and turned to the right. It looked like it was coming back for another attack.

The first thing that came into my head was that the P-51 was teasing me. Imperial subject Shinsuke Yamanaka was being toyed with by the barbarians. The next thing that occurred to me was that the P-51 couldn't keep this up much longer. I remembered the mimeograph stencil of a notice from Defense Headquarters, "What You Need to Know about the P-51" that I made for block group leader Takahashi: "Because the P-51s are departing from Iwojima, they have to carry additional fuel tanks, which means they can only fly over the mainland for fifteen or twenty minutes." And this P-51 was probably on its way home right now, so it could only have enough fuel left to hang around here for another five minutes. In other words, the P-51 was in the same situation as Shinsuke Yamanaka, wondering when it was going to run out of fuel. It might come at me another time or two, but that was it; after that, it would have to hurry back from the shores of our Empire to the squadron leader that was circling over the ocean several dozen kilometers away. And that squadron leader was a B-29. The B-29 was the homeroom teacher, and the P-51s were the primary school students on their class field trip. That meant that if I could just dodge another one or two runs from the P-51, I'd be safe. This was what I was thinking, anyway. Of course I wasn't just standing in the middle of a road or running through a wheat field considering my options. The moment I saw the P-51 bank off to the right, I jumped back into my truck and drove full speed ahead up the gradually rising road leading to the pine grove.

The reason that I concluded that the P-51 was on its way home was that I remembered what I'd been told in Mabashi. When they said that "the enemy is heading north from Ogasawara and the Izu Peninsula," you could count on the fact that they would fly in over Suruga Bay, pass Mount Fuji and appear in the Keihin area. And they'd return flying over Katsuura. This P-51 was lolling around on its way back to Katsuura. Recently Shoichi said, "We know the route they take when they leave, so we should plant some mines in the sky. Or just put a big mist net over the area." He's right.

When I was close enough to the pine grove that I could distinguish the tops and the trunks of the individual trees, I turned the truck decisively into the wheat field. In other words, left, left, left—I'd escaped in the same direction three times. I was planning to move away from the truck and flatten myself on the ground, but I didn't have time. The P-51 let loose with one or two hundred rounds like thunder over the road I'd been on and flew off. Keeping hold of the handle of the truck, I pressed my chest against the dashboard. When I cautiously lifted my head, I saw several little clouds of dust above the road. The enemy was using his machine guns. The blood in my body ran cold.

I kicked the starter backward several times, got the engine running, and drove back to the road. I opened the accelerator full throttle and sped forward. My rear end bounced up and down on the seat, the springs squeaking loudly. The nose of the P-51, low in the sky to my right, was pointing toward the Edogawa. If he'd been planning to head for Katsuura, he'd have to be pointing in the opposite direction. He was coming back to take another run at me. But by now the pine grove was just in front of me, so my throat and my knees felt a little better. While in the wheat field, I'd experienced a terror as if someone had my throat in a death grip; my knees were shaking, like I was standing in cold water.

But the moment I drove into the pine grove, the terror came back, like a painful burn flaring up again on my skin. It wasn't a real pine grove—just two rows of pines planted in a straight line from north to south, with an occasional third row in places. I'd been looking at it from the west, so it had appeared to be a broad belt of green stretching for some distance, but if I had been able to see it from north or south, it would have looked like just one or two trees. I couldn't hide here. And on top of that, the pines were thin and frail looking, their branches sticking out hesitantly as if they wanted to avoid touching the tree next to them. The branches had few needles, and you could see the sky through them. I cut through the rows of pines, aiming for another grove that I could see beyond them—a real pine grove, deserving of the name. Having just seen the fake grove, it was clear at a glance that this next one was the real thing. There were also dense clusters of elms and firs mixed in with it, which set off the green of the pines even more distinctly. If I could just make it to that grove, my three-wheeled truck and I would get out of this in one piece. I was sure of that. Another reason urging me toward the grove was that I noticed the smoothness of the ground leading up to it. It was as flat and even as a playing field. Though it was the size of several soccer fields combined, there wasn't a single dip or depression; and, quite conveniently, there were ropes on either side of me, extending to my goal. The shortest distance to the grove was to drive straight between them, and the terrain couldn't have been any easier to drive on. What was this place? A training field for the army engineering school? But the school was south of here, next to Matsudo. A crop field prepared by students mobilized to increase agricultural production? But a field with nothing planted in it at a time like this, when the national policy was focused on increasing agricultural output, was unthinkable. I spotted a large thatched roof in the middle of the pine grove that was my only hope, but just at that moment, the engine of my truck began to sputter and misfire and a big plume of white smoke shot out from beneath my seat. I guess I shouldn't have driven at full speed up that last hill.

As I stepped out of the truck, I must have been having some kind of mental lapse, because I pulled the toolbox out from beneath the truck bed. Looking back at what I must have been thinking, which of course I hadn't been, I feel sorry for myself. I was still five hundred meters away from the safety of the pine grove. I saw another one to the north, but it was a kilometer and a half away. To the south there was a cultivated field, but that was five hundred meters away, too. And to the west, the fake pine grove I had just left was also five hundred meters back. And there it was, floating in the clouds beyond the fake pine grove—that dark shape. In other words, I was standing, all alone, in a vast open space without a single blade of grass, two thousand meters north to south, a thousand meters east to west. There was no way to avoid that P-51. I was in a much better situation when it was chasing me along the road through the wheat field. Helplessness and terror grew in me until they were as round and fat as one of the sweet potatoes Matsudo is known for. I couldn't just sit there waiting for the P-51 to come for me; I'd go crazy if I didn't do something, anything. And so I pulled the toolbox out from under the truck bed.

The sound of the P-51's engines grew. At that instant, I decided to turn around, face the plane and just laugh scornfully at it. But instantly I felt ashamed of myself. The same blood of an Imperial subject that beat in the hearts of the Special Attack Forces pilots, the world's most glorious heroes, ran through my veins. Aren't our heroic champions, giving their life to take out a battleship with the flying bombs they're riding in, striking fear into the hearts of the enemy? In Okinawa, soldiers and civilians have united as heroic comrades to stave off the enemy, who far outnumber us, and are giving living proof of the principle of loyalty. The enemy might come at me with the latest fighter jet, but after all, I have a screwdriver. But more importantly, I have the lineage of the spiritual power of heroic champions. I'll concentrate my entire being into my eyes and glare at the enemy. I'll destroy the P-51 with my glare. I stood by my three-wheeled truck and faced directly west.

I felt as if Kinuko were standing alongside me. Next to her was her father- and mother-in-law, the Furusawas. My brother and his wife were behind them, whispering to each other. I heard my brother's voice. "Shinsuke, if glaring doesn't bring the plane down, dive to the right just before he gets within range. You can save your life in that final second."

"I think he should jump to the left," said Mr. Furusawa. "He's been lucky with the left up to now, so he should stick with that."

"It's a tough call."

"No, it isn't. The pilot hasn't been paying attention to the direction you're escaping in, so he's not going to be thinking about that."

"Still, I think he should switch to the right this time."

"Do you want to bet on it?"

"Sure, why not?"

In the two or three seconds that the head of the pilot in the cockpit of the P-51 grew from the size of a poppy seed to a sesame seed, Furusawa and my brother bickered. It's Kinuko whom I should turn to, I thought, and as I stood there glaring at the P-51, I moved a step closer to her. The pilot's head suddenly grew to the size of a bean. My time has come, I said to myself, when suddenly a sound like five or six giant fireworks going off in succession roared from behind me. The P-51 wobbled, a piece protruding from its belly, a thread of smoke spewed out as the plane skimmed over the ground to my left and slid off to the southeast. My body followed as I watched it go. The grove of elms, firs and pines fell silent, as if in a deep sleep. I collapsed where I was, and for the first time I noticed that my pants were wet...

My candle is about to go out, and looking at my watch, I see that it's already 2 A.M. on May 30th. I'll tell the rest of the story after I've had a chance to get some sleep.

May 30

After a short while, I noticed three bicycles approaching. The riders seemed to be in their forties. They were wearing military pants and cotton undershirts, with military helmets on their heads.

"Hey, he's alive." One of them, with a long, thin face shaped exactly like an ear of corn, stopped his bicycle right next to me.

"You gave us quite a scare, suddenly getting out of this truck right in the middle of nowhere."

I explained that I didn't have any choice, since the radiator broke. He said to the other two: "Will you go to the motor corps and tell them to repair this truck?" Then he pointed to the luggage rack on the back of his bicycle. "Climb on. If we loaf around here too long, one of the Ps will get us. Though actually, with you as a decoy, we were able to make a hit on that P back there, so it's really not right to say you were just loafing around."

"Decoy?" I straddled the luggage rack and held him around the waist. His undershirt smelled like earth. "What do you mean?"

"You're putting me in a tight spot." He silently pedaled the bicycle, following the path laid out by the ropes, for a few minutes, then he nodded and said: "Hitting the plane, you really deserve the credit for that. So as a certificate of commendation, I'll give you a general sort of rundown on the situation." He paused, then continued in a more formal tone: "And anyway, everyone in the area has put in volunteer labor to reinforce this airfield, so it's not as if it's a secret to any of them. As long as the Ps don't hear about it, there's no problem."

"Wait a minute. This is an airfield?"

"Yup. Matsudo Airfield."

"No wonder it's so flat."

"I'm a member of the Tenth Pilot's Squad of the Sixth Airfield Battalion— Oops, I shouldn't have said that. Please forget I ever mentioned it. Anyway, my name is Tadashi Tanaka."

I told him my name and asked: "But I don't see any planes."

"They're all scattered and hidden in bunkers."

"Ah, I see. Beyond the pine grove. There's another forest beyond the pine trees. So it's like a natural hanger?"

"That's not what a bunker is. You pour concrete over an earth foundation, then you build a curved wooden roof over it, cover the whole thing with thirty centimeters of earth and plant pear trees on top— Oops, please just forget I ever mentioned that too."

"What about runways? All I see in every direction is bare earth."

"Paved runways are like sending an announcement to the enemy."

"I see."

"But it's bad when it rains. The plane's wheels get stuck in the mud and we can't use the field at all. Oops—"

"I've already forgotten you ever mentioned it. So this is an airfield in preparation for when the attack on the mainland happens. When the enemy flies in over Kujukurihama Beach, you send up planes from here to smash the attack and teach them a lesson."

"..."

"Just forget I ever mentioned that. But Mr. Tanaka, you don't seem like a soldier. I don't know what it is, but..."

"More like a farmer, right? We members of the Airfield Battalion grow our own food. We're the ones working the fields around here. We're farmer-soldiers. We even make our own charcoal. Oops—"

"You never mentioned it."

"No, that's okay, I suppose. It doesn't really matter either way."

The bicycle entered a tunnel of pine boughs, shaded by a soft green light. All of the trees were very tall and straight, thickly branched and densely needled. A house with a thatched roof stood in an open area among the pines about 330 meters square. Piles of plane bodies and wings sat in front of the house. They were all made of plywood.

"Do you build your own planes, too?"

"Don't be silly. Those are fake Kawasaki Ki-61s. They're decoys. To attract the Ps. Now, will you take a look from here at where you were before?"

He led me to the edge of the pine grove. There was a patch of clover about two meters wide. The ropes ended at the patch of clover. There were depressions at the end of each rope and machine guns camouflaged by pine boughs were installed in the depressions.

"We removed the guns from a reserve aircraft and installed them here, twenty-five meters apart. Taking the distance between the two weapons as the center point, we draw a line to the pine grove in front of us, in other words, due west."

"I see."

"With that line as the central axis, we line up fifteen fake Kawasaki Ki-61s."

"So that's it. The two ropes are for lining up the noses and tails of the planes."

A small truck appeared from far to the north of the pine grove, picking up speed as it headed for my three-wheeled truck, raising a trail of yellow dust stretching out behind it.

"The Ps have no idea that the planes lined up down here are fake, so they attack along the pathway marked out by the ropes. Firing their machine guns or anti-aircraft weapons, they pass over from west to east, thinking they'll be able to take out fifteen planes in a single run, so they fly directly along the rope pathway. What easier target could there be for us? From here, it's as if the P-51 is motionless. It works the same way if they attack from behind, from east to west. We just follow them with our fire."

So I led that P-51 to these anti-aircraft guns, all by myself. I certainly did deserve a certificate of commendation.

"We've been working day and night to finish the decoy planes so we can line them up here sometime this month. This was a great test run for us. Of course, I'll have to ask you to keep this decoy strategy completely secret."

"Sure. So, did you bring down that P-51 earlier?"

"We know one shot hit it, that's for sure. But…"

"But what?"

"Well, we might have just hit the auxiliary fuel tank… But a hit is a hit. And we did hit it."

Fifteen minutes later, my radiator was repaired. Planning to get after-the-fact approval from Dr. Yoshida, I gave the corps members ten rice balls for their noon lunch.

"What a treat! We haven't had rice in ages. Basically, we live on gummy wheat porridge mixed with sweet potatoes."

Members of ground crew corps have to make do with wheat porridge because white rice is reserved for members of the flight corps. Apparently, Corpsman Tanaka told me, unless fliers eat a diet of white rice, they can't control their flatulence when they're up in the air. He also told me that the 53rd Matsudo Air Corps worked almost entirely on a night shift. They get up in the evening and go to sleep in the morning. If any of them had some business that had to be done in daylight, they were required to wear dark glasses and the room they slept in was completely curtained off with opaque curtains. But this started to lead to a series of mental breakdowns among the soldiers, and it had been very hard to watch. As a result, the 53rd Matsudo Air Corps was gradually being taken off the night shift. Having been reminded one last time that I couldn't mention this to anyone, I left the Matsudo Airfield. As I was about to depart, Corpsman Tanaka said to me in a low voice, "Can I lend you a pair of pants? There's no wind here and they haven't dried. It must be very uncomfortable."

"Once I start driving, there'll be wind. But more important," I said, lowering my voice as well, "please never mention that I wet my pants."

And that's what happened on the morning of May 29th.

An article in the *Mainichi Newspaper* today caught my eye.

The B-29s that attacked on the nights of May 23 and 25 seem to have changed their strategy on May 29 and launched a large-scale daytime air raid for the first time. On May 29, approximately five hundred B-29s accompanied by one hundred P-51s departed from the Marianas and, heading north over Ogasawara and the Izu Peninsula, entered the skies over Honshu from Suruga Bay, flying past Mount Fuji at an altitude of roughly five thousand meters and attacked Yokohama and sent sub-squadrons to Kawasaki and Shinagawa in several waves. As in night air raids, the enemy dropped incendiary bombs, aiming at burning our cities, and Yokohama suffered considerable damage. From 9:30 to 10:40 A.M., the enemy flew off from the vicinity of Katsuura. The special features of this attack are that it occurred during the day and employed incendiary bombs, as well as that it marshaled the largest number of B-29s since the enemy began its attacks on the Homeland. We must be fully prepared to fight against the apparently well-equipped enemy bases and their obstinate determination.

This, of course, was just a general description of events. The article then went on to report that small numbers of planes also attacked areas in the Tokai region and southern Kyushu, and closed with the headline: "Three Planes Downed in Chiba Prefecture":

DATELINE CHIBA. The large battalion of B-29s and P-51s that attacked on May 29 crossed over from the Keihin area toward Tokyo Bay, the majority of them departing over the Boso Peninsula toward the South Pacific, but three planes were downed, one outside Kamatari Village outside Kisarazu, another in Oikawa Village in Isumi County and the third in Shiratori Village, Ichihara County. There was no damage.

One of those three planes must have been my P-51. I went to Kiyoshi's room and got a map of Japan and a bamboo ruler and started to check. I discovered that Shiratori Village, Ichihara County is to the southeast of the Matsudo Airfield. Corpsman Tanaka had hit his mark. He hadn't just hit the auxiliary fuel tank—he had made a direct hit. And who was it that gave him this opportunity to exercise his skills? Me. Shinsuke Yamanaka.

Today is the seven-day anniversary of the deaths of Kinuko, my brother and sister-in-law and the Furusawas. Being able to write in my diary today that I helped bring down an enemy plane on this special occasion is a cause for celebration. Today's entry is the best offering I can make to the deceased. After presenting it at the Buddhist altar, I intend to go to Jigenji Temple in Senju Naka-cho. That's where the Furusawa family grave is.

May 31

The elder Mrs. Furusawa has been staying at our house since yesterday evening.

Our house is relatively large for Nezu. Soon after I took over the family business, my father said, "I'm not going to be one of those old retired guys who sits around doing nothing. I plan to keep making fans until the day I die.

"Shinsuke," he said, "whenever someone asks who's the best fan maker in Tokyo, the answer's always the same—'Ibasen in Nihonbashi.' I can't stand that. I agree Ibasen makes good fans. They're durable. The designs are very stylish. And what makes it worse they're inexpensive. But I think we can do as well or better. Especially you—you've got a good head on your shoulders, you're hard working and enthusiastic, and most of all, you enjoy making fans. The only missing ingredients are sales and design. If we can just take care of those, we'll be more than a match for Ibasen. So I want you to leave the fan making to me for a while and concentrate on sales.

He sold a rental property we owned in Nezu Suga-cho and bought ten *tsubo* of land from a neighbor, using it to add on to our workshop. He purchased a new color printer. Saying he wanted to hire more people, he divided the upstairs into two rooms for the additional workers. Though he had said he was turning over the business to me, there he was all these making major changes, and I couldn't figure out what was going on. Something was funny. I persuaded him to have a checkup. The doctor said he was suffering from a form of mania often seen in the elderly. The weight of the family business is lifted from their shoulders. They feel relieved and liberated. That's fine and dandy, but some people become a little too liberated, get carried away, and go completely off their rocker. That's what happened to my father.

The year after he added on to the workshop, he was jostled in the crush around a portable shrine during the Asakusa Torigoe Shrine festival, got knocked down and later died from the injuries. One of the parishioners of Torigoe Shrine was a toy wholesaler, and my father went to deliver some fans that the toy dealer had ordered as a promotional give-away to his customers. Either he got drunk or he was overcome with one of his manic fits, and the next thing we knew he'd tucked his summer kimono up into the sash and, joking around with the men carrying the portable shrine, was fanning them with a fan, when he got knocked over in the crowd. One of the festival organizers made his way through the crush to pick him up, and he found my father firmly grasping one of the fans he'd gone to deliver, twitching it back and forth in a kind of convulsion. Not everyone may agree with me, but I think he had a happy life and I envy him. Anyway, he was able to keep doing what he loved right up to the end, which makes him more fortunate than me.

I want to make fans but I can't. The times are against me. My artisans and apprentices have all been drafted, and the color printer has been requisitioned and melted down into bullets. The only thing our workshop, which faces the street, is used for is the regular meetings of the block group, and the extra workshop my father built is filled with junk. The two rooms above it are empty. That's why I said our house is actually quite large. But it can't compare with Furusawa Enterprises. Their house faces a two hundred *tsubo* garden and they have five or six spare rooms. It's the difference between a tennis court and a ping-pong table. Or if they're a stable, we're a rabbit hutch. But old Mrs. Furusawa said to me: "Would you let me stay at your house for a few days?"

She must have some reason for her request. Without a special reason, why would someone choose to stay in a cramped rabbit hutch with no real garden to speak of? Come to think of it, she's been talking strangely since yesterday.

From two in the afternoon yesterday, the interment ceremony for the ashes of the deceased was conducted at Jigenji Temple in Nakamachi, Senju. The only remaining structures in the temple are its gate and a little Benten Hall, six square meters, the rest having burned down in air raids. A barracks, nine square meters, has been thrown up next to Benten Hall as a temporary Main Hall, and that's where the sutra recitation and the incense offering took place. The sutra recitation was interrupted by a spate of driving wind and rain, and five or six wooden memorial staves fell over with a plaintive sound. The walls of the barracks were made from the memorial staves. The intensity of the rain grew, extinguishing the priest's voice—naturally, since the roof of the barracks was made of fire-blackened corrugated tin.

When the rain had slowed down to a drizzle, we interred the ashes in the grave—though of course there were no ashes, neither for Kinuko nor the Furusawas. So instead we interred the rice bowls that they'd used every day. I'm planning on choosing an appropriate day to take Kinuko's soup bowl and inter that in the Yamanaka family on the grounds of Yofukuji Temple in Nippori. I'll do the same with something for my brother and his wife. On the way back from the grave to the temporary Main Hall, old Mrs. Furusawa said to me: "Someone said, 'You can't stay sad forever.' It's frightening to think of it, but I believe it's true."

"I wonder. Whenever I even see or hear the word *kinu*, I think of Kinuko and tears well up in my eyes. I think that will be true as long as I live. I'll never go to Kinugawa Hot Springs. I never want to see another film starring Kinuyo Tanaka. Because—"

"Because they both have the word *kinu* in them."

"That's right. I'd spend my whole time at Kinugawa crying, and whenever Kinuyo Tanaka appeared on the screen, I'd burst into tears."

"But Shinsuke, haven't you laughed even once in these last seven days?"

That gave me pause. For example, on the morning of May 29th, I did laugh there in the pine grove at the Matsudo Airfield. When I heard that airmen who didn't eat white rice were unable to control their flatulence at high altitudes, I laughed. Not only that, but I made a vulgar rejoinder of my own, saying that the cockpits of B-29s must really stink, since the staple food of the Americans is wheat.

"I think that the survivors should try to forget their sadness as quickly as they can. You can't go on living if you spend all your time grieving. Of course you have to remember the dead. But I don't think becoming preoccupied with them helps anyone."

I'm sure the priest would have raised his eyebrows at this remark, but she just bustled off to the temporary Main Hall.

When we got back to the Furusawa house from the temple, there was saké waiting. All the relatives were there, so at first the atmosphere was solemn, but gradually things loosened up as people started talking about recent events, and the mood got quite lively when the conversation turned to the black market, until it finally ended up in a shouting match when someone suggested that we were losing the battle for Okinawa. Though we Yamanakas are related by marriage, we're latecomers to this family, so I just sat there listening. Eventually old Mrs. Furusawa came up to me and said: "What can I do to make sure that your family remains close to us?"

I had no idea how to reply to this sudden question, and as I sat there in surprise, she continued: "You're too reserved. That's why now that Kinuko is no longer with us, you'll stop coming by. Eventually, you'll be like a stranger, and then we'll have no relationship whatsoever."

"That won't happen. After all, Kinuko is interred in your family grave."

"I hope that when you come to Jigenji to visit her, you won't fail to stop by and see us, too. I'm not saying I think you're cold-hearted. I'm just saying that I'll be lonely, and I'll want to see you from time to time. Isn't there any way that I can tie you to the Furusawa family?"

And so she came to stay with us. I'm glad that she likes us, but is that the only reason? No. I think she has something else in mind. That's my intuition. And she brought a *to* of white rice as a gift. I can't complain about that.

June 1

From tonight, there are two new people living in our house—a total of seven altogether. On top of which old Mrs. Furusawa seems to have taken a liking to us and has been staying with us since the night before last, making for a very bustling household. Both of the two new residents are lovely young ladies. Kayoko Makiguchi is tall, with a fine profile. She doesn't say much, but Fumiko tells me that Kayoko's father was an oil wholesaler near the Yotsuya Police Station. An incendiary bomb hit their house in the May 25th air raid, and it went up in flames. The entire family was killed, except for Kayoko, who was at work at Tokyo Station. Though, of course, Tokyo Station was also destroyed in the air raids that night. Built at a cost of 2.8 million yen, the three-story, redbrick, Renaissance-style structure, which survived the Great Kanto Earthquake, has been almost completely reduced to a pile of ash and rubble by a rain of incendiary bombs. Through it all, though, Kayoko and a hundred other students of the Tokyo Station Girls High School protected the freight elevator on the platform from going up in flames with a bucket brigade. While she was fighting that fire, however, her family was killed.

The story of the other girl, Kumiko Kurokawa, is much the same. According to Takeko, her family worked for the Iwasaki family in Takanawa, and when a storehouse on the estate received a direct hit during the May 29th air raid, three hundred bales of rice caught fire. The Kurokawas were in charge of the warehouse, and tried to get the bales out of the burning building, but on one of their trips inside a falling rafter pinned them down and they died in the fire. Like Kayoko, Kumiko was also on duty at Tokyo Station that day, so she survived.

This is the meaning of total war, I suppose. In this total war, these two girls had become orphans, with almost precisely matching fates.

"The Iwasakis are directors of the Mitsui Conglomerate, aren't they? I think it's the responsibility of the Iwasakis to look after Kumiko," said old Mrs. Furusawa, after the histories of our two new housemates had been presented. "Please don't misunderstand me, my dear," she went on. "I'm not saying that having you live here will be a burden for the Yamanakas. I'm perfectly willing to provide for your needs myself, if it comes to that. What I don't understand is why the Iwasakis seem to have abandoned you, when by rights you're their responsibility. After all, when it comes down to it, your parents gave their lives for the Iwasakis. Yet they let you leave without a word. Don't you think that's odd?"

"No one from the main house even attended my parents' wake," said Kumiko, "That's the only reason." She tended to be very quiet, but on this occasion she spoke up quite clearly, a light flickering briefly in her narrow eyes.

"So you left the Iwasaki estate of your own free will."

"That's right."

"I can see why. What cold-hearted people."

Kumiko stared down blankly at the seam in her cotton trousers.

Since the major air raid on March 10th, any sign of feeling or animation was gradually fading from the faces of everyone in Tokyo. The other day a legal scholar and member of the Imperial Academy named Shigeto Hozumi was talking on the radio about this, and praised us, saying, "It's as if the residents of Tokyo have attained Buddhist enlightenment. They know that they might die at any moment, so nothing affects them any longer. That's the reason the faces of Tokyo residents have become serenely expressionless. They say that battle is the father of invention and the mother of culture, but it turns out it's also the uncle of moral character. Whenever I see one of these expressionless city dwellers, they look like enlightened beings to me and I proudly regard them as my comrades."

When someone's clever at dishing out the praise you can't help but feel good, even if you have no idea why. Still, there's no escaping the fact that an expressionless young girl is a very pitiful sight. They're at an age when, under normal circumstances, the most trivial things send them into peals of happy laughter, but to see a young girl unable to even lift the corner of her cheek in the faint beginnings of a smile is not a sign of enlightenment, it's a sign of having absolutely nothing left to care about. It's because they don't have any poetry, any chocolate, any pretty clothes, any love. In other words, they have no youth. They don't have that much longer to live anyway. Can't someone, somewhere, grant them just a moment, no matter how brief, of youth? As my last memory of this world, I'd like to see a young girl smile.

June 2
The light rain that dripped from the eves at dawn became a downpour by noon. A bad Sunday for those living in underground shelters. And it was cold, too, harkening back to the first days of spring. That reminded me of my diary entry for March 9th. As I recall, that night I wrote something like this: "In normal years, after the Peach Blossom Festival, mustard flowers blossom here and there on Ueno Hill, but this year the snow that fell in February still remains on the ground in shady areas. It almost seems a portent of disaster ahead, and it's unsettling. This lingering cold is a sign of an impending calamity, a change in the heavens. I know saying things like that puts me at risk of being accused of spouting inflammatory nonsense in a time of national emergency, but since December 8, 1941, the newspapers have ceased to carry any weather reports, so I can't help it if I resort to thinking superstitious thoughts." Unfortunately, my premonition seems to have come true. That night, after I closed my diary, a cautionary alert siren sounded—the prelude to the terrible tragedy of the predawn hours of March 10th.

Today I want my premonition proved wrong. That's what I was thinking about as, this afternoon, I made my way over to the Nezu Miyanaga-cho Neighborhood Association offices. Before going in, I carefully read a notice posted on the board by the entrance: "Concerning Neighborhood Residency Registration." I've read it several times before, so I had it nearly memorized, but you can never be too careful. If I made a mistake filling out the forms, I know the Neighborhood Association leader would only take delight in calling me on it, clucking his tongue and wagging his finger in my face, and I was fed up with that.

Concerning Neighborhood Residency Registration

A neighborhood register recording all residents of the neighborhood is kept in order to expedite the distribution of goods and services in the area and other needs of daily life. In the following cases, all residents are required to submit the necessary forms to update or revise the register:

1. Births, deaths, marriages, divorces, hiring or firing of employees, the arrival or departure of cohabitants, or any other events that result in changes of the number of individuals living in a household.
2. The arrival or departure of a household in its entirety.
3. The establishment of a new residence in the neighborhood.

Before he even saw my face, the Neighborhood Association leader, sipping tea with his legs curled around a hibachi, said: "I expected you here last night. You have two young friends of Fumiko and Takeko staying with you since then, don't you? You're supposed to submit the forms for any changes in residence within the day that they occur."

As usual, he had all the latest information. Silently astonished, I placed the air-raid victim identification papers of Kayoko Makiguchi and Kumiko Kurokawa on his desk.

"Of course, since it's you, Mr. Yamanaka, there's no point in making a fuss about it. Or I should say, rather, that it would be positively wrong to do so. You're such a generous, warm-hearted person—the likes of which we rarely see these days. The official rations are delayed or never appear at all, and black-market goods are so expensive as to make your eyes pop out. Everyone is doing everything they can think of to reduce the number of mouths they have to feed, and here you are, willingly adding two to your little family! Not just anyone would do that. You're an example to us all."

"I don't deserve your praises, I'm sure."

"You most certainly do. You're a model citizen for everyone here on the home front."

"They both have very unfortunate circumstances, and I felt I had to help them if I could. That's all."

"What impressive modesty. There are 22,000 Neighborhood Association and Hamlet Associations in the country today. As you know, they're all under the supervision of the Imperial Rule Assistance Association. Part of the duty of us Neighborhood Association leaders is to report on virtuous citizens to the leaders of the Imperial Rule Assistance Association once a year. This year I plan to nominate you, Mr. Yamanaka."

"I appreciate that, but I only did what anyone in my position would do."

"Then why doesn't everyone do it?"

"I don't know…"

"I'll tell you why. Because they can't afford black-market prices. Your little truck is in great demand right now, I'll bet. You can make several hundred yen a day with it. Unfortunately, the rest of us don't have an Aladdin's lamp like you do. We don't have a bottomless cornucopia that can produce the flow of treasures that your little three-wheeled truck does. Much as we want to feed our families, we can't. But you don't have that problem, do you?"

Just as I suspected, he was setting me up for something.

"And we don't have powerful relatives, either. You, on the other hand, have an influential patron in Furusawa Enterprises. That's why you can do what all of us wish we could, but can't manage to. But all that aside, you're still quite a fellow. Though you could just as easily ignore them, here you are reaching out with your big heart for these air-raid victims. You're an example for everyone in Miyanaga-cho. Please take care of the two new girls in your household."

"I'll do my best."

"Yes. And it's in your interest, too."

"What?"

"Well, you're going to be losing a daughter again soon, aren't you?

"I don't know what you mean."

"You mean Fumiko isn't going to the Furusawas to take Kinuko's place? That's why old Mrs. Furusawa is staying at your house now, isn't it? Fumiko may be getting married and leaving for Senju, but you've added two girls to your household, so you shouldn't be too sad. Why, it's divine providence that two new girls should suddenly fall from the heavens into your household at precisely this moment."

So that was it. Old Mrs. Furusawa's remarks about "You can't stay sad forever" and "Isn't there any way that I can tie you to the Furusawa family?" were her way of hinting that she wanted Fumiko to step in as Kinuko's replacement. I may be slow, but in my defense, it's only three days past the first seven-day anniversary of Kinuko's death, and my heart is too filled with sorrow to even imagine such a proposal.

"When Fumiko gets married and leaves for Senju, excuse my vulgarity, you'll be living high off the hog again. Would you be giving up your trucking service then? When you do, can I ask you to allow me to offer a new home for your three-wheeled truck? It just so happens that the executive director of the Kanto Region Stockpiled Goods for Supporting the War Effort Council is an old friend of mine from middle school, and when I went to see him the other day, on the fifth floor of Mitsukoshi in Ginza, he asked me whether I knew of anyone with a three-wheeled truck to spare."

He had a lot of nerve, basically suggesting that I was selling my daughter so I could "live high off the hog," as he so boorishly put it. "I intend to support my family as long as I have breath in my body," I said with a force that surprised even me. "And my truck isn't 'to spare.' It's being used to help keep daily necessities circulating on the home front."

As I turned to leave the office, the Neighborhood Association leader's voice followed me with a nasty ring: "It seems that when you were looking at the bulletin board earlier, you didn't see anything except the notice about neighborhood residency registration, but you'd better look more closely. Your duty as a resident is to read the entire board once a day. There's an important meeting tomorrow. Anyone who fails to attend will be regarded as unpatriotic."

In the very middle of the board was the notice in large letters:

INAUGURAL CEREMONY FOR THE THREE
TROOPS OF THE NEZU
NATIONAL VOLUNTEER CORPS

Time: 8:30 A.M., June 3 (Sunday). As announced in the circulating notice of May 27 (Sunday), but delayed one week for additional preparations.

Place: in front of Nezu Gongen Shrine

All men from 16 to 65, all women from 12 to 45, with the exception of the sick or pregnant, are required to be present.

"I'm aware of it. I read the circulating notice," I said. "And by the way, I also happen to know that the Imperial Rule Assistance Association is being disbanded and replaced by the National Volunteer Corps." I saw the Neighborhood Association leader nod. "What happens to the policy of recommending virtuous citizens to the Imperial Rule Assistance Association, then? It's just going to disappear, isn't it? Promising things that you know will never come about, just to butter up a resident—you don't miss a trick, do you? I had no idea we had a fox living here at the base of Ueno Hill."

He threw the dregs of the cup of tea he was drinking on to the earthen floor of the entryway.

When I got home, my wife was on the verandah mending a sock, a burned-out Matsuda light bulb inserted in the heel.

"Why don't you just make that into a cleaning rag?" I said, sitting down beside her. "The whole sock is so threadbare that patching it won't do any good."

"But there's an important meeting tomorrow. You can't very well wear wooden sandals."

"Yes, a National Volunteer Corps wearing wooden sandals would be very strange."

"This is the only pair of socks you have, so darning is the only option, I'm afraid."

"The house is so quiet."

"Old Mrs. Furusawa has taken them all to Senju. As soon as you left, Tadao showed up with some beef. We can't make sukiyaki here, of course."

If any of our neighbors smelled beef cooking, there'd be a big fuss. Toward the end of last month, an incident of just this kind occurred in Yanaka Shimizu-cho, Shitaya Ward, next to Nezu. A certain incense seller happened to come by two hundred *momme* of beef. Before they started cooking the sukiyaki, the family pretended they'd gone away, shutting their sliding wooden outer doors and turning off all the lights. You can hide many things, but not the aroma of beef cooking. The neighbors gathered around the incense seller's house. Someone shouted, "It's unpatriotic to pretend not to be home so you can eat sukiyaki!" When the retired head of the incense shop heard the word "unpatriotic," he lost his temper, leaped outside and started shouting: "It's the duty of every loyal subject to stay strong and healthy for the final battle for the Homeland. Those who are too stupid to find nourishing food and who allow themselves to degenerate into thin weaklings will be useless when we have to fight to defend our country. They're the real traitors!" The man who had called the retired incense shop owner unpatriotic struck the old man, who was toppled by the momentum of the blow and fell and hit his head on the concrete. And that's how the smell of beef cooking not only drew the entire neighborhood but resulted in a fatality.

"They're safe at the Furusawas," she said. "You could cook fermented dried fish there and no one's close enough to smell it."

"By the way, did old Mrs. Furusawa say anything to you?"

"You mean about Fumiko?

"Yes."

"She asked me if we'd let Fumiko marry Tadao. To take the place of Kinuko."

"What did you say?"

"That'd I couldn't say anything until I'd talked it over with you and Fumiko. And I added that, for my part, I appreciated the fact that she'd done us the favor twice of regarding one of our daughters as a suitable match for her grandson."

"Hmm. I guess the problem now is how to present this to Fumiko."

"It seems that she knew what it was all about from the moment Mrs. Furusawa asked if she could stay here for a few days. As she was leaving earlier she said to me, 'I always get Kinuko's hand-me-downs... Her picture books and toys, her book bag and dresses, her shoes... I grew up with her hand-me-downs. I was hoping that at least my husband would be brand new.'"

"So she doesn't want to marry him, I guess."

"No, that's the kind of thing you say when you've already decided to accept."

"Is that how it works?"

"Though Fumiko did make one condition."

"What's that?"

"She said, 'I don't want to marry Tadao until after the hundred-day anniversary of Kinuko's death. I wouldn't feel right marrying him before that.'"

"Looks like everything's already been decided, without me. Not that I mind, especially," I said, moving to my desk.

"Let's go visit Kinuko's grave in the next few days and tell her about this."

As I exchanged my celluloid glasses for my reading glasses so I could write in my diary, my wife turned on the light for me.

June 3

I went to Nezu Gongen Shrine early. There are two hundred stone posts on the shrine grounds lining the pathway leading to the sanctuary. The posts are five *sun* square and one and one-half *shaku* tall. Each pillar was donated by one of the shrine's parishioners; the fifty-sixth pillar from the entrance is inscribed with "Kankichi Yamanaka," which is the name of my father.

Sitting on my father's pillar as I watched the members of the National Volunteer Corps arrive, I noted that two out of three were women. Most of the men were elderly, over fifty. According to the papers, the National Volunteer Corps—the entire populace, mobilized to defend the Homeland when the enemy lands—is going to consist of two corps, the Volunteer Corps and the Battle Corps. As it said on the bulletin board outside the Neighborhood Association office, the Volunteer Corps will consist of "all men from sixteen to sixty-five, and all women from twelve to forty-five, with the exception of the sick or pregnant"; among those, "men from age fifteen to fifty, and women from age seventeen to forty" will be selected as members of the Battle Corps. When the time comes to defend the Homeland, this Battle Corps is supposed to do the actual fighting with the invading army. Unfortunately, it looks like Nezu's Battle Corps is going to consist entirely of women, because, as I've noted before, there are almost no males under fifty in Nezu. Of course at night healthy males return from their places of work or forced mobilization, but they're already members of the Battle Corps wherever they're working or mobilized. Our only hope is that the enemy doesn't attack Nezu during the day. We can't defend our neighborhood with a battalion made up entirely of women.

Eventually the various Neighborhood Association leaders, starting with the Hongo Ward leader, began to gather in front of the shrine and the inaugural ceremony began. The wind has been blowing continuously since last night, and there was an earthquake at dawn, but by morning the strong wind of the night before, powerful as an autumn typhoon, had tapered off into a refreshing spring breeze.

According to the opening remarks of the ward leader, the governor of Tokyo will also serve as the headquarters commander of the Tokyo National Volunteer Corps. The ward leaders will be battalion commanders, the Neighborhood Association leaders will be company commanders, and the block group leaders will be platoon leaders. In other words, the system was exactly the same as it was before when it was the Imperial Rule Assistance Association, the Neighborhood Association and the block association. The only difference was that it's all military style now. Anyway, that's my impression. Next, the Neighborhood Association leader—I mean, the company commander—spoke. He was followed by a Lieutenant Kiyohara, an adviser from the Tokyo National Volunteer Corps Headquarters. For what seemed like several minutes after ascending the platform, Lieutenant Kiyohara just glared at the members lined up in the Nezu Miyanaga-cho Battle Corps. He seemed extremely displeased. What could be the matter? Standing in the Nezu Miyanaga-cho Volunteer Corps, I sneaked a glance at the Battle Corps to my left. There was only one man in it. And that one and only man was none other than Gen the tailor, who has a bad right leg. He was constantly shifting back and forth, as if his leg hurt.

"You there! I know you have a bad leg, but can't you stand still for five minutes!"

"I can't," replied Gen without hesitation.

"Is that so? Step forward. I wonder if shaving your head in punishment would help. It's as messy as a rat's nest."

Gen walked to the front of the line, shifting his shoulders broadly left and right as he dragged his leg. The lieutenant came down from the stage, and when Gen reached him, he rapped Gen lightly on the head. "Do you know why the samurai shaved their heads? To let the steam out, that's why. To keep their heads cool under all circumstances, so they could handle any situation that arose in a calm, rational manner—that's why they shaved their heads. You're going to have to take a lesson from them, aren't you?"

"Yes."

"Why don't you shave all your hair off to commemorate your induction into this Battle Corps?"

"I will."

"Good. Now, are you absolutely certain of victory?"

"Yes."

"And are you sure of that?"

"Yes. I'm absolutely certain of victory."

"Good. So, what do you think of the present situation? Our former allies Germany and Italy have thrown down their weapons and signed a declaration of unconditional surrender. The fighting on Okinawa is going badly, and the news from the front is desperate. Moreover, enemy air attacks are intensifying. The majority of the Imperial capital has been destroyed, and both Nagoya and Osaka have suffered severe damage. On top of that—this was in today's newspaper, so I'm sure you're already aware of it—the enemy president, Truman, boasts that from June he intends to increase U.S. air power to three and a half million, and naval forces to three million, and he's going to concentrate them on attacking Japan. What do you think about this? The Empire stands at the crossroads between victory and defeat, don't you think?"

Suddenly the residents of Nezu filling the area in front of the shrine all nodded their heads, some vigorously, some less so, resembling nothing so much as a pumpkin patch in an earthquake.

They were all so familiar with the words, "the Empire stands at the crossroads between victory and defeat," that they just automatically nodded in recognition. It was one of the favorite sayings of former Prime Minister Kuniaki Koiso. Navy Minster Mitsumasa Yonai also used to say something very much like it. "The victory or defeat of the Imperial realm will be determined by whether or not we can overcome the challenging situation we presently face." Surely, most of the people nodding were remembering these declarations. I remembered them both myself, and that's why my headed nodded with the rest of the pumpkins.

"Just like you said—I believe that the Empire stands at the crossroads between victory and defeat."

"Are you sure?"

"Yes. I'm sure."

"Do you all agree?" The lieutenant directed his question at all of us. Another earthquake rippled through the pumpkin patch.

"And at the same time, you all have complete certainty of victory. Is that what you think?"

We all shouted "yes" so loudly that the birds in the shrine precinct trees flew up into the sky in surprise.

"Then you need to think again!" He dashed back to the platform, stomping on the wooden boards with his high boots. "You'll never be able to defend the Imperial realm with that attitude." Mystified, everyone turned to the person next to them and murmurs of puzzlement rose in the air.

"You're nothing but a bunch of mindless idiots!" shouted Lieutenant Kiyohara. "On the one hand, you're wringing your soft little hands that the Empire stands at the crossroads between victory and defeat, and on the other, you're one hundred percent certain of victory. Is there anything rattling around in that empty space between your ears? Or do you have shit for brains? How do you even manage to get dressed in the morning? Now listen up! Don't you see how impossible that is? If you're one hundred percent certain of victory, how can you be worried that the Empire stands at the crossroads between victory and defeat? That means you only believe that your nation has a fifty percent chance of victory. Or to put it in the reverse..."—and here the lieutenant slowly turned his head from right to left, inscribing an arc of 180 degrees, glaring at the residents of Nezu—"…it means that those who whine that they're worried about the victory of the nation are unpatriotic, because they imagine a fifty percent chance that the Empire will be defeated. No one, not even you idiots, can believe one hundred percent in the nation's victory and fifty percent in its defeat. With that attitude, how do you expect to be able to defend the Emperor? You, over there—the one with the hair like a rat's nest. Your brains are as messed up as your hair. Do you understand now?"

Gen scratched his head in puzzlement and then said in a loud voice: "Yes, now I see. Boy, you certainly got me there!"

The lieutenant just stood there glaring at Gen, but a moment later all hell broke loose. The Miyanaga-cho Neighborhood Association leader—I guess from today I have to call him "troop commander"—ran up to Gen and shouted: "How dare you speak to the lieutenant like that! 'You got me there!' is no way to respond to such a fine moral lesson!" and, nearly choking with rage, he slapped Gen across the face. Fortunately the lieutenant had the presence of mind to bring the situation under control, calling out, "Let's all sing 'If I Go Away to Sea'!" If he hadn't, the Neighborhood Association leader would probably have wrestled Gen to the ground, and I doubt he'd have stopped there, probably climbing on top of him and kicking him until someone pulled him off. If that happened, I decided instantaneously, as a member of the same block group, I'd join the ruckus to protect my friend—though if it had really come to that, I don't actually know if I would have the courage.

As I was singing "If I Go Away to Sea," I felt a different kind of courage rise up within me. I remembered visiting Nezu Gongen Shrine during a festival, carrying three-year-old Kinuko on my shoulders. My hair got all sticky from the cotton candy she was eating. Kinuko must have looked forward to having her own child with Tadao. She probably wanted it to grow up strong, and to take it herself to the shrine festival on September 21st. She'd point out the stone pillar to the child and say, with a touch of pride in her voice, "Look, that's the name of your great grandfather." When the child was older, she'd explain, "The path in front of Nezu Gongen is called 'S Path.' Great writers of the Meiji period like Soseki and Ogai used to stroll along that path." She died before her time, leaving all these and countless other wishes and dreams unrealized. As I sang "If I Go Away to Sea," I felt those intense desires of hers form in my heart. "Let me take revenge on my daughter's enemy. I'll fight the enemy when they land. Give me the courage to die in battle with the enemy." These were the prayers I found myself making to the god of Gongen Shrine.

The nice thing about "If I Go Away to Sea" is that it's so gloomy. Whenever there's an announcement of a major victory in the war on the radio, if it's an army victory, they play "Army Drill March." If it's a navy victory, it's "Battleship March." And when it's a joint army-navy victory, they play "Against Ten Thousand Foes." But all three of them are so cheery. It's like they're making fun of us. On the other hand, I think "If I Go Away to Sea" is a perfect match for the feelings of the surviving residents of Tokyo.

After that, we were all given a piece of chocolate about the size of the king in Japanese chess. A big phonograph player was brought on stage, and we were told to listen to the sound of B-29s flying overhead as we ate our chocolate bars. The chocolate was made from potatoes, they told us. Karafuto Agricultural Development Company in Rutakacho, Karafuto, had invented a process for obtaining high-quality dextrose from potatoes, which they poured into the shape of chocolate bars.

Lieutenant Kiyohara explained that it was an important part of the diet of pilots and submarine crews. "From today, you are champions of the National Citizens Volunteer Corps. You're soldiers on the front lines, right alongside the pilots and submarine crews. That's why you're able to eat this chocolate that has been developed to provide nutritional sustenance to the soldiers on the front lines. It takes six or seven potatoes to make a single bar of this chocolate. Eat slowly and savor it."

It didn't taste bad.

Nearby someone muttered, "Instead of this crummy little piece, I'd rather have had the six or seven potatoes boiled nicely."

The recordings of the B-29s were boring.

There was narration by the NHK announcer Shuichi Fujikura, which started out: "NHK recording engineer Nagatomo and his team made this recording over a period of eight days from February 22nd to 29th, hiding in Mount Takao valley, Kaohsiung, Taiwan. It's a daring recording capturing the sound of B-29s flying overhead, starting with one plane and gradually increasing to eleven." To the accompaniment of the sound of the planes, Fujikura continued: "A single plane makes a heavy *gun-gun* sound like the ground rumbling, which you can feel in your gut, occasionally alongside a *do-do-do* like the sound of a drum beating. With each additional plane, the reverberations intensify, and the frequency of the *do-do-do* sound increases. It's very easy to distinguish the light *buuun* sound of our fighter planes from the heavier *guuun* of a B-29."

To tell the truth, if you ask me, this "daring recording" is complete fiction. The announcer says that the sound of eleven planes is "powerful," but for the past three months we've spent hundreds of hours living under huge squadrons of B-29s—and not eleven planes, but hundreds. The sound at such times isn't a sound at all—it's a material presence. It's like being shut inside one of the giant drums of Nezu Gongen Shrine while the drum is being beat with hundreds of drumsticks. Or like being a pickle pressed down under a heavy stone. It's enough to drive you mad. Add to that the sound, like an evening shower, of incendiary bombs falling, and the sound of the shells exploding like beating on a piece of tin three millimeters away from your ear—all of it continuous, never stopping. A big squadron of B-29s, bringing all this fire and noise with it, is like a giant flying hell. It can't be compared to anything as ordinary as "the ground rumbling" or "the sound of a drum beating."

There were a few parts of the recording that were interesting, though. Because the recordings were made in the mountains of Taiwan, there were some funny coincidences. It was strange to hear the birds in the mountain forests calling out *Cuckoo! Cuckoo!* when the B-29s flew over with their *guun-guun*, and the white-eye mejiro answering the *do-do-do* with their peeps of *chiichiku-chiichiku*, as if they were laughing. I was eating my potato chocolate and smiling at this just as a woman about my age dashed from the shrine precincts waving her arms over head, shouting, "Hot! Hot!" Her arms were deformed and twisted like a mountain yam, covered with welts.

"That's Setsu. She's been taken in by the fishmonger Uogin in Nezu Aizome-cho."

"Her house burned down on March 10th. Everyone else was killed. She's the only one who survived."

We moved from the shrine precincts to Sendagi-cho. We've been ordered to begin our service in the National Citizens Volunteer Corps by planting a vegetable garden in a burned-out section. Our block group—now officially known as the Eighth Platoon of the Miyanaga-cho Company—has been assigned to an area of about fifty *tsubo*. Our job was to plant sweet potatoes. The Tokyo National Volunteer Corps Headquarters has decided to turn the residents of Nezu into farmer-soldiers, transforming burned-out urban wastelands into fields and waiting there to strike the invading enemy forces. And not only Nezu—Shinobazu Pond in Ueno has become a rice paddy, and the garden in front of the Imperial Diet and the prime minister's residence was a farming field. In other words, the Buddhist priests of Ueno, and the Diet representatives and ministers, too—everyone has become a farmer-soldier.

The first thing you notice when you look out over the burned-out areas of the city is the number of safes and stone lanterns. In the fifty *tsubo* assigned to our block group, we found one safe and three stone lanterns. We removed them, as well as the scorched sheets of tin and roof tiles. The hardest things were the porcelain bases of toilets. It took five hours to clear all of these out of our field. If you subtracted the time we went home to eat lunch, I guess it was just a little over four hours.

Once we reached the stage of actually turning over the soil with our shovels, it was fun. Whatever you found was yours to keep, and I found a hammer head and a bucket of charcoal. Gen, working next to me, grinned ruefully when he dug up a gas burner. There's no gas in Nezu these days. So a gas burner is a treasure that's useless.

"You've drawn the short straw today, that's for sure," I said as I handed him a pair of copper-plated scissors I had just dug up. "First you got tricked by the lieutenant, then slapped across the face by the Neighborhood Association leader. And now you dug up that gas burner. Please accept these scissors as a sign that your luck has changed."

"Thank you," he said, accepting them gratefully, and adding, "but I'm glad he slapped me."

"Huh?"

"I was so close to laughing out loud that I didn't know what to do. That slap helped me get control of myself again."

"What was so funny?"

"The lieutenant told me to shave my head, right? That was it. On May 29th, five days ago, there was that big air raid in Yokohama, remember? During the raid, several B-29s strayed into the downtown area and, instead of dropping bombs, they dropped leaflets. A guy I once apprenticed with picked one up and showed it to me. It said: 'Residents of Tokyo! Sorry for the patchy cut we've given you so far. We'll shave your head nice and smooth very soon.' I almost burst out laughing when the lieutenant said the same thing."

When the rubble of the area was starting to glow red in the sunset, we called it quits. Sweet potato starters are supposed to arrive next Sunday from the Hongo Ward Battalion. Looking at the sunset as I walked home, I suddenly thought of a time forty or fifty years ago when there were hardly any homes here in Sendagi; it was mostly lotus ponds, rice paddies, and farmers' fields. My brother and I used to come out here almost every day to catch minnows. As the capital's population grew, the fields were replaced by homes. And now the city was returning to vegetable patches, though the rice paddies weren't back yet. I felt as if I had just had a very long dream. Getting married, the war, the air raids, the death of Kinuko and my brother—they were part of a dream. Awake again, I was four or five years old. I was waking up, wearing my toddler's apron and wiping the drool from my mouth, in our old house, before the renovations. My mother was bringing me a slice of cold watermelon.

June 4

At noon my wife and I went to meet my father-in-law at Ueno Station. We went from there to Yofukuji Temple in Nippori. After saying, "It's too bad about Kinuko and your brother and his wife..." he fell silent. When we told him that it looked like Fumiko would be taking Kinuko's place, he was quiet for a while, and then murmured, "In normal times that would be unthinkable, but... well, things are different now." Once again he fell silent.

No trace of Yofukuji remained. It had been destroyed in the air raid of the night of April 15th. The head priest, wearing a national civilian uniform with gaiters wrapped over his low shoes, pointed to a pile of roof tiles in the corner of the temple garden and said with a rueful smile, "The 'water mark' roof tiles were no match for incendiary bombs." Two years ago, a new roof had been put on the temple with the "water mark" tiles recommended by the Imperial Rule Assistance Association. The advertising slogan at the time went: "Each tile has the *kanji* for 'water' burned into it. The flames of the incendiary bombs won't dare come near these roof tiles!"

"Why not complain to the Imperial Rule Assistance Association? Of course, it's gone out of business and now it's called the National Citizens Volunteer Corps."

"I'm to blame." Pulling a Buddhist surplice over his uniform, the head priest led us to our family grave. "We're the ones who believed that kind of nonsense in the first place."

The graves weren't burned.

I placed the plectrum of Kinuko's favorite shamisen in the grave. It's made from boxwood. I also placed a matching pair of rice bowls in the grave for my brother and sister-in-law. The entire time the priest was chanting the sutras, my father-in-law's shoulders trembled. After Yofukuji, we went to the Furusawas family temple, Jigenji, in Senju Nakamachi.

Her eyes red with tears, my wife murmured, "Kinuko, don't be angry. Fumiko is going to take your place. Please don't be angry with Tadao, either. The Furusawas are short-handed, and they need someone who can run the household. So Fumiko will be marrying Tadao. Please watch over her."

In my own heart all I said was, "I'll avenge your death."

My father-in-law continued to weep silently.

We went from Jigenji to Furusawa Enterprises. My wife immediately entered the kitchen to join old Mrs. Furusawa and Tokiko. They must have been winding up the arrangements for Fumiko's marriage to Tadao. My father-in-law started playing Japanese chess with old Mr. Furusawa. I sat down next to Tadao at the counter of the store.

"Why don't you leave Nezu and move in here?" Tadao asked me. "We'd be happy to have you. It would be a great help."

"We can't do that. It may not be much, but we still have our own family to run. But Tadao, do you know a good company I could get a job at?"

"A company?"

"A big company, if possible."

"The big companies are mostly military suppliers."

"That's even better. I'd like someone to hire me and my truck as a combination." I explained that the situation for a small trucker like me, which had become as perilous as walking a tightrope over a yawning chasm. "I'm stopped every other day by the military police. This happened a lot in the last week. The question is always the same: Where did you get the gas in your tank? After that, they always search the truck bed. I've never carried anything illegal, and I have no intention of doing so in the future, so having them search the truck doesn't frighten me. What frightens me is the questions about the gasoline. Small truckers receive almost no gasoline rations. The big freight firms get all the gas. I just save up as much as I can and then use it as sparingly as possible. But if I admit that I've saved any up, then I'd be in big trouble."

"They'd accuse you of hoarding a precious commodity. And then they'd prohibit you from working."

"That's it. When you've been prohibited from working, it's all over. The next day you get a visit from some official who introduces himself as a representative of the Kanto Region Stockpiled Goods for Supporting the War Effort Council and says that a three-wheeled truck mustn't be allowed to sit idle, offering to purchase it at a fair price."

"If not the Supporting the War Effort Council, it'll be someone from the Kanto Military Supplies Comptroller Division, or the Defense Communication Facilities Bureau. I can see how the Municipal Economic Agency would also want it. And yes, of course—don't forget the Police Department Special Security Battalion."

"What's that?"

"A special volunteer battalion established with the mission of exercising special powers in an emergency. They were first formed in May in Nihonbashi Hisamatsu-cho. The battalion commander, Tetsumaru Kumase, is supposed to be quite a tiger, doesn't hesitate to stop a car driving down the street. Then he'll confiscate it on the spot."

"I have to remember to stay away from Hisamatsu-cho." Even if I manage to somehow avoid having the truck confiscated, getting my hands on gasoline is still the problem. Small tuckers basically receive zero gasoline rations. I could install a charcoal-burning engine on the truck, but it's so big it would take up seventy to eighty percent of the truck bed. If there's no room to load anything into the truck, what's the point of having it? "When you consider all these things, the easiest thing is just to work for a big company. The company supplies the gasoline, and with an official Imperial registration number on my windshield I won't be stopped by the military police."

"Would you be willing to work for us?"

"I'd prefer to work somewhere else for a while and save up gas." My hope was to sock away a cup of gasoline for each *ri* I drove. If I didn't do that, I could be left high and dry in an emergency.

"Well, let me ask two or three companies we do business with," Tadao said, though he didn't seem very happy about it. With the phone book in hand, he entered the booth at the end of the counter. Personally, I wouldn't have minded working for Tadao, who is a very easy-going young man, but I can't allow myself to impose any further on the Furusawas. For starters, it would place Fumiko in a difficult position. I went into the living room to take a look at the chess game going on between old Mr. Furusawa and my father-in-law.

"One to three, and I'm losing," said old Mr. Furusawa. If they were already on their fourth game in less than an hour, they had to be playing a very strange "speed chess."

"I always start with the determination that this time I will absolutely win, but I guess determination isn't enough. You need skill and brains, too."

"It's the same with a war," said my father-in-law, slapping a knight on the board in a move to place his opponent's king in check. "You need both supplies and brains."

"You seem to be a thinker of very dangerous thoughts," said old Mr. Furusawa, stroking his chin. At that moment, Fumiko entered the room accompanied by Takeko, Miss Makiguchi, Miss Furukawa, and Kiyoshi and Shoichi. Mr. Furusawa had invited everyone to dinner, based on the assumption that Fumiko would agree to the marriage. After saying hello, the girls went into the kitchen, and Kiyoshi and Shoichi sat in a corner with a notebook.

"Working on another poem?" I asked, peering over their shoulders. "I don't care what you write, but please promise me you won't throw it into the Neighborhood Association office again."

"This time we're serious," said Shoichi, half-turning to me. "Me and Kiyoshi are writing our death poems. We're trying to condense our last will and testament into 'one score eleven' syllables."

"One score eleven" is an archaic way of saying thirty-one.

"Think how upsetting it would be if you were too anxious when the time came, and you couldn't compose a good poem. If you had too many syllables, you'd leave a record of shame for future generations. Brave as your last deed might be, if your poem is a dud, people will suspect that the whole thing was just a goof. You only die once, so you want to do it up right. That's what me and Kiyoshi were talking about just now."

How far I've come from my hometown, to strike down the foe from over the waves.

How bitter my resentment should I fail to strike true, as I throw my body against an enemy tank.

I set out now, following in the path of the valiant exploits of warriors of old.

Though I be reborn seven times, I would give each life to protect the beautiful empire of Japan.

I go to battle as my sovereign's shield, with stalwart faith that my comrades will follow.

As long as others follow in my footsteps, the hallowed Empire of Japan will long endure.

Why should I not fall, as the cherry blossoms do, for the sake of my Sovereign?

Born in his August Majesty's glorious reign, I now give my life for my Sovereign.

Countless tragic lives of warriors cast away, one atop the other, to defend the hallowed Empire of Japan.

A man's sole path to valor is in selfless service to his Sovereign
and his parents.
I become a Yamato cherry blossom petal to serve as my
Sovereign's shield.
To defend my country, I go now to the place of death so
graciously bestowed upon me by my August Sovereign.

"Pretty impressive," I said, kneeling in formal position. "I feel like
I've heard some of them before. A few of them are a bit clumsy, but
in general, they're pretty good."

"Father, be careful what you're saying," said Kiyoshi, raising his
eyebrows. "These are actual death poems composed by Special
Attack Forces soldiers."

"We copied them out of the newspaper as a guideline for composing
our own," added Shoichi.

"Why didn't you tell me? If I'd known they were the real thing,
I would have approached them differently. Though I guess it's my
fault. When I thought I'd heard them before, I should have asked you
if they were the real thing. I would immediately have read them with
more respect." Deeply regretting my error, I read the next one.

I set forth to battle to offer all in the land of the rising sun a
Sunday without rising.

"That one's mine," said Kiyoshi. "Of course I know it needs a lot
of work. The idea is that by throwing our bodies against the enemy,
we can prevent their attack for a day and all the girls of the land of
the rising sun will be able to enjoy a day off. Do you like it?"

I didn't dare say a word. As is true for the poems of all the young
men of the Special Attack Forces, no matter how faulty their verses,
their ideals are impeccable. Their fearlessness at sacrificing their
young lives is indescribably lofty. That's what moved me. Every
time one of these young men sets out to the front or courageously
blows himself up, the high-ranking military officials and the
commentators declare on the radio and in the newspapers how
noble they are and praise them with flowery phrases. But when

you look at the lives of the old men saying those things, what do you find? The high-ranking military officials are safely protected in concrete bunkers. The commentators and intellectuals are living the bucolic life of gentlemen farmers in the countryside, tilling a little vegetable plot—for themselves and their families, not the nation. Their words might be lofty, but their spirits are base. And what about me? Though I might be prepared to die, I don't dare compare myself to these young men, who are ready to give their lives at the drop of a hat. We've been raised with the idea that everyone can expect at least fifty years of life, which represents an unbridgeable gap separating us from these youths, who have accepted a mere twenty years as their full span on earth. They are heroes; we are cowards.

The last poem in the notebook was:

I do not compare myself to the warriors of old, but just once I'd
like to sing at Tokyo Station.

"Takeko told me that Keisuke Yasokawa will be singing in the plaza in front of the ticket gate at Tokyo Station," said Shoichi, explaining his poem. "And Hamako Watanabe will also be performing there. I'd like to have the chance to do that before I die, sing in front of the crowds at Tokyo Station. It must feel great. Do you think I'm a sissy, Mr. Yamanaka?"

"No, I don't."

"I'm glad."

"But why do we have singers performing in the plaza in front of the ticket gate now?

"Well, according to Takeko, one reason is to improve the frantic mood at the ticket gate, and another is to entice people whose jobs are in the Marunouchi area to come to work."

It's true that the word is people haven't been showing up for work in the Marunouchi area. While the average job attendance rate for Tokyo is seventy-point-two to seventy-point-six percent (in other words, one in four is absent from the workplace), it's only fifty percent (that's one in two) in Marunouchi. It's fallen even lower since the air raids on May 25th and 26th, to about forty percent. This is essentially the collapse of the home front, and commentators have decried it as a betrayal of the soldiers on the front lines. But this is certainly a strange policy for solving the problem.

"Was this the idea of Stationmaster Amano?"

"Actually, it was two novelists," said Fumiko, bringing in the charcoal brazier. "Masao Kume and Yasunari Kawabata. They went to see Stationmaster Amano the other day about it."

"Nobuko Yoshiya went, too," added Takeko, carrying in the sukiyaki pot with its delicious odor. The bottom gleamed with oil, and a piece of golden, braised fat skidded around the center of the pot.

"They say that singers live very well."

"Yes, they're treated like regimental commanders."

Miss Makiguchi brought out a heaping platter of beef, and Miss Kurokawa carried in the konnyaku noodles.

"That's funny, that's better than the treatment a Special Attack Forces pilot gets," said Tadao, coming in from the store counter area. He was holding a piece of paper that he handed me. It read, "Be at the Akasaka Dormitory of Nippon Soda Company, Ltd., tomorrow morning, 8 A.M. A delivery to the north Kanto region. Imperial registration number 562."

I am very pleased and grateful. I no longer have any need to fear the stop-and-search operations of the military police. My gasoline will be taken care of. And I have put one over on the Neighborhood Association leader, who's planning to turn my three-wheel truck over to someone for a profit.

Soon after we started eating, Shoichi turned to me and asked, "Mr. Yamanaka, why do death poems have thirty-one syllables? Why aren't there death haikus?"

I thought about it, but couldn't think of a good answer, so I said: "You got me. Give me two or three days, and I'll find out for you."

"That's all right," said Shoichi. "I was just wondering. I don't see why a hero couldn't just as well say farewell to this life in a haiku. Kiyoshi, when my time comes, I'm going to write a haiku."

"Do what you want, Shoichi," said Kiyoshi casually.

The girls reacted very differently. They looked at each other, and pushed the beef in the sukiyaki pot over toward Shoichi and Kiyoshi. "You'll be going to Yasukuni Shrine soon, and you'll never be able to eat beef again. Enjoy it now," said Tokiko, speaking for them all.

At last I understood the motivation behind Shoichi's question. It was his strategy for getting more beef.

June 5

Today, unusually, I left home without more than glancing at the newspaper. The headlines on the front page had frightened me: "The Battle for Okinawa at a Critical Juncture," "Bitter Fighting on Every Front," "Gap in Military Force Gradually Widening," "No Room for Optimism."

I took my father-in-law to Ueno Station. As we said our farewells, he said to me, "They shouldn't write headlines like that. 'No Room for Optimism'—who in their right mind is optimistic about the war these days? If anyone was ever optimistic in the first place, it was only during the first year of the war. Since then, the majority of people have been pessimistic, if you ask me."

He's right. Recently, no matter whom you talk to, all you hear is depressing, negative opinions. If you want to hear an upbeat opinion in Miyanaga-cho, you have to go to the Neighborhood Association office.

"The only ones who are optimistic are the big cheeses. It's pretty pointless to preach to us ordinary subjects about being overly optimistic. I'd like to tell them where to get off. Anyway, take care of yourself," my father-in-law said. And with that he went to the end of the long line snaking out from the ticket window.

I went to the Akasaka Dormitory of Nippon Soda Company and met with a member of the office staff, Kyoichi Eguchi. I think he is about four or five years my junior. Oddly, since no one favors the national civilian uniform more than employees of big companies like Nippon Soda, he was wearing a suit. He told me that the freight I was carrying was secret and loaded it into my truck himself. There were five pieces. They were about four *shaku* by three *shaku*, and less than five *sun* thick, and very carefully wrapped in waxed paper and hemp string.

"Do you know Yokokawa on the Nakasendo Road?"

"Where the Usui Barrier used to be?"

"That's right. The boss has a country place there. There's a caretaker. Deliver these to him."

"All right. They're paintings, aren't they?"

"Don't ask questions. Just keep your mouth shut and deliver them to Yokokawa. On your way back, go through Maebashi and check into the Aburaya Inn in Hon-cho. The proprietor of the inn will give you a package. Bring it back here by tomorrow afternoon. Here's your pay, the money for the inn, gasoline and a little something extra."

The orange crate he loaded into the back of the truck last held ten containers of gasoline, each of them five *go*. He also have me two envelopes, one larger than the other, and a small bag.

"There are five *go* of brown rice in the bag. No one can stay at the Aburaya Inn unless they bring their own rice. It's the same at inns everywhere. That's it."

He slung his emergency bag over his left shoulder and walked briskly off, probably to the office. I opened the envelopes to check on their contents. The larger one had an Imperial registration plate and a narrow strip of paper with expert calligraphy, "Vehicle of the General Affairs Department of Nippon Soda Company, Ltd.," and stamped with the company seal. I took a few grains of rice from the rice ball that would be my lunch and attached both documents to the bottom edge of the windshield, at left and right. The smaller envelope contained two fresh, clean 100 yen bills and one ticket for the sumo tournament at Meiji Shrine on June 7th, the day after tomorrow.

Low clouds continued to darken the sky, but I was so happy that my employer was taking care of the gas that the weather didn't trouble me. I followed the outer moat from Akasaka to Suidobashi, and drove northwest from there, through the devastated areas of Hakusan, Sugamo, Itabashi and Shimura. The engine seemed to be running fine.

I crossed Todabashi Bridge into Saitama Prefecture. It's one of the famous spots on the Nakasendo Road, and I should have been able to see mountains everywhere—Mount Tsukuba ahead, the mountains of Chichibu to my left, with Oyama and Mount Fuji behind me. But today everywhere only looming gray clouds could be seen and I missed the opportunity to enjoy the famous mountain views.

After Omiya, the driving suddenly became harder. For one thing, the road was bad. It was as bumpy as being on horseback. I didn't want to break an axle, so I slowed down and made my way with care.

Another reason I had to drive carefully was that from Okegawa there were a lot of people on the road. About every *cho* or *cho* and a half, I encountered people walking along the roadway. Most were elderly couples. There wasn't a single young couple, and very few were in their thirties or forties. The majority by far were couples in their fifties or sixties. They all appeared to be dressed pretty much the same way, the men in national civilian uniforms and work tabi, and the women in cotton work trousers and wooden clogs. All the men were carrying large bundles on their back. The women, as if agreed upon, had smallish bundles on their back, but also carried shopping bags in their hands.

Maybe one in ten couples was pulling a cart or other small conveyance, though none of the carts was very full, usually containing two or three bundles bound up in wrapping cloths with a traditional design of twining vines.

At first I thought a local old folks' home was evacuating its residents to the countryside. But after passing dozens of couples, there seemed to be no end to them. The most disturbing thing about it was that everyone had their backs turned to Tokyo. At Kumagaya there was an air-raid siren. I asked a civilian air-raid warden wielding a fire hook like a sword about it, and he told me that planes had been spotted over Nijima. As a precaution, I got out of the truck, deciding to wait and see. The old couples, however, just kept moving forward, pressing on to the northwest at a steady pace, one foot after the other.

After the all-clear was sounded, I started the truck up again. It was already noon. About one and one-half *ri* out of Kumagaya, I spotted a towering zelkova tree. I decided to eat my lunch under its shade. From Akasaka to the zelkova was about seventeen *ri*, which had taken me a little less than four hours.

Under the zelkova, I noticed a large earthen mound. That is, a hexagonal stone fence surrounded the mound, and the zelkova rose from the center of the mound. The tree must have been about thirteen meters high and four meters in circumference. Nailed to the trunk was a board with the wording, in black ink:

> Nakasendo Nijima Village Ichiri Mound
> This zelkova is three hundred years old.
> Don't hurt it.
> The Village Chief

Adjacent to the mound a couple sat around a pot that they were eating from. Glancing at them from the corner of my eye, I guessed that they were one of the couples I'd seen walking along Nakasendo Road. The man seemed to be about sixty, his wife my age. Their shoulders were white with dust. The button at the fly of the man's trousers was open. "You're fly's open," I blurted out.

"It's open on purpose," he said with a smile. "If you leave it open, you don't get chapped thighs. If you look at the men who have their fly buttoned, they're walking bow-legged—proof that their thighs are chapped. Of course, it's no big deal. If you wash the chapped skin and sprinkle tooth powder on it, it's fine. But why waste tooth powder?"

"You're an experienced traveler, I see."

"You get experienced fast. This is the fifth day we've been on the road."

"Where are you coming from?"

"We left from Shibuya, Tokyo, on June 1st."

"And where are you headed?"

"To my family home in Kashiwabara, Shinshu, first. If things don't work out there, we'll try her hometown, Okunimachi in Yamagata." He placed his hand gently on the shoulder of his wife, who was carefully scraping grains of cooked rice off the lid of the cooking pot.

"I don't think they'll want us staying a month in Kashiwabara. We'll probably end up going to Okuni."

"Walking all the way?"

"Yup. Enjoying the scenery along the Japan Sea. We should get there by the Obon Festival in August."

"You're not taking the train?"

"Do you think anyone can get a long-distance train ticket these days?"

"We waited in line for a week at Shibuya Station," said his wife, speaking for the first time. "Scalpers keep cutting in and you end up in the same place in line no matter how many days you sit there. The line never moves. If you say anything, they beat you up. Just when you think the line is finally moving, a B-29 flies over. Once an air-raid siren sounds, you have to start all over. And even if you try to get a ticket through the back door, money doesn't cut it anymore. The going price for one long-distance ticket is one *to* of rice."

"If you manage to get a ticket somehow or other, your problem's still not solved," the man went on. "The first hoop you need to jump through is a reserved seat ticket, which you need in addition to the regular ticket. Even officials on public business or employees of big companies traveling for business have a hard time getting their hands on those. For ordinary folk like us? Well, it's about the same as trying to catch the moon by scooping up its reflection in a pond. And—at least this is what I've heard—from the 10th of this month the Transport Ministry is going to cut the number of passengers allowed on trains by half. I figured we could wait a hundred years and never get a ticket. So me and the wife decided to walk, pulling this cart."

Our four young women who work for the railway had said as much after dinner last night. The Ou Line was the worst hit; there had been only two round-trip long-distance trains, and now there was only going to be one; only the military and those working for factories producing military supplies would be able to travel. In other words, the number of passenger trains would be reduced and freight trains increased in order to push the shipment of military supplies even more. And the national and private railways of the Tokyo area would start restricting ridership during commuting hours (6:30–8:30 A.M. and 6:30–10:30 P.M.) to people going to and from work. All other riders would be kept off the trains unless they had special circumstances—the idea being to reduce electricity consumption.

"Now if by some miracle you were able to get both a ticket and a reserved seat," the man continued, "what are you going to do about your baggage? They won't let you bring anything large onto the trains, and only those who have the documents showing they've been evacuated because their homes have been demolished by the government are allowed to ship the minimum amount of household effects by train. If you go to a small-freight delivery service, you've got to pay black-market rates."

I found myself wincing.

"Listen: I was told that it would cost 15,000 yen to take just this stuff to Kashiwara. Gasoline was extra. I'd have to hand over six or seven *sho* of gasoline to the crooks. I'm an umbrella maker. Where's someone like me supposed to get gasoline? I told the guy if I had some way of getting gasoline, I'd throw it on his three-wheel truck and set a match to it. People like me, without money or connections, if we want to evacuate, we have to foot it, using these legs our parents gave us."

"Do you have any children?" I asked.

"Three boys."

"They must be able to help you out."

"All three were drafted. I have no way of knowing if they're alive or dead, but I stayed in Shibuya this long because I wanted them to be able to rest and recuperate in the house they were born and raised in if they ever came back from the war. If I evacuated the year before last, or even last year, it would have been much easier. Evacuees were being treated much better then. I've only got myself to blame for staying on in Tokyo so long."

"I can't see how it's your fault. Where will you sleep tonight?" I asked.

"We don't have any plans. When it starts to get dark, we'll stop wherever we happen to be. Last night a farmer in Konosu let us sleep in his barn."

"The farmer said he envied us," said the wife, the "military mother" who had sent her three sons off to war, picking at the grains of rice stuck to her husband's lap.

"'I'd like to take a trip with my wife, too,' the farmer told me. 'It'd be like a honeymoon,' he said. Hmph. We're just trying to survive, but to others it's romantic."

"Aren't you being a little too talkative today?" his wife smiled.

"Yes, you're right," said the umbrella maker, tapping his deeply wrinkled forehead with his right middle finger and looking at me. "The three rules for a long journey on foot. Number one, keep up a steady stride. Number two, don't drink too much water. Number three, don't talk too much. That's what I'm going to do now."

I placed four or five Hikari cigarettes into the umbrella maker's lap and stepped down from the mound. As I gave the starter of my truck a kick, I glanced at the luggage in the old couple's cart: a wicker trunk and two large cloth bundles. One bundle was probably bedding; the other had handles of paper umbrellas protruding. The couple was probably counting on trading the umbrellas for rice along the way. There were fewer than twenty umbrellas; how far would the supply take them? As I looked at them, the umbrella maker was bowing to me, a lit cigarette in hand. The "military mother" waved, the box of matches in her hand.

The road from Hongo was freshly repaved, which made for easy driving. From Annaka it began to rise, so I stopped every *ri* and let the engine cool off to keep it from overheating. There were a lot of soldiers at Matsuida. The rumor that military headquarters are going to be moved into the mountains of Shinshu must be true. If the enemy lands somewhere on the Kanto Plain, this Nakasendo Road, linking Kanto to Shinshu, will become the Ginza Avenue of the fighting.

I don't really care what happens to the paintings of the president of Nippon Soda Company, but I do care about that elderly couple. They've already given their three sons to the war, and I don't think they owe the nation a whit more. Even if they're the last two Japanese alive, I want to see them live out their days peacefully to the end.

At 3:30 P.M., having driven thirty-three *ri* without a mishap, I arrived at the company president's second house in Yokokawa. I handed the paintings over to the surly caretaker and returned by the road I'd come by as far as Takasaki. Tonebashi Bridge in Maebashi was under repair and closed to traffic, so I detoured to the north and entered Maebashi over Nakanohashi Bridge. I registered at the Aburaya Inn, and by the time I'd bathed and eaten, the seven o'clock news had begun. I'm listening to Enoken's *Gozonji Isshin Tasuke* as I write this.

There's no trace of the odor of smoke or ashes in Maebashi; the air is indescribably fragrant and refreshing. The streets are quiet, and it's very calm and relaxing. The bath at the Aburaya Inn is made with cedar, and I felt like a king soaking in it. After the charred ruins of the city, everything here is an absolute delight. The only complaint I have is the fleas. I went to the desk to ask for flea powder, and the proprietor apologized, "We're so short of help that we haven't been able to do a thorough cleaning for the last two years." Then she added: "There are so many military supply factories in the area, and every able-bodied person is working at one of them. Oh, that reminds me—Mr. Shimoyama from the military clothing factory brought some fabric from the Maebashi warehouse..." And she pulled out a bundle tied up in a wrapping cloth from behind the counter.

June 6

When I finally returned home after delivering the fabric to the Nippon Soda Company, Ltd., employees' dormitory in Akasaka, the Neighborhood Association leader was waiting for me. "Just let me wash my hands," I said from the yard. "I'll only be a minute." He turned his long face away with a dismissive jerk.

When I was in the bathroom, my wife stuck her head in and whispered: "I served him tea but he just dumped it out in the garden. He won't say a word to me. I'm frightened."

"I wonder what he wants."

"Mrs. Igarashi, the dentist's wife, told me that someone threw another anonymous letter into the Neighborhood Association office. Maybe that's it."

"Maybe Kiyoshi is up to his old tricks again."

"He and Sho must have done it. They're the ones who wrote that poem the other day."

"Yes, and it wasn't bad, either."

"Don't side with them. You'd better get out there."

"Is Kiyoshi at school?"

"Yes. Tonight he'll be sleeping over at the factory. Sho, too."

"Well, that settles it. They must be the culprits. They arranged it pretty cleverly so that they could escape without a scolding."

I went out to greet the Neighborhood Association leader very humbly.

"It's just like the time with the poem," he snapped, slapping a sheet of paper down on the tatami. "Paper from the same Kokuyo notebook, with a watermark, and the same sparrow-track writing. The notebook belongs to your son Kiyoshi, and the handwriting is that of Sho Takahashi. Right? Can you deny it?"

The page contained a haiku with a brief preface explaining the circumstances of its composition:

Should two young men of Miyanaga-cho, who have earned a reputation for their brilliance, set off to the perils of the battlefield, their last words might be the following poem:

The lives
of the young warriors—
fodder for horses.

"Ah," I said.

"What do you mean by that? This is no time for poetic appreciation. I know that a certain very small minority of the residents of Miyanaga-cho refer to me, Kiichiro Aoyama, as 'the horse' or 'horse face.' In other words, the horse in this haiku is me. So the poem means 'We're going to give up our lives in the war, not for Emperor and the Empire but for the likes of Kiichiro Aoyama, and the only reason that he can go on with his comfortable life is that he's living off the blood of young people, who are nothing but his fodder.' This is preposterous."

"Are you sure you're not taking this too personally?"

"This isn't just an insult to me. This poem has the smell of sedition."

"It's just a silly little haiku. For starters, there's not even a seasonal word."

"Let me be perfectly clear. This poem is unpatriotic."

"It's just a bad parody of Basho's 'The roadside mallow—fodder for horses.' It's a joke."

"This is no joke. This is the germ of an idea that is a reprehensible crime."

"They're just playing around."

"And what would happen if the military police learned of it?"

"Look, the reason I said, 'Ah' earlier is that I realized the reason why an ordinary haiku won't serve as a soldier's farewell poem. A haiku is too short and can't express the fullness of one's thoughts. That's why you need a kind of foreword to set up a haiku."

"So you're determined to try to protect them."

"I think it's related to the difference between waka and haiku— one is lyric, the other is anecdotal. This is an important trial run for them, don't you think?"

"An important trial run!" The Neighborhood Association leader hit me on the knee with his pipe. "Do you really mean that?"

"And there's some truth to the content. I'm not saying it's about you, but in general the more important a person is in society the more they're dependent on the blood of our young soldiers..."

The Neighborhood Association leader glared at me with the astonishment of a child who had seen his first magic trick by the Great Tenkatsu. He grabbed the sheet of paper and left the house waving it above his head like a banner.

June 7

"I have no regrets."

Nothing could describe my feelings better today. The heavy rains that started falling in the afternoon have by now—as I'm writing these words—grown into a raging tempest. It is 9:30 in the evening. The storm is so violent that one could imagine the world is coming to an end, but if I shut my eyes, I see in my mind's eye the decorative aprons of the sumo wrestlers, in every color of the rainbow, edged in silver and gold embroidery, and I feel completely satisfied and at peace. That's right—for the first time in a long time, I went to see sumo. And the ticket I received from Eguchi at Nippon Soda Company was a rare prize, a first-class seat. I was so close to the action that I could almost reach out and touch the topknot of my favorite wrestler Terunobori; and besides that—I still can't believe this—the seat came with a two *go* bottle of blended saké.

I wonder if the banging I've been hearing at the front door is the wind. I'll have my wife go take a look. Right now, I can't bear the thought of even a single moment's interruption in recording what I witnessed at the first day of the Meiji Shrine Sumo Tournament as completely as I can. I don't know how much longer I'll be alive, but as long as I am, I intend to read and reread what I set down about this glorious day whenever I'm feeling depressed. I know it'll be a source of great comfort to me. Even if I have to stay up all night, I've got to get this recorded to the last detail.

Well, I arrived at the Ryogoku Sumo Stadium at 4:30 in the morning. During the major air raid on March 30th, the stadium

September 28
Yesterday, September 27th, I was released from the Yokaichiba Prison in Chiba Prefecture. I don't have it in me to write more than that single line today.

September 29
There's a plain in the north of the Boso Peninsula about one hundred kilometers from east to west and eighty kilometers north to south, ranging from about twenty to forty meters in elevation. Most of it's in Shimofusa, so it's usually called the Shimofusa Plain, and on the southeast edge of it, where it touches Kujukurihama Beach, there's a town called Yokaichiba. It's known for its sardines, a special variety of giant burdock, garden nurseries and swamp parsley. It's a marshy, damp place. I arrived home from the prison there after nine o'clock in the evening the night before last. Feeling a sense of relief that our house still stood and hadn't been burned down, I knocked on the outer door. When my wife saw me through the glass, she dropped to her knees in complete astonishment. Then, still on her knees, she released the latch and slid the door open.

"Everyone said that political prisoners were sent to Okinawa. I had set June 23rd as the day of your death, the day Okinawa was conquered by the Americans, and I've been praying for the repose of your soul every morning and evening at the Buddhist altar."

That was the first thing she said.

And the first thing I said was, "That's impossible." I had sent letters to my wife, secretly, avoiding the surveillance of the fifteen guards at the prison. A certain Koga, an official from the Yokaichiba Town Office who visited the prison on city business, came up to me once while I was gutting sardines in the work area and murmured in my ear, "I can help you contact your family. Of course, there's a risk in it for me, so I won't do it for free. How about two gold fillings for each letter?"

He passed me a worn-down pencil and an old receipt. I wept tears of joy at his kindness, and I wrote on the back of the receipt in letters no bigger than a fly's head: "I'm serving a prison term in Yokaichiba-machi, Sosa County, Chiba, for violating the National Defense Law. I'm pretty sick of the menu, which is nothing but sardines, but thank heavens I'm well. I'm praying for your safety. Shinsuke Yamanaka."

Then I yanked two gold crowns from my back teeth, with considerable bleeding. When Koga appeared at the prison again a few days later, I gave him the note and the crowns. Of course I had written my address on the back of the receipt as well. When I was arrested, I had eight gold teeth. I have only two now. In other words, I paid Koga to deliver messages to my family three times. It was a shock to hear that not one had gotten through. He must just have pocketed the gold.

"I wrote to you," I said to my wife, "but the messages never got here. I'll tell you about it some other time. Right now, I really want to take a bath." I took off my straw sandals and crawled toward the living room. "No," I called out to my wife, "before a bath I need something to eat. Please." Panting, I collapsed over the hibachi. Then I noticed that, next to Kinuko's funerary tablet, was a plain, unvarnished wooden one. And my diary was laid out in front of the tablet.

"I'm sorry," said my wife as she lit the charcoal brazier in the kitchen. "I looked everywhere for a black lacquer funerary tablet with gold letters, but it was impossible, so I made do with that."

I took the funerary tablet and the diary down from the Buddhist altar.

"I'm glad my diary is safe. I had reconciled myself to it being confiscated by the Special Higher Police."

"When they came, I had a brainstorm and stuck it in the fuel hole of the bathtub."

When they came! That was 113 days ago, at 9:30 in the evening on June 7th, just when I was starting to record what I'd seen in my front-row seat on the first day of the Meiji Shrine Sumo Tournament at the Ryogoku Sumo Stadium. I had gotten as far as:

Well, I arrived at the Ryogoku Sumo Stadium at 4:30 in the morning. During the major air raid on March 30, the stadium

When I got to that point, my wife let out a scream from the shop. "The Special Higher Police are here for you!"

Nothing good could come of them getting a hold of my diary, I thought. Of course, it's just the ordinary diary of a an ordinary fan-maker, with nothing special written in it, but it does contain a lot of very clear references to the black market, as well as gripes about the government and the military. Everyone says these things, but as long as they remain as speech, they fade and disappear into nothing after they're uttered. It's another thing entirely to put the same words down in writing, and I couldn't expect to get away with it. Praying that my wife would cleverly dispose of the diary, I shoved it across the floor into the kitchen as I went in to the workshop.

Two men wearing rubber raincoats were standing in the entryway. One had a handlebar mustache and the other a little bristle mustache like Hitler. The one with the handlebar said, "I'm Kobayashi from the Special Higher Police Division of the Police Department. Apparently you are engaging regularly in unpatriotic speech and actions. Four days ago, you were heard walking around the grounds of Nezu Gongen Shrine telling people, 'Whenever a young man goes off to the front or offers his life in the line of duty, the top military officials and intellectuals say in the newspapers and on the radio how wonderful it is and praise the young men with flowery words, but it's all phony.' And you went on, 'But what about when you look at the actual lives of the top brass and the intellectuals who are praising the deaths of our young men? The military leaders are all safe inside concrete bunkers. The intellectuals have all evacuated the cities and laying low in the countryside, planting their vegetable gardens, and putting everything they grow on their own plates or those of their families. The big shots are full of flowery speeches, but they have no principles. The higher up they are in society the fatter they're growing on the blood of our young men.'"

"It was the Neighborhood Association leader Aoyama who reported me, wasn't it?"

"No."

"Yep, it was him without a doubt."

"No, it was someone else in the neighborhood, other than him. And not just one person. We've has reports from several individuals."

"I swear to the god of Nezu Gongen, I never said anything like that to anyone on the grounds of the shrine. The only thing I said to the Neighborhood Association leader was…"

"So you admit you said it."

"Uhhh…"

"And that's a clear violation of the National Security Act. You're coming with us." The man with the handlebar mustache grabbed my collar. At the same instant, the one with the Hitler brush stepped up into the house with his boots on. When I think about it, it must have been during this back-and-forth that my wife and stuffed my diary into the bathtub fuel hole. I never knew she was so quick-witted.

The afternoon of the following day, June 8th, I was at the Yokaichiba Prison gutting sardines. In a room in the Metropolitan Police Department, Detective Kobayashi's superior, the Home Ministry Police Bureau Security Division Home Affairs Officer, informed me of the secret regulation that permitted "the immediate arrest, punishment and even execution of thought criminals who have violated the National Security Act," and with that I was summarily dispatched to the countryside near Kujukurihama Beach. I was never told where I was being sent. I know I need to write in detail about the more than one hundred days I spent in prison, but the truth is that I simply don't have the physical strength to sit in front of my desk for several hours on end pushing my glass-tipped pen. I have to write a little each day.

To return to what happened after I got home the night before last: my wife made me an omelet. It was an unimaginable treat after having eaten nothing but sardines for so long, but as the ache in my empty stomach began to dissipate, I began to taste something vaguely artificial in the omelet. For starters, the entire thing was bright yellow. This was not an omelet as I remembered omelets. There should have been little white spots of egg white mixed in with the yellow.

"I made it with powdered eggs," explained my wife, as I looked carefully at the edge of the omelet, examining it from every angle. "Fumiko got the powdered eggs, made just from the yolks, from an American. Since it's one hundred percent yolks, it's completely yellow."

"How did Fumiko come by it?"

"Fumiko's working at the Imperial Hotel. Takeko, too. And so are Kayoko Makiguchi and Kumiko Kurokawa, the two girls staying with us. Important Americans are staying at the hotel, and they're very generous…" she went on as she was cleaning up in the kitchen.

"So they're okay, then."

"Yes, they're just fine. The four of them will be back Monday morning. Let's see, today is Thursday, the 27th, so that will be the morning of October 1st."

"They stay at the Imperial Hotel?"

"Yes, they sleep there. In the big air raid on May 25th, the south wing and the main portion of the banquet hall burned down, remember? Apparently they're incredibly busy cleaning up the site and taking care of the guests in the part of the hotel that's still in operation."

"What's Kiyoshi doing?"

"He's studying English conversation at the church over in Yotsuya. Sho Takahashi is with him. He says that the teacher is an American missionary."

"I see. And how about Tadao at Furusawa Enterprises? Is he all right?"

"Yes, yes, he's fine. Oh—that bath is ready now. We have the most wonderful soap. Fumiko got it from the Americans. Not only does it get you cleaner than you could ever have imagined possible, it smells so nice."

I didn't care about how clean the soap got me or how nice it smelled as much as the simple fact that it didn't hurt to rub it against my skin. For the longest time the soap we've had here in Japan was mixed with clay or sand or something, and if you weren't careful when you soaped up, you'd scour your skin ragged. The girls used to say it was like a dull old grater, and complain about the marks it left on their legs. I always used to kid them and tell them not to make a fuss, that they should be happy to have any soap at all, given the state of the world. But this soap was different. It was as smooth and slick as a peeled boiled egg. I drifted off, and with my exhaustion, I actually fell asleep in the tub for about five minutes. Then I climbed into the futon spread out at the rear of the living room and went soundly to sleep.

For an entire day and a half, up to after noon today, I was out like a light. My wife tells me that I got up several times to use the toilet, slurp down a little rice gruel with instant eggs, and drink a bit of grated apple juice, but I don't remember it. I have a very faint memory of holding my glass-tipped fountain pen, which felt as heavy as a log, and writing these lines in my diary: "Yesterday, September 27th, I was released from the Yokaichiba Prison in Chiba Prefecture. I don't have it in me to write more than that single line today."

I also think I might remember old Mr. and Mrs. Furusawa looking in on me and saying how glad they were that I was still alive, and that they were staying on our second floor. Then I think Kiyoshi might have come in and said "How are you?" to me in English. And one more thing: I think I remember Tomoe, the wife of the saké brewer in Toride, looking at me with tears in her eyes, but that must have been a dream. There is no reason that she would have come rushing all the way from Toride to look in on me. I must be secretly attracted to her; that's why I dreamed about her.

This afternoon, before opening my diary, I asked my wife two questions. This was the first one: "I seem to remember old Mr. and Mrs. Furusawa thanking me for letting them stay on our second floor. Did something happen?"

"Not really."

"But Mr. Furusawa supposedly hates staying at other people's homes."

"Furusawa Enterprises took a direct hit from an incendiary bomb. So they moved for a while with Tokiko to Yagiri, where they have their retirement home, but Mr. Furusawa wanted to be back in the city, and so from the end of August they've been here. The place in Yagiri isn't really suited for old people anyway."

"Why not? It should be very peaceful there."

"Yes, it should be, but right now it's being used as a store."

"I see. So Tadao must be running the business from Yagiri now."

"Yes, that's it."

On my way back home in the full train from Yokaichiba, I heard people saying that Tokyo was completely bombed out, and even on June 7th, my last day in the city, it was extremely strange that our home in Nezu Miyanaga-cho, and Furusawa Enterprises in Senju, should still be standing, so I wasn't really surprised at what my wife said. In fact, I thought that the inevitable had just finally taken place. I was happy that Tadao and Tokiko were safe. My second question was: "What happened to the three-wheeled truck?"

"Someone from a place with a long fancy name, the Kanto Region Stockpiled Goods Something-or-other, came and took it away. Oops, I shouldn't say he took it, or I'll get in trouble. He gave me 55 yen in cash for it."

"It cost 6,500 yen on the black market, and they gave us 55 yen! You can't buy three bars of soap for that."

"He said that was the price when the national authorities were buying it."

"It's thievery. And when did that something-or-other association guy come?"

"The afternoon of the day after they took you away."

"June 8th. Just as I thought—he was behind it."

Kiyoshi has just come home. The grandfather clock says 5 P.M. I'll leave off writing any more until tomorrow. I'm exhausted just gripping my pen.

September 30
The Yokaichiba Prison occupies a piece of land about 850 *tsubo* in area. Surrounded by a high concrete wall are five low wooden buildings, about as sturdy as cardboard boxes left out in the rain. Only two of them really deserve to be called buildings at all—the office and the workroom. The other three are in such bad shape that even a cow or a pig would protest being kept there. The roofs are so leaky that when it rains, puddles form on the floor. We slept in the building that had the fewest leaks. There were fourteen of us "thought criminals." We were all embarrassed by the label. For example, "thought criminal" Yoshikawa, a wooden sandal maker from Sahara, was dragged away by the Special Higher Police because when he was drunk on two *go* of blended saké, he blurted out at a meeting of other sandal makers: "The Emperor not only makes us pay high taxes, but he also took my two sons from me, and no matter what the holiday I never get even a pair of underpants in return." Yoshikawa, who had only graduated from elementary school, used to say that they could bang on his head as much as they wanted,

but he'd be more surprised than anyone if they managed to knock anything as fancy as a "seditious thought" out of it.

A nearsighted fellow named Nishino, a part-time teacher at the Chiba Prefectural Nobara Agriculture School, said to two or three of his students while they were working in the fields, "They're always declaring 'Victory! Victory!' in the newspapers and on the radio, but if we're always winning, why are all my friends dying. It's very painful. We've been fighting in China for eight years, but we're still not in control. I don't think we have what it takes. I don't know how we can defeat the Americans and the British." That's how he violated the National Security Act. Nishino said he had doubts because he really loved his country, but just having doubts qualifies as having a "seditious thought," and the prison warden and the jailers treated Nishino as "the most dangerous thought criminal at the prison."

The most pitiful guy there was a Korean named Minoru Hirano who had worked as a laborer in Koiwa, Tokyo. He was pulling a cart past the police box at the west end of Ichikawabashi on the way to Edogawa and happened to be singing a popular song to himself: "Pity the poor Korean / He lost the war and his country / His house was flattened in an earthquake / *Pewashanko, pewashanko* / Pity the poor Korean / Picking up trash for 5 sen a day / Not enough to fill his belly / *Pewashanko, pewashanko*." The cop in the police box arrested him on the spot, saying "It's arrogant and condescending for a Korean to sing a popular song that Japanese sing to ridicule the Koreans," and handed him over to the Special Higher Police. Hirano tried to defend himself by saying, "The song describes our situation perfectly, that's why I liked to sing it all the time." But the Special Higher Police would have none of it. They branded him as a dangerous ringleader of the traitorous rebels plotting to overthrow Japanese rule of the Korean Peninsula and restore Korean independence, and dumped him in the Yokaichiba prison.

The warden of the prison was very dedicated to his work, and so determined to cleanse our heads of our dangerous, seditious thoughts that he declared we had to come up with a minimum of one patriotic slogan a day to demonstrate our change of heart. He hung up a large blackboard at the entryway of the workroom, and the rule was that by the time we left for our evening meal each of us had to have written our daily slogan on the board. If one of us failed to do so, we were punished as a group and there was no supper. So not only did we have to work processing sardines from five in the morning to five at night, until our bodies were as worn-out as old straw sandals, but at night we had to come up with our new slogans for the next day, which often kept us up halfway through the night. It would have been one thing if all we had to do was invent a new slogan, but the warden added conditions.

"You're thought criminals—political prisoners—who are here because you violated the National Security Act, which forbids any communication revealing state secrets or providing information to the enemy, talking about events that compromise public security, obstructing or attempting to obstruct the nation's economy, or inciting traitorous ideas. As your warden, I know you succumbed to these dangerous, unpatriotic thoughts in a moment of temporary weakness and that now you're spending your days purifying yourselves, filled with profound gratitude to the Emperor and living as upstanding Imperial subjects. But you need to express your newly purified condition to the public. They won't forgive you unless you clearly announce your conversion in words, for all to hear. Your slogans are your declarations of conversion. Once you've composed one or two thousand slogans, they'll stand as a big, fat testament to your change of heart. Express your determination to cleanse yourself in the form of these slogans. Anyone who fails to write a new slogan for three consecutive days will be regarded as an unrepentant traitor and will go without food for three days."

The moral lessons the warden repeated to us on a daily basis only made the job of composing the slogans harder. For one thing, none of us had ever had any dangerous, traitorous thoughts in the first place. Nothing is harder than to deny something you've never felt. But none of us wanted to have our food taken away, so every day we each came up with a new slogan affirming our reformation:

Talk about your determination to win, and keep secrets to yourself.

B-29s are the devil's handiwork, and Zero fighters are the acts of the gods.

What you're eager to write, the spies are eager to read.

Gratitude to the Empire surpasses gratitude to your parents.

The moon in the east, the sun in the west, and the Emperor in the middle.

When the black market flourishes, our world grows dark.

American and British devils, your arms are too short to fight us.

I'm sure the warden wouldn't like to admit it, but his prison was less a place of purification and reform for thought criminals than it was a sardine factory. Everyone knows that Kujukurihama Beach is one of the two major sardine-fishing grounds in Japan. But for many years, sardines were looked on as trash fish, and about eighty percent of the sardines were pressed for oil, which was made into oil cakes that were shipped throughout the country to be used as fertilizer. But immediately after the funeral of Naval Marshal General and Commander of the Combined Fleet Isoroku Yamamoto, the new slogan "Vindicate the marshal with increased food production" was proclaimed, and from that point on people began to look at the worthless, lowly, trash fish, the sardine, in a different light.

"Vindicate the marshal with increased production"—now that's a real slogan. The cabinet information officers are true pros, after all. Bringing new land into cultivation is not the only way to increase food production. Taking a different look at foods that no one would ever even consider eating in the past was a brilliant way to increase food supplies. So why not turn to this "garbage of the sea" as a new source of nutrition? And so research facilities sprung up along the seacoast from Kujukurihama Beach to Choshi. I say "research facilities," but they were really little more than bait and tackle shacks with fancy new signs slapped on them—pretty much what you'd expect when the subject of the research is sardines. The Yokaichiba Prison was the center for these new research facilities. After all, the labor was free. We were told to make sardine bread by grinding up sardines in flour. The yeast reacted badly to the fish and we couldn't get it to ferment no matter what we did, so sardine bread always ended up as a hard ball of dough. So they changed the name from sardine bread to sardine balls and sold them to the military base food canteens and military goods factory cafeterias in Chiba Prefecture. Nobody liked them, so after a month we were told to stop making them. Next was sweet sardine jelly, but that was abandoned as a failure at the experimental stage. Mixing yam paste and ground sardines produced a very strange result.

The food taster was an old fisherman from Urayasu who'd been sent to the Yokaichiba Prison for saying at his block group meetings: "I don't understand why Colonel Tateo Kato, leader of the Hayabusa Flight Squadron, was promoted two steps up to major general and immortalized by the government as a 'God of War.' He only took down one plane in his final battle over the Bay of Bengal. And three others in his squadron were shot down. Compared to him, my son, who went missing in action in North China, is the better man." This old guy was always bragging: "There's nothing worse than someone who complains about the food. I can eat anything short of horse manure." That's why he was picked as the product taster. The prison thought it had the ideal guinea pigs for the Sardine Food Products Development Project. If someone got food poisoning, what did it matter? We were prisoners. Which is why the prison became the research center for the project. When the old fisherman ate a roll of the sweet sardine jelly he vomited three times, had diarrhea for five days and was in bed for two weeks.

Our attempts at sardine-filled wafers, sardine crackers, sardine steamed buns, sardine candies, sardine crunchies, sardine crispies, sardine cakes and sardine gelatin delivered equally questionable results. In fact, all of the Sardine Research Centers along the Kujukurihama coast only succeeded with three products: sardine buckwheat noodles, sardine wheat noodles and sardine powder. But because of the shortage of buckwheat and wheat flour, the only new product to actually be manufactured was sardine powder. We dried the sardines on the roofs of the buildings, then ground them up roughly with a mortar and pestle and dumped the result into a medicine grinder to get a finer powder. Apparently tuberculosis sanatoriums around the country occasionally asked for it.

Aside from the sardine powder, we also made seven other kinds of sardine products. We made dried whole sardines by sprinkling the fish with rock salt, letting them sit overnight, then rinsing them off the next morning and drying them in the sun. We also split sardines at the gut and salted and dried them the same way as a kind of dried sardine fillet. We prepared sardines by the same method but put four on a skewer, through the eyes or the jaw, to dry, for another two products. The warden offered a reward of three white rice balls to any prisoner who could make one thousand skewered sardines in a single day. Even the most dexterous could only do eight hundred or eight hundred and fifty a day; obviously the warden knew this, and that he'd never actually have to award the prize. It was just a free way of motivating us. But interestingly, every day two or three prisoners met the goal. Nishino, Hirano and I came up with our own system, and we won several times. Anyone who could add could pull it off. For example, if the final results for a certain day were:

Yamanaka	650
Nishino	700
Hirano	750

no one would win. So from about noon, I'd give Hirano 110 and Nishino gave him 150, a total of 260. So now the result was:

Yamanaka	540
Nishino	550
Hirano	1,010

Hirano would get the reward of three rice balls from the warden, and he'd give one to me and one to Nishino. All three of us got the reward. The success of our system, however, was only temporary; the warden soon canceled this reward. Someone was always breaking the target of one thousand rice balls, but the total efficiency of the operation never improved, and he realized he was being played.

We also made dried baby sardines, seasoned dried baby sardines and salted sardines. Combined with the other four products, that made seven—all seven of them traditional, tried-and-true forms in which sardines were eaten, meaning that the war came to an end without anything coming of this attempt to develop new sardine products at Kujukurihama Beach.

All the time I was there, not really being able to say if I was a thought criminal or just a live-in employee at a sardine factory, I kept wondering why Nezu Miyanaga-cho Neighborhood Association leader Kiichiro Aoyama ratted me out to the Special Higher Police. Then one evening, about ten days after my arrival at the prison, I happened to see a three-wheel truck from the Yokaichiba Town Office drive into the prison grounds to pick up some dried sardines, and I realized—he'd been after my three-wheel truck the entire time. He'd said to me, "When you give up your trucking service, can I ask you to allow me to find a new home for your three-wheeled truck? It just so happens that the executive director of the Kanto Region Stockpiled Goods for Supporting the War Effort Council is an old friend of mine from middle school, and he's looking for a three-wheeled truck." No doubt he sniffed around everywhere he could, and mine was the only truck he could find. When his old school chum got what he wanted, Aoyama earned himself a nice little windfall for his good deed. I wanted to get out of prison and find anything, even circumstantial evidence, to get my revenge on him before I died. That's what kept me going. To tell the truth, I made two attempts to escape from the prison, at the end of June and in mid-August. I was brought back both times, but my motive in each case was to confront Kiichiro Aoyama and land at least one good solid punch to his narrow horse face.

The whole story of those two escape attempts will have to wait for later. But the fact that the Kanto Region Stockpiled Goods for Supporting the War Effort Council showed up less than a day after I'd been kidnapped meant one thing and one thing only: that Kiichiro Aoyama was behind the whole thing. I'll bust his door down at six o'clock tomorrow morning and get him before he's awake. That's the only way to prevent that smooth-talking old fox from squirming his way out of this.

October 1
In an odd reversal of fate, it was Aoyama who arrived at my door just as I was waking up. He showed up at 5:30 and set down a wide, slim pamphlet on the floor of the shop, saying: "Thank you for all your effort. I heard from Special Higher Police Detective Kobayashi that you'd returned from Yokaichiba, but I delayed stopping by to pay my respects until the month was over. I didn't want to impose on you when you were still recovering. But today is a new month, the first day of October, and it couldn't be a more fortuitous day for your return to society. After all, everything starts from 'one.' I brought you this little gift to celebrate your rehabilitation."

A lot of the people riding the train on the way back to Tokyo had the same little book, and here in the city, it seemed that one in ten were clutching it as they walked through the streets. This instant bestseller bore the title *A Guide to Japanese-English Conversation.*

"The publisher, Seibundo Shinkosha, is laughing all the way to the bank with this. It's only been on sale for two weeks, and it's already sold more than two million copies," Aoyama said.

"There must be some shameless pamphleteer out there. It's only six weeks since the American and the English were devils," I said.

"It's not public yet, but they say that the Japanese language is going to be outlawed."

"What? That's unbelievable."

"I have it from a very reliable source. General MacArthur is going to make a declaration outlawing Japanese within the year. Did you see the newspaper the day before yesterday? The one with the picture of the Emperor standing next to General MacArthur?"

Of course I'd seen it. MacArthur was playing the big man, with his hands on his hips. And the Emperor looked so pitiful, especially the way his hands hung limply at his sides. He may have been forced to accept unconditional surrender, but he is our revered leader, and I'd like to see him with his arms straight and his fingers extended. Or he could have given MacArthur what he got and put his hands on his hips, too. When you compared the photographs we used to see of the Emperor on horseback with this, well, it brings tears to your eyes.

"The Emperor's visit to the American Embassy on the morning of September 27th is apparently related to the plan for the wholesale outlawing of the Japanese language."

"I don't want to believe that."

"I suppose whether you believe it or not is up to you. But Mr. Yamanaka, remember that the Japanese Empire banned the native languages in Korea, Taiwan and Manchuria. I think the Americans will do the same to Japan. Oh, that's right—I have another little gift for you. Go to the Metropolitan Police Department at 8:30 this morning. Detective Kobayashi wants to hire you. As a matter of fact, I went to the Metropolitan Police Department and suggested it myself. I think you'll be very pleased with his offer."

I was about to say, "I'd rather have my three-wheel truck than a job," but by that time Kiichiro Aoyama was already out of my house and standing in the middle of the road. He's so quick. As he faced me, he bowed deeply and said, "I hope I can make up for any past offenses with these two presents. My sincere apologies."

It's getting near seven. I'd better get going to the Metropolitan Police Department. There's something I want to say to that Detective Kobayashi, too. By the time I get home, Fumiko and Kinuko should be back.

October 2

I got a job yesterday. I'm working in the Administrative Documentation Section of the Metropolitan Police Department. I'm a contract worker, making mimeograph stencils, for 160 yen a month. To be honest, it's quite a relief. And also yesterday, I had the shock of seeing the Supreme Commander of the Allied Forces General MacArthur, up close and in person. And the even bigger shock of observing my fellow countrymen looking up at him as if he were their dear, loving father. Where did the countrymen so lustily singing "The Song of the Decisive Battle of the Philippines," published in the *Yomiuri Shimbun* last October, disappear to? The next thing I knew, I was standing in front of the Daiichi Seimei Headquarters Building, where MacArthur could surely hear me singing at the top of my lungs:

The dawn of Asia, glowing with victory in the decisive battle
Young cherry blossoms not begrudging their lives
Blooming luxuriously in the Philippines.
Come Nimitz, Come MacArthur;
If you dare show your faces, we'll send you to hell.

The police grabbed me and took me to the Marunouchi Police Station.
Then this evening I learned that while I was away in Yokaichiba
Prison, two or three tragedies befell my family. And so it is that I will
never forget the events of the two days of October 1st and October
2nd, 1945. If there is a decisive moment in my life, it may well be
those two days, so I intend to record what occurred from yesterday
morning in as great detail as I can.

I arrived at the Metropolitan Police Department a little before eight
in the morning. Having a few minutes to spare before the agreed-
upon time, I told the receptionist that I was Shinsuke Yamanaka
from Nezu Miyanaga-cho, that I had an appointment with Special
Higher Police Detective Kobayashi, and that since I was early I'd
be waiting in the sun at Sakuradamon, next door. The view of the
National Diet Building from Sakuradamon was a shock. The area
around the building is razed. There is nothing but a striped pattern
of burned ruins and green trees. There was a constant roar of engines
above and the reflected forms of planes appeared and disappeared in
the soupy green water of the palace moat.

"What are those American planes doing at this hour?" I asked
Detective Kobayashi, who had joined me. This question was by way
of a greeting.

"The U.S. Strategic Bombing Survey Headquarters must be taking
aerial photos."

"What's that?"

"They're gauging the effectiveness of their strategic bombing
during the war. They compare prewar aerial photos with photos of
the ruins. And I'm not Special Higher Police Detective Kobayashi
anymore, by the way," he said very politely. "From September 26th,
I'm Internal Affairs Clerk of the Documentation Section of the
Tokyo Metropolitan Police Commissioner. As a matter of fact, my

last act as Special Higher Police Detective was to call the warden of Yokaichiba Prison on the afternoon of September 25th to pressure him to release you as quickly as possible. So please just wipe your memory clear of any detective named Kobayashi in the Special Higher Police Force."

Kobayashi certainly had balls. This blatant attempt to make me feel grateful for getting me released from prison was outrageous. He and his cronies were the ones who slapped that ridiculous "thought criminal" label on me in the first place and threw me into prison without even a hearing. I certainly didn't owe him anything for getting me out, and he had a lot of nerve suggesting I did. "You're the ones who owe me, buddy," I said to myself, glaring at him. "You could throw yourself at my feet a hundred times and I wouldn't be satisfied."

"It was the fault of the times. That's how things were done then," he said, walking toward the police department building.

He showed me to a three-story wooden structure in the back. There were two doors next to each other. The door on the left was bigger. A newly painted wooden sign hung over it: "First Cavalry Division Military Police Headquarters Military Police Liaison Office Quarters." The door on the right was smaller. The sign hanging over it said: "Tokyo Metropolitan Police Department Documentation Section Annex."

"Up to now this building was the Police Commission Consultation Center, an office that assists with the personal issues of police department employees. It helped with things like building a new house, applying for school loans for their kids, even divorces. There was a company store on the first floor."

"And now American military police is being quartered here?"

"The U.S. forces commit a lot of crimes," said Kobayashi in a low voice, opening the door on the right, revealing a descending staircase. "The U.S. military was having a hard time dealing with the situation, and eventually they realized that sharing information with the Police Department was the most effective way to bring the disorderly conduct under control. On the average, GIs commit forty-five crimes each day in Tokyo, and another twenty or so in Yokohama. The military police were way overextended, so they decided to set up a Military Police Liaison Office within the Tokyo Metropolitan Police. About fifty MPs are quartered upstairs."

There was a glass door at the bottom of the stairway, though there was no glass in the frame. Beyond it was a wooden-floored room about sixteen tatami mats in size. The windows were high up toward the ceiling, so apparently the room was a half-basement. The windows were glass, reinforced with Xs of heavy paper.

"This used to be the dining hall. The kitchen was next door," said Kobayashi, pointing to wall on the right. The wood wall was new. "In fact, it's still the kitchen. The meals for the military police are prepared there."

There were two desks in the middle of the room facing each other, and another desk to the left with a mimeograph machine sitting on it.

"The GIs pull some of the damnedest stunts, too. The other day two of them hijacked a streetcar going from Tsukishima to Tsunohazu in Shinjuku. They boarded at the Hibiya stop, forced the driver off at gunpoint, and raced the streetcar at full speed all the way to Shinjuku."

"Why would they do such a thing?"

"A Jeep was racing along with the streetcar. Apparently they had some kind of a bet, to see which was faster, a streetcar or a Jeep."

"I didn't see anything about this in the morning paper."

"It's not easy to write about things that cast a bad light on the U.S. military," Kobayashi said, as he pulled the string for the light hanging above the desk with the mimeograph machine. "Those are the orders from Emperor Moatside, so that's that."

"Emperor Moatside?"

"Our blue-eyed leader. MacArthur. His orders."

A mimeograph backing board and a mimeograph stylus were on the desk.

"According to the Nezu Miyanaga-cho Neighborhood Association leader, you're a real pro at making mimeographs."

"I used to do that at Daiichi Tokosha on Suzuran-dori Street in Kanda."

"If you were working there, you're obviously first rate." He took a sheet of newsprint—cheap paper made from straw—out of a drawer and handed it to me. "Please make a stencil and mimeograph it by noon. I need one hundred copies. If you do a good job, we'll hire you as a contract employee. Think of this as an employment examination. I know it's rude to give a test like this to a copyist who worked at Daiichi Tokosha, but those are the rules, so I hope you won't be offended."

"You're saying I'm going to be working for the Police Department."

"The salary is 160 yen a month. That is also set by the rules. Do you have a problem being a contract worker for the Police Department?"

"That's not it. I'm just a little concerned about what kind of work it is."

"It's mimeographing. Work starts at seven in the morning. You'll find manuscripts waiting for you on the desk. Most of them will be data and information related to the Allied Command. You'll be mimeographing the information that General Headquarters thinks people in various departments and divisions of the Metropolitan Police Department need to be aware of. I'll come back at noon to check on things. And then you're done."

For a half-day's work, 160 yen isn't bad. In these crazy times when two chickens cost 100 yen, a *kamme* of beef is 200 yen on the black market, and black-market saké is 250 yen a *sho*, and a *to* of new rice is 420 yen delivered, you can't live on 160 yen. But it's a solid job, and it's only in the mornings. If I can find another place to work in the afternoons, we might squeak by. Eventually I hope that I can call on some of my old connections, acquire fan-making materials and start producing flat and folding fans again. The GIs seem to like folding fans. There's a real demand for them as the perfect Japanese souvenir. I can keep working on contract at the Police Department while making preparations to return to my original profession. It's a plan. Looking at the memo in my hands and envisioning how I'd lay it out, I rejoiced at my sudden good fortune. And I said to myself, "Okay, Kobayashi, you owe me a hundred supplications, but because you found me this job, I'll reduce it to fifty."

The sheet of newsprint he gave me bore the heading: "List of Buildings and Facilities to Be Commandeered by the Allied Command." And the list was as follows:

Daiichi Life Insurance Building (General Headquarters)
Norin Building (Economic and Scientific Section)
Hibiya Imperial Insurance Building (Allied Forces Tokyo District Military Police Command, Command Staff Detention Center, Legal Affairs Bureau)
Sanshin Building (71st Communications Division)
Ginza Matsuya (PX)
Hattori Clock Shop (8th Division PX, Economic and Scientific Section)
Shirokiya (PX)
Ogura Building (PX)
Ginza Shokan (Receiver Island)
Kurosawa Building (American Red Cross Chapter)
Tokyo Takarazuka Theater (Allied Forces Ernie Pyle Theater)
Hogakuza (Allied Forces Private Theater)
Imperial Hotel (quarters for Allied Commander, colonels, State Department officials, reparations delegations representatives)
Daiichi Hotel (quarters for the GHQ officers)
Sanno Hotel (U.S. officers' quarters)
Hirakawa-cho Manpei Hotel (quarters for U.S. military captains)
Yaesu Hotel (quarters for male civilian employees)
Marunouchi Hotel (British military personnel quarters)
Seikyudo Building (U.S. military personnel quarters)
Fukoku Life Insurance Building (hotel)
Residence of Prince Kan'in (U.S. military family housing, Jefferson Heights)
Site of the Infantry Air Headquarters/Armory (for the construction of U.S. military personnel housing, Palace Heights)
Kaigyosha (CIC officers' quarters, Mitori Hotel)
Gakushi Kaikan (U.S. Far East Air Force Command officers' quarters)
Shinko Seikatsukan (quarters for U.S. female civilian employees, Hilltop House)
Shufunotomo Company (quarters for U.S. military women)
YMCA (quarters), YWCA (quarters)
Ajinomoto Building ("Continental Hotel")

Tokyo Shoken Torihikijo ("Exchange Hotel")
Nomura Bank ("River View Hotel")
Mitsubishi main building (U.S. Military Post Office, U.S. Military women's troops)
Mitsubishi building No. 10 (U.S. Military Tokyo Supply Corps)
Tokyo Kaikan (quarters, Union Club)
Yurakucho Matsuda Building (quarters for Far East Air Force officers)
Yurakaukan (commissioned officers' quarters)
Akashi Kokumin School (Continental Hotel)
Gunjin Kaikan (officers' quarters, Army Hall)
Kaijo main building (women's quarters)
Kaijo new annex (U.S. Air Force quarters)
Kazoku Kaikan (American officers' quarters, Peers Club)
Seiyukai Honbu (Non-Commissioned Officers' club)
Kahoku Kotsu Building (Allied Forces club)
Ginko Shukaijo (Bankers Club)
Nippon Times Company (*Stars and Stripes* newspaper)
Hoso Kaikan (Civil Information and Education Section and Allied Forces Radio WVTR)
Meiji Seimei Building (Far East Air Headquarters)
Hotei Building (Far East Air Force Offices)
Tokyo Bank (U.S. Navy Headquarters)
Tokyo Kogata Jidosha (Far East Navy Operation and Maintenance Office)
Showa Building (British Commonwealth Forces)
Shisei Kaikan (Civil Censorship Detachment)
Home Ministry (Civil Censorship Detachment)
Finance Ministry (General Headquarters Officers quarters)
Ministry of Agriculture and Forestry (General Headquarters quarters)
Municipal Police Department Liaison Office (Military Police quarters)
Kempeitai Shireibu (441st Counter Intelligence Corps)
Tokyo Central Post Office (Civilian Censorship Detachment Postal Censorship Department)

Tokyo Central Telephone Bureau (Eighth Army International Telephone Exchange/Civilian Censorship Detachment Telephone Interception Department)
Tokyo Central Telegraph Bureau (Eighth Army Information Processing Detachment/Civilian Censorship Detachment Telegraph Department)
Chosen Bank (Statistical Data Section)
Taiwan Ginko (Economic and Scientific Section)
Mitsui main building (Foreign Service)
Nihon Yusen Building (Allied Translation and Interpreters Service)
Mitsubishi Shoji Building (Health and Welfare Section/Natural Resources Section)
Mistubishi building No. 11 (U.S. Army Kanto Civil Affairs Headquarters)
Kokubun Building (Public Health Office)
Gunjin Izoku Kaikan (Chapel Center)
Tokyo Seihyo Factory (Icemaking Supply Facility)
Kan'i Insurance Bureau (Eighth Army Hospital)
Seiroka Hospital (U.S. Army Hospital)
Hibiya Park (Doolittle Baseball Field/Moonlight Garden)
Jingu Gaien Ballpark, Pool and Stadium (Stateside Park)
Kokumin Sports Facility (U.S. Army Sports Club)

The following facilities have not yet been assigned:

Ministry of the Navy
Osaka Building
Toa Dobunkan
Josui Kaikan
Nichifutsu Kaikan
Jiji Tsushinsha
Kanda Police Facility
Yanase Automobile
Naigai Building
Teikoku Theatre Naibu Shidokan
Nihon Kaiin Ekisaikai (Shibakaigan Dori)

Yotsuya Kasumicho YMCA
Tokyo Sixth Corps Barracks (Akasaka)
No. 7 Taiheiei (Aoyama)
Naval Medical Academy (Tsukiji)
Naval Accounting School (Shinagawa)
Prisoners Detention Center (Omori)
Toritsu Tsukiji Hospital
Teikoku Seimei
Matsumoto Ro (Hibiya)
Dainihon Heiki
Fuji Kokuki Company
Showa Aeronautical Company
Kokudo Keikaku Industries
Tachikawa Airplane Factory
Haneda Airport
Tachikawa Airport
Chofu Airport
Tama Airport

I managed to include all of this on a single stencil. I was also very careful in the mimeographing process. When attaching the stencil to the mimeograph frame, an amateur just uses the hooks bordering the frame, but that's not really sufficient. The paper will move, just a little, as you apply pressure with the roller, and the words will be blurred as a result. Even if you manage to avoid blurring, the writing will be too heavy, because the paper moved, and you lose all the flavor of handwritten characters. What I do is melt some of the wax at the edge of the stencil, and then quickly attach the stencil to the frame, using the soft wax as adhesive. Another trick for making the lettering as clear as possible is to mix a little white ink in with the black, and stir it thoroughly—the white ink is my "secret ingredient." I might be able to get white ink at Daiichi Tokosha, but I didn't have the time, so I tried to get the same effect by making sure not to apply too much ink to the roller and moving the roller as steadily as possible. Of course smooth bond paper would take the ink a lot better than the cheap newsprint I was working with, but there was no smooth bond to be found anywhere.

I'd just finished mimeographing seventy copies when Kobayashi returned. Seeing my work, he let out a little gasp of admiration: "I can't believe you managed to fit it all on a single page."

"If I'd made it two pages, we'd have to use twice as much ink and newsprint. That's wasteful."

"I'm grateful. But still, it's amazing how you got it all in there."

"Yes, but it's not too hard to read, is it?"

"It's clearer than printing. I'm sure the section chief will hire you without another word."

"I hope so. But according to this, the Americans are taking over every important place in Tokyo. A chill came over me as I was copying it. It's like Tokyo is no longer Tokyo."

"That's right. All of central Tokyo has become American territory. The only thing they don't want is the burned-out places. And I'm pretty sure this 'America inside Tokyo' will keep expanding. I've heard that all surviving private homes of any reasonable size are going to be requisitioned by the Americans, which means all of Tokyo will be America before you know it. The high-ranking military personnel are bringing their families over from the States, and they'll be living in the residences they requisition. The War-End Central Liaison Bureau is being swamped with requests from the U.S. forces for buildings and personal residences in good condition."

"They've got some nerve. If they knew they were going to need buildings and homes so badly, why'd they bomb the crap out of us the way they did?"

"Shhh." Kobayashi put his finger to his lips and raised his eyes to indicate the ceiling above us. "It's forbidden to criticize the Americans here. There are five second-generation Japanese in the military police who understand every word we say, and support staff from the Translation and Interpretation Division are always walking around, inside and outside the building. You'll be in big trouble if they hear you say anything like that. The staff of the Translation and Interpretation Division is ridiculously good at Japanese, too. They even vary the dialect they speak depending on the day."

"What?"

"Kyoto dialect the day before yesterday, Kumamoto accent yesterday, then Matsuyama dialect today. I'm from Ehime, so that really got to me. I asked the guy where he learned Matsuyama dialect, and he replied by reciting whole pages of Natsume Soseki's *Botchan*. They're absolutely unbelievable. You can't drop your guard for a minute."

"How long is the Occupation going to last?"

"Basically forever, I guess. If you work on that assumption, you won't go wrong. From now on, if you want to get ahead you're going to have to kiss up to the Americans. Hurray for the U.S.A.!"

According to Kobayashi, the basis for assuming that the Occupation would last forever is that the GHQ is planning to rename all of Tokyo's main streets. In fact, the main streets from Ginza to Tsukiji in the east, Tokyo Metropolitan Police Department in the west, Shinbashi in the south, and Tokyo Station in the north had already been given English names, and if you didn't know them, you couldn't communicate with the GIs. Showa Dori is now Dark Avenue. I jotted down some of the other new names that Kobayashi told me about:

Avenue X: Yaesu Dori from the Yaesu exit of Tokyo Station to Reiganjima.

Avenue Y: The road from Babasakimon through Kajibashi, crossing Showa Dori, passing along Echizenbori to the east side of Eitaibashi Bridge.

Stick-up Avenue: Starting at the Daiichi Seimei Building, where the GHQ is located, passing by the north exit of Yurakucho Station, going from Jitsugyo no Nihonsha to Nishi Ginza, crossing Ginza Dori and Showa Dori, passing through Kibiki-cho and Akashi-cho to the ferry to Tsukuda.

St. Luke's Avenue: The street starting at Yomiuri Newspaper Building in Nishi Ginza, passing Toho Seimei and the Okura Building Annex leading into Ginza, along the Matsuya Annex to Higashi Ginza, up to Showa Dori.

Exchange Avenue: The street starting at the Ginza Church in Nishi Ginza, known as the place where Toyohiko Kagawa often sermonized, passing in front of Ginza Florida and the Maruga Soba Shop out to Ginza Dori, alongside the PX at Matsuya into Higashi Ginza, until it runs into Showa Dori.

Avenue Z: The street passing in front of Tokyo Metropolitan Police Department, Hibiya Crossing, Asahi Shimbun Building, Sukiyabashi, Ginza 4-chome, Miharabashi, through Tsukiji, and on to Tsukishima.

St. Peter's Avenue: The street starting at the Imperial Hotel, passing in front of Taimei Kokumin School, the Western clothes store Ichibankan, and running into Ginza Dori.

Embassy Street: The street starting at the American Embassy in Toranomon and passing in front of the Ministry of Education before leading on to Shinbashi Station.

Times Square: The area around Shinbashi Station.

Four Letters Square: The area under the tracks at Yurakucho Station.

Poker Street: The street leading from Sukiyabashi to the Yaesu exit of Tokyo Station.

New Broadway: Ginza Dori.

Avenue A: The street running in front of the Daiichi Seimei Building, where the GHQ is located. Following it south, passing through Tamura-cho Crossing, Shiba, and on to Shinagawa, and to the north, through Marunouchi and Otemachi on to Ochanomizu.

Yes, it looked like the Allied Forces intended to be in Japan for the long haul.

"Do you know which Japanese government agency is the most important?" Kobayashi asked.

I'd just been released from prison in the countryside of Chiba four days ago. I was like Rip Van Winkle. How could I know that?

"I'll tell you. It's the War-End Central Liaison Bureau of the Extra-Ministerial Bureau of the Foreign Ministry. It's the only agency of the Japanese government that has direct contact with the command of the Allied Forces. All the GHQ's requests go through this bureau before they're passed on, and all Japanese government requests go through this bureau before they're communicated to the GHQ. It's like the track switch of a railroad. You've got to know English if you want to work in this bureau—the perfect place to make friends with Americans. Stands to reason these bureaucrats are going to be the ones running Japan some day, and stands to reason they're going to do what's right for America. I tell you, the American Occupation is here to stay."

"You're really thinking far into the future, I see."

"I like to think ahead."

"Too bad you didn't think ahead when it came to the defeat of Imperial Japan. If you had thought that, maybe you wouldn't have had me sent me to prison."

As a scowl came over Kobayashi's face, I finished the hundredth mimeographed sheet. From the room next door came the sound of pots and pans and the aroma of heated lard. My stomach rumbled.

"Let me treat you to lunch," said Kobayashi, knocking on the wall three times. "But in return, keep the sarcasm to yourself from now on." Three knocks came back from the other side of the wall. Kobayashi knocked twice back. The person on the other side knocked once.

"What kind of code is that?"

"The first three knocks is a greeting, kind of like 'Hello.' The next two knocks means 'Two servings, please.' The old guy's last knock means, 'Got it.'"

"The old guy?"

"I brought the former proprietor of the Hongo Bar here to cook for the MPs; his kitchen's on the other side of the wall. You've heard of the Hongo Bar?"

I knew the Hongo Bar very well. It wasn't far from Nezu Miyanaga-cho, and in my mid-twenties I used to go there almost weekly. It was a tiny place, with just three tables and five stools at the counter. But small as it was, it and the famous Ginza restaurant, Rengatei, were the two most popular Western-style restaurants around. Rengatei was the first Western-style restaurant to come up with the idea of serving finely sliced cabbage along with deep-fried breaded pork cutlets. The innovation spread like wildfire, and Western-style restaurants everywhere began serving the cabbage with the cutlets. Only the Hongo Bar served a different side dish—freshly boiled potatoes. You melted a pat of butter on the steaming potatoes and ate them with Akahata sauce. This really went well with the pork cutlets. This was about twenty-five years ago, around 1920.

The Hongo Bar was famous for another thing—its shelf of sauces next to the counter. There was every kind of Worcestershire sauce you could want, from Akahata to Indian, Athena, Hato, Oriental, Mitsukan, Ikari, Tengu, Union, Kikkoman, Shiratama, Haguruma and Toritsu. Plus the proprietor's own special sauce. You could use any sauce you wanted.

Otora-*chan*, the waitress at Hongo Bar, was very popular. She was a real beauty with a light complexion, hair styled in a bun and a meisen-weave kimono with the sleeves tied back. Her arms were graceful and beautiful. I think many of the Hongo Bar's customers went there just to look at her. She had a nice voice, too. She'd say to the cook behind the counter, in a voice as cool and clear as a silver bell, "Three pork cutlets and one order of beef and onions over rice and croquettes." And without a word, the cook would drop the breaded cutlets into the kettle of boiling oil. They had their timing down perfect.

The potatoes were such a popular side dish that the proprietor opened branches in Kanda and Asakusa, but I haven't heard any mention of the Hongo Bar in the last four or five years. I hadn't heard the rumor that it became a restaurant licensed to serve people with ration coupons.

"I see. So that renowned cook is here now."

"In the first weeks of September, I was sort of a 'cook wrangler.' The War-End Central Liaison Bureau came to us and said, 'The

Special Higher Police are good at finding and catching people. Use your skills to round up all the best cooks in Tokyo.' So I went everywhere I could think of—Fugetsudo Mikasa Kaikan, A-1, Printemps, Izumotei, Yashimatei, Chuo Tei, Toyoken, Koyoken, Rengatei... everywhere in Ginza. In Shinjuku I went to Hayakawatei and Nakamuraya. Tawaraya and Beniya in Kagurazaka..."

"And?"

"I came up empty-handed. The cooks had all either evacuated or been killed in air raids, and after ten days I only found two cooks. Then I heard that a whole band of cooks were living in a swampy area out past Abiko, in Chiba Prefecture."

Why were so many cooks living together out there? To sum up Kobayashi's story, a little before the fighting with America began, the authorities established a Greater Tokyo Union of Restaurants and Drinking Establishments. It was the largest union in all Japan, with members from 45,000 businesses. As the war escalated from the China Incident to the Greater East Asian War, food supplies were getting shorter day by day. Aside from the restaurants licensed to serve people with ration coupons and the high-class restaurants, which managed to get foodstuffs one way or another (the high-class places having their own black-market routes), most restaurants were on the verge of going out of business. At that point some big cheese said to the restaurant owners, "You've consumed a lot of our foodstuffs up to now. I think it's time you started actually producing some, to pay for your sins." And so they were formed into a Food Production Increase Patriotic Unit and they set to work reclaiming the land in the Abiko area.

In the Tokyo metropolitan area, they planted potatoes in Koganei, Kinuta and Jindaiji. Abiko is far away. Since it's a nationally sponsored project, the train fare is free, but even so they had to travel by freight train. And after arriving at Abiko Station, they still had to walk another six kilometers. The swampy land they'd been assigned to cultivate was overgrown with reeds. Reeds have deep roots. The restaurant owners gradually began to steer clear of their little patch of swamp. Instead they went to Koganei and Jindaiji, which were closer and where the work was easier, and they sent their cooks to Abiko in their place. Thinking to save the time of the long commute, the cooks took up residence there. They came to like their new home, which had the added benefit of no air raids. They soon came to take on the job of cooking for village gatherings, which pleased the villagers. They became skilled at making unrefined saké, which was another plus. They won the hearts of the local kids by baking cakes and sweets with the ingredients they could find on hand. In time, with the help of the children, they built a pond to raise frogs, which they ate, and the cooks became indispensable members of the local community. The cook on the other side of the wall, the former proprietor of the Hongo Bar, was the leader of these chefs in exile.

"The old man said that he liked living in Abiko, and was planning on spending the rest of his days there; he had no intention of returning to the bombed-out wasteland of Tokyo. He was very stubborn and I had a hard time persuading him. I just kept repeating how badly we needed someone with his talent for the new Japan. It took me five days to get him to change his mind."

"And now he's cooking for the American MPs in Tokyo."

"That's right. The Allied Forces in Tokyo are being fed by our nation's top chefs."

"In addition to taking over our buildings, our public facilities, and our streets, they've taken over our cooks, too."

"That's right."

"I guess Japan really did lose the war."

At just that moment there were three knocks on the wood wall. Kobayashi crouched down to the floor and gently moved the lowermost board aside, took a pack of Hikari cigarettes from his jacket pocket, and shoved them across to the other side.

"There are still six in the pack. I hope that's enough, just for today."

"That's fine," replied a husky voice, as a plate heaped with white rice appeared, covered with sliced meat slathered in thick gravy. Another plate followed.

I never expected to find the Hongo Bar's hayashi rice in a place like this.

My afternoon was busy, as Kobayashi showed me around the headquarters, took me to the head of the Documentation

Section for an interview and had me write out my resume. I didn't leave the Tokyo Metropolitan Police Department until 3:40 in the afternoon. Just as I approached Hibiya Crossing, I noticed a crowd of maybe five or six hundred people. They were standing in front of the Daiichi Seimei Building, which has been requisitioned as the Supreme Command GHQ of the Allied Forces. MPs and Japanese police were also on the scene. Maybe some kind of trouble? The crowd was absolutely silent. Most of them were standing with their hands clasped lightly together in front of them. They were almost disturbingly well-mannered. The mood was almost reverent.

"What are you all doing?" I asked an elderly gent standing at the edge of the crowd, with a derby on his head. Binoculars hung from his neck.

"We're waiting for him."

"Him?"

The man took a step back and looked me over from top to bottom. "General MacArthur, of course," he said.

"Oh, I see."

"You haven't a clue, do you? My guess is that you're not from Tokyo."

"Maybe I'm not. I just landed back here again a few days ago."

"That's what I thought. Well, the fact is, a crowd about this size gathers at the front entrance to the Daichi Seimei Building four times every day."

"Four times a day?"

"At ten in the morning, General MacArthur leaves the American embassy to start work here at the GHQ. At two in the afternoon, he returns to the embassy to eat his lunch. At four in the afternoon, he returns here to work. And at eight at night, he goes back to the American embassy. We gather here to welcome him and see him off on each of those occasions."

"You're really up on it, aren't you?"

"I've been coming here every day since September 18th. September 18th was the day that General MacArthur began working here. If you come here, you can learn a lot of things. For example, the general gets up at eight in the morning."

"Well, he's sixty-five, isn't he? That's kind of late for someone his age, don't you think?"

"Just listen. After he gets up, he plays with his oldest son, Arthur, who is eight. Then he eats breakfast. After he goes home at eight at night, he watches a movie with his wife, whose name is Jean, and his aides. He has a special fondness for westerns. At twelve, after reading from the Bible, he goes to sleep.

"Excuse me for asking, but what do you do?"

"I used to be a barber. Presently, I'm the proprietor of eight barbershops in Tokyo. Though I leave the business up to my daughter and her husband."

"So you're retired. You don't see much of that these days. I envy you."

"I'm not retired. I'm determined to become General MacArthur's barber and work as hard, or twice as hard, as any man."

The elderly gent pushed his binoculars over his shoulder and undid the buttons of his overcoat. He was wearing a jacket with seven or eight pockets that held scissors, combs, razors, and ear cleaners.

"They say that the barber shop beneath Daiichi Seimei Building is going to become the barbershop for the PX soon. They're going to be considering candidates for the position. It's said that only those who've worked as a barber for more than three years at the Imperial Hotel will be eligible, which means I'm qualified, because for five years, from the end of the Taisho into the start of the Showa era, I was a barber at the Imperial Hotel. I gave up the post I've held for a very long time as the head of the Neighborhood Association so I could come here every day and observe the general's hairstyle."

A whistle blew sharply. The mass of people parted, and a black luxury sedan slid silently into the gap. The guards on both sides at the bottom of the three stone steps leading up to the building entrance lifted their rifles and stood at attention. The barber raised his binoculars to his eyes. From the rear seat of the car appeared a military cap stiff as a steep cliff. Decoration made from gold braid was applied to the front of the cap, and beneath that was a long face wearing sunglasses.

"Those are Ray-Ban sunglasses," said the old man knowingly. "Ray-Ban sunglasses were originally made for U.S. pilots, and now they're manufactured by the optics company Bausch & Lomb. They make all the glasses for the U.S. forces. In other words, Bausch &

Lomb are the eyewear contractors for the U.S. military. The eagle made of gold braid on the front of his cap goes very well with the sunglasses, don't you think?"

MacArthur was wearing a dark brown uniform. Just before his well-polished shoes were about to touch the stairway, MacArthur turned back to the people who were applauding. I hate to praise an enemy general, but he was a good-looking man. He resembled a slightly more long-faced Chiezo Kataoka, with a higher bridge to his nose. The area around his left breast pocket glinted in the autumn sunlight. I could make out a single silver star.

"The general hasn't had a haircut for the past five days," said the old man as MacArthur disappeared into the main entrance.

Suddenly, I felt a burning sensation rushing wildly through my veins. Half of it, I think, was anger at how easily people could change their minds. The other half was anger at the insult to the spirits of those who had died at the front or were killed in the air raids. Wasn't it just six weeks ago that everyone was screaming, "Destroy the American and the British devils"? And now this? If people can change so easily, why didn't they change before Kinuko was killed by an incendiary bomb? Or even before that, the day before the massive air raid of March 10th? The hot, burning sensation rose to my throat. All right, if we lost the war, we lost. But those who'd been shouting "Destroy the American and the British devils!" should at least take some responsibility for what they'd done. I wanted them to accept their role as a defeated people with some dignity and integrity. If this old man next to me had the spare time and energy to worry about the haircut of the enemy general, why didn't he do something about the haircuts of the homeless orphans living in Ueno Station? Before I knew it, I was singing: "Come on, Nimitz, MacArthur, show your faces, and we'll send you off to hell..." I was crying out in my heart that, I, at least, don't change so easily.

This morning I was released from the Marunouchi Police Station. It was only because of Kobayashi that I got away with spending the night there. Apparently he had to pull a lot of strings on my behalf. After sleeping until evening collapsed over my desk at the Documentation Section Annex, I felt a little better and went home.

But the story my wife told me during dinner really knocked the wind out of me. I didn't have the energy to lift my pen, so I just crawled into my bed. I got up in the middle of the night and was able to write this much, but I just can't bring myself to set down what I heard from my wife yet. It's too cruel. I'm going to wait a while.

October 3

A band of low pressure moving through the Korean Strait and across the Japan Sea took a sudden turn and headed east-northeast. As a result, since this morning a baby typhoon has settled over Tokyo. It's a very moody child, and after pouring heavily, it suddenly will stop, leaving clear blue skies in its wake. Then just when you think the storm has passed, heavy rain begins to fall again. When I left the house, the skies overhead were blue, so I headed from Nezu Miyanaga-cho toward Ueno Station without an umbrella. When I got out at Yurakucho Station, a light rain had begun to fall. By the time I was at Hibiya Crossing it was pouring, and when I arrived at the Tokyo Metropolitan Police Department I was soaked to the bone. Drying myself off in the Documentation Section Office, I looked out the window and rays of sunshine were streaming brightly down. So I spent the morning being teased mercilessly by the baby typhoon.

But why am I writing about the weather in such detail? When I think about it, it might be because at last the "Today's Weather" column has returned to the newspapers. And the fact that the radio has started announcing the weather again like it did before the war, after the twice-daily news reports at noon and 7 P.M. In the three years and nine months since December 8, 1941, when the weather reports in the newspapers and on the radio were canceled, we Japanese have been trying as much as possible to avoid mentioning the weather. In Nezu Miyanaga-cho, Neighborhood Association leader Aoyama sent out a notice saying, "Even when conversing with friends on the street, please avoid remarks like 'What nice weather today' or 'Too bad it's raining.'" This was the reason: "The walls have ears and the doors have eyes, and you never know where an enemy spy might be lurking. If the spy hears the weather and reports it to enemy headquarters, it will damage the reputation of

Nezu Miyanaga-cho and be a blot on our honor forever." As I think about it now, this doesn't make sense. If a spy wanted to report the weather in Tokyo to enemy headquarters, it would be much faster to simply look up at the sky than to eavesdrop on the conversations of people in the street. But at the time, everyone had completely swallowed the Cabinet Information Agency's warning that "This Is a War of Information," and no one pointed out the gaping hole in the Neighborhood Association leader's logic.

At first, everyone was genuinely perplexed. Deprived of their usual greetings about the weather, neighbors would often find themselves facing each other on the street, hemming and hawing as they searched for something to say. Eventually they overcame this discomfort, learning to use remarks about delayed rations or their plans for evacuating as a kind of casual greeting—information that would certainly have been far more useful than the weather to any spy who might have been listening.

Well, anyway, that's why having the weather report back is so special—even fascinating. Which is why I'm writing about it in such detail. On the radio, in addition to the weather report, NHK's second broadcast channel has been revived. The second channel was canceled the day after the weather report, in other words, on December 9, 1941. Since then, I'd gotten used to there being just the single channel; now that I can suddenly pick between two, it's rather confusing. Tonight's radio presented a particularly tough choice. On the first channel, Chieko Takehisa was reading Hans Christian Andersen's *Picture Book without Pictures*; the second channel was broadcasting Koshiro Matsumoto in the play *The Picture Book Taikoki*. If you listened to one, naturally, you couldn't listen to the other. It was a strange situation, like finding someone else's wallet but losing your own at the same time. Kiyoshi said, "They're both picture books, so what difference does it make?"

A sealed letter was sitting on my desk at the Metropolitan Police Department Documentation Section Annex. A note was attached to it. In thin writing, the note said: "Mr. Shinsuke Yamanaka: Please make a stencil of this letter. Clerk Kobayashi." I put a stencil master on the stencil frame and then saw with surprise what was written on the envelope: "To General MacArthur." There was a stamp on the envelope. To be precise, there were two neatly applied five-sen stamps with the portrait of General Heihachiro Togo. They were clearly canceled with the date "1945-9-25." It was, without a doubt, a letter. But the fact that it was addressed simply with a name made it very odd for a letter. I hesitated for a moment. But when you consider it, General McArthur is the most famous person in Japan right now. You wouldn't really need an address. I turned it over to look at the return address. It said "Kakutaro Tashiro, Okawamura, Nishimatsuura-gun, Saga Prefecture." The regular, blocky handwriting matched the name. The letter read:

Kakutaro Tashiro
September 25, 1945
To General MacArthur,

Greetings:

As a Japanese citizen, I would like to express my sincere appreciation and gratitude for your tireless and energetic efforts since your arrival in administering postwar Japan, as well as your labors to transform Japan into a democratic nation and for world peace. I am a simple country person. As they say, country folk are unschooled in manners. If what I am about to write is rude or offensive in any way, I ask for your pardon in advance. I speak without deceit or pretension. I merely disclose, with utter frankness and straightforwardness, what is on my mind.

On December 8, 1941, when I read the Imperial declaration of war against the United States, I jumped with joy. I cheered "Banzai!" three times in a loud voice. I felt a deep sense of relief and satisfaction. I expressed my emotions in a poem: "We can no longer delay in attacking America and England / if only for the sake / of the One Hundred Million citizens of Greater East Asia."

Ignorant and unschooled as I am, I had no knowledge of the relations between Japan and the United States at the time of the war's outbreak or their international relations prior to that time, and I was only aware of the information that was presented in the Japanese newspapers and on the radio. I believed that the

United States and England were hateful countries, with which Japan could never peacefully coexist. Why? Because they had tried to isolate and alienate Japan from the rest of the world and were truly despicable regimes that wanted to rule the world as they saw fit, and we had to put the fire out before it got started. We had to win the war by whatever means possible, and endure whatever had to be endured to do so. That was what I believed and why I obeyed the orders of the government, whatever they might be. But the war went badly for our nation, and Okinawa, where I believed we would somehow halt the enemy's assault, finally fell. The prime minister, Kantaro Suzuki, said that Kyushu was our turning point, that if we met and fought the enemy at Kyushu we would defeat them. This reassured me. If we succeeded in defending Kyushu, the fatherland would triumph, and so we, the ordinary people of Kyushu, pathetically decided to become soldiers and give our lives for our country. I began to contemplate stabbing my two sweet grandchildren to death, because I was afraid that their pleas to me not to join the fighting would soften my determination.

Then, at last, August 15 arrived. I listened to the Imperial declaration of the end of the Greater East Asia War with unimaginable pain. But later, when the truth surrounding those events was revealed in the newspapers and on the radio, I concluded that Japan's defeat was a foregone conclusion. Moreover, having observed the peaceful fashion in which your nation's forces, in accord with the Potsdam Declaration, have occupied our country as its new rulers, all of my previously held opinions have evaporated like the wind, and I regret my earlier foolishness daily. In particular, I have no words to express my gratitude for the enormous degree of forbearance, transcending all thoughts of revenge, that you have exhibited in the measures you have taken. I have one additional request of you. According to the newspaper, on September 19, the U.S. Senate Committee on Military Affairs considered a call from Georgia Senator Russell for a resolution to inquire into the Japanese Emperor's personal responsibility for the war. I was so shocked by this news that for several days I felt immobilized.

Then, realizing that I must try to do whatever I could to prevent this, I decided to write a letter directly to you.

General MacArthur, the Emperor is a supreme and irreplaceable being. He is higher than a god. He is the focus of our national religion. Though I hesitate to draw any profane comparison, if we are a ship, he is our rudder. If anything should happen to the Emperor, our people would lose all sense of purpose and direction. The Emperor must not be punished. If anything happens to the Emperor, we will lose our will to live. The Emperor's responsibility for the war must not be brought up. In Japan we have the saying, "Plowing the field but forgetting to sow the seeds." The moment the Emperor is held responsible for the war, all of your good governance will be transformed to tyranny. I beg that you will expend every effort to insure that no resolution inquiring into the Emperor's war responsibility will ever come before the Senate again. If public opinion in the United States is so strongly against the Emperor that it cannot be controlled, I wish to be allowed to take his Imperial majesty's place. If you tell me to leap off a skyscraper, I'll gladly do it. If you tell me to jump over Niagara Falls, I'll do it. But in exchange, the Emperor must not be harmed. Please listen to this plea from an old man. In closing, I pray for the success and happiness of you and your country.

It took me about an hour to finish the stencil. As I was holding it up to a window to check whether I had made any errors, Kobayashi walked in.

"You have finished the stencil already? You are such a fast worker, Mr. Yamanaka."

"A professional stencil maker should be able to finish this in thirty minutes," I replied.

"I know your false modesty is just meant to annoy me," said Kobayashi sarcastically.

I ignored him and asked, "Does MacArthur get a lot of letters like this??

"Yes. And the number is growing every day."

"What are they about?"

"Most of them seem to be reports of war criminals. About a third of the letters and postcards sent to the Allied GHQ belong to that category. The next most common are calls for reform of the rationing system and for increased food allotments…"

Kobayashi went on to inform me that the rest of the letters, in order of quantity, expressed gratitude for the elimination of restrictions on the press and other human rights; complaints that, under their former leadership, the Japanese people weren't told the truth; calls to suppress the black market; praise for the fine equipment of the American forces; requests for reform in the educational system; arguments for the necessity of women's suffrage; and advice about the threat posed by the Soviet Union.

"Among them, there are some rather peculiar letters. There was a postcard that said making saké available to everyone should be the top priority, before any other reform. 'The Japanese people are facing a period of tremendous change, the postcard said, and they couldn't be expected to get through it sober.'"

"I understand the feeling," I said, nodding as I applied the roller, which resulted in me smudging one copy.

"A lot of people write saying that they want cigarettes. 'The Japanese people are forced to make do with bad-tasting food, and not enough of it, but a lousy meal can be transformed by a nice smoke afterward.' The writer of one of these letters asked that some of the cigarettes of the Allied Forces be distributed to the Japanese, and he sealed the letter with in blood. Speaking of blood…"

Kobayashi pointed to the letter from Kakutaro Tashiro sitting on the desk and continued, "Did you notice that this letter was written in blood?"

Holding the roller, I looked over toward the desk. The ink was a rust color. These days, most of our ink was of poor quality and changed to a shade of oxidized red soon after it dried, so I hadn't noticed that the letter was, in fact, written in blood.

"What you'd expect from Saga, the land of the samurai spirit. Don't you agree, Mr. Yamanaka?"

"I guess so… But why are letters addressed to the Allied High Commander here at the Metropolitan Police Department Documentation Section? These are classified, aren't they?"

"The Allied High Command has a Translation Section that translates all the letters into English. As soon as they're translated, Emperor Moatside reads them. He likes to read letters that praise him. And in his quest for letters like that, he scans all the letters addressed to him. When he comes across something he thinks is important, he passes it on to us. That's how it works."

"What makes a letter important?"

"First, it praises MacArthur. Second, it has content that can't be ignored. This particular letter praises MacArthur, so it fits the first requirement. The content is a cry to save our Emperor. This, it seems, is something that hasn't appeared in letters up to now. So it fulfills the second requirement. And that's why it gets sent from Horibata over by Hibiya to here at Sakuradamon. We're going to need you to make stencils of letters and postcards like this almost every day, I think."

Kobayashi gently placed the letter from Kakutaro Tashiro inside his jacket. "Treat them carefully. We have to return them to the Supreme Commander for the Allied Powers—SCAP, they call it— the next day. But come to think of it, you haven't said anything about this letter, Mr. Yamanaka. There are still some admirable members of the older generation in Japan, don't you think?"

"I don't know," I said, removing a completed copy from the frame. "We fought our hardest and lost; I think it would be better for us to just lie down and take what's coming to us, like a fish on a chopping board. This may be a strange way of expressing it, but I think we should show some integrity and face the music. To me, this letter seems to be currying favor. The way he flatters MacArthur is astonishing. And to offer yourself in place of the Emperor... well, that's just conceited, don't you think? The Emperor is the Emperor, and I'm sure he has his own idea of what he's prepared to do..."

"You really do sound like a thought criminal after all..." said Kobayashi, his eyes flashing coldly for a second.

As I handed the mimeographed copies over to him, I got my own back. "I wonder if any of the letters arriving at SCAP in Horibata complain about the outrageous methods of members of the former Special Higher Police? It seems to me that there should be plenty."

"Yes, there do seem to be a good number of letters of that sort," said the former Special Higher Police officer with a wry smile, his previous friendly expression returning as he walked out of the room.

That was the only work I had for the day. I had extra time. Should I go to Shinjuku and take a look at the Ozu-gumi Market everyone was talking about? Kiyoshi said that he'd spotted Tonbo Coffee there. I don't know what they're selling it for at black-market prices, but if I emptied out my wallet, I thought I should be able to buy four or five pieces. Tonbo Coffee is a candy that first started to become popular in the 1910s, when I was in my early twenties. It looked like an ordinary sugar cube, but if you examined it closely, it had the image of a dragonfly stamped on it. When you popped it into your mouth and bit into it, the bitter taste of coffee spread throughout your mouth. It was really just a sugar cube with powdered coffee in it. If you put two or three of them in a teacup and poured hot water over them, it turned into a cloudy, dark beverage. It did, in fact, taste like coffee. I liked it a lot, and I always had four or five cubes stashed in my pocket. But then, I think it was in 1914, the confectioner Morinaga came out with their famous milk caramels, gradually driving Tonbo Coffee off the shelves of the candy stores. The price of the caramels—5 sen for a box of ten caramels—was good, but the packaging was the decisive factor. Even adults loved the catchy package design and the fact that the caramels were individually wrapped in paper. On top of that, hordes of imitation caramels popped up on candy store shelves like bamboo shoots after a rainstorm, and Tonbo Coffee disappeared completely.

My next encounter with Tonbo Coffee was in the spring of 1940. I had gone to Yonezawa in Yamagata Prefecture in search of fan-making supplies, and the candy store opposite the place I was staying was selling Tonbo Coffee. Though I had gone to buy bamboo strips, I forgot entirely about the bamboo and came back with five jars of Tonbo Coffee on my back. At first we ate them as snacks, me and the kids, but eventually sugar became very hard to find, and the Tonbo Coffee became our sugar. That's why for a certain time the boiled pumpkin at our house tasted of coffee. So I was thinking of going to Shinjuku to see if I could be reunited with my beloved Tonbo Coffee.

I also had a reason to visit the Imperial Hotel, which was nearby.

Both Fumiko and Takeko have gotten jobs there. And Kayoko Makiguchi and Kumiko Kurokawa, the two young women for whom my wife and I are acting as foster parents, are also waitresses there. I wanted to go visit their boss and pay my respects.

After thinking about it for some time, I decided to do neither. There was somewhere else I needed to go. I didn't want to, but I should go there and join my palms in a gesture of prayer.

I got off the train at Ueno Station and headed down Showa Avenue toward Minami Senju. As I approached the place where the Furusawa Enterprises had been, my legs grew stiff and heavy, as if they were being held to the earth by a magnet.

"There was an air raid on Senju on the evening of August 8th." My wife's solemn voice of the night before once more sounded in my ears. "There were sixty-four B-29s, and they dropped more than 180 incendiary bombs on Senju, Hoya and Nerima."

This was my wife's reply to my question about the absence of Tadao, and whether he had had some kind of falling out with Fumiko.

"One of the bombs made a direct hit on the main building of Furusawa Enterprises. It was a large bomb. The building took a direct hit. Tadao and two employees were in the building. When we got there, there was nothing left."

I couldn't hear what she said after that, because her voice was choked with tears. Hearing what was going on, old Mr. and Mrs. Furusawa came downstairs from the second floor and continued the account in my wife's place.

"Your wife told you this when you returned from the prison in Yokaichiba. She told you that Furusawa Enterprises in Senju had taken a direct hit from an incendiary bomb," said Mrs. Furusawa, gently massaging my sobbing wife's back. "And then she told you that Tadao was away at their retirement place in Yagiri, working at their temporary factory, as I remember. But that was a white lie, because she was so worried about you. You were so debilitated at the time. Not only physically, but you seemed to be on the verge of losing your sanity. You just kept rambling on and on incoherently, as if you were delirious."

"Your wife said to me, 'My husband seems to be on the verge of a mental breakdown.' I told her, 'You can't tell him what happened right now. He could crack.' It was my advice, so if you're going to be angry at anyone, I'm the one you should blame," said Mr. Furusawa, bowing his head. "Kinuko called Tadao to the other world. That's what I think. I know they're both very happy there together now."

I asked him what he meant by that. Mr. and Mrs. Furusawa took turns explaining.

"As you know," started Mr. Furusawa, "August 8th was a Monthly Commemoration of the Imperial Declaration of War Day, the solemn day each month when we remind ourselves of the meaning of this sacred war and reinforce our will to fight. Furusawa Enterprises closes early on the 8th of every month, and the family and employees sit down for a special meal of beef to build up their strength. The idea behind it was that we would make sure we were well-nourished, so that when the time came, we could serve our country with all our might. So we had closed the business at three o'clock that day..."

"And then your wife came by with Fumiko and Takeko..." continued Mrs. Furusawa, picking up the thread of the narrative, which went like this:

Without anyone saying it in so many words, they all decided to pay a visit to Jigenji that evening before dinner. The Urabon Festival of the Dead was near, and while they were at it, they could clean Kinuko's grave. But just when they were about to leave, Tadao said he'd stay home. He was going to be marrying Kinuko's sister right after the observance of the hundredth day anniversary of Kinuko's death. Kinuko wouldn't like it if Tadao visited her grave with her sister. Of course, he was joking about Kinuko being jealous, but he said he just felt it wouldn't be right to visit Kinuko's grave with Fumiko, and he'd go later, by himself, to pay his respects. Everyone agreed that was reasonable, and they departed for Jigenji, leaving Tadao behind. When they arrived at the temple, a warning *kan, kan-kan* sounded. The warning *kan, kan-kan*, and then the air-raid alarm *kan, kan-kan-kan-kan* that had sounded for the last five days, August 4th, 5th, 6th, 7th and now the 8th, but the only actual attack was on August 5th, and that had taken place in Hachioji, so they all ignored the warnings and started weeding the grave plot. After about ten minutes, the *kan, kan-kan-kan-kan* warning sounded clamorously. They took refuge in the Jigenji bomb shelter. The priest's wife served them barley tea, saying they must be bored waiting in the shelter. Someone said, "This area is safe today, I'm sure. Lately the B-29s seem to have their sights set on the area around Hachioji and Tachikawa." Everyone agreed, and they emerged from the shelter. It was 4:15, and time to start preparations for the evening meal. "All right, let's get to work and finish cleaning the grave," said Mrs. Furusawa, when there was an unpleasant whining sound and a thick column of mud rose up from a paddy field about one hundred meters to the east of the graveyard. They only saw it for an instant, for a brilliant flash of light and a huge explosion followed, blinding and deafening them—

"That's when two large bombs fell on Senju. At the same time. We saw one of them. The other one fell directly on Furusawa Enterprises."

"In other words, this is what happened, Shinsuke. To save our lives, Kinuko led us to Jigenji. And she arranged for Tadao to stay behind at Furusawa Enterprises, so he could join her in the other world…"

"Do you see, now, Shinsuke? Now you know what I meant when I said that Kinuko called Tadao to join her in the afterlife. Without a doubt, those two are happy together again."

"If I didn't believe that, it would be just too tragic. I couldn't go on living," added Mrs. Furusawa.

Recalling their words, I stood before the site of the former Furusawa Enterprises. Nothing recognizable remained. Nothing but an eerie hole, thirty meters in diameter and about ten meters deep. Suddenly it began to rain. Heavy ropes of rain mixed with the mud on the slanted sides of the hole and raced to the bottom. Thinking that the baby typhoon had grown into a young man in the half-day that had passed since morning, I stood there in the rain.

October 4
Today there was another sealed envelope on my desk in the Metropolitan Police Department Documentation Section Annex. Unlike the one from yesterday, this one had a very detailed address written on it:

"General McArthur, Former President's Office, 6th Floor, Daiichi Sogokan, Yurakucho, Kojimachi-ku." The office and floor were even included. People are still uncertain how to spell MacArthur, so you see all kinds of variations, like this one. Kiyoshi and his friend Sho insolently call him "Mac." The newspapers use "MacArthur," and radio broadcasts swallow the first "a" somewhat, sounding more like McArthur. I myself have no idea which one was correct.

The sender of the letter was Tokuzo Takagi, at 1-66 Narimune, Suginami-ku. It read:

September 29, 1945

Dear General McArthur,

General. Please forgive my rudeness in sending you this letter in spite of the fact that you don't have the slightest idea who I am. Let me begin by introducing myself. I'm an ordinary citizen. I run a small pharmaceutical company. I have an interesting idea concerning the reports that on September 19, the U.S. Senate Committee on Military Affairs discussed a resolution to inquire into the Japanese Emperor's personal responsibility for the war.

General. I would like to request that you take the Emperor with you to Washington, D.C. With your assistance, the Emperor should do two things while he is there. First, he should sincerely apologize to the U.S. Congress and President Truman. He should apologize for his responsibility for the war and pledge before the Congress that the people of Japan will dedicate themselves to the establishment of world peace. I would like to request that you act as his protector when he is before the Congress, and that you arrange for his flight to the United States.

General. I ask that the Emperor's apology and pledge to the U.S. Congress be broadcast in its entirety, live, to the entire United States and, indeed, the world. And when I imagine the scene of the Emperor and President Truman shaking hands, through your intercession as a go-between, and this moment also being reported live to the whole world, I feel a thrill in my chest. Victors and defeated transcending their former enmity is the first step to true peace. I would like to ask you to play the role of an intermediary in this, and to arrange for the broadcast with the radio stations.

General. On the way back from the United States, I would like to suggest that you and the Emperor visit the countries of Asia. I know that you have toured Asia as an aide to your father. You also fought bravely in many parts of Asia during the last war. For you, traveling through Asia will be a pleasant, nostalgic journey. But for the Emperor, it will be a painful one. He will not enjoy it, since he will be apologizing to all the countries that we harmed during the war. Still, this is necessary. What I would like to request of you, General, is that you comfort the Emperor in the profound distress he is certain to experience on this journey.

General. If the Emperor fulfills all these conditions, who could think of pursuing the matter of the Emperor's war responsibility? In my humble opinion, he should be allowed to quietly live out the rest of his days. Or perhaps he will wish to retreat from the world and take Buddhist orders. As a Buddhist priest, he may wish to visit the surviving family members of the soldiers killed in the war, or the family members of the civilians killed by the incendiary bombs and naval bombardments. In this case I would like to ask that the General do nothing at all. Just leave the Emperor alone. My sole wish, and that of all Japanese, is that the Emperor be left in peace.

Paying my humble respects to the photograph of the Emperor visiting General McArthur,

Tokuzo Takagi

Arriving just when he expected I'd have finished my work, Kobayashi asked me, as he had the previous day, what I thought of the letter. I said I liked it better than the one the day before. Kobayashi said, "It's a ridiculous letter. This guy's crazy, thinking that the Emperor should be sent on such a long journey. He deserves to be punished," he spit out, glaring at the return address on the back of the envelope.

That night, pulling my desk over toward the entryway to write in my diary, I noticed a man with a rucksack over his suit and wearing a military cap looking at me intently. He had a face like a wrinkled eggplant, but with a friendly smile; lightly holding the bill of his cap, he bowed several times. I immediately recognized him as someone I knew from somewhere—somewhere in my past.

"In 1935, I worked at Tamaru Radio Shop in Kanda. My name is Ishii."

At the time I was obsessed with radios. Wanting to assemble a radio on my own, for about three months I was a regular customer at Tamaru, in hot pursuit of radio parts. In the end it proved to be too difficult for me, and I gave up without completing a single set, but Ishii had stuck with me while I was still involved with my project, generously helping me out.

"I remember you. You were always very helpful."

"You do remember me, then! Thank you."

Ishii removed his hat and bowed formally. His hair had gone completely salt-and-pepper. Back in the day, he had a luxuriant head of thick, black hair.

"I have a radio repair shop in Nakoso, Iwaki," he continued, setting his rucksack down on the earthen floor of the entryway. His left arm seemed injured. "During the big air raid on March 9th, the left side of my body was burned. In 1936, I left Tamaru to open my own radio shop by the train stop at Morishita in Fukagawa. Everything I own was destroyed in that big air raid. I'm just barely getting by now, in my wife's hometown."

"You've had it tough."

"No tougher than anyone else. Anyway, sir, would you be able to put me up for one night? I'm in Tokyo to buy radio parts, but Tamaru is full of others just like me, here in the city for the same purpose, and there's no room for me there. I walked from Kanda to Ueno checking the streets for an inn, but there aren't any."

"Yes, that's right. There are no more inns in Tokyo."

"I was planning on spending the night in Ueno Station, but it's a miserable place. The homeless sit there staring at you the whole time. They gather around you and gape."

"They say that every other day someone collapses at Ueno Station. The homeless there don't even have the strength to beg anymore."

"I suddenly felt frightened. And then just as suddenly I remembered that one of the customers who used to come to Tamaru Radio Shop in the old days lived in Nezu Miyanaga-cho, so I crossed over the hill at Ueno and made my way here to find you."

"You were lucky that you came through Ueno while it was still daylight. When it gets dark, there are dogs there."

"Dogs?"

"Packs of wild dogs. Homeless people are often attacked and killed by them. General MacArthur's personal guards, the First Cavalry Division, are supposed to take on the dogs in the near future."

"Is that so?" Ishii used his hat to wipe the perspiration from his face. He inserted his right hand into his rucksack and pulled out a sack of rice, some autumn eggplants, some myoga ginger and some edamame, and set them on the step into the house. "This is my payment for my lodgings. There is a *sho* of rice there. Can I have some rice for my dinner and breakfast and two rice balls for my lunch from it?

"All right," I said. I brought the food that Ishii had taken from his rucksack into the kitchen, where my wife, who was cutting sweet potatoes into cubes, waved to me with the knife and whispered: "I heard what you were saying, but are you sure it's safe? There's a new kind of scam going around. Since there are no inns in Tokyo, a lot of people come looking for places to stay, resorting to the flimsiest connections, just like this man. When people see the rice and vegetables they offer, they decide to become instant inns. But the next morning, their guest has disappeared. Startled, the homeowners search their closets and find that kimonos and other valuables are missing. They say this is happening quite frequently."

"Ishii isn't that kind of person."

"You know him well?"

"Like I said, I met him five or six times ten years ago, at the radio shop in Kanda."

"Is that all?"

"At any rate, I accepted, so I can't go back on my word," I said, and left the kitchen. But perhaps because I was bothered by what my wife had said, I welcomed Ishii into the house with a rather bluff, intimidating voice. Ordinary homes pretending to be inns, and guests who are actually burglars in disguise. Special Higher Police officers masquerading as clerks in a Documentation Section, and our despised enemy MacArthur adopting the guise of our savior. The whole world had turned into some kind of crazy carnival funhouse. Anyway, we'd know if he was a crook by tomorrow morning, so I decided there was no point worrying myself too much about it.

October 5
The number of letters arriving at the Tokyo Metropolitan Police Department Documentation Section Annex from SCAP grew day after day. Today there were ten. The content of the great majority was, much like that of the following postcard, a plea for the Emperor's life:

> His Imperial Majesty is the very life of the people of Japan. If the Emperor were to disappear, the Japanese people themselves would disappear. Please, even if you punish the military leaders and heads of the financial conglomerates who played a major role in the conduct of the war as criminals, I beg that you do not treat the Emperor as a criminal.
>
> —Kenjuro Yoshiwara, Shimogomura, Shimoge-gun,
> Oita Prefecture

About one in five is more like the following:

> Our Great Liberator General MacArthur, please harken to this heartfelt plea of an ordinary citizen. I humbly request that you immediately abolish the crime of lèse-majesté. The Emperor is a human being just like us. He's neither a god nor a monkey. It is completely unacceptable that a mere lapse in form of speech referring to the Emperor, a human being like any other, should be punished as a crime. When it comes down to it, the Emperor is no more than the descendant of the kingpin of a foreign people who invaded our land centuries ago and conquered the indigenous people. It's completely unreasonable that we should be banned from speaking freely about this Emperor. We do not recognize the need to protect the Emperor, who is just another

wealthy individual, with special laws. I believe that we should choose our own leaders freely. Perhaps because we've had Emperor worship pounded into us through the education we received from the days of our youth, we support the Imperial system blindly and without complaint. If this is allowed to persist, wily and unscrupulous individuals are certain to exploit it. Please immediately make known to all the true and unadulterated history of our country and awaken the Japanese people from their delusions. And please make it possible for us all to live as equals. I'm thirty-one and a technician who has graduated from a state technical school. I regret that I never mastered English.

One more thing. In Japanese we have the words "Imperial edict" or "Imperial proclamation." These words should be outlawed immediately. As long as these words exist, there's always the chance that we'll be forced to take part in some future idiocy. I was in the army for three years, and I was harmed hundreds of times by the words "Imperial edict." Though I was innocent of any offense, I was mercilessly beaten in the name of the Emperor and years of my life were wasted. As a result, my youth was spent without any opportunity to make a positive contribution to either my comrades or humanity. I regret this to the point of tears. And in addition, you should get rid of the name of the House of Peers, and the institution it refers to. Am I mistaken in my thinking? If I am, I will readily correct myself, but I won't do that until I hear a convincing argument that persuades me I'm in the wrong.

Ichiro Sato
6 Araijuku, Omori-ku, Tokyo

I didn't like either of these kinds of letters. I can't see why, less than two months after the war is over, anyone should be playing up to the enemy general this way. It makes my skin crawl. If making the stencils weren't my job, I'd throw the stylus away and tear up the letters.

For starters, I hate America. American bombs killed my brother and his wife. They killed my oldest daughter and her husband. My daughter's father- and mother-in-law were also killed by direct hits. I'll never forget my bitterness as long as I live. I'm disgusted at hearing the big boss of those murders referred to as "our great liberator." I'd rather die than ask him for anything. We Japanese should have more backbone. Of course, I know there are millions of people who feel the same way as I do in the places laid waste by the Japanese army—on the Korean Peninsula, the Chinese mainland and the islands of Southeast Asia. Japanese will have to spend the rest of their lives under their hateful glare. If one of them were to say, "I hate the Japanese. The least you can do is let me give you five or six good kicks," we'd have no choice but to let them kick us, without a word of protest. And we Japanese should show some backbone then, too.

As I was making the stencil with the stylus, the former proprietor of the Hongo Bar, who worked next-door making food for the MPs, came over with a half-loaf of fresh-baked bread for me.

"All the MPs are out on duty," he said, "so take your time and enjoy it. I baked it myself." He also brought me some butter. I ate the bread as if I were going to devour the entire world—though I did save half of it, to bring home to the family.

"Are the MPs out because GIs have been causing trouble again?"

"They shot five Japanese to death in Ueno Park. They were drunk, and they wanted to do some shooting practice, I guess. You're from the area, so I'm sure you know, but the homeless are gathered around the statue of Saigo in the park. At dawn this morning, about ten drunken GIs got five homeless men to go with them into the woods, tempting them with the promise of chocolates. They tied the men to trees, blindfolded them, and put apples on their heads."

"Like William Tell?"

"It was some kind of bet."

"That's horrible."

"So now the MPs are out looking for the soldiers who did it. By the way, I happened to hear something from one of the MPs. You might want to think about going back to your original profession as a fan maker, Mr. Yamanaka. The Tokyo Metropolitan Economic Agency is rushing to establish a Souvenir Goods Retailers Association."

According to what the former proprietor of the Hongo Bar heard, the city has decided that they had to make the travel experience of the Allied soldiers and other foreigners who'd be coming to Tokyo more memorable by offering a wide range of fine souvenir items that would appeal to them. They've designated thirty-seven retail outlets for the souvenirs, including Mitsukoshi Department Store in Nihonbashi, Shinjuku and Ginza; Matsuya in Ginza and Asakusa; Matsuzakaya in Ueno and Ginza; Shirokiya in Nihonbashi; Isetan; Takashimaya; Kyugetsu Sohonten at Kuramae; Yamato Shokai in Ginza; Shobido in Kanda; Hattori Clock Shop; Kyobunkan; and Mikimoto in the Imperial Hotel. Further, they'd specified some forty souvenir categories to be offered, including flat and folding fans, traditional parasols, decorative *hagoita* bats, dolls, postcards, reproductions of Japanese woodblock prints and other "exotic" items. But even though they came up with a list, the actual goods were not available. So the Municipal Economic Agency Materials Division has turned to the Allied Forces for help, and is busily requisitioning the necessary raw materials and rounding up the craftsmen to make the products.

"In other words, the city government is going to see to it that the craftsmen are provided with the materials they need. The supplies for making one thousand dolls have already been delivered to Kyugetsu in Kuramae. From now on, any businesses in which the Allied Forces have a hand are certain to hit the jackpot. Why don't you, Mr. Yamanaka, present yourself to the Tokyo Metropolitan Economic Agency as an accomplished fan craftsman? I'd be happy to ask the MP I heard this from if he'd push your application behind the scenes. If you get designated as one of the official manufacturers and start making fans, you'll be sitting pretty in no time."

"Why are you being so kind to me?"

"Well, we're here working under the same roof. Of course, I might have to present the MP with a little gift or something, just to motivate him, if you know what I mean. Not money. Do you have some antique calligraphy or a painting scroll that's been in the family for generations?"

"Are the MPs taking bribes?"

"They're human beings, after all. But this isn't a bribe, it's a thank-you gift. Anyway, the thing they like most of all is women. The best thing would be if you knew some pretty war widow."

I thanked him, but declined categorically. I didn't want any Americans using fans I'd made. I'd rather die than sell them my fans. If they wanted souvenirs, they could have cardboard printed with a map of Japan. They could fan themselves with it, and it would last longer than a fan.

"For a Japanese, you have no ambition," said the former proprietor of the Hongo Bar.

I replied, "No, for a Japanese, I have too much pride." After he left, I regretted sounding so high and mighty.

When I got home and told my wife about this, she was furious with me. Why, she asked, when we have so many free hands here to do the work, did you turn down such a promising offer? Frowning fiercely, she said she simply couldn't understand what I was thinking, moving toward me as she struck the tatami in frustration. I've been with her for twenty-four years, and this is the first time I'd ever heard her speak so angrily. Where has she been hiding this temper all these years?

"You say we have a lot of free hands in the house, but everyone already has a respectable job," I said, looking at my wife in puzzlement. "Fumiko and Takeko, as well as Kayoko Makiguchi and Kumiko Kurokawa are waitresses at the Imperial Hotel. And now that Tomoe from the Yamamoto Saké Brewery is staying with us, she, Tokiko Furusawa and Sen-*chan* are working in the Accounts Department of the Japan Water Company. Those are all perfectly good jobs. I can't ask them to quit to become my assistants making fans."

"I want them to quit their jobs. If they did, we'd have plenty of workers, wouldn't we? Besides, the Imperial Hotel has been taken over by the Americans. Working as a waitress at the Imperial Hotel is playing up to the Americans. If you're so proud of being Japanese, they should quit immediately, shouldn't they?" said my wife.

"You say that because you don't know about the origin of the Imperial Hotel. It was built to be Japan's Official Foreign Guest House. Funds came from the big conglomerates, and the land was provided by the Imperial Household Agency and the Foreign Ministry, too. The idea was to make it like the great hotels in Paris and London and New York. So it's a great honor to work there. Many of the waitresses are well-bred girls from good families, and it's not rare for a girl working there to marry into a wealthy family, either."

"When you start spouting off like that, I have nothing more to say," muttered my wife, and indeed, she said nothing more. I saw tears in her eyes. I sensed that she was concealing something. In the hundred days since I was charged with violating the National Security Act and had been packed off to prison, something had happened in our family. Whatever it was, it had changed my wife. There seemed no point in asking, since her mouth was shut tight as a clam.

The Furusawas are up in their room chanting *nembutsu*, and neither Kiyoshi nor Sho is back yet. The girls are at work. So here I sit alone at my desk in the back room, listening to the rain. Washbasins, buckets, pots and bowls are set out on the tatami to catch the leaks. I was surprised when suddenly the sound of the raindrops falling in the various vessels seemed to be playing the song "If I Go Away to Sea." It made my spirits sink farther. I switched the location of one bowl and a washbasin.

October 6
Today there were fifteen letters from Horibata—actually all fifteen were postcards, so I had finished making my stencils by noon. I decided to go to the Imperial Hotel. This morning, the rain finally stopped; it's been raining for three days. I was so happy to be able to walk the streets without an umbrella that I found myself humming, "The flower of love blooms from a single cup of coffee..." The reason why I was feeling so light-hearted as I walked the several hundred meters from the Police Headquarters to the Imperial Hotel was, I think, because I had hopes of tasting some real coffee. After all, four people living in our house are waitresses there. Surely I'd be able to have a cup of real coffee.

I first began drinking coffee when I was fifteen, in my third year of middle school. That year, 1911, several coffee shops opened— Café Printemps in Hiyoshicho, Kyobashi, Café Lion at the Ginza intersection, and Café Paulista at Sojurocho, Kyobashi. A cup of coffee was 5 sen and a donut another 5. I liked the fact that for just 10 sen you could spend a half-day there without so much as a cross look from the proprietor, and my friends and I used to go there on a daily basis. Café Lion also served liquor and an extensive menu of food, so I wasn't comfortable staying too long there when

I was only spending 10 sen. And the thirty waitresses at Lion were all very pretty. They wore white aprons tied in front, with a pencil tucked into the bow. It was just too stimulating for us middle school students. There was also something rather vulgar about the way the bronze lion statue on the first floor let out a roar each time a hundred glasses of beer were sold.

At the Café Paulista there was an American-made player piano, and the waiters all wore matching uniforms. Their English pronunciation was perfect. When they called out your order, they did it in English, just as if we were in America: "Three coffees and three donuts." The rumor was the waiters got daily lessons from an American pronouncing the numbers one to ten. Someone suggested that maybe they didn't know how to pronounce any number higher than ten, so one day eleven of us went there and each of us ordered a cup of coffee. The waiter said in a thick country accent: "That's the first time customers have ordered so many cups of coffee at once!"

We were merciless: "Where are you from, hayseed?"

"Hanamaji, Iwate," he replied embarrassedly, lapsing into his heavy local accent. We watched as he went to call out our order at the counter. He was shaking as if he was sobbing. I regret what we did to that poor guy.

After I took over the family business and got married, I usually drank coffee in Asakusa. There was a branch of Paulista there, but I used to go to the Hakujuji coffee shop and the Hatoya coffee shop next to the Kinryukan Theater. Hakujuji had very tasty Western-style sweets. The best thing about Hatoya, beside its being cheap— everything was 5 sen—was that you always ran into a famous artist there. I'm sure there were other nice places that I never went to—at that time there were more than two hundred coffee shops in Asakusa alone. Oh, that's right—I used to go to the Los Angeles coffee shop by the ward office, too. Once I saw Jun Takami and Rintaro Takeda choking back tears of emotion as they listened to the record of Debussy's *The Martyrdom of Saint Sebastian*. Kafu Nagai was there that day, too. He was holding court with a group of artists, talking loudly between bites of a sandwich. I wondered if Nagai had a rivalry going on with Takami and Takeda. Anyway I remember sitting there speechless watching all three of them.

Coffee began to taste bad in 1939, just about the time the song, "A Cup of Coffee," by Ko Fujiura and Ryoichi Hattori, became popular. Two years before that, the Imports and Exports Extraordinary Measures Act was passed, and coffee was subjected to import restrictions. From that time on, the only coffee available in Japan was "standard coffee." That was supposed to make it sound like the genuine article, but that was the name given to it by some official in the Agriculture and Forestry Ministry. We called it "substitute coffee." Of all the types of substitute coffee, the stuff made out of lily or tulip bulbs tasted the most like real coffee. Next came banana, sweet potatoes and millet, in that order. Then, quite far down the line, came soybeans from Korea, wax tree fruit, Chinese sicklepod and corn. The worst was pressed soybeans and fava beans. During the war, I drank a foul beverage made from the parched fruit of the lacquer tree, while trying to imagine it was made from real coffee beans. But I wonder why I'm spending so much time writing about things to eat and drink in this diary? It must because the food that's available to us is pitiful.

An MP was standing at the employee's entrance to the Imperial Hotel, talking to a fat foreigner in a suit. Next to the foreigner stood a middle-aged Japanese man wearing glasses and smoking a cigarette. I assumed he was the interpreter for the foreigner and said to him, "I want to see my daughters. Both of them work here. So do two young women who are staying at my house." Of course I also told him who I was. At first he seemed to ignore me, but when I said I worked for the police department and produced my business card, his attitude suddenly changed.

"It's Saturday, and it's almost noon. Employees are off at noon, so let me take you to the employees' waiting room," he said obsequiously. Another smarmy Japanese, I thought, but I kept quiet. He said something to the foreigner in the suit, and then gestured for me to follow him. The fragrant odor of real coffee permeated the corridor, which soon became a stairway leading to the basement level. I stepped down the stairs, deeply inhaling the fragrance of the coffee, filling my whole body with it.

"The fat American in the suit is Joseph Markham Morris," said the man with the glasses. "He's my boss, but he's a hick who knows nothing about the hotel business, so it's not easy working for him."

"Who is this Morris?" I asked.

"The new hotel manager. Actually, he'll be the manager from next month. In preparation, he's scurrying madly around the hotel like a mouse."

"I know the hotel's been requisitioned by the Allies, but it's still Japanese property, isn't it? Japan's official guesthouse. Isn't it strange for it to have an American manager?"

"Maybe, but that's the way it is. General Marshall, the chief of staff of the U.S. Armed Forces in the Far East, established an Internal Committee for the hotel, and from November it will be in charge of operating it. The plan is to run it as a first-class hotel under military rules and regulations. Do you know what Mr. Morris's business was back home? A butcher! I'm not saying there's anything wrong with being a butcher, but you don't want a butcher managing a first-class international hotel. Apparently, back in the States his employees were always stealing meat from him, so all he does here is inspect and inspect."

"Inspect?"

"He searches the employees. He seems to think the employees are stealing sheets and food, and that's all he cares about. He's always stopping employees wherever he runs into them—in the hallways, or in their break rooms—and having them searched. His favorite thing is searching wastebaskets. He's terrified that someone is going to drop something they want to steal in the trash, so they can get it outside the hotel and make off with it. I don't care how bad the food-shortage situation is, this is the world-famous Imperial Hotel. Our employees aren't that sort of people."

"Are you one of the hotel employees?

"My name is Okita. I work in the manager's office."

Three of the walls of the space he led me into were made of new plywood. There was no ceiling. I could hear hammering in the distance.

"A U.S. Army work detail is rebuilding the South Wing that was burned in the bombings. They're also renovating the banquet room. They're rebuilding the things they destroyed. You've got to hand it to them."

"This is underground, isn't it? I think it's directly below the main dining room. I didn't know there was a room below the main dining room."

"It's not a room, actually. It was once a swimming pool. Morris's policy is to convert as many as possible of the employees' common rooms and night watchmen's rooms on the aboveground floors into guest rooms, so he divided up this swimming pool with plywood walls. The Japanese employees are stuffed down here, below ground."

"Was there a pool in the Imperial Hotel? This is the first I've heard of it."

"No one knows about it. It's never been used. It's no surprise that you've never heard of it. Actually, during the Great Kanto Earthquake, the ferroconcrete pillars around the pool took a serious shock, and cracks appeared in the surrounding walls. So the pool never saw the light of day. Please wait here a moment."

The Imperial Hotel didn't have a very good reputation before the Great Kanto Earthquake. For starters, there were rather unsavory rumors about the architect, Frank Lloyd Wright. Some intellectuals said that his work was outdated. An educator complained that Wright was an adulterer, having left his wife and six children to run off to Europe with a widow who was a client of his, and that such an immoral individual should not be allowed to design Japan's premier hotel. Some architects said that Wright had bad karma: After returning from Europe, Wright used money from his mistress to build a new studio, Taliesin, which a servant set on fire two years later, axing people as they tried to escape the flames. Wright wasn't at Taliesin that day, but his mistress was, and she was one of the madman's victims. Supposedly it was Wright's building that had driven this servant mad, and it was unthinkable that Wright should be designing the Imperial Hotel.

But work on the new wing has began anyway. (The main building of the hotel had burned down in 1922, so this new wing later became the main building.) Even so, the new hotel was unpopular. Many people thought it was an embarrassment because, instead of being a respectable six or eight stories tall, it was only three stories tall, with one section four stories tall. Others said that the geometrical designs engraved on the oya stone were sinister. When the hotel was finally completed, there was this announcement in the *Yomiuri Shimbun*, which for some reason I kept. It is dated July 3, 1923:

> The modern hotel, a magnificent structure across from Hibiya Park, is 10,000 *tsubo* in area. The 150 rooms are each equipped with baths and telephones. There are over 400 bedrooms, a banquet room that can accommodate 1,000 guests, a theater with 1,500 seats, a dining room seating 500, five ballrooms, a dozen smaller banquet rooms of various sizes, a roof garden, an indoor pool, a grillroom and a post office. It is completely furnished with all the latest conveniences. Made from ferroconcrete and brick, it is safe and fireproof. The hotel serves Western food, offers Western laundry services, cross ventilation devices and elevators, as well as daily room cleaning service. It is fully electrified.

In the margins of the announcement, I had scribbled in pencil how much things cost: Special rooms with private bath started at 8 yen a night, per guest; breakfast was 2 yen, lunch 3 yen and dinner 4 yen.

The reputation of the Imperial Hotel changed dramatically after the Great Kanto Earthquake. A special opening ceremony for the hotel was scheduled to begin at noon that day, but just as the five hundred important government officials and leading citizens who had been invited were arriving, the earth shook violently. When the earthquake was over, the only buildings still standing in the area were the Imperial Hotel and the Tokyo Station Hotel. All the other first-class hotels—the Seiyokan in Tsukiji, the Grand Hotel and the Oriental Palace Hotel in Yokohama, the Hakone Hotel, the Atami Hotel and the Hakone Fujiya Hotel—either burned down or collapsed. The Imperial Hotel gave out free rice balls to the earthquake victims, as well as offering them refuge—free of charge, naturally.

And that's how the myth of Wright as a great architect was born. The only damage the Imperial Hotel suffered was three broken windows. After the earthquake it stood triumphantly "like an unsinkable battleship." But now I have learned that the earthquake had, in fact, rendered the swimming pool unusable.

Four years ago, I attended the wedding reception for the heir to the Ibasen fan makers, a colleague of mine, at the Imperial Hotel.

Receptions at the Imperial Hotel were conducted in a unique fashion, the guests being led first into the hotel's theater. While waiting for the reception to begin, we were entertained with comic monologues, rakugo, to get us in the proper mood. That was the standard practice there. Top artists performed at these pre-reception entertainments. Musei Tokugawa was there for the Ibasen reception, and he recounted "The Story of the Imperial Hotel," which I found very interesting.

Apparently Wright got the idea for the hotel's foundation from watching a man deliver trays of soba noodles. The ground in the Hibiya area is a soft, alluvial mud the consistency of tofu, and one would have to sink the foundation piles to a considerable depth in order to reach solid ground. It could be done, but it would be prohibitively expensive. Strolling through the Yurakucho neighborhood as he pondered this problem, Wright saw a soba deliveryman cross the street with a tall stack of soba trays balanced skillfully on the outstretched fingers of his right hand. "That's it!" cried the architect, clapping his hands. "I'll sink a giant foundation like the right hand of that man into the mud, and set the hotel on that. The hotel will be like a battleship floating on the sea of mud. If there's an earthquake, the mud will soften the shock of the quake. A floating foundation is the solution to the alluvial mud." This was the story related by Musei (although I've learned it may be questionable).

Then Musei told this story about the hotel manager Tetsuzo Inumaru. There are five ballrooms in the Imperial Hotel. It would have been a waste not to make use of them, so Inumaru held a ball in one of the ballrooms each Saturday night. In May the year after the earthquake, seventeen rightist extremists stormed into one of these balls, wielding swords. They started yelling that the American Congress had passed the Immigration Act of 1924, so if Americans were going to persecute Japanese immigrants to America, then Americans living in Japan should expect the same. American products should be boycotted, and anyone who was dancing with an American was a traitor and was going to be killed on the spot. These balls were immoral and unpatriotic!

Then the rightists began to dance the White Tiger Corps sword dance. Inumaru, who had remained calm while this was happening, ordered the White Russian Imperial Hotel Orchestra to play the Japanese national anthem, *Kimi ga yo*. He shouted to the rightists, caught up in their sword dance, "How disrespectful, dancing when the national anthem is being played! *You* are the traitors!" The rightists snapped to attention and began singing the national anthem. When they'd finished, they gave three ceremonial cheers for the Emperor and exited the ballroom, strangely subdued.

Inumaru also introduced many Western-style innovations to the hotel, including wedding receptions and Christmas parties, the grillroom, and the fine restaurant Prunier. Naturally, he didn't merely import Western customs; he also instituted unique hotel operations that other hotels soon adopted. Adding a ten-percent service charge to the bill was the best known. He eliminated the troublesome practice of tipping, and distributed that ten-percent service charge to the employees as an addition to their salary. Today first-class hotels around the world have adopted this practice, which was originated by Inumaru.

Under Inumaru, the Imperial Hotel became known as one of the top five hotels in the world. For the five or six waitress positions available, there would be a thousand applicants. As far as the qualifications were concerned, inner beauty came first, outer beauty second. But with the hotel's standards so high, there was always a bevy of lovely waitresses waiting to serve guests in the banquet.

"I'm afraid you've made some kind of mistake," said Okita, as he returned to me. "No one by the name of Fumiko Yamanaka, Takeko Yamanaka, Kayoko Makiguchi, or Kumiko Kurokawa is employed at this hotel."

"That's impossible!"

"I checked the employee roster. No one by any of those names is listed there."

"I can't believe that!"

"I also checked with general affairs. They gave me the same answer."

"But all four of them say, 'I'm off to the Imperial Hotel' when they leave the house in the morning. Last night they were on night duty, and they didn't come home."

"What did you really come here looking for?"

"What?"

"Wasn't coming to see your daughters just an excuse to get inside the Imperial Hotel? If you're trying to find something out, you need to follow the proper procedures. Please don't come here again under false pretenses. Mr. Morris is a first lieutenant in the army and an executive member of the hotel's administrative committee and the Allied Forces General Staff Office."

"I need to get out of here," I said.

"I'll be more than happy to escort you to the exit."

I was confused and perplexed. I couldn't understand what was going on with the girls' not being on the Imperial Hotel employee roster, and the encounter with Okita left a funny taste in my mouth. I was standing there when a young woman of rather flashy appearance passed me, and then suddenly stopped. It was Kayoko! At home, she always dresses modestly, but the Kayoko standing before me was extremely … "glamorous," I suppose, is the word. Her lips were red with lipstick, and she was wearing not her cotton trousers, but a dress.

"Mr. Yamanaka, what are you doing here?" she asked in a tone at least three times as coquettish as I'd ever heard from her before. "You surprised me."

"I'm the one who's surprised. You've all been lying to us, haven't you?"

"Huh?"

"Fumiko, Takeko, Kumiko, and you—the four of you. I just left the hotel manager's office, and I was told none of you work here. What are you hiding? Where are you really working? What are Fumiko and Takeko doing?"

"Mr. Yamanaka, please don't speak so loudly," Kayoko said as she waved to the MP at the service entrance. The MP waved back.

"Be careful. We don't want to attract unnecessary attention, do we? This isn't something we can easily talk about here. Let me treat you to a cup of coffee inside."

"But you don't work there."

"As a matter of fact, I *am* an employee. I'll explain it over coffee, Mr. Yamanaka."

The MP nodded to us as we entered through the service door. She must have been an employee after all, I thought, since he didn't question her. Kayoko led me to a third-floor sitting area. Alongside the highly textured wall of oya stone and scratch tile, fancy chairs were set around small tables. There was only one other person there—an American civilian intently reading a book. Kayoko left me, saying she was going to get us coffee, and while I sat there surveying my surroundings, a waiter walked through, calling out "Paging Mr. Galbraith, Mr. Galbraith." The American civilian acknowledged the page, and departed. I guessed someone had come to see him. Kayoko soon returned with two cups of coffee on a brass tray—a rare sight these days. There were four blindingly white cubes of sugar on the tray. As I lifted my cup and inhaled the perfume of real coffee, it was as if the sign on the wall of the Paulista coffee shop in Sojurocho was reflected on the surface of the dark liquid: "Black as a Demon, Hot as Hell, Sweet as Love."

"Fumiko, Takeko and Kumiko are resting," Kayoko began. "It would be mean to wake them, so I'll explain for all of us."

"Huh? Did you say something?"

"Oh, Mr. Yamanaka, I can see you're lost to the world in your cup of coffee! I said that Fumiko and the others are sleeping in the employees' nap room, so I'll explain for them. There are two categories of Japanese who work here at the Imperial Hotel. First, the Imperial Hotel employees, who are the waiters and waitresses and the maids, and all of them wear uniforms—some of which are terribly worn out and shabby, I must say. The Japanese office staff, of course, wear suits. The other category, well, there's a hotel administrative committee that was established by the Americans…"

"I heard about the committee from Mr. Okita."

"Well, then you know. There are a large number of Japanese at the hotel who are employed by the administrative committee. For example, in the kitchen. Right now, the only source of food for the hotel is the U.S. Army Field Ration Section. In other words, the U.S. Army makes the operation of the hotel possible. And the head of the kitchen is an American. So are the kitchen workers. The majority of the Japanese cooks working alongside them are employees of the administrative committee."

"The Americans don't trust the original employees of the Imperial Hotel, then."

"Maybe that's it. I think it might be more that they don't want the hotel staff telling them, 'That's not how we do things at the Imperial Hotel.' As a result, they hired a large number of Japanese who had no previous connection to the Imperial Hotel, and they're transforming it into a hotel that operates the way the Americans prefer. After the South Wing and the Banquet Hall were bombed, the hotel stopped operations and employees had no job, but even if you called all of them back, there wouldn't be enough of them and maybe some wouldn't want to come back. So new employees had to be found. The hotel administrative committee took charge of that task."

"So you're all employed by the committee."

"That's right."

"And what sort of work are you doing?"

"We're companions."

"What's that?"

"You might find it hard to understand, since it's a job that hasn't existed in Japan, but, well, you might think of us as female attendants. Only officers of the rank of colonel or above are allowed to stay at the Imperial Hotel. Even an ordinary colonel won't do; you also need to be head of a department of the GHQ. If you're not, the hotel is off limits. We take care of those important men. We make sure their baths are the right temperature, we shine their shoes, iron their slacks, and show them around Tokyo in their free time. That's our job."

"I see. That's very demanding, I'm sure. But none of you speak English, do you?"

"We can communicate well enough through gestures."

"I see," I said, draining my coffee cup. "I wonder if I couldn't ask you to treat me to a cup of real coffee from time to time. It's one of my favorite things."

"Certainly—although I'd need four or five days' advance notice. But Mr. Yamanaka, please don't say anything about our work to the neighbors. If they know what we do, everyone will be after us to help them get an in with the GHQ."

"I understand. Well, give my best to the other three. Thank you for the coffee."

It was strange, given my anger at the Americans, that I accepted having my daughters work for them with such alacrity. But it was all right with me. Hating the Americans was my duty to the dead, but the girls had their own lives. I had no need to force my feelings on them, nor any need to rearrange my life to match their beliefs. As I walked toward Yurakucho Station, I found myself humming "A Cup of Coffee" again.

October 7
Today is Sunday, and the Tokyo Metropolitan Police Department Documentation Section Annex is closed. I enjoyed sleeping in, and after having sweet-potato porridge, my wife and I aired the tatami. With all the rain lately, the tatami were as soaked as pieces of wheat gluten floating in a bowl of soup. They were so wet that if you could wring them out, water would come gushing out. I have to plug up those leaks in the roof with something, but there is no "something" to be had. The only material I can count on getting my hands on these days is the morning newspaper, but you can't repair holes in the roof with newspaper. So for the foreseeable future, on sunny days, we, like all the residents of Tokyo, have to air out our tatami. And to tell the truth, the newspaper already has a very important use: toilet paper. There is no way we can sacrifice that.

After putting the tatami out to dry, just as I was taking a rest, Neighborhood Association leader Kiichiro Aoyama appeared. "One of my tenants at the Eiwa Apartments was applying to the city for temporary housing, and I went along with him to see how things worked, but it was a real mess. Absolutely hopeless," he said, stepping up onto the wood floor of the workshop. "A staff member of the city's Housing Department working at the Ward Office said that the only things the city can supply are twelve timbers for the framing and twenty boards. You have to roof the place yourself, find your own tatami, but he said there wasn't any shoji paper or window glass anywhere in the city right now."

"At least, the city will send over a carpenter over, right?"
"Yes, the city will send you a carpenter…"
"Well, that's something to be glad for."

"If you want an 'instant carpenter' who doesn't have any experience," and with that Aoyama launched into how the city's Housing Department and the Housing Authority was giving demobilized soldiers a crash fifteen-day course in carpentry. The first class had graduated, and the authorities were now canvassing for places these "instant carpenters" could be put to work. "It's all backward. Rather than needing carpenter to build houses, they're trying to build houses to give carpenters a job. Doesn't make sense—especially when there're so few supplies to begin with."

"So what did your tenant end up doing?"

"He asked the Housing Department official if a house built by 'instant carpenters' would be able to withstand strong winds. The official said they couldn't guarantee that, but if he was worried about it, then he should find a real carpenter on his own. So my tenant ..."

"Gave up?"

"I told him to at least make the application. You can buy the roof framing and the boards at the government-set price, so they're cheap. If the house blows down, you can sell the wood as kindling and you won't lose any money."

"Oh."

While Aoyama was going on, I got the urge to toy with the guy. I figured, after all he did to me, I owed him something back. "I'll bet a shiver must have run down your spine when you heard seven o'clock radio news last night," I said devilishly.

The Neighborhood Association leader looked at me with the startled gaze of a great horned owl.

"You didn't hear? Baron Kijuro Shidehara received the imperial command to form a cabinet. In the next few days, there's going to be a Shidehara cabinet, and of course the count will be prime minister. I'm sure Baron Shidehara remembers how you insulted him."

"I insulted Baron Shidehara? What are you talking about? He's a count and I'm just an ordinary citizen. How could I have ever even met him, much less insulted him?"

"But you have met Baron Shidehara. I was with you."

"When?"

"One year ago."

"Where?

"At Nezu Gongen Shrine. You shouted to him, 'Drop dead, you dirty traitor!'"

The Neighborhood Association leader's eyes now had the nervous glance a sewer rat. But he still didn't seem to remember the incident. So I reminded him: It was at our air-raid drill, and the Neighborhood Association leader was going on about the false rumors going around that the enemy was dropping gold rings and caramels instead of bombs, and that the Japanese government was going to move to Manchuria so that the Japanese mainland would become the final battlefield. The Neighborhood Association leader was lecturing us on our duties as warriors on the home front when an elderly gentleman walked by. He had a large nose and mouth, a graying mustache and round, wire-rimmed glasses that were as big and shiny as glass orbs. He was wearing a felt hat and a suit and walking with a slender cane, which he tapped on the paving stones as he walked.

"The handle on your cane is silver, isn't it?" the Neighborhood Association leader called out to the man, who stopped and smiled.

"Yes, it's silver."

"That's disgraceful. Why haven't you donated it to the government?"

"I made an exception for it. It's a family keepsake. I donated all the rest of my precious metals. So I've done my duty as a subject."

"No, you haven't," shouted the Neighborhood Association leader, stepping down from the orange crate he'd been standing on and walking straight up to the old man. "Holding on to a family keepsake is a sin of spinelessness. You should be ashamed of yourself."

The old man laughed loudly. "Spineless? Well, I guess I'm spineless whatever I do, then."

The Neighborhood Association leader was caught off guard by the "surprise attack" of the man's laughter. He stood there, furious, as Mr. Takahashi from the newspaper's photography department told him quietly: "Mr. Aoyama, please stop. The elderly gentleman is former foreign minister Baron Shidehara."

At that time, Baron Shidehara, had just been hounded out of government for being part of the faction considered to be too friendly to the Americans and the British, denounced as "a mouthpiece for spineless diplomacy." Hearing that this was the disgraced diplomat, the Neighborhood Association spat out venomously, "So you're still alive. I'd have thought that you had long ago been executed by a national hero, for the good of the nation. Why are you wandering around here?"

"I live in Komagome, and I sometimes take a stroll through this area," the baron replied.

"Your hat and your suit are proof enough that you're a traitor. We don't want traitors like you in our neighborhood. Because of you, the Imperial forces are suffering. You should have drowned yourself in Shinobazu Pond the day that war was declared."

"Thank you for your advice," said the baron, touching the brim of the hat and lifting it slightly. "But I'm only halfway through my diplomatic memoirs, and until I'm finished, I won't die, no matter who tries to kill me." As he walked away slowly, the Neighborhood Association leader shouted at his back: "Your memoirs aren't worth feeding to a dog. Drop dead, you dirty traitor!"

Having heard this much, Aoyama spoke up nostalgically, "Yes, I remember that now. I was really fired up then."

It's no easy thing to take revenge on someone like our Neighborhood Association leader, who is so skillful at editing the past.

"Anyway, I came to ask you something today," he continued in a low voice. "A man named Yumitaro Obayashi will be stopping by soon. If you have a free moment, please listen to what he has to say."

"Free time is just about the only thing I have plenty of. What does he want to say to me?

"Please let him tell you that. I will, however, tell you a little about him. He used to be a lumber dealer in Kiba, Fukugawa. He was drafted to work in a military supply factory in Gotanda, and while he was lodged there, his wife and two daughters were killed."

"In the air raids, you mean."

"Yes. They took a direct hit in the air raid on March 10th, Armed Forces Day. You lost your daughter in an air raid, too, didn't you, Mr. Yamanaka?"

"My daughter, and most of her in-laws' family."

"I'm sure you'll get along. Anyway, lend an ear to what he has to say."

"Is he an acquaintance of yours?"

"We sat next to each other at the Taito Ward Elementary School in Asakusabashi." Then the Neighborhood Association leader took something shiny out of his pocket and placed it on the floor. It shone because of the cellophane it was wrapped in. "These are Lucky Strike cigarettes. Smoke them with Obayashi. I smoke this brand because the package looks like the Japanese flag," said the Neighborhood Association leader as he left.

The Neighborhood Association leader's fellow student from elementary school arrived a little before noon. His complexion was as dark as smoked meat, and he was quite tall. He was wearing a brown suit that was deeply faded, making him look exactly like a telephone pole left standing in a bombed-out area.

He introduced himself, then asked for a cup of hot water. "I brought some rice balls," he said, removing a package wrapped in bamboo sheath that contained four rice balls. "Two of these rice balls are for you." Without thinking, I snatched them from him. I gave one to old Mr. and Mrs. Furusawa, and shared the other with my wife. In return, we served Obayashi some sweet-potato porridge.

After we had eaten and were about to light up a couple of Lucky Strikes, Mr. Obayashi suddenly said: "If what I am about to say were to leak out, not only my life, but yours, too, Mr. Yamanaka, would be in danger. So I must begin by asking you to promise not to mention this to anyone." He startled me so that I let my match go out—which was a shame, since matches remain a precious commodity these days.

"Do you hate the air raids, Mr. Yamanaka?"

"Of course… If I had wings, I'd drop bags of excrement over the entire American continent, even if it took me a hundred years."

"Well then, would you be willing to press charges against America?"

This time I broke the matchstick I was using to light my cigarette. His words surprised me so that I struck it with too much force.

"During the recent Great East Asian War, the air raids on Japan clearly violated international law. MacArthur, who calls himself Emperor Moatside, is looking for some excuse to eradicate Japan's leadership class by impeaching them as war criminals, but we can get the jump on them by charging the Americans as brutal monsters who committed crimes against humanity. What do you think?"

"Before what body are you going to charge them?

"The court of international public opinion."

"International public opinion? That seems pretty nebulous to me."

"To be more precise, then, we can charge them before the counties that remained neutral in the last war. Our earnest and righteous plea will spread from those neutral counties to the rest of the world. Eventually, international public opinion will be swayed."

"I'm sorry, but I don't believe that's possible."

"I have faith in international law." His voice was low, but it was intense enough to drive a five-inch nail into concrete.

Concentrating, I was finally able to light a cigarette. It was a real shame, though. In spite of these fine cigarettes, I was so upset that I couldn't even taste them.

"Air raids are supposed to be conducted against military targets—that's the rule as established by international aviation law," he went on. "Military targets are military bases, antennas, air fields, hangars, military factories, military storage facilities, government buildings and offices, rail yards, railways and street car lines."

"Yes, I know that."

"It's forbidden to rain down bombs on anything except such targets. In July 1932, at the Geneva Disarmament Conference, the participants agreed on an absolute ban on air strikes against civilian targets. This was the only achievement of the Geneva Disarmament Conference."

"May I present a counterargument?"

"A counterargument?" It was Mr. Obayashi's turn to break a match. It seemed that it never occurred to him that someone who had suffered so terribly from the air raids would disagree with him. "I don't mind if you offer a counterargument," he said, "but if you are going to say that indiscriminate bombing of civilian targets is acceptable, your deceased daughter will turn over in her grave."

"You've said that only military targets can be attacked and it's prohibited to kill civilians, but isn't that an impossibility in actual practice? Rail yards are of necessity located in densely populated areas. There are no rail yards deep in the mountains, away from all human habitation. This is even truer of government buildings and offices. The Military Supplies Ministry isn't going to be located in the back reaches of the countryside, where it's three *ri* to the nearest barber and five *ri* to the fish market. So let's say that military pilots follow international law and only drop their bombs on military targets. But what happens if a breeze should blow at that moment? Carried by the wind, the bomb will miss its intended target and explode over the heads of civilians. Who could blame the pilots in such a case? The military pilots are following international law. But you can't put the wind at that time in the defendant's chair at an international tribunal. With foot soldiers, this rule about military targets can be observed, but when it comes to air raids, is it really possible?"

"On August 15 and 16, 1863, Admiral Kuper of the Royal British Navy led seven ships in an attack on Kagoshima," Mr. Obayashi responded, once again starting down a strange path. "In those two days, the British ships launched 350 shots. They were all aimed at Japanese artillery guns installed on the shores of Kagoshima Bay. But when Admiral Kuper returned in glory to his homeland, he was summoned before Parliament. He had also fired on the town of Kagoshima, it turned out, and Parliament tried to impeach Admiral Kuper, because the town of Kagoshima was a civilian target, and shelling it violated the laws and customs that civilized nations should observe during wartime."

"What happened?"

"There were repeated inquiries, which hundreds of witnesses testified at. The result was this: The ships commanded by Admiral Kuper were firing at the Satsuma domain armaments under conditions of high waves and strong winds. Given those conditions, precise aim was impossible, and it was unavoidable that a small number of the British shells should overshoot their targets and land in populated civilian areas. Moreover, the houses of the Satsuma domain were made of paper and bamboo, and as a result were highly flammable."

"A convenient decision for the British."

"You could say that. But the important thing is that Parliament's inquiries recognized that in wartime it is only acceptable to aim at military targets, and if civilian targets were unavoidably also hit, it wasn't the fault of the gunners. It's important because the decision in this case regarding Admiral Kuper later became the fundamental principle of international artillery battle law."

"But we're talking about air raids, not artillery battles."

"Still, as a result of the Kuper incident, the principle of restricting attacks to military targets was reinforced and from there adopted as the guiding principle for air raids as well, becoming a rule of international law. Mr. Yamanaka, the air raids that America launched against the Imperial realm of Japan completely flouted this principle. The atomic weapons dropped on Hiroshima and Nagasaki are the clearest examples. These massive and incredibly destructive bombs inflicted first- and second-degree burns on everyone within a four-kilometer radius; where on earth is there any military base with a radius of four kilometers located within a city? Could any government buildings, rail yards or factories occupying an area with a radius of four kilometers be located within a city? The answer is no. In other words, these atomic weapons by their very nature, flout the principle of restricting attacks to military targets. In the face of those weapons, the distinction between military targets and civilian targets is annihilated. Yes, those monstrous weapons are a fundamental challenge to international law. And the carpet bombing that Americans inflicted on Tokyo is identical in principal to an atomic weapon."

"All right. You've persuaded me a little." I struck a match and lit a cigarette.

"Good. Would you be interested in coming to Atago Shrine in Ojima, Joto Ward, at eight in the evening the day after tomorrow?" asked Mr. Obayashi, rising. "A large number of people like you should be there." And with those words he disappeared from the workroom like the wind. Seventeen Lucky Strikes were left. Enough to last me for a week.

October 8

My work mimeographing at the Police Department Documentation Section Annex is going smoothly. I've gotten much faster with the stylus. I think I must be one and one-half times faster than I was at the start. It's not that I've gotten more skillful. It's really due to the backing board of the mimeograph machine. It's like new, and the grooves are very deep. You can write very quickly and easily. Also there's a bottle of benzene at the annex. When the grooves start to fill up with wax, the benzene cleans them out nicely. When I think of that, I can write even faster.

But though my efficiency has risen, I still finish my work at about the same time each day, around noon. The amount of work has increased. Up to now, most of my time has been spent making mimeographs of letters that Japanese sent to General MacArthur, lent to the police headquarters for a single day by the GHQ in Horibata. But from the latter half of last week, I've also been making stencils of handouts with the title "Occupation Forces Security Reports." For example, today I had three of them:

At about 2 P.M., yesterday, Sunday October 7, while jinrikisha operator Yoshikichi Konno (age 52) was cleaning his jinrikisha adjacent to Namiyoke Shrine in Odawaramachi, Kyobashi Ward, two U.S. military men with brass major insignia assaulted him and took his jinrikisha. The two U.S. officers, taking turns pulling each other, headed for the Imperial Hotel, and left the jinrikisha there at about 2:30 P.M.

After 3 P.M., on October 7, while housewife Hatsue Saito (age 42) of Kojimacho, Asakusa Ward, was removing laundry from a pole where it had been drying under the eaves of her home, three solders rode up in a Jeep and stole the red underwear belonging to Hatsue and her daughter Yuko (age 21), tied it around their heads, and drove off cheering and squealing.

At 4 P.M., on October 7, witnesses reported that three U.S. soldiers in a Jeep grabbed two young women at the Akasaka Mitsuke intersection, tossed them in their Jeep, and drove off toward Ichigaya. According to some witnesses, the screams of the two young women soon changed to coquettish laughter.

When printing these "Occupation Forces Security Reports," I had to call Document Clerk Kobayashi. He was concerned that Shinsuke Yamanaka would take copies of these reports out of the office. I had to print fifty copies of them. When I asked who read them, he replied, while stamping each of the copies with "Confidential" in red, "The top leadership of each ministry, and the top leadership of the War-End Central Liaison Bureau. And of course the top leaders of the Police Department."

"And do these criminal acts get investigated?"

"We have no choice but to leave that up to the blue helmets." "Blue helmets" was police slang for the American MPs. "The best we can do is dangle these printouts in front of their noses and gently suggest that they consider looking into them."

At about noon I looked up and saw blue sky above my head for the first time in a long time. Following its invitation, I went to Ginza. Ginza Dori had been somewhat cleaned up. The depressing mood there right after the air raids, when it was singed and smoldering, was gone. It was filled with people selling things. An old man in a suit was selling dolls for Girls' Day. An old woman had a samurai helmet laid out on a cloth and was sitting, waiting for a buyer. A man with a national civilian uniform cap was there with three bonsai trees, and a woman was selling a brightly colored wedding kimono. They were all hoping to attract a buyer from among the U.S. military personnel flooding the Ginza. I couldn't imagine that anyone would be interested in the old advertisement posters for wine and saké, but in fact, they were selling well. I was surprised to see ten posters sold in the blink of an eye. Apparently the soldiers are drawn to the girls on the posters, which will probably be tacked up on the walls of their barracks that very night.

An American nurse walked up briskly, tossed a half-smoked cigarette onto the ground, and stopped before a young man selling a saké flask and cups. Her jacket and slacks were almost identical to a male officer's. A major's insignia sparkled on her right collar. You could tell she was an army nurse because of the Red Cross insignia on her left collar. She bought one saké flask and a sake-serving ladle for three packs of cigarettes. Maybe she was planning to use them as flower vases. After she left, a middle-aged man leaped over with lightning speed and picked up the cigarette butt she had discarded.

Soldiers were gathered in front of the Hattori Clock Shop at the Ginza 4-chome intersection, which had become the PX for the Eighth Army. Two young Japanese women, dressed like office workers, walked past the soldiers, holding hands. Another young woman, who might have been a coworker of the first two, stopped in front of the soldiers, looking hesitant, as if afraid to walk past them on her own. The GIs called out something, and then one of them beckoned her to come sit in the space beside him. The two young women holding hands embraced each other, aghast. "How awful!" they screamed, "What shall we do?" Yet at the same time they sidled closer to the soldiers. It seemed very clear that they had wanted the soldiers to call out to them all along. Several soldiers advanced slowly toward the two girls, holding out chocolates and cigarettes. One of them must have said something, for suddenly there was an explosion of laughter. The small crowd of Japanese observing this from a short distance—and I was one of them— also laughed, not having any idea why the GIs were laughing, but somehow being caught up in the mood. The girl who was alone, with the hesitant expression, looked at the two happily squealing young women enviously.

Yet just two months ago this sight would have been unimaginable. I no longer understood the Japanese people, myself included.

In the area from Sukiyabashi to Yurakucho, several groups of students were selling mimeographed printouts to passersby. They were booklets teaching English conversation. I bought one being sold by Keio students to see what it was like. On one side was printed:

Gumonin.
Haiyu.
Sankusu.
Wayugoin.
Tosuku.
Shiyuafunun.

On the other side was the expression in actual English:

Good morning.
How are you?
Thanks.
Where are you going?

To school.
See you afternoon.

Then this explanation:

With this system, if you want to start learning English right
now and don't want to do it through reading, you can do it by
listening. Just read the katakana over and over. Find a friend and
try reading it together. As you repeat it again and again, your
tongue will get used to pronouncing English. You don't need
to be embarrassed that you can't write English.

Uekiapu.
Wataimu izutona?
Itsu nain
Remi suripu mō
No—
Esu
Noo!
Izu torein ausai?
Fuain!
Zen aisuripu.
Wai?
Bikozu aimusuripi.
Za bīn suppu getenkoru.
Ōraiōrai.
Gumonin ma.
Gumonin pa.
Gumonin to nekisudoa.
Gumonin to horutaun

The conversation above is written in English as follows:

Wake up.
What time is it now?
It's nine.
Let me sleep more!

No.
Yes.
No!
Is it rain outside?
Fine!
Then, I will sleep.
Why?
Because I'm sleepy.
The bean soup getting cold.
All right, all right.
Good morning Ma.
Good morning Pa.
Good morning to next door.
Good morning to whole town.

How are you doing? Have you gotten accustomed to English pronunciation? When your tongue is moving freely, we'll teach you to say whatever you want in English. Next time we'll study a daytime conversation. Please come to the same place next week. We'll be selling the daytime conversation text. If you have any questions about the present installment, feel free to ask them at that time.

Keio University English Conversation Study Group Streetcorner Promotion Unit

I don't know if 1 yen a sheet for this stuff is expensive or cheap, but at any rate, it was selling very well. But again I couldn't help thinking: Who would ever have imagined this just two months ago? Mimeographed English conversation handouts selling like hotcakes? Is this 180 degree turn really all right? I just don't know.

That night the rain fell mournfully. I went over to the block group leader Takahashi's house for our regular meeting. The only thing on the agenda was surrendering guns and swords. MacArthur's headquarters had ordered that any family possessing guns or swords immediately hand them over. Igarashi, the dentist, said: "We've already turned anything like that in long ago. And if anyone was still hiding any, the way things are now, they'd have been traded in for food before now."

We nodded in agreement, and in just a few short minutes the meeting was over. After that we sipped weak tea and let the flowers of gossip blossom. I told Takahashi what I had seen that day in Ginza, and wondered aloud why things had changed so dramatically, and whether that was right.

"They may seem to have changed, but that's just on the surface," Takahashi said.

This response took me by surprise.

"For example, look at the members of the Shidehara cabinet. We still have a war minister and a navy minister, just like before—Sadamu Shimomura is the War Minister and the Navy Minister is Mitsumura Yonai. Though the Imperial army and navy have been disbanded, the real foundation hasn't changed in the least. And take the release of thought criminals. The ruling ideology of the nation was completely discredited when we were defeated, so we Japanese should have released all thought criminals on our own at the moment we surrendered. That would have been the right and natural thing to do. But their release was only decided four days ago. And they were only released at the command of the Supreme Commander for the Allied Powers. Nothing has changed. We don't want to change anything. A force stronger than we are, the Allied Powers, has appeared, so we just obediently follow their wishes. As long as the Allied Powers don't ask us to change something, we have no intention of changing it. We bow down to those who are more powerful than us. That's all it is, in my opinion."

As I sat there silently, not fully grasping Mr. Takahashi's meaning, Gen the tailor said in a consoling tone: "It's different for your family, Mr. Yamanaka. You're unique. That's why you think that the world has changed so much."

I didn't understand. "What do mean, we're different?"

Startled, Gen said: "If you don't think you're different, that's fine."

"I don't like that," I persisted. "What's so different about us?"

Suddenly the usually very mild-mannered Takahashi announced: "The regular meeting of the block group is over. It's raining hard now. Please take care on your way home."

At home I told my wife what had transpired at the meeting. "What happened in our family while I was packed away at the Yokaichiba Prison?" I asked. "It must be something, from the strange thing Gen said and Takahashi's odd attitude. Tell me the truth."

"Nothing happened," said my wife evenly. "We just tried to find a way to keep from starving to death. Do you want an omelet for a snack tonight?" Cradling the can of dried egg powder in her arms as if it were a precious treasure, she went into the kitchen. Twenty-four years of living together should not be underestimated. When you've been side by side for twenty-four years, you know at a glance when someone is trying to hide something. I'd find out what it was. Maybe she'd gotten heavily involved in the black market and been caught by the Economic Police? By the time the fried eggs were done, the sound of the rain had lessened, and in its place, somewhere crickets were chirping.

October 9
It rained all day today. Atago Shrine in Ojima, Joto Ward, was a shabby shrine, and the roof of the shrine office leaked. Until just recently—in other words, during the war—Shinto shrines enjoyed unstinting government support, and it was rare to see one in such poor shape. Ten people had gathered for the meeting, all middle-aged men. Yumitaro Ohashi opened by saying, "I appreciate you coming in spite of the rain. I'd like to start by proposing a name for this group: 'Association to Demand Compensation from the United States for their Sadistic and Indiscriminate Bombing, including the Use of Atomic Weapons.' Does anyone have any objections?"

Since Kinuko and the majority of the Furusawa family were deprived of their lives by U.S. bombings, I believe I can say that I'm second to none in hating America. But America won the war, and it is the leader of the Allied Powers presently occupying Japan. They have the guns. It seems reckless, to say the least, to make any demands for compensation; at best, they'd just dismiss them. At worst... I pressed my hands down on my chest to suppress the palpitations.

"I lost my family while I was in Tokyo for work. My wife, my oldest daughter and her two children—four family members—

were killed with a single stroke when the bomb was dropped on Hiroshima," said a man wearing a black felt hat, beneath which a head of graying hair peeked out. "That's why I was invited to this meeting, but is there really any chance of achieving anything?"

"If there wasn't, I wouldn't have approached you all."

"I teach Japanese literature at Hiroshima Teacher's College, and I don't know much about international law, but can we really sue the United States government?"

"I think there is a way to do it."

"We're just a gathering of private individuals. No matter how far we press it, in the end, what can we do? Does international law recognize the rights of private individuals? Aside from where they are especially recognized in treaties, it's my understanding that under international law, it's only nations that have rights."

"And so we need to involve the Japanese government in our case. I believe we need to force our government to sue the United States government for compensation."

"Oh yes, our government..." said the teacher from Hiroshima with a low laugh. "It would be great if our government had the courage to do that."

"We may have been defeated, but we're still a nation, aren't we? And though August 15th stands between them, the nation before that day and the nation after that day are the same nation."

"Yes, I guess so. Though it's a defeated nation, it's still a nation. It still exists."

"If that's the case, this carries weight," said Obayashi, pulling a newspaper clipping from the pocket of his faded brown suit. "This is a protest from the Imperial government to the U.S. government published on the front page of Tokyo's *Asahi Shimbun* on August 11th. I'm sure you've all read it already, but I believe it's very important, so I would like to read it aloud."

I hadn't read the August 11th paper. I couldn't, because I was in prison at the time, so I listened intently.

On August 6, U.S. warplanes dropped a new kind of bomb on the city of Hiroshima, killing a large number of residents immediately and utterly annihilating the majority of the city.

Hiroshima did not possess any special military defenses or facilities, and was just an ordinary regional city. It had no special nature as a military target, and U.S. President Truman's statement that the attack was aimed at destroying factories producing port and shipping facilities and at disrupting transportation networks notwithstanding, given that the bomb was dropped from a parachute and exploded in the air, it is clear that the Americans were fully aware that the bomb would wreak destruction over a vast area, making it impossible to target specific facilities, as the president claimed. And with regard to the actual destruction caused by the bomb, it affected an extensive area, and in the aforementioned area it killed indiscriminately, taking the lives of combatants and noncombatants alike, of both sexes and all ages, who were mercilessly exterminated by the powerful blast and extreme radiant heat produced by the explosion. Not only was the area affected completely and powerfully annihilated but the injuries inflicted on the individuals within that area were of a degree and cruelty heretofore unseen. The fundamental principles of international law regarding warfare restrict the choice of methods of warfare even in attacks on enemy combatants, and prohibit the deployment of weapons, projectiles, or other materials that cause unnecessary pain and suffering. In the treaties and protocols concerning the regulations for land combat, this is specifically outlined in Articles 22 and 23. The United States has repeatedly since the start of this war emphasized that the deployment of inhumane weapons and methods of combat are regarded as unacceptable by the peoples of civilized nations, and has declared that it would not employ such inhumane methods and weaponry as long as its opponents similarly agreed to forgo them. But the bomb employed by the Americans on this occasion, because of its indiscriminate and brutal destructive powers, far exceeds the destructiveness of poison gas and other outlawed weapons. The United States has chosen to ignore international law and the fundamental principles of human decency, and through indiscriminate air attacks on numerous cities of the Japanese Empire has killed innumerable civilians of both sexes and all ages, and burned shrines and temples, schools, hospitals and homes. This new attack, in which a weapon of unprecedented force, a bomb of incredible and indiscriminate destructive power such has never been seen before has been employed, is a new crime against humanity. The government of the Empire of Japan, speaking for itself as well as for all humanity and civilization, impeaches the government of the United States and solemnly calls upon it to immediately cease and desist the deployment of this inhumane weapon.

As I listened to Obayashi read this, for some reason I was reminded of the favorite story of old Shinsuke who lived in the tenement house in Hama-cho, a property my father used to own. I don't know how it came about, but most of our renters were stagehands at the Kabuki Theater, and old Shinsuke was a prop master. His one claim to fame was that when he was young he was a favorite of the legendary Kikugoro V. Whenever he brought the rent over, he would tell the same story as he drank a cup of my father's saké until his eyes turned red.

"In *The Firemen's Fight*, there's a scene when Kikugoro V, playing Tatsugoro, the leader of the firemen, returns to the stage along the hanamichi runway and sits down beside a hibachi at stage left. Kikugoro was incredibly particular about the precise placement of the cushion that was set in front of the hibachi. If it wasn't in exactly the right spot, he used to chew us prop managers out. He'd say: 'It was an inch too far to the right today,' or 'Today it was a half-inch too far to the rear.' A lot of truly great actors are like that. Of course there are plenty of quite mediocre ones who just pretend to be first rate and make all sorts of unreasonable demands, too. I decided to put Kikugoro V to a test, to see if he really deserved his reputation for greatness. One day, I measured the exact placement of the cushion with a ruler and marked it with ink before placing it precisely where it belonged. My plan was that if Kikugoro still fussed over it, I would know that he was merely complaining to complain and I would be able to snicker behind his back that he's a phony. I'd show him the marks on the stage floor and say, 'I put it exactly where you asked, as you can see; is this wrong, too?' exposing his hypocrisy. When the curtain went down that day, he came up to me and said,

'The cushion was in exactly the right spot. Please put it in the same place every day. I was able to give a fine performance and I'm feeling good. I'd like to treat you all to some saké.' That's what they mean when they talk about being on your mark on stage. From that time on, I observed Kikugoro's performances more carefully, and he was always right on his mark. For example, in one play he had to slide up beside another actor, look him in the face, react with surprise, and fall back, placing both his hands on his knees as if bowing in respect. When he fell back, he always landed squarely on the low seat where he had been sitting before he slid up to the other actor. Though he never looked back to check on the seat's location, and without relying on the stage assistants to move the seat so he would hit his target, he always landed his rear end right back on that seat. It was like he had eyes in his ass. But to get back to my original story, when Kikugoro took us to the promised restaurant, he suddenly said: 'Shall I offer you, as an appetizer to go along with our saké, a little amusement by reading the menu for you? Reading it straight would be dull, so I'll tell you what: I'll make you cry. All right? Now, of course there's no one here beside me, but just imagine a girl sitting here. I'm her father. I'm going to sell her into prostitution in Yoshiwara. I'm begging her to accept this terrible hardship so that we can afford medicine for her mother, who is gravely ill, and tuition for her younger brother. I'll read the menu in that tone. Prepare yourselves, because I'm going to have you bawling your eyes out.' Art has a frightening power. He read the menu hanging on the wall from right to left, with just the right intonation, and his voice was that of a grief-stricken father trying to persuade his beloved daughter to accept a hard fate. How I wept!"

Just as old Shinsuke wept as Kikugoro V read the menu, I wept as Obayashi read the Japanese government's protest aloud. Kikugoro transformed the ordinary words of a menu into a tragic and heartrending speech through the power of his art, but Obayashi, through his anger and grief at the loss of his wife and two daughters in the indiscriminate attack, transformed the stiffly formal government protest into a living, breathing eulogy. And nothing could have prevented his audience, all of whom had lost loved ones in air raids, from weeping. No one spoke for a time; we were all busy dabbing at our eyes with handkerchiefs. Finally the professor at Hiroshima Teacher's College removed his felt hat and said to Obayashi: "I'd like to apologize for my earlier skepticism. I agree that we should try our best, as you suggest, to make the Japanese government do something about this. But given the nature of this matter..." he said, pausing before continuing in a quiet voice, which caused us to come in closer to him, forming a small circle around him so as not to miss what he said, "it's critical that no information about our group be leaked to the outside. Just think what might happen if the GHQ at Horibata got wind of it. We'd be snatched up and sent off to Guam or Saipan. We'd spend the rest of our days doing forced labor. To avoid that, we need to make our preparations in the strictest secrecy."

He was right. We all nodded in agreement. "We need to be especially vigilant that we all remain loyal to the cause. Secrets are spilled by turncoats. Yes, that's it..." The professor pulled a sheet of newsprint from his bag and began to write fluidly with a thick fountain pen. "Since our first meeting is being held at the offices of a shrine, let's write a sacred oath. Everyone can sign it and pledge their loyalty."

Obayashi read the oath first and said, impressed, "Just what you'd expect from a professor of Japanese literature." The sheet of paper was passed around for all of us to read:

With the establishment of this Association to Demand Compensation from the United States for their Sadistic and Indiscriminate Bombing, including the Use of Atomic Weapons, we submit this oath to Atago Shrine, Ojima, Joto Ward.

Fifty-five days after the defeat of our nation, life is slowly revisiting the mountains and rivers. But the flowers will not bloom again, and the streams have flowed into the ocean and will not return. We do not know where our loved ones are, but hear only their voices raised in melancholy lamentation. Do not weep, our kindred spirits, do not weep, our comrades. Listen to the plan of those who are late in following you in death, and your myriad sufferings will be extinguished. We vow to strike terror in the heart of the American government, so that you, the departed spirits, may rest in peace.

October 9, 1945

We borrowed the professor's fountain pen and signed our names. Then we placed the oath before the shrine's altar and prostrated ourselves repeatedly. If anyone was disloyal after signing this, they would be terrible cowards and shameless villains who had betrayed both the gods and their comrades. After deciding to meet on the fifteenth of every month, we disbanded.

I traveled with the college professor from Kameido to Akihabara. He was staying in the home of his wife's family in Wakabacho, Yotsuya, which had survived the air raids.

The Sobu Line heading toward Tokyo was astonishingly empty. All the seats were taken, but there were only fourteen or fifteen riders standing in each car, the first time I'd seen a train this empty in years. At Kinshicho, three young men wearing students' caps got on and began to speak to those in the car:

"The GHQ will be outlawing the use of the Japanese language in the near future."

"English is going to replace Japanese as the language of daily life."

"I'm sure that some of you will say that can't be possible, that no one can learn to use English so suddenly."

"That's perfectly reasonable, but with the right method, English is surprisingly easy to master."

"Here's a highly effective textbook for fluency in English. You've got nothing to lose by giving this here *Lectures for Completely Mastering English Quickly* a try."

"You'll be amazed at how easy it is."

"It's mimeographed, but it has thirty-six pages and a cover. We'll sell it to you at cost, only 15 yen."

"Numbers are limited, however. We're forced to limit our sales to five to a car."

"The Japanese language may soon be outlawed, after all."

The students easily sold seven or eight copies and then got off the train at Ryogoku Station.

"Our Neighborhood Association leader has said General MacArthur is going to declare a complete ban on the Japanese language. Is English going to become our new national language?" I asked the college professor.

"It's not impossible," he replied. "Until just recently, Japanese national policy was to make Japanese the international language. It wouldn't be at all strange if America were considering doing the same thing for English. In particular, we tried to establish Japanese as the common language of the Greater East Asian Prosperity Sphere. We put a lot of effort into making Japanese the national language of Singapore, Malaysia, the Philippines and the Korean Peninsula. It seems instinctual for the victors to try to force the vanquished to adopt their language. To tell the truth, I was previously deployed in Seoul, where I taught at the state-run Seoul Law School. I read *The Tale of the Heike* with the students for an hour each week. The Korean language was banned from all textbooks. The order from the governor-general's office went something like: 'The people of the Korean Peninsula, in order to strengthen their awareness as loyal subjects of the Japanese Emperor, and to express that awareness in every aspect of their lives, must all learn the national language and use it in their daily lives...'"

"What happened if anyone used Korean?"

"When a middle school student was caught using Korean by a teacher, he was placed on indefinite suspension for the first offense, and was expelled for the second offense."

"That's very strict."

"Ordinary citizens were forced to repeat the 'Pledge of Subjects of the Japanese Empire' thirty times."

"The Pledge of Subjects of the Japanese Empire..." I had heard of that somewhere.

"'One, We are subjects of the Japanese Empire, and we pledge our loyalty to our great country. Two, as subjects of the Japanese Empire, we pledge mutual cooperation and strong solidarity. Three, as subjects of the Japanese Empire, we will foster endurance and self-reliance and promote the Imperial way.' This was the pledge for students in middle school and above, and for the citizenry in general. Of course the pledge was written in Japanese. There was also a version for elementary school students. It went, 'One, we are subjects of the great empire of Japan. Two, we will work together to demonstrate our loyalty to His Majesty the Emperor of Japan. Three, we will persevere and train ourselves to become fine, strong subjects.' The governor-general of Korea made people repeat this pledge everywhere. At schools, of course, but also at government offices, companies, movie theaters, banks, factories, department stores, and anywhere else people gathered you could hear voices repeating the pledge. Now we Japanese may be forced to sing 'God Bless America.'"

"*Goddo* what?"

"America's favorite national song. '*Goddo buresu amerika, rando zatto ai rabu, sutando bisaido haa, ando gaido haa...*'"

I didn't have a chance to hear the lyrics to America's favorite national song to the end because the train pulled into Akihabara Station. I walked from Ueno Station to Nezu in the rain, the words repeating in my brain: "What goes around comes around, what goes around comes around, and now it's Japan's turn..."

October 10

When I had finished mimeographing the letters from Japanese people to General MacArthur lent to the police headquarters by the Horibata GHQ and the "Occupation Forces Security Reports" and had handed them over to Kobayashi, a middle-aged man appeared in the doorway and said, "Hello. It's been a while. Clerk Kobayashi from the Documentation Section told me you were here and showed me the way."

I recognized the voice—it was Kyoichi Eguchi from the office staff of Nippon Soda Company. He had asked me to deliver some goods to the company president's vacation house in Yokokawa on the Nakasendo Highway in early June.

"Mr. Kobayashi's very considerate."

"You wouldn't know it by looking at him, but he used to be a fearsome detective for the Special Higher Police. But how did you discover that I worked here?"

"I stopped by your home in Nezu, and your wife told me that if I had urgent business with you I should come here."

"So what is this urgent business?"

"Yes. Couldn't we talk about it outside?"

"Not before noon. I don't know what it is you want to discuss, but can't we do it here?"

"I'd rather not." Eguchi came closer and whispered, "Actually, it's about a black-market deal."

"I'm not a police officer, and next door is a kitchen, where the cook is busy preparing lunch and doesn't have time to eavesdrop on us. Upstairs is the barracks for the American MPs, and our voices won't carry that far. So you can relax. What is it you wanted to talk to me about?

"You have a three-wheel truck, don't you?

"It was confiscated."

Eguchi let out a sigh.

"But I still have a fair amount of gasoline left."

"That's great. As long as that's the case, we should be able to work something out. If, Mr. Yamanaka, I was able to get my hands on a three-wheel truck, would I be able to prevail upon you for some gasoline and your driving skills? Perhaps you know that there was a naval fuel storage depot at the Kanazawa Bunko Museum in Yokohama. In the hill behind the depot, there's a half-built storage facility for firewood and charcoal, and seven bales of rice are hidden there. I want to go and get them. I'll give you two bales for your trouble. How about it?"

I stood there flummoxed for a moment. A bale of rice sold for 1,500 yen on the black market. Two bales would bring me 3,000 yen. That much money for a trip to Yokohama was unbelievable. It was a godsend, an incredible stroke of good fortune. My monthly salary for a half-day's work right now was less than 200 yen, which meant that in one round trip I could make half a year's wages. It would have been ridiculous to refuse. But at the same time, it seemed too good to be true.

"Those rice bales are navy property, aren't they? Is it all right to take them?" I asked.

"There is no navy any more. So now they don't belong to anyone," said Eguchi evenly.

"But maybe someone else has already discovered them?"

"There's no need to worry about that. Nakagawa sealed up the storage facility with a wall of earth, so that you can't see the entrance at a glance. But someone who knows what to look for can see it right away."

"Who is Nakagawa?"

"A naval officer from my home village. He was the person in charge of building the storage facility."

"I'm having a hard time understanding the situation."

"Nakagawa was ordered to build this storage facility in mid-July. He got fifty middle school students from Yokohama assigned to him, and they dug a tunnel in the hill behind the fuel storage depot. But before they could get very far, the war ended. And the next day, the newspapers were carrying the Tripartite Agreement, the Potsdam Declaration, issued by the United States, Great Britain and China in the newspapers. As a result, the staff at the navy fuel storage facilities fell into utter confusion."

"Why?"

"Didn't you read the Tripartite Agreement?"

"At the time I was in a prison in the countryside in Chiba; we didn't have any newspapers to read. You remember when I delivered the goods for the president of your company? Two days later I was arrested for violating the National Security Act. I was completely innocent, but it didn't matter."

"I see."

"I was released on the 27th of last month—not yet two weeks ago. I still feel out of touch with what's going on." So much so that, it occurs to me now that as I was leaving the prison, the warden said to me: "Our Fatherland has been defeated by the Allied Forces of the United States, the United Kingdom, the Soviet Union and China. We have surrendered unconditionally. Engrave that on your heart and rehabilitate yourself completely."

I had replied sarcastically, "I think it's going to be very difficult for someone who hasn't committed any crime to rehabilitate himself." And I remember thinking at the time, "Just what you'd expect of the Japanese Empire—unconditional surrender." But I was confused what that meant. The warden cleared that up: "Unconditional surrender doesn't mean that the victor doesn't attach any conditions for the vanquished, it's the opposite. The vanquished agrees to do whatever the victor says, without any conditions."

That's how out of touch I was with the events surrounding August 15th. Nor am I alone, since on the train from Yokaichiba to Chiba, several of the passengers thought unconditional surrender was a wonderful thing because we wouldn't have to pay any reparations.

Political terms really are hard to understand.

"Well, at the end of the Tripartite Agreement," Eguchi continued, "it says—and when they read this, the military officers and enlisted men were all suddenly transformed into common thieves—that after the Japanese military has laid down its arms, each man is to return to his home and find a way to lead a peaceful and productive life. 'We're disarming! We're going home!' The military facilities were all suddenly a hive of activity. One navy pilot petty officer in particular was busy. In his seaplane he was flying to Gunma one day, to Shizuoka the next day."

"What for?"

"His superior officers were from Gunma and Shizuoka. So at a landmark in Gunma, the pilot drop packages of rice, sugar, clothing—by parachutes. Then he'd do the same thing at a landmark in Shizuoka."

"I see."

"It goes without saying that he didn't forget to drop a few parachutes over his own home in Saitama."

"That's terrible."

"This pilot petty officer is small potatoes. A lieutenant at the naval fuel depot commissioned three trucks to make a delivery to his home in Chiba. That Nakagawa I mentioned drove one of the trucks, and then used it to drive on to his home in Hachinohe. The trucks belonged to the naval fuel depot. Naturally, Nakagawa's truck wasn't empty. He carried ten drums of gasoline with him. Today he's one of the leading players in the black market in Hachinohe. Yesterday I received a special delivery letter from him." Eguchi pulled an envelope out of his pocket and showed me the letter. The heading read: "Naval Fuel Storage Facility." Mr. Eguchi's young friend had not only stolen a truck and gasoline.

Greetings. I'm glad to hear that you are well. Excuse me for broaching this so suddenly, but I have some information that I wonder if you'd be willing to buy from me for 3,000 yen. There is an excavation for a tunnel to store charcoal and firewood in the hill behind the Naval Fuel Storage Facility at the Kanazawa Bunko Museum. I hid seven bales of rice in the tunnel and left it there when I returned home, and I am too busy with my business to go and get it. There are three pine trees growing on the hill, and the tunnel is directly below the roots of the pine on the right. I filled the entrance with earth, so you'll need to look carefully. I propose to give you this information in exchange for 3,000 yen. That's cheap, but I feel I owe you a favor. Please stop by when you're back in town. I can let you watch movies for free. Actually, I built a movie theater. Only the first three rows have chairs; the rest is earthen-floored. I can fit any number of customers in. I had the Naval Fuel Storage Facility sell me the projector that was in the auditorium.

Best regards

The part about buying the projector was extremely suspicious. No doubt he just walked off with that, too. The fact is that our Imperial army is nothing more than a gang of thieves. It's depressing.

Eguchi returned the envelope to his pocket and laughed. "Visit the black market. Aside from the food, take a close look at everything else for sale—the clothing, shoes, sugar, biscuits, leather belts, light bulbs. They've almost all been stolen from military supplies and dumped on the black market. The pots and kettles and lunch boxes and dishes are all made from duralumin and aluminum that planes are made of. These materials were embezzled and channeled into the black market. All the supplies that the military bought during the war under the fancy moniker of 'military necessities' were filched by officers and enlisted men and can now be found on the black market. And those goods are what is sustaining our lives now."

"But they're all so high priced."

"Yes, that's true. However, Mr. Yamanaka, no matter how expensive they might be, if they're indispensable to our survival, we have to find some way of purchasing them. And those expensive but indispensable products are piled up on wooden shutters people take down from their houses to make an instant black market stall. We should be thankful. During the war, we couldn't purchase anything unless we had special connections. But now we don't need connections. All we have to do is go to the black market, where they're waiting for us. Isn't that great? Of course it makes you angry when high-ranking officers and giant military supply factories are moving huge quantities of goods in the darkness or trading them between each other. But when it's low-ranking officials and ordinary soldiers selling off no more than the amount they can carry away in their own two hands, and that amount finds its way into our open-air markets, I think that's to our advantage. I don't think it's such a bad thing." Eguchi's words rang with conviction, which was only natural, it seemed to me, since he was about to join the ranks of the black-market merchants.

"Do you know, Mr. Yamanaka, how many Japanese are presently out of work? Since I work in the general affairs department of my company, I pay attention to this sort of thing. More than ten million people are presently unemployed. More precisely, the figure is from twelve to thirteen million. Since the population of the nation is eighty million, and twelve or thirteen million are out of work, it's a truly desperate situation."

All of the demobilized soldiers automatically joined the ranks of the unemployed. Some seven million Japanese soldiers streamed back to Japan from overseas. Almost none of them have work. The factories producing military necessities have shut down. The only factories still in operation are producing foodstuffs, pharmaceuticals, electrical appliances and farm equipment, but raw materials are in short supply, so even they are going out of business or cutting down on the number of employees. The widespread unemployment was common knowledge, but the actual figures left me dumbfounded. I had no idea the number was so high.

"Still, all these unemployed people are somehow getting by. How do you think they're doing it? The fact is, many have found their way into the black market. In other words..."

"They're black marketers..."

"That's right. Without the black market, Japan would be really black. Anyway, when I'm able to arrange for a three-wheeled truck for you, I'll let you know."

"All right."

"Maybe the day after tomorrow."

"I'm free every afternoon. But you probably can't do it unless it's a Sunday, am I right, Mr. Eguchi?"

"The absentee rate at companies in Tokyo is over thirty percent," he replied, once again producing figures. "The day after pay day, the absentee rate rises to over fifty percent. Why do you think that is?

" . . . "

"There's just one reason. Everyone takes off work to look for food. Or to put it another way, looking for food is always a reason for taking off work. Well, see you in a few days."

"One question first, please. Why did you decide to ask me to help you go get this rice? Nippon Soda Company is a big company. There must be plenty of people you could ask to do this with you."

"I'm fed up with trying to deal with the people here. When I asked you for help last time, you did a good job. I remembered that. I'm counting on you," said Eguchi, politely lowering his head.

After dinner, when I told my wife about this, she wasn't as pleased as I had imagined she'd be. In fact, she said, rather indifferently, "I'd rather you didn't do anything dangerous."

"We've been in the red for a long time, haven't we? You've probably been selling your kimono to make ends meet. The money from this little job will last us for months."

"I actually don't know if we're in the red," replied my wife. "I haven't been keeping a household account lately." Then she excused herself to go to Kiyoshi, who'd come home from school at noon with a stomachache. He was in his room groaning. When my wife rubbed his stomach, the groaning stopped.

Normally, I would have exploded and say how dare she talk to me like that, but I didn't want to involve Kiyoshi, so I quieted my anger and began to write in my diary.

Still, my wife's attitude is very strange. Twelve people are living in our house. There are two separate household accounts actually, one being for the corner house group, with seven women: Sen-

chan, Tomoe (the widow of the proprietor of the Yamamoto Saké Brewery in Toride), Tokiko Furusawa, Kayoko Makiguchi, Kumiko Kurokawa and my daughters Fumiko and Takeko. All are employed, so they can manage without going into the red.

It's this household that's in trouble. Of the five of us—old Mr. and Mrs. Furusawa, Kiyoshi, who is a student at Municipal Fifth Middle School, and my wife and I—I am the only one with a job. And I've just started working; I haven't received any salary yet. We have to be in the red. So why is my wife so unconcerned? Did she have some kind of Aladdin's lamp hidden in her dresser drawer?

October 11

Last night, while I was writing in my diary, Kiyoshi's stomachache worsened, so I put down my pen, carried him to the cart and pulled him to Juntendo Hospital. The young doctor's diagnosis was acute appendicitis. His appendix was inflamed. Unsure of the next step, my wife and I agreed that she would stay at the hospital and I would go back home. As I was using the toilet in front of the office, the doctor who had diagnosed Kiyoshi walked in.

"He'll need surgery, won't he?" I asked.

"We'll try as much as possible to flush it out first."

"What do you think caused it?"

"Well, it looks like *Montag* appendicitis to me."

"What's that?"

"Monday appendicitis. German doctors call it that as a joke. Since Sunday is a day off, people tend to overindulge—to eat and drink too much. They suffer the aftereffects on the next day, and they get an inflamed appendix on Monday. Overexertion and overeating can cause appendicitis."

He must be a quack, I thought, glaring at him. How could anyone be overeating these days? But I decided not to ask any further questions.

At noon today I went directly from the Tokyo Metropolitan Police Department to Juntendo. My wife was asleep in a chair in front of Kiyoshi's room. Awakening her, I asked, "How is he? Is the surgery over?"

She shook her head. "The doctor said he's trying to flush it out."

"Is it working?"

"No, he says."

"It doesn't make any sense. If they can't control the infection, they need to operate."

"The doctor says he'd like to operate, but…"

"I don't understand."

"They don't have any fuel, he says. So they can't sterilize things. You need a lot of boiling water to perform surgery, it seems. The surgical equipment, surgical gowns, the bandages and gauze, the sheets—you need to boil a lot of water to sterilize them. But they don't have any coal."

"So what's going to happen to Kiyoshi's appendix?"

"He says it looks like they're going to get a coal delivery on Monday. The strategy is do everything they can to try to control the infection up to then."

"Is that a strategy?"

"Juntendo is one of the more fortunate hospitals. Tokyo Imperial University Hospital doesn't even serve food to its patients. They were tearing down the old wooden buildings on the hospital grounds and using them for fuel, but they've used them all up and they don't have anything left to burn." Her exhaustion seemed to affect her usual reserve, and my wife was talking up a storm. "It turns out Kiyoshi did overeat. The day before yesterday, he and Sho Takahashi went over to the Imperial Hotel to see Fumiko and the others, he told me. They brought him into the employees dining hall, where he stuffed himself to the gills with the Americans' leftovers."

"I see. So it was *Montag* after all. I guess I'm glad there are no quacks at Juntendo."

My wife seemed very tired, so I sent her home, telling her to send Fumiko or Takeko around later with some lunch and my diary. I waited until near evening, and finally Tomoe appeared.

"Fumiko and Takeko are on night duty again."

"Oh. Thank you." I found it difficult to talk to Tomoe, but I eventually became even more uncomfortable with the silence, so I started making innocuous small talk: "How is your job? Are you used to it by now?"

276

"I find myself thinking about my children several times a day, and it makes me sad. Aside from that, it's fine."

Her two children were in Onahama, with her brother's family. She sent 100 yen a month for their care. Her late husband's father was in a mental hospital in Ichikawa. She was paying for that, too, so things could not be easy for her.

"You seem to spend many nights at work. Is it very busy?"

"Yes, it's dizzying."

"Do you get paid extra for working at night?"

"Yes, very generously."

"Well, then it's worth it."

"Yes, yes, I suppose so."

"Why don't you bring your children here? I know the Furusawas would be pleased. They'd treat them as if they were their own grandchildren. My wife loves children too, so please, feel free."

"I can't," said Tomoe, stiffening into stone. "I can't possibly do that." She backed away. I guess one shouldn't mention Tomoe's children to her. It makes me feel bad. I wanted to chase after her and apologize, but just at that moment Kiyoshi started groaning and instead of following Tomoe I rushed to the nurse's station.

October 12

Mr. Eguchi from Nippon Soda Company arrived at the Documentation Section Annex an hour ahead of the agreed-upon time. I couldn't let him wait in the annex, because, at least officially, my work of cutting stencils and mimeographing security reports concerning the Occupation Forces is top secret. Promising to meet him at noon in front of the Home Ministry, I had him leave. He immediately returned and asked, "You have the gasoline, don't you?" I tapped the two one-*sho* cans I had sitting under the desk and assured him that I had three liters.

Most of the reports for the day were about selling cigarettes on the black market. There's been a rash of cases of Occupation officers and enlisted men selling cigarettes to Japanese in the back alleys of the Ginza. They sell cigarettes because they wanted money, and as soon as they get their hands on any money, they're off to the nearest Special Comfort Facility.

The GHQ authorities have said that they will severely punish the illegal activities of their officers and enlisted men. We, as the Japanese police, must also investigate and charge with equal rigor the Japanese who try to purchase the cigarettes.

A comment to this effect appeared at the end of the list of incidents. The following rather strange report was among those I mimeographed:

At 3 P.M. on October 11 (Thursday), a GHQ/SCAP Civil Information & Education Section officer, accompanied by a Japanese-American interpreter, appeared at Sensoji in Asakusa and ordered that the temple be dismantled. When the astonished temple administrators asked why, they were told that the officer had heard the interpreter translate Sensoji as "War Temple," and angrily decided that this was an inexcusable expression of militarism. After purchasing a fortune at the temple office, he left before 4 P.M.

A short while after noon, I was driving a three-wheeled truck from the Home Ministry toward Yokohama. For the first time in a while, the weather was clear and the skies were blue. And today's reward would be two bales of rice. Before I noticed it, I was humming to myself. Mr. Eguchi, hanging on next to the driver's seat, said in a happy voice: "This will get my family through the winter." He told me that there were seven at his house, their daily ration was just two bowls of rice, and the rations were often ten or even twenty days late. So they managed by buying three or four *kan* of sweet potatoes on the black market each month. In the morning they had sweet potato rice, followed by sweet potato lunch, and in the evening a small bowl of rice gruel with sweet potatoes. This was the menu in the Eguchi house lately. It seemed pretty good to me.

"These days in Tokyo, I don't think there are that many families that have three meals a day."

"My oldest daughter is an office worker at the Daiei Film Studio," said Eguchi, "and she contributes her entire salary to the household, which helps a great deal. And my wife doesn't seem to mind selling her kimonos, which also comes in handy."

"I envy her working for Daiei. She must be able to watch as many movies as she wants."

"I guess she's too busy to do that. She's responsible for scouting new acting talent, and as many as two hundred people apply for an audition every day. Most of them are soldiers returning from overseas or men and women who used to do factory work, she says. One applicant was a former army officer who filled in his application in blood. At the end he wrote: 'If you don't hire me, I will be so humiliated as a man that I request you destroy my enclosed resume and photograph.'"

As we chatted on about this and that, we crossed Rokugobashi Bridge and entered Kawasaki. We drove through an expanse of collapsed walls and rubble spread out over charred earth. Here and there were leafless trees and steel frames twisted into strange shapes.

"My daughter says that a disproportionate number of the female applicants are former employees of Kanagawa Prefecture. She's already seen fifteen or sixteen. Daiei thought this was odd and found it was connected to Japan's defeat. On August 16th, a department chief at the prefectural headquarters declared that they should evacuate all their female employees."

"There were those rumors that the occupying soldiers were certain to rape all our women—was that it?"

"Yes. The department head had fought at the front lines in southern China, and he insisted that from his own personal experience the invading soldiers were going to violate the women of the occupied territory. Kanagawa Prefecture Governor Hisao Fujiwara gave all female employees of the prefectural government three months' severance pay and forced them to resign, telling them he hoped they would all start a new life in the countryside, away from where the occupying soldiers are stationed. 'Please fiercely guard your chastity as pure Japanese maidens,' he said. But while people watched fearfully as the soldiers of the Occupation Forces arrived in the country, most of them turned out to be very gentlemanly. They weren't the barbarians that they were rumored to be. And the former Kanagawa Prefectural government employees began to crawl out from their hiding places."

"And some of them applied for jobs as actresses?"

"That's right. In fact, Kanagawa Prefecture is a very strange place. Have you heard the story about the monument to Admiral Perry in Uraga?"

"No, what's that?"

"Toward the end of the war, the leader of a men's division of the Imperial Rule Assistance Association in Yokosuka burst into the office of Governor Fujiwara, angrily demanding to know why the monument was allowed to remain standing. 'Perry was a lawless American admiral who forced Japan to open up to the rest of the world. Why are we commemorating his landing in our country?' The governor agreed and asked the Yokosuka Imperial Rule Assistance Association men's division to tear down the monument. Then he had a new monument put up with the words 'Monument to Rouse the Spirit of the People' in the calligraphy of Soho Tokutomi. But then the war ended, and the prefectural officials and the members of the Imperial Rule Assistance Association were shaking in their boots, afraid their actions might end up placing a noose around their necks. So how did it all end? One night the Yokosuka Civil Engineering Chief, on the orders of the top officials of the prefectural government, put the old monument back in place."

"I'd like to laugh it off as incredibly ridiculous, but we're doing the same sort of thing. Three years ago, in the fall of 1942, the newspapers handed out those labels that said 'American and British Devils,' and we all pasted them up on the pillars in our houses. I wasn't home on August 15th, but my wife said that the first thing she did after hearing the broadcast of the Emperor surrendering was to peel that label off. I think I would have done the same if I'd been home. We're the same as the Kanagawa Prefecture officials. Our nature is to always follow the crowd, changing our ways of acting and thinking in a snap."

"Yes, we're very… adept, aren't we?"

"I suppose that's it."

"But I think that from now on we shouldn't be quite so adept, maybe, which is why I intend to hate the Americans and British for a long time."

Mr. Eguchi looked at me with a startled expression. I am sure that if I could have told him about the Association to Demand Compensation from the United States for their Sadistic and Indiscriminate Bombing, including the Use of Atomic Weapons, his surprise would have changed to agreement, but as we have all pledged strictest secrecy and proffered our formal oath before Atago Shrine, I couldn't. Instead, I "adeptly" changed the subject. "So what happened to that men's division leader after that?"

"He's been lucky. He started a souvenir shop for the Occupation soldiers. It's a great success. Actually, he's my cousin," he said, scratching his head in chagrin.

Yokohama had been very severely hit, too, though the area around the docks isn't so bad. A lot of buildings survived there, and American soldiers stand at armed sentry duty around the entire area. Sentries are posted around all of Kannai.

"It looks like they purposely didn't bomb the harbor. In other words, they knew far in advance that they'd win and decided not to destroy the facilities and buildings that they'd need later," I said, half to myself.

Eguchi murmured in agreement, "They planned it all along. They're very smart."

When I tried to enter Isezaki-cho along a back road, a police officer leaped out and said: "For the next two weeks, this road is closed. Go around." The Eighth Army, under the leadership of General Eichelberger, was building an airport.

"Can they build an airport in two weeks?" I blurted out. I guess I must have sounded rather sarcastic, because the police officer scowled at me fiercely and replied: "Nowadays everyone treats the police like fools. If they say they can do it in two weeks, who are you to doubt it?"

I apologized and turned the three-wheeled truck around.

After driving through an area of single-story houses we came to a huge facility on the left, enclosed in a wire fence. This was the Naval Kanazawa Bunko Museum Fuel Depot. Four U.S. Army sentries were standing at fifty-meter intervals. About two hundred meters

away there was a hill about fourteen or fifteen meters high. This was
the hill behind the depot that Eguchi had been talking about. A field
separated the depot and the hill. Four or five children were walking
about with a bag sewn out of hand towels.

"They're catching crickets and grasshoppers," Eguchi said. "They
dry them, roast them and grind them into powder, which they eat as
a source of calcium. I wish we had a field like this near our house, so
we could catch bugs to eat, too."

Following Eguchi's directions, I stopped the truck. The hill has
two or three indentations, which blocked our view of the sentries
and, I assumed, blocked their view of us, so we could get on with
our task without worrying. Eguchi took a wooden shovel out of the
truck and walked toward an area on a steep incline of the hillside
where some black earth was visible. I took a pole from the truck,
which I was going to use to break through the earthen wall.

We finished in less than thirty minutes. Everything went smoothly.
At one point some of the children came to see what we were doing.

"We're making a big cave here where you can play when it rains," I
said. "So just go back to catching bugs." But instead of going back to
the field, they went home and reported that two men were digging
a hole in the hill, which created a major problem for us on our way
back. So I guess everything didn't go so smoothly after all.

We loaded the seven rice bales into the back of the truck, covered
them with a straw mat, and tied them firmly in place with straw rope.
We started the truck and were driving through the nearby residential
area when suddenly something that looked like a pole with a clothed
tied to its top came toward us. I slammed on the brakes. Looking
more closely, I saw it was an old lady. She strutted up to us like banty
rooster, stood directly in front of the truck and said, in a raspy voice:
"We heard from the children. You've got some contraband that you
dug out of the hill in your truck, don't you? It's probably rice."

I saw women coming out of all the nearby houses. There were
about ten or so, all in their thirties or forties.

"Drop it here and take off," said a voice from the crowd of women.
"Thieves."

"You're the thieves," shouted Eguchi. "I paid a lot for this rice.
It's mine."

"Shall we go to the police, then?" said the old woman who had stopped us, shoving her leathery face into ours. "It's not the kind of rice you want to take to the police, is it?" she said.

"What right do you have to threaten me? Who are you, anyway?"

"We're the members of the Nishi Oshiba District Citizen's Foodstuffs Management Committee." A dirty towel wrapped around her hair like a headscarf, she pressed in on us, sticking her chest out aggressively. "We've been waiting to expose anyone dealing with sequestered navy stores. There are a lot of navy facilities in the area, so we've been on the alert. If we confiscate anything, the residents of Nishi Oshiba will purchase it is at the official price. We don't intend to make any profit, and we'll contribute all the money to the national treasury. We're not thieves."

I remembered reading about people trying to form a Citizen's Foodstuffs Management Committee in the Kurihama district of Yokosuka. The officials weren't pleased about it, and the committee was never actually set up, but a considerable majority of the residents remain strongly committed to the idea. That strange organization apparently exists here in the neighborhood by the Kanazawa Bunko Museum. Kanagawa Prefecture really does have all sorts of things going on.

I whispered to Eguchi: "The longer we stay here, the bigger this is going to get. Let's leave them one bale and get out of here. Pretend we're going to unload them all, and toss one bale off the truck. That's when I'll start the engine. Be careful not to fall off the truck—and be sure none of the other bales fall off, either."

Going to the back of the truck, Eguchi said loudly enough for everyone to hear: "Why do I have such bad luck?" He began to loosen the rope, and I got down from the driver's seat, pretending to help. Taking the bait, the old woman with the leathery skin went around to the back of the truck. Given the times, everyone would be eager to see the contents of a bale of rice, touch it, put a few grains in their mouth, and bite down, even if the rice was raw. If I were in her place, I'd have gone to the rear of the truck, too. Eguchi steadied himself and kicked one bale of rice down off the truck. That anyone could bring himself to kick so precious a thing was shocking, and in that moment I leaped into the driver's seat.

I accepted the sacrificed bale of rice as my own loss, dropped my bale off at my house in Nezu a little after six, and when I arrived at the Nippon Soda Company Employee Dormitory in Akasaka, the seven o'clock radio news had begun. As I accepted an invitation to join the family for sweet-potato gruel, I ventured something that had been troubling me since our escape: "I hope those women don't report the truck's license number to the police."

"Don't worry. I promised to give the truck owner two masu of rice. He'll cover for us."

"How?"

"If the police come to his house and ask him what he was using his three-wheeled truck this afternoon, he'll say: 'On October 12th? That was the day my truck was stolen. But whoever took it left it in the alley behind my house that night. I don't know what they used it for, but at least they're honest thieves, because whatever they used it for, they returned my truck when they were finished.' How's that?"

"You're a very smooth operator."

This year is one of the worst harvests in forty years, since 1905; on top of that, millions of Japanese are returning from overseas. Yet the government has offered no effective strategy for dealing with this food crisis. Recently the Minister of Agriculture caused great public anger when, asked by a reporter what the government planned to do, he answered, "We'll just have to plead with the farmers, and maybe they'll give us some food." He seemed oblivious to the fact that the reason the reporter asked the question in the first place is that the farmers, our only lifeline, don't have any rice either. Since that time I've been telling myself that unless I was very careful, we wouldn't get through the winter. In Tokyo, in particular, about ten people a day starve to death. I'll have to learn to be just as smooth an operator as Eguchi.

Just then Eguchi's daughter, who works at the Daiei movie studios, came home. She is a real beauty, somebody you'd expect to be working as an actress, not in the front office. After saying hello, she smiled and went into the next room, singing a song about a red apple.

"What's that song?" asked one of her sisters.

"It's the theme song for a movie. A new actress, Michiko Namiki, sings it in this film called *Zephyr*. I saw it today. It's a nice tune, isn't it?"

"Is that one of your company's films?"

"Unfortunately, no, it's a Shochiku movie."

Eguchi and I left the house as the radio announced that it was eight o'clock. With the two masu of rice, I drove as far as Rokujizo on Hitotsugi Street, where Eguchi had me stop at a vegetable shop. "The proprietor of this shop owns the truck. Just park it behind the store," Eguchi said, thanking me, then politely bowing his head and entering the shop.

Walking to the Akasaka Mitsuke Subway Station, I passed several people singing the song about the red apple that Mr. Eguchi's daughter had been humming. In the lyrics was the phrase, "Lifting my lips to the red apple." Everyone is hungry.

October 13

When I awoke and opened the sliding wooden shutters, it was so foggy outside that I couldn't even see the eaves of the house next door. An hour later the fog completely lifted, and the sky was clear and blue. Just looking up made me feel refreshed and happy. I invited Mr. Furusawa to take a stroll with me on the grounds of Nezu Gongen.

"I don't deserve your kindness," he said.

"Inviting you for a walk hardly qualifies as a kindness. But Mr. Furusawa, when you were back in Senju, were you especially friendly any of your farmer clients?"

"Well, since Furusawa Enterprises sold farm implements, naturally I knew a lot of farmers. Why do you ask?"

"Maybe we can buy food from them. I'm afraid we won't make it through the winter unless we can make one or two solid connections."

After a pause, Mr. Furusawa said in a strange voice that could equally have been either happy or sad, "I don't think that will be necessary. Fumiko, Takeko and Tokiko at the Imperial Hotel are working hard. Every time they come home they bring back butter, sugar or dried eggs. Those are all precious commodities that can be traded instantly for rice and vegetables."

"But they're just hotel waitresses. I don't think they'll be able to bring that kind of stuff home forever."

"Maybe not. You never know when they might get caught." He paused rather conspicuously before continuing: "It all comes out in the end. No matter how cleverly you lie, it only works for a while, and the truth raises its head from beneath the lies eventually."

I had no idea what he was referring to, but he said it in such a solemn voice that for a moment I was horrified.

"I was on very good terms with one farming family in Kashiwa," he said, returning to a more normal tone. "I'll write down the name and address for you later."

What was it he wanted to say to me? Hoping to understand the meaning beyond his words, I looked intently at him.

"The cicadas are still buzzing," he said, looking at the tips of the branches above and picking up his pace. Indeed, a cicada was making its rasping trill somewhere.

When we got back from our walk, there was a special delivery postcard from Mitsukoshi waiting. It read: "The photograph you recently had taken is ready for pickup. Please bring your receipt." It had to be Kinuko's wedding photograph. The ceremony was May 4th. It had taken five months to develop one photograph, a sign of how short they were on supplies.

Today's "Occupation Forces Security Reports" were about prohibiting U.S. soldiers from certain areas. One of them began:

As is well-known, on October 10 the GHQ issued an order banning U.S. military personnel from beer halls, restaurants,or Special Comfort Facilities under the jurisdiction of the Police Department for the foreseeable future. On October 12, the GHQ sent a following request to the Police Department for its cooperation in enforcing the order issued on October 10 with special thoroughness. Each precinct shall now increase the number of officers patrolling such gathering places, and if U.S. military personnel are observed in banned facilities, quietly suggest that they depart. If they do not, immediately call the MP Liaison Office of the Police Department.

What was particularly interesting to me was the reason the GIs are banned from these facilities, which was explained as follows:

According to what we have been able to find out, there have been several cases in which U.S. soldiers have gone blind drinking methanol alcohol in saké bars and beer halls, and the GHQ has decided to keep the ban on military personnel from such establishments until the problem of adulterated alcohol has been resolved. The reasons for the closing of the Special Comfort Facilities have not been specified, but the failure to carefully monitor the health of the women employed there is regarded as the cause. According to our investigations, approximately 2,500 to 2,600 American soldiers have contracted serious cases of venereal diseases. We will here repeat the off-limits facilities: houses of assignation in the five locations of Oji, Senju, Shinagawa, Yoshiwara and Shinjuku, a total of fifty-seven proprietors; places of assignation in the twelve areas of Arai, Ikebukuro, Hakusan, Mukojima, Shinagawa, Shibuya, Yoshicho, Oku, Tachikawa, Chofu, Juniso and Gotanda, 205 proprietors; Special Comfort Facilities in the six areas of Tateishi, Terajima, Shin Koiwa, Kameari, Musashi Nitta and Tachikawa, 123 proprietors; Special Comfort Facilities in the six areas of Komachien, Korakuen, the site of the former Nihon Gakki, Fussa, Miharashi and Gokurin, six proprietors; the total of the entertainment facilities listed above being located in twenty-nine areas, 391 proprietors. The high-class comfort women who are serving the Imperial Hotel (GHQ officers lodgings), the Sanno Hotel (U.S. military officer lodgings), the Yaesu Hotel (male army civilian employees' lodgings) and the Marunouchi Hotel (United Kingdom military personnel lodgings) are regarded as being free from venereal disease, but it is important to strictly watch the many streetwalkers that infest the areas around train stations between Oimachi and Yurakucho. It would be wise for us to take action before we are instructed to do so by the GHQ.

When I reached the mention of the Imperial Hotel, my stylus slipped. Realizing that Fumiko and Takeko were working in such a dangerous place, I made a mistake and spoiled the stencil.

On my way home from the Documentation Section Annex, I stopped at Mitsukoshi. After receiving the photograph, I put on my reading glasses and looked at the faces of the bride and groom. It is a wonderful likeness. Both Tadao and Kinuko look ready to burst into a smile. When I smiled back, it almost seemed they would reply. But neither of them were alive. An emotion of overpowering bitterness rose from the depths of my being. My vision was clouded and I could no longer see their happy faces.

Dabbing at my eyes with a handkerchief, I walked out the side entrance until I was under the blue sky again. A group of people had gathered there. Standing on tiptoe to look over them, I saw a man in a ragged national civilian uniform sitting up formally on a rush mat. On his lap a little boy of two or three was playing with a boiled potato. A little girl of four or five years of age was seated next to him, perfectly aligned with him. She was looking down, and a cardboard sign was hanging around her neck. It said:

Children For Sale

Shoko (4 years old) 800 yen

Kazuo (2 years old) 500 yen

Someone shouted angrily from the crowd, "No matter how hard things are, it's against the law to sell your children." Another person shouted: "What kind of a parent are you?" The man slowly lifted his exhausted face, revealing dark bags under his eyes, in the direction of the voice. As he did so, our gazes met. Seeing my eyes, still wet with tears, he said in a low but very clear voice: "Thank you."

October 14

Shouldering a rucksack with a bag of rice, I set out for Tamagawa Oyamadai Station on the Tokyu Oimachi Line. Mr. Furusawa said that if we visited the Kobayashis, they might be willing to sell me a *to* of rice, so we headed out there together. When the Furusawas were flourishing as government-approved dealers of fertilizer and agricultural implements—just a half-year ago—they had a friendly relationship with the Kobayashi family, and they had provided them with spades, sickles and other equipment on the quiet.

"Mr. Kobayashi sold the stuff to others, so he made out very well. It's time to get the favor returned today," said Mr. Furusawa confidently. I took a can of dried eggs, soap and cigarettes from one of the care packages that Fumiko and Takeko had brought back from the Imperial Hotel. These are cardboard boxes about fifty centimeters square, containing such daily necessities as needles, thread, buttons, toothbrushes, towels, socks, as well as foodstuffs like soup, biscuits, butter, peanuts, chocolate, coffee and sugar. When the girls first opened one of them, I gasped, a shiver of excitement running down my spine. The U.S. government sends out tens of thousands of these boxes every day for the U.S. staff working for the Occupation, and they are piled up to the ceiling in the unused pool in the basement of the Imperial Hotel. We sure picked a fight with one hell of a country.

The road leading south from Oyamadai Station is uphill. A small shopping district hugs both sides of the street. Most of Setagaya Ward, except for one strip from Sangenjaya to Shimokitazawa, is nearly untouched by the air raids. There is none of that acrid, burnt odor of the bombed-out areas of the city to assault your nostrils there. The row of shops stops at the top of the hill, from where you can see a gently sloping expanse of vegetable fields stretching out to the Tama River, glinting in the sun like a knife. Near the riverbanks is a golden area of rice fields, dotted with the figures of people harvesting the rice. Here and there you can see woods, with thatched roofs and bamboo groves nearby. The weather was beautiful when we arrived, and I could hear chickens clucking peacefully. All in all, it was like a painting. While every morning one or two people are found dead from starvation in the area around Ueno Station, here in the same city, the scene is... bucolic. I found myself half-appalled at this thought, as Mr. Furusawa walked down the other side of the hill and arrived at a large bamboo grove. Seven or eight chickens were scratching about; startled by our presence, they dashed off into the bamboo grove. An old man rushed out of the thatched-roof house armed with a pole. He ran up to us and cried: "Are you back again, you chicken thieves?"

This energetic old fellow was the retired head of the Kobayashi family. "The homeless kids are always coming by and stealing our chickens," he explained by way of a greeting, and led us into the house. Apparently, the kids use fishing poles, baiting the hooks with worms to draw the chickens near. When a bird swallows the worm, they reel it in and stick a tatami needle through the skull behind the ear. They're fast as lightning and they've already made off with ten chickens this month, Mr. Kobayashi said. He opened the sliding door of the living room so that from inside the house he could see the veranda, the yard and the bamboo grove, and he began to prepare some tea for us, remaining very much on the alert for chicken thieves the whole time. Something in the living room flapped lightly in the faint breeze that stole in from the open window. A curtain of 100 yen notes was hanging stretched out across the decorative alcove.

"My granddaughter is getting married," said the old man, pouring the tea. "That's the dowry. Three hundred notes. Well, I haven't seen you for a long time, Mr. Furusawa. Everyone is well, I hope?"

Mr. Furusawa replied that his son, daughter-in-law, his grandson and his grandson's wife had all been killed in the air raids, and only he, his wife and a granddaughter survived. The old man, who had been taking a jar of deep-fried sweets out of a drawer, paused and asked about the store in Senju.

"It took a direct hit. The bomb blasted a huge hole where the store was, and it's become a pond, filled with rainwater. They say people fish for carp there."

Kobayashi quietly placed the sweets back in the drawer and closed it. "Where are you living now?"

"My wife and my granddaughter and I are all staying with Mr. Yamanaka here."

"What a stroke of misfortune," said the old man.

As Mr. Kobayashi continued what he was doing, Mr. Furusawa pressed up to him, bowed his head, and came to the point: "Will you sell us some rice or vegetables?"

I spread out seven 100 yen bills in the shape of a fan on the low table in the room.

"At the black market in Ueno, the going rate for one *sho* of rice is 70 yen. Would you be willing to sell us one *to*?

The old man glanced over at the curtain of 100 yen bills hanging in the living room. "I'm happy to say that we're not short of cash right now. Anyway, if I dispose of any rice or farm produce without my son's permission, he'll raise a fuss."

"How about if I throw in some dried egg powder?"

"We have twenty chickens. Why would we eat dried egg powder?"

"And some American cigarettes."

"My son and I both smoke pipes."

"How about soap?" I slapped several bars of soap down onto the table. "Everyone needs soap."

"We have enough soap to be selling it ourselves." He walked into the living room and lifted up the bottom of the curtain of 100 yen notes. Five or six bricks of laundry soap were lying on the floor of the decorative alcove, tied with a string. The legs of a new sewing machine were also visible. "It's not cheap to marry off a girl. By the way, Mr. Furusawa, you wouldn't happen to have any spades or sickles or anything along those lines, would you?" He came back to the table and took his pipe out of his tobacco pouch. The bowl was brass, but the mouthpiece was silver. "No one would be stupid enough to sell their rice or produce now when we all know the price will go up this winter. But if it was a matter of exchanging it for spades or sickles, well, that's something else altogether."

As Mr. Kobayashi inhaled deeply through his pipe, his neck wrinkled like a turkey's. I don't know what the mental connection was, but at that moment I was reminded of two newspaper articles I'd read. One was about how, according to a survey conducted by the Ministry of Posts and Telecommunications, while the savings accounts of people with salaried jobs were disappearing at an alarming rate, those of farmers were growing; the other was a report from the Treasury Ministry announcing that three times as many rural residents as city residents had restaurant bills of over 10 yen, the cut-off point for adding tax to the bill.

"Shinsuke, do you remember the wedding of my grandson Tadao and your Kinuko in May this year?" Mr. Furusawa turned and asked me. It was such a sudden change of topic that before I could say anything, he went on: "There was as much sukiyaki with Yonezawa beef as anyone wanted to eat, as many Hikari cigarettes as anyone wanted to smoke and a hundred bottles of beer. The souvenir for the guests was two light bulbs, a package of dried squid, a bag of dried sweet potatoes…"

"Yes, and a string of laundry soap."

"Honestly, what's made you think of the wedding?"

"Well, I guess I'd have to call it incredibly extravagant, or, well…"

"The words you're looking for are vulgar and pretentious," said Mr. Furusawa, staring at the curtain of 100 yen bills. "I realized that when I saw those."

"I don't see how it's any of your business," said the old man, tapping the tobacco out of his pipe bowl into the hibachi. "All we're doing is sending off my granddaughter into marriage with a splendid ceremony, with money we've earned. We don't care what anyone else has to say about it. During the war, the government not only robbed me of all the rice I grew but took away my son and grandson, too. What's wrong with us enjoying the springtime of success that has finally come our way?"

Mr. Furusawa was already out in the yard by this time. I scooped the objects I'd placed on the table back into my rucksack.

"It would be rude to let you go without a little gift, so let me give you some advice," said the old man as I rushed to shove my feet into my wooden sandals. "Catch some grasshoppers and crickets on your way back to the station. A lot of people from the city come here to do that. We don't eat them, so take as many as you want."

Without responding, I stepped into the yard. I caught up with Mr. Furusawa just after I'd passed through the bamboo grove. He was carrying a strangely full rice bag, which seemed to be clucking excitedly.

"It was a very friendly bird," he said, "and it followed me this far. As far as I'm concerned, it's a little payback for all we did for them during the war."

The train ride home turned into quite a rumpus. Startled by the sound of the train, the chicken started thrashing wildly about in the bag and Mr. Furusawa, taken by surprise, dropped it. The bird stuck its legs out of the opening and began dashing around the train car. The other passengers saw nothing but a bag running around, which of course was even more surprising. Fortunately, it was a Sunday afternoon and the Oimachi Line train was fairly empty. If the bird had started running about a crowded train at Ueno or Shibuya, it would have been snatched up in an instant. I mean, it only takes two hours for a bicycle stolen in Ueno to show up in the black market by Shinbashi Station, freshly repainted in bright blue enamel; three hours after a double-breasted suit is pinched in Shinjuku, it's being hawked in the crowds of Asakusa, refashioned into a single-breasted version. There are dozens of similar instances like this every single day. In five minutes, a loose chicken would find itself being served up to a customer on top a bowl of noodles. We felt bad about it, but we got off at Kuhonbutsu, the station after Oyamadai, walked behind a temple near the station and strangled the unfortunate fowl.

We started cutting it up as soon as we got home. As we were tenderizing the meat with a wooden mallet over a pickle-pressing stone used as a cutting board, a B-17 Flying Fortress took up its daily course circling over Asakusa and Hongo at an altitude of about five hundred meters. From a giant speaker attached to the tail, music poured down on us, together with the roar of the plane's engines. The day before yesterday it was Schubert's "Unfinished Symphony," yesterday was Beethoven's "Pastoral," and today was Offenbach's "Orpheus in Hell."

While I appreciate the American's attempt to comfort our devastated spirits with beautiful music, how does it not occur to them that up until quite recently the roar of a B-17 Flying Fortress was always accompanied by a storm of incendiary bombs, splitting the air with a piercing sound like a thousand shrilling flutes? My first reaction to any plane flying overhead is fear, not comfort, and I felt a powerful urge to dash to the dugout shelters in Ueno Park. It's one of the cases where you really mean it when you say, no, honestly, the thought is more than enough.

Yet, today's musical selection was oddly appropriate: we below suffering hellishly from hunger, as Orpheus's gift of music poured down from the skies above.

October 15

This morning was soup with chicken meatballs again. It's the second time in a row since last night, and given the times we live in, I'm nothing if not grateful, but the reason that it was left over is that none of the working women returned home for dinner last night, which troubles me a little. They all seem to be very busy—Fumiko, Takeko, Miss Makiguchi and Miss Kurokawa working as waitresses at the Imperial Hotel, and Sen-*chan*, Tomoe and Tokiko Furusawa working at the Accounting Office of the Water Department—but they do have a home, and I think they should come home from work every day. They shouldn't be staying overnight at their jobs unless it's absolutely necessary.

"We're acting as the foster parents of Miss Makiguchi, Miss Kurokawa and Tokiko Furusawa in particular, so you should lay down the law to them," I said to my wife on my way to work. "We have a duty to supervise the daily lives our two daughters and those three girls. We shouldn't shirk that until they've each found their proper place in life."

"They're all adults, so let's just let them do as they please," replied my wife briskly, beginning to clear the table. The radio and newspapers are talking a lot these days about women's suffrage, but it seems to me that may have influenced my wife to become a bit too lax in her dealings with the girls. I'm going to have to have a serious talk with her about it soon.

Clerk Kobayashi came into the room carrying the day's portion of letters to General MacArthur and "Occupation Forces Security Reports" while I was cleaning the built-up wax from the interstices of the mimeograph backing board with an old toothbrush. "Can you write in smaller characters today?" he asked.

"Yes, I suppose I can if I try. Why?"

"Paper shortages. I'd like you to write it in characters small enough to fit everything on one page." He recounted the roll of sheets of newsprint as carefully as if they were 100 yen notes. There were fifty sheets, which he placed softly on the desk. "For the time being, you can't waste a single sheet."

"The time being?"

"Until the Economic Police succeed in raiding some warehouse and confiscating a stash of black-market newsprint."

"That's discouraging."

"Yes, it's pitiful. How is the Documentation Section supposed to operate without paper?"

"Actually, I was planning to ask you for twenty or thirty sheets of newsprint today."

"Impossible. Why do you want newsprint, anyway?"

"I stitch it together into a notebook for my diary. Writing in my diary is my sole pleasure in life. I haven't missed a day since this May—aside, of course, from the time I spent in the prison at Yokaichiba after you had me arrested."

"It must be brimming over with nasty things you've written about me."

"No one will ever know. I don't even allow my wife to read it. When I die, I'll have it placed in my coffin, and it'll accompany me to the next world. So you have nothing to worry about. And I also say some nice things about you in it, too."

"I still think there's something sinister about a person who keeps a secret record of events," said Kobayashi, with an expression as if he had a bitter taste in his mouth, leaving the room. Having failed to get my hands on the newsprint I wanted, I placed the stencil on the backing board in a disgruntled mood. Today's "Occupation Forces Security Report" was:

At 8 P.M. on October 13, Saturday, children stole several cardboard boxes containing cigarettes and canned goods from a Jeep parked near Yurakucho Station while the U.S. soldier driving it chatted with a streetwalker. The soldier noticed the boys, chased after them, and caught them, and after spanking them two or three times released them. When he had finished talking with the streetwalker for another ten minutes or so and tried to start his Jeep, the engine wouldn't fire correctly. Upon inspection he discovered that the lid to the gas tank had been stolen and the gas was mixed with urine. Similar events occurred this weekend in Shinbashi, Ueno, Shibuya and Shinjuku, all attributed to homeless children. The GHQ Civil Information and Education Section Colonel H.W. Allen, Assistant Adjutant General, has asked how long the Japanese government intends to ignore these homeless children, so we had better round them up right away.

There was also a letter to Emperor Moatside. It was rather long:

Your Excellency. I humbly give three cheers for the long life of Your Excellency, General MacArthur, and pray for the health of all the military staff of your honorable nation. I am little more than a nameless old man, but I pride myself on one thing. I have a great knowledge of onomancy, and last night, I applied my skills to interpreting your name and arrived at the following results, which I would like to share with you. I will be deeply honored if my humble efforts should please you.

If we were to write your family name in characters, we would use the three characters *matsu* (pine), *ku* (forever) and *asa* (morning). In Japan, the pine is a felicitous symbol. For example, we celebrate the advent of the New Year with pine-bough decorations. We also place pine boughs in the decorative alcove or other conspicuous locations at weddings and similarly festive occasions, a custom that derives from the fact that the evergreen pine has been revered as a symbol of faithfulness and long life since ages past. Before the war, there were popular restaurants throughout the town that served broiled eel, and the ranks of pine, bamboo and plum were used to indicate the quality of the food. It goes without saying that pine was the top quality. Looking further back into the past, during the Edo period, *matsu* referred to the top-ranking woman in a house of pleasure. As you can see, the pine represents good fortune, constancy, long life, quality and excellence.

Ku, or for ever, means enduring. And the last character, *asa*, meaning morning, also has the meaning of "reign," as in the reign of Emperor Suiko or the reign of Emperor Kanmu. In other words, the last name Matsu-Ku-Asa can be interpreted as meaning: "His Excellency General MacArthur is the most excellent and superior of rulers, and his reign will endure and prosper for ever."

As I read it I muttered to myself, "Good grief, not another of those garbled, nonsense theories," and I stifled a yawn. This kind of letter, employing the same lame theories and flattery slathered on thick enough to cut with a knife, has been especially common lately. Just last week I had cut a stencil of an obsequious letter signed by someone with the title, "Gifu Prefectural Assembly President." He wrote MacArthur's name with the characters *matsu* (pine), *ka* (auspicious) and *sa* (aid), but the rest of the letter was nearly identical to this one. This game of writing Western names in characters was very popular both before and during the war as well. I remember a radio broadcast by a Ministry of Education official named Nobuo Odagiri on the *Inspirational Lectures on Current Affairs* program in the fall of 1941, four years ago, suggesting that Roosevelt's name means "loose belt," and that Japan had nothing to fear from a country whose president was as useless as a loose belt.

The reason I remember this particular broadcast is that the second half was really something. The voice of the Ministry of Education official suddenly rose in pitch and he began to shout:

Recently I visited the Fifth Municipal Middle School and asked fifty first-year students to write out the lyrics to our national anthem, *Kimi ga yo* [The Emperor's Reign]. The results were shocking; only twenty-three, less than half, were able to do so correctly. It's unforgiveable that the younger generation, who will shoulder the future of the Empire, should be so ignorant! They wrote especially ridiculous versions of the line, "until a pebble grows into a boulder." Some wrote, "grows ever bolder," which might be understandable, in a way. Another wrote, "grows into a bowler"; others wrote "glows in two colors," or "groans on their shoulders." Five students actually wrote "go into boaters." What's that supposed to mean! But I'm not sitting here in front of the microphone to criticize the students of the Fifth Municipal Middle School. Do you, the adults listening to this program in front of your radios right now, the subjects of Imperial Japan, know the lyrics to our national anthem, *Kimi ga yo*? That's what I'm asking. "May the glorious reign of our Emperor endure for a thousand, even eight thousand generations. We pray that it will flourish until a pebble grows into a boulder, and even longer, for moss to grow on that boulder." This is our national anthem! Although "a thousand, even eight thousand generations" expresses an infinity, even that is not long enough for our Emperor's reign, so this is followed by the lyric, "until a pebble grows into a boulder," adding yet another infinite expanse of time, and even that is not enough, so this is followed by the lyric, "with moss to grow on that boulder." *Kimi ga yo* is a hymn dedicated to the eternity of the Emperor's reign, but in our country, the Emperor, the realm and the people are not to be considered separately. The three are one. When the Emperor flourishes, the realm flourishes, and when the realm flourishes, the people flourish. In our national polity, loyalty to the Emperor is also loyalty to the nation from the people who are praying for its success and prosperity. Since times of old, loyal ministers have always loved their country. This unchanging and eternal spirit fills *Kimi ga yo*. But only by correctly remembering the lyrics can one apprehend this lofty spirit.

To get back to my original topic, while the war was going on, it was popular to come up with derogatory or funny ways of writing MacArthur's name, such as with the characters for "serious" "pain" "penniless" "scoundrel" (*ma-ku-a-sa*) or writing Churchill with the characters for "spill the tea" (*cha chiru*). This way of thinking spread to all sorts of baseless theories why we were certain win the war. One of these theories was that as long as battles were fought at night, Japanese soldiers had a clear advantage over the Americans because Americans were white, which made them easy targets, while we Japanese would blend into the night. Another was that in an air war, we Japanese had a clear advantage because our short legs fit better in aircraft seats than white people's long legs, and we're also used to crouching over the privy. Army and navy headquarters were releasing this kind of this kind of "information" on a daily basis, so it was only natural that these "explanations" would become a popular trend. I, too, fell prey to this nonsense, spreading the reasons for our victory around every time I heard a new one. But after August 15th, I stopped. Plenty of Japanese, including those in very high places, however, are still carrying on the nonsense, only now to curry favor with the enemy generalissimo. I'm sorry, but to me this is far uglier than an ancient geisha, her face powder slathered on like wet plaster, mincing in front of a client, cooing and shaking her hips in an attempt to be seductive. I pushed my stylus through the motions of copying this letter with a feeling as disagreeable as if my crotch were infested with scabies, our national blight.

In the second half, the letter suddenly picked up steam:

As my interpretation of your name indicates, you are a great leader. I believe that the Japanese would be incredibly fortunate if Japan could be ruled by such a world champion as yourself and the United States of America, the land that gave birth to you. It matters not to me whether Japan is assimilated into the United States or whether it remains under its rule in some other form. I do not say this out of any desire to sell out my country, but because I deeply love my country, and I believe that either union with or becoming a protectorate of the United States represents salvation for the Japanese people, in their exhaustion and degraded moral condition. If we could be governed by Your Excellency and your nation, all of the difficult problems confronting us—the food shortage, energy shortage, traffic problems, degeneration of morale and the threat of communism—would be instantly resolved. Whether we keep the Imperial system or not is an issue of no significance. In fact, it could be solved by having you become our emperor. What becomes of the Imperial system is of little weight when compared to restoring security to our lives. Your Excellency, have pity on the Japanese people. Though you may reprove me for saying so, if Japan is allowed to remain on its present course, the Communists will gain power and we will become a nation of Reds.

One page of the letter remained to be copied. Glancing ahead to the name and address of the letter writer at the end, I was as astonished as if a bomb had exploded right next to me. The letter writer was "Kiichiro Aoyama, Nezu Miyanaga-cho, Hongo Ward." That our Neighborhood Association leader, an Imperialist to the marrow of his bones, could have written such a letter to Emperor Moatside! I threw the stylus down and stood in shock, staring at the rusty brown seal in blood at the letter's end.

"Have you finished the stencils?" asked Kobayashi, his voice bringing me back to my senses. Somewhere in the distance I could hear the roar of a B-17 Flying Fortress.

"I'll be done in five more minutes."

"You're a little slow today!"

"My mind wandered. I'm sorry."

"Will it be all right if I wait? Oh, by the way, I found some spare newsprint on one of the bookshelves of the Documentation Section." Kobayashi pulled three sheets out of his jacket. They were a bit yellowed and very wrinkled.

"They were stuck at the back of the shelf, so they're not in perfect shape. This should last you ten days, right?"

"It'll last maybe three days."

"You must write an awful lot in that diary."

"I have nothing else to amuse me. I humbly accept your kind offering. Thank you," I said, starting to cut the stencil again. The roar of the approaching plane was accompanied by the notes of Beethoven's Fifth Symphony. Suddenly there was applause, whistling and foot stamping from the MPs' room above. It was like they were holding a celebration.

"The Americans really seem to like the Fifth Symphony," said Kobayashi, looking up toward the ceiling. "One out of four times, that's what they broadcast on those flights."

"There's a reason for that," said the former proprietor of the Hongo Bar, who was carrying a tray with enamel cups of coffee. "The *da-da-da-da—*, *da-da-da-da—* at the start is the Morse code sign for 'V.' 'V' stands for 'Victory.' So, the Fifth Symphony is a victory song. That's why they get so excited whenever they hear it."

There was plenty of sugar in the coffee, and it roused my spirits sufficiently so I could finish copying the Neighborhood Association leader's letter.

October 16
Today I finished my work in a half-hour, because there were just two "Occupation Forces Security Reports."

On October 12, the GHQ ordered the Metropolitan Police Department to supply them with fifty luxury passenger automobiles. The Metropolitan Police established an automobile supply service at the Transport Office, and they are inspecting some twenty or thirty automobiles each day looking for suitable prospects, but only one or two a day pass muster. As of today, October 13, we have only been able to secure thirteen automobiles. The GHQ has expressed their dissatisfaction with these results, and on October 15 they repeated their demand, noting that there are plenty of automobiles in perfect condition driving about on the streets of Tokyo and expressing disbelief that we were unable to fulfill their request. In response, the police will be sending out six-man squads to the various areas of the city to confiscate automobiles, but in addition all police officers are called upon to be on the lookout for automobiles on their way to and from work, and if a suitable candidate is spotted, write down the license plate and report it to the Transport Office. If the automobile passes inspection and can be handed over to the GHQ, the officer who reported it to the Transport Office will receive a reward of udon noodles or dried squid.

Major Victor Clark, a civilian official with the 386th Unit stationed in the Kumagaya District, visited the Kumagaya Police Station on October 14 and communicated the order that the prefectural residents should immediately be instructed to begin driving on the right side of the road. He also communicated the decision that the Army would not punish soldiers of the Occupation Forces for selling cigarettes, as follows.
Operators of vehicles of the Occupation Forces will be driving at higher speeds and driving on the right side of the

road, following American custom. As such, Japanese drivers (including bicycle riders) must heretofore obey the same rule. Pedestrians, however, may continue to walk on the left as they have always done. They should avoid any potential collisions by making mutual visual contact in advance.

Since cigarettes are the private property of the soldiers of the Occupation Forces, the army will not punish soldiers for selling them. The sale of any U.S. Government goods, such as gasoline, tires, clothing, food (including candy), is, however, prohibited.

The order to begin driving on the right is quite likely to be adopted in Tokyo as well, so please begin making the necessary preparations to implement this with all relevant officials so that no one is taken by surprise if this instruction is suddenly received.

I was chuckling to myself when Kobayashi walked in.

"Cars on the right and pedestrians on the left. If a collision seems imminent, they avoid it by 'mutual visual contact in advance.' I like that part. It's so optimistic. Also, the fighting's over, but nothing has changed, has it?"

"Yes, everyone's bellies are still empty," said Kobayashi perfunctorily, as he ran his gaze over my mimeograph. "Prices just keep going up. That hasn't changed, either."

"I wasn't talking about that. I was talking about the confiscation of vehicles. A half-year ago, the police decided they wanted my junker of a three-wheeled truck, and to get their hands on it, they sent a Special Higher Police detective and had me thrown into prison." Of course, that Special Higher Police detective was none other than Kobayashi. "Even with the fighting over, the Police Department is still in search of vehicles. During the war, it was for the Emperor, and now it's for the Moatside Emperor."

"I'd like you to go down to the storage area in the basement to help out," said Kobayashi, completely ignoring my sarcasm. "I'll join you as soon as I distribute these reports."

In the dark basement area beneath the main building I found a man, his nose and mouth covered with a cloth tied around his head, slapping books energetically together, producing a smoke-like plume of dust that was visible in the shafts of light from the small windows near the ceiling. My eyes quickly got accustomed to the gloom. The storage area was about the size of two elementary school classrooms, and it was filled to the ceiling with bundles of books tied with string.

"I'm the proprietor of the Kondo Bookstore in Kanda. Thank you for your patronage," the man said, removing the cloth over his nose and mouth to greet me. There was the flash of several gold teeth as he spoke. He had a large, red, rather misshapen face, somewhat resembling a yam. When I told him that Kobayashi had sent me to help him, he was delighted. "Excellent! You help me sort the books. Marx goes here, and Eitaro Noro there. Lenin's over here. It's quite simple, really."

"So they're all Red books, then?"

"Yes, all the books here are Red books. At the beginning of this month, on MacArthur's orders, three thousand political and thought criminals were released. Since then customers have been flooding into Kanda asking for books by Marx, Hajime Kawakami and Kiyoshi Miki. I've been visiting police headquarters and stations all over town, knowing that if any books had survived, that's where they'd be. Look," the proprietor of the Kondo Bookstore in Kanda said, pointing to the area of the storage room, "the entire used-book section of Kanda can keep going for a half-year on what they've got here."

"So these books belonged to…"

"Yes, they were confiscated from people arrested for thought crimes. Or more accurately, they're a portion of the confiscated books."

"A portion?"

"Yes, when the police made arrests, they confiscated all the books the suspects had. Among them was a lot of books that had nothing to do with communism or socialism—there were plenty of works of literature, poetry collections, books of natural history and science. As a matter of fact, that made up the majority of the confiscated books. Those books were sold long ago. One of my good customers was a prosecutor with the thought police, and he used to come and sell me a truck-full every month. The books down here are the books that we couldn't put in the shops until now... Oh, here's another Malthus," he said, tapping the book in his hand. "The Special Higher Police couldn't tell the difference between Marx and Malthus."

"Are they that different?"

"Marx is the founder of communism, and Malthus is a staunch critic of socialism. They're as different as snow and mud, east and west. No one wants to buy Malthus these days."

The book by Malthus, whose title, *An Essay on the Principle of Population*, was printed in gold leaf, was tossed to the side, and the proprietor of the Kondo Bookstore in Kanda busied himself with another pile.

"I'm really not qualified to sort the books, so I'll just do the dusting," I said, proceeding to slap books together.

Suddenly the proprietor stopped what he was doing, seeming to be dumbstruck by something. He was staring intently at the flyleaf of a book. Maybe he'd come across a rare find. He began to tremble. "It's *his* writing..." he said, his face pale as if he had seen a corpse, all traces of his former cheeriness gone. "Look, look at the writing."

A page of manuscript paper was tucked behind the flyleaf. The first three lines were blank, but the fourth began: "It is often said that the special feature of Shinran's thought was that it humanized Buddhism. That's probably true, but—" And it ended there. The rest was blacked out by a huge X. Each component of his *kanji*, his Chinese characters, was written with sharp, straight strokes, and they seemed stretched out vertically—giving the appearance not so much of a clumsy hand as that of a child. In the blank space to the left was written in large characters: "People end up where they belong."

In the lower left corner, in small characters, was the name "Kiyoshi Miki." Even I recognized the name, and I let out a gasp myself. I certainly don't know much about philosophy, but I did know that Miki regularly contributed articles to the newspapers, and he also wrote editorials on current events for the magazine *Bungei Shunju*, which I used to read. In an old issue, he wrote a very stimulating article in which he used what had happened to Riichi Yokomitsu as a starting point to take the police and the bureaucracy thoroughly to task. I remember that I even told my wife she should read it, promising her it would give her the same refreshing uplift you get from drinking a glass of sharp cider.

This is what happened: Riichi Yokomitsu, the "god of novelists" who is very popular with young people, was stopped by the police late one night. They refused to let him go even when he told them his name, but when he announced that he was a professor at Meiji University, he was released. Everyone knows that Riichi Yokomitsu is a great novelist, while hardly anyone knows that he's a university professor. Nor does his university position have much to do with his real profession. But when it comes to the police, the hundred relevant matters speak less than the one irrelevant one. They care more about social status and titles than the actual contribution someone is making to Japanese culture. And in some cases, even being a university professor wouldn't be enough; you have to be teaching at a national university instead of a private college. In many situations, minor administrative officials in the bureaucracy outrank a private college professor. Miki wrote that until we rid ourselves of this reverence for bureaucrats, until we stop going with the tide without asking questions, and until we stop blindly worshiping material goods and wealth, real national solidarity is nothing but a dream. Miki's argument gave extremely satisfying vent to the outrage and frustration we feel on a daily basis, pushed around by the police and petty bureaucrats.

Sometime after that article, Miki disappeared from the pages of the magazine. But from October this year his name appeared in newspapers—in an obituary: At the end of September, forty days after the war came to a close, the philosopher Kiyoshi Miki died in Toyotama Prison. The cause was acute nephritis brought on by a heavy infestation of scabies. The newspapers said that he was discovered at three in the afternoon, collapsed on the floor of his cell, his clothing bloodied. It was believed that his scabies were so uncomfortable that he scratched himself until he bled.

"Whenever Mr. Miki visited my store, he emptied out my shelves," the proprietor of the Kondo Bookstore in Kanda said. "That's how much he loved books. He stopped by after his philosophy lectures at Bunka Gakuin and his work at Iwanami Shoten publishers. Did you know that the famous Iwanami Paperback Library series was his idea?"

I did not.

"He had a very sharp sense about publishing. He used say: 'I'm the excitable type. I get easily carried away. I want to stop having to come up with all these book ideas and publishing programs and just shut myself away in my study.' He used to have noodles delivered to my shop for lunch—always ordered the same thing: he called the wheat noodle soup topped with toasted rice cakes 'power udon.' He used to say to himself: 'I'm strong, I just have to believe in myself.' I remember his dark expression and gloomy voice, and the way he ate, not like he enjoyed food but with this kind of determination that he had to eat for fuel. Using your mind to make a living—there's nothing worse."

The bookshop proprietor softly closed the book and lifted it to his forehead in a gesture of reverence. It was a difficult-looking book with a title something like *The Transition from the Feudal to the Bourgeois World View*.

"I'll give it to his daughter," said the proprietor, dabbing the corners of his eyes with a handkerchief. "I'm certain this possession of her father's will only make her weep, but she should have it."

"What was Miki like?"

"He lost two wives, and had a sad family life. His daughter is still a student. He must have deeply regretted leaving her behind."

No doubt that had to be true. I can't compare myself to a great philosopher, but I know that the only thing that kept me going when I was locked away in that prison was my wish to see the faces of Fumiko and Takeko once more. Kiyoshi is a man, and I knew he'd be able to take care of himself, but I felt a powerful duty to make sure that my daughters found good partners for the rest of their lives, and that kept me alive. It would have been tragic to me if because of failing health or some other circumstance I were to die before my daughters' future was assured... I know that the ghosts of middle-aged men aren't the stuff of romantic fiction, but that's what I'd become, remaining in this world as a spirit to protect and watch over my daughters. Thinking of how that philosopher father must have felt, worrying about his daughter's future as he scratched his scabies scars in his prison cell, I was overwhelmed by a terrible sadness, and I sunk to the floor.

But what was the meaning of that single line the philosopher left behind in this book—"People end up where they belong"? Did he have a premonition of his death even before he was arrested? Maybe it is simple-minded to interpret this as a parting message to his daughter, but maybe it meant something like, "I'm joining your mother now, and eventually you'll be here with us as well, so until that time live your life to the fullest and enjoy it while it's yours."

I thought about this all day. One thing for sure, though: Miki should have been released from prison immediately after the war ended. If he had, he wouldn't have died of scabies. What were his friends doing in those forty days he remained in his cell? Why didn't the magazines and newspapers he wrote for petition for his release? Of course you could say tat everyone had their hands full just taking care of themselves, and that would apply equally to me as well, I know.

October 17
As I was coming home from the Metropolitan Police Department after noon, I happened to run into my neighbor, Mr. Takahashi, who works in the photography department at the newspaper, in front of our house. "How's work?" I asked.

He replied with his usual embarrassed, wry smile, "Up to now I've been taking photographs of Special Forces pilots before they set out on their final missions, but lately it's all Communists—street demonstrations led by Communists who're being released almost every day from prison. From August 15th, the heroes of the people have switched from the Special Attack Forces to members of the Communist Party. I'm having a hard time adjusting to this change."

"Just don't think about it too deeply, and make us an interesting paper to read."

There are all kinds of stories about daily life that could be written up. For example, at the Fifth Municipal Middle School that Kiyoshi attends, all the kids wear their most beaten up wooden sandals to school, and when they take them off at the door, they hide one of the sandals in a place that's as hard to find as possible. This is the only way to avoid having your sandals stolen! Now that kind of article would be not only interesting but useful. Or, for example, I heard from the former proprietor of the Hongo Bar that lately there's been a rash of all-too-clever bicycle thefts. The thieves ride away on the bicycles to the farthest reaches of places like Katsushika or Setagaya. Those who are really confident of their stamina go as far as farm villages in Chiba or Saitama Prefecture. They have a picnic, and then they exchange the bicycle for food in the village and return to Tokyo by train... I was telling Mr. Takahashi these things because I wanted to be friendly, but then he suddenly interjected: "As a matter of fact, I was just thinking of quitting."

This is not a subject to be discussed standing on the street, so I invited him into our house and asked my wife to bring us some coffee from our Occupation Forces care package. Mr. Takahashi has been a generous, good neighbor, and he loves coffee, and I thought it might comfort him.

"I think the entire top management of the *Asahi Shimbun* will be replaced," he began. "The president, the chairman, all the directors, and the heads of the editorial department, as well as the managing editors will all resign. I'm one of those who've been responsible for the photography department, so I bear responsibility, too..."

"What responsibility?"

"For the war. If you're going to expose the culpability of the military cliques, the business conglomerates, the politicians, the bureaucrats, and all the others who kept the war going, you need to start with yourself."

"I think the newspapers tried to do their best. You might say you bear the culpability for what went on the front page. But if readers looked closely at the second page, they could always find small articles that were calling out softly to them, 'This war is a mistake,' 'The declarations of the Imperial headquarters are lies,' 'It's entirely possible that we're going to lose.' If you look back on it now, that's very clear."

"But criticizing the war secretly in back-page articles is pointless," Mr. Takahashi said without hesitation. "From the time of Konoe's New Political Order, the press was completely in bed with the government. The formation of the Axis alliance of Japan, Germany and Italy, which became one of the causes of the war, was our last opportunity to criticize the government, but we never made a single attempt to resist. We need to take responsibility for that... I spent all my time taking pro-war photographs. That seems to be jinxing me now, and whenever I try to take a photo of a Communist Party demonstration, it's out of focus. I don't know how to explain it, but it's like my shame at what I've done makes my finger shake when I'm going to press the shutter, and I just feel unable to take photographs anymore. I don't have the right to do so..."

"But what will you do when you quit?"

"I suppose I could get by for a time by selling off my equipment. I wouldn't mind setting up on a street corner and taking photos of GIs, but I'm not sure if I could do that with my shaky shutter finger," Takahashi sighed.

As my wife brought in the coffee, she listened to our conversation. She sat down next to me, her shoulders drooping.

At this, our door slid open, and Nezu Miyanaga-cho Neighborhood Association leader Kiichiro Aoyama poked his head into the entryway. "What a wonderful smell. May I join you? And Mr. Takahashi, you're here, too. That's perfect. I have something I want to talk to both of you about. This is very convenient."

My wife went to the kitchen, presumably to bring this miserable hypocrite a cup of coffee. I would rather serve him a brew made from the dirt under Takahashi's fingernails, I thought angrily to myself. "What was it you wanted to talk about?" I asked flatly.

"Kiyoshi Yamanaka and Shoichi Takahashi seem to have an irresistible attraction to objectionable literature, don't they?" he said, pulling a scrap of paper from his jacket. "This is the third time." He spread the paper out between Takahashi and me. "This was stuck to the glass sliding door of the Neighborhood Association Office."

I read the writing carefully. It was an obvious parody of the Imperial Rescript on Education. For future reference, I record it here:

Know ye, our neighbors: Our Neighborhood Association leader, assiduously collects Neighborhood Association dues and devotes himself to cutting off our official rations. Our Neighborhood Association leader excels at eating, excels at talking, while secretly cadging our Neighborhood Association dues, from generation to generation persisting in this vice. This is the glory of our Neighborhood Association leader, and herein lies the source of our destitution.

Ye, the poverty-stricken residents of our neighborhood: Having separated you from your parents, causing the loss of your brothers and sisters, carrying on an adulterous affair, selling out his friends, bearing himself in obstinacy and narrow-mindedness, extending his corruption to all, abandoning learning and cultivating the black market, and thereby trivializing his intellectual faculties and becoming crazed with gambling; furthermore, advancing the practice of thievery, evading the police; cultivating brute force and filling his rucksack; should emergency arise, he runs down the railroad tracks, and thus supports runaway inflation. So shall he not only sell his wife's clothing, but also the apparel of his forefathers. These are the deeds of our Neighborhood Association leader.

In the way of relations, our Neighborhood Association leader's wife is sickly, and our Neighborhood Association leader has long kept his distance from her. Dissatisfied with this, he has acquired a mistress, whom he keeps out of the neighborhood, and plays beddy-bye with. One day playing paper-rock-scissors with his mistress, he was discovered by his wife, and humbly begged her forgiveness.

The 17th day of the 10th month of 1945

—Strictly Anonymous

As the Neighborhood Association leader slurped his coffee from the cup my wife had coweringly handed to him, he smiled and sucked his tongue in satisfaction, the sound gradually shifting to a clucking. "Since this October, there have been strikes at five schools—Mito High School, Saitama Prefectural Chichibu Agriculture and Forestry School, Shizuoka Prefectural Fujieda Agriculture School, Kanagawa Prefectural Yokohama Commerce and Industry Training School and Hokkaido Otaru Industrial School. Oh yes, I forgot another very important school—the sixth would be the private Ueno Girls' High School, where the students striked because they accused the principal of illegally disposing of the produce grown in the school's vegetable garden. Can you believe it? Girl students on strike. It's a sign the world is coming to an end."

Having drained his cup of coffee, the Neighborhood Association leader flipped the cup over in his palm of his hand, tapped it, then noisily licked up the last drop. Everyone in the neighborhood knows that when he makes a theatrical flourish of this sort, trouble is brewing and he is ready to drop one of his bombs. Which, of course, he did.

"Two foolish junior high school students living in our neighborhood went to join the girls in their strike. Kiyoshi and Sho," he said, his voice rising. "The girls surrounded the vegetable fields with something they called a 'picket line' and sang school songs. An Azabu Middle School student accompanied them on the harmonica and a Fifth Municipal Middle School student stood nearby waving a red flag. Looking into the matter, I've learned that Sho has been absent from Azabu Middle School these past five days. Kiyoshi has been absent from Fifth Municipal Middle School for the last four. Did you know that?"

I looked at my wife, who shook her head slightly. But Takahashi was not to be cowed. Glaring angrily at the Neighborhood Association leader, he launched a counterattack: "You said, 'looking into the matter,' if I heard correctly. Is that the job of the Neighborhood Association Office? Do you think you're an officer of the Special Higher Police? In case you haven't noticed, they've been disbanded."

"Our job is simply to keep an eye out so the children living in the neighborhood don't go astray. Now I don't mean to imply that Kiyoshi or Sho are bad kids. But they do tend to get a bit carried away, especially when they decide to do things like support the strike at the girls' high school or write something inflammatory like this and stick it to my door. You have to bear that in mind and watch over them accordingly. This is a good opportunity for you. And let me just add that I do not have a mistress or anything as fine as that. It's true that every three or four days I visit a woman in Komagome Sendagi-cho, but I want to point out that she is the daughter of my dear teacher, she is a very unfortunate soul who lost her husband at the southern front during the war and her children during the air raids..." As the Neighborhood Association leader spoke, his eyes took on a dreamy haze and grew red in the corner—just like the poem in the Hundreds Poems by a Hundred Poets game: *Though I would hide it, In my face it still appears—My fond, secret love…* "All I do is bring her something useful I happened to come across in the black market. I leave it at the door of her apartment and I leave without a word. At any rate, if your boys do this kind of thing again, I'll be forced to take the appropriate steps."

"I'll give Kiyoshi a severe warning," said my wife, bowing deeply and taking away the cup. I dipped my head very slightly, following my wife's lead. Takahashi swung his air-raid supplies rucksack over his shoulder as he rose and, after bowing to all three of us, said, in a quiet voice: "I don't have the courage to scold our children. You seem to think the world's coming to an end, Mr. Aoyama, but we adults are the ones who brought this about, and I don't think we have the right to be telling the children what they should or should not be doing," and with that, his head down, he left with deliberate slowness, as if counting each step.

"You intellectuals are always doubting yourselves, so even your children take advantage of you," said the Neighborhood Association leader, pulling a Lucky Strike out and lighting it. My wife brought out an ashtray. Tossing the burned match into it, the Neighborhood Association leader said: "By the way, Mrs. Yamanaka, have you thought about what I was telling you earlier?"

"Yes, it's a very nice offer, but…"

"She hasn't turned it down, has she?"

"As a matter of fact, she has."

"How stupid. What a waste."

"I'll go get the photograph for you." As my wife went into the living room, the Neighborhood Association leader said, his face flushed, "Shinsuke, you need to speak to your daughter about this again. After all, this fellow is the eldest son and heir of a landowner in Setagaya. The house is 50 *tsubo* in size. With people in Tokyo living in barracks, old bomb shelters, or at best an apartment four-and-a-half mats in size, a 50 *tsubo* house is like a palace. Not only would she be marrying into wealth but the young man is a university graduate and an official at the Foodstuffs Corporation. As you know, they're the ones who handle all the rice and barley that the government buys from the farmers. She'd have white rice three meals a day, as well as for snacks. It's a life of luxury, a dream come true…" He stood up suddenly. "How can she refuse? I don't understand."

"Neither do I," I said. "After all, this is the first I heard of it."

"What!" the Neighborhood Association leader leaned forward in such surprise that I thought he might knock me over. "She refused this proposal without consulting you? Is that acceptable to you?"

"Apparently she doesn't feel like getting married yet."

My wife returned with a large portrait photograph. I grabbed it from her and looked at the man, who was very handsome, maybe two-thirds as good looking as a younger Shin Saburi.

"He fell for Fumiko at first glance. He ran into her in Hibiya, followed her, and rushed into the Neighborhood Association Office, pleading with me to introduce her to him. All Fumiko would have to do is give it the nod, and this would be settled tomorrow."

"I'm very sorry," said my wife.

"Or is it perhaps that there's some reason that Fumiko can't get married at all?" asked the Neighborhood Association leader, his eyes narrowing sharply.

I was surprised to see my wife lift her eyes to meet his inquiring gaze head on with a nasty glare of her own. "None at all," she said," spitting out the words in a voice as cold as ice. This was the first time I'd ever seen her like this.

After the Neighborhood Association leader left, I could only sit there dazed.

"There's nothing to worry about," she said to me. "Fumiko said she didn't want to marry him, so that's the end of it… I'm sorry, though, that I didn't talk to you about it. Please forgive me." She began picking up the cups and returned to her normal demeanor.

"I don't know what's going on in this house lately. I want to talk to Fumiko about this. Will she be home this evening?"

"She comes back tomorrow night," my wife replied as she was putting away the dishes.

October 18

I'm writing this at seven in the evening on Thursday, October 18, 1945. I'm the only one at home. My wife, the Furusawas and Kiyoshi are all staying at my late brother's house down on the corner.

It's extremely quiet; the only sounds are that of the rain striking the shingles on the roof and the scratching of my glass pen nib on the Western-style writing paper I'm using. But I'm only quiet on the outside, while my heart within is rocking as violently as a tiny boat about to be crushed by pounding breakers. I have an earthenware teapot with water in it next to my desk, and every minute or so I raise it to my lips and take a sip of water. I'm worried about what might happen if I don't cool myself down. I'm still burning with anger inside. If I don't control it, I feel I'll explode into a ball of flame, go dashing to the house on the corner, and start beating my wife and daughters. And then I'll have to take Kiyoshi on again, who will leap in to stop me. My right hand is hurt, making it difficult to write. That's my punishment for hitting my wife and daughter. The back of my skull is throbbing. When Kiyoshi leaped on top of me and flipped me over, my head hit the charcoal brazier; I wonder what that bump is punishment for? At any rate, on this October 18th of the year of Japan's defeat, the Yamanaka family has been destroyed. What I am about to write may transcend the boundaries of a diary, but nevertheless, record it I must. Because this diary is me. This hundred or more pages of Western paper stitched together is Shinsuke Yamanaka. How can I possibly lie to myself?

I would like to record today's events with accuracy, to the best of my ability. I may be in a state of utter confusion, not knowing what my purpose for living from tomorrow onward will be, but by clearly recording today's events, perhaps I'll discover some kind of guide for my future. In writing in my diary up to now, on numerous occasions I've been able to discover order, principles and laws that had been concealed from me in the confusion of daily life. I pray that this will be the case again today.

As always, this morning just before seven I left home with three roasted sweet potatoes given to me by my wife. Walking at a leisurely pace as I ate, I arrived at the Metropolitan Police Documentation Section Annex at precisely 8:10. The annex is located in a corner of the first floor of the First Cavalry Division Military Police Barracks, within the police headquarters. Separated by a thin wall is a kitchen where the meals of the MPs are prepared. My daily routine is to stick my head into the kitchen and ask the cook for some water and any coffee that has been left by the MPs, and, if I'm in luck, one or two Lucky Strikes. I sharpen the point of my stylus on the unglazed bottom of a teacup and use an old toothbrush to clean the wax that has accumulated on the backboard of the mimeograph. I have decided to walk from Nezu to Sakuradamon to avoid the crowded morning trains. I don't mind the crowding myself, since it's something we all have to put up with, but I'd be in terrible trouble if my eyeglasses got knocked off my face and trampled. There isn't any place to buy eyeglasses, and even if there were, they would cost several dozen *to* of rice. So I choose safety over convenience, and I walk to work in the mornings. The right temple of my eyeglasses fell off some time ago, and I've replaced it with a shoestring. That makes riding in a crowded train extremely risky.

After eating the second sweet potato this morning, just as I was arriving at Yushima Kiridoshi-cho, I saw a Jeep approaching from the direction of Okachimachi, women's voices raised in laughter pouring out of it. I was fond of three-wheeled trucks and automobiles from the days of my youth—which is why, for a period toward the end of the war, I decided to try to earn my living by driving a three-wheeled truck—and when I saw one driving by I always stopped in my tracks and watched until it was out of sight. I am especially fascinated by Jeeps, and whenever I see one of those little four-wheel-drive vehicles that can make their way easily through mud and up steep slopes, I feel deep in me that our defeat in the war was inevitable. To over generalize, I think you can say that the Japanese Empire was defeated by three weapons: the B-29, the atomic bomb and the Jeep. The three sacred regalia were as meek as a lamb compared to those three. While thinking those same thoughts somewhere in the back of my mind, I watched the Jeep come closer, until a voice called out, "Mr. Yamanaka, good morning!" as the Jeep pulled to a halt right in front of me.

It wasn't a GI in the driver's seat. He must have been some kind of officer because he had three medals on his right sleeve that looked like arrows pointing upward.

"We have meat," said a woman in the passenger seat, smoking a cigarette as she turned toward me, dangling a package tied in string before my eyes. It was Sen-*chan*! In the back seat, Tokiko Furusawa, Kayoko Makiguchi and Kumiko Kurokawa smiled slightly at me—

their smiles a complex mix of emotions—three parts astonishment and three parts embarrassment, two parts guilt and two parts affection.

"When will you be getting home?" asked Sen-*chan*. She had been the mistress of my brother who lived down the street and who had been killed by a firebomb. I suppose by some reckoning that justified her familiarity, but this wouldn't do. She was in her early thirties and had striking features, while I was a man in his late middle age, with half-white hair and broken eyeglasses. The combination was certain to attract undue attention.

"The same as always. About half past one."

"Well then, we'll start the sukiyaki at about three. Make sure to come home hungry!"

"These days, I'm always hungry."

"Don't eat some cheap rice gruel or stew on the way home."

"I won't. I'll look forward to it," I said, even as I wondered how those working for the Imperial Hotel and those for the Japan Water Company happened to be in the same car.

"We stopped by the employees' cafeteria at the Imperial Hotel for breakfast," Sen-*chan* said, reading my mind. "Tomoe went back to the office. She's going to be away from work for ten days, so she has a lot to do before she leaves. I told her to just take off and go to her children in Onahama and we'll take care of everything, but she's very dedicated."

"If only she could wait another ten days."

The news lately is that from October 25th, it's going to become much easier to buy train tickets. During the war, there were numerous travel restrictions under the banner of insuring transportation for those making important trips, and those regulations were still in place. One of the policies, "Investigations into Reasons for Traveling," was extremely unpleasant. At the ticket window, the station official would ask you in the condescending manner you might use with a small child, "Where is it you want to go?" and proceed into inquiries of whom you were going to see, veering off in such strange directions as whether you had a daughter, whether the daughter was a beauty, and if she was "easy" or not, until you couldn't tell if you were buying a train ticket or being grilled by the police. It would have been one thing if, after submitting to this humiliating procedure, you were able to buy a ticket, but in most cases it ended with a rude dismissal along the lines, "If that's your business, you can take of it through the mails. Don't bother us with such petty requests in the future." But recently the Occupation Forces' insistence on the "democratization" of everything seems to have made its way into the heads of the top officials of the Tokyo Railway Administrative Office. With the jumbled excuse that now, after the war, there are no longer any "important travelers" and the business of all travelers is equally urgent, they'd decided to cancel the "Investigations into Reasons for Traveling" policy, but from now on, apparently, it's going to become incredibly easy to buy railway tickets. The requirements that you apply to purchase tickets a day in advance and specify which train you will be traveling on will be also dropped. All you'll have to do now is go to the station and get a form for buying a ticket, present your form at the window and buy the ticket.

"Was Tomoe able to get a ticket?" I asked.

"She used a connection, so it's okay," replied Sen-*chan*, her cheeks vibrating like gelatin with suppressed laughter. "You seem to have a thing about Tomoe, don't you?

"Don't be silly. Where are my daughters?"

"It looks like they haven't finished work yet," said Kayoko. "But I think they'll be home by noon."

"All right. Speaking of which, I have a favor to ask. Please don't drive all the way back to Miyanaga-cho in the Jeep. We have the neighbors to think about, you understand."

"Of course we do," said Sen-*chan*, who had been communicating something to the soldier in the driver's seat with words and gestures, turning toward me and handing me a small package. "We always have them drop us off at Shinobazu Pond. We're not stupid."

"Remember, Mr. Yamanaka, it's sukiyaki tonight," said Tokiko, waving from the Jeep as it sped off. I raised my hand in response, which was when I was astonished to notice myself holding some Lucky Strikes. Cigarettes are an important tool of the trade for someone who cuts stencils. A lighted cigarette is extremely useful in making a correction on a stencil. The first thing you do is take the round end of the stylus and press it over the error, smoothing it out, and then you hold the lighted end of a cigarette close to it and melt the wax. The wax pours into the area on the stencil where you had made a mistake, and you can write over it. That's why people who cut stencils light a cigarette each time they make a mistake. The cigarettes of recent times, however, that are made by taking apart old cigarette butts and rerolling the tobacco don't burn smoothly, and they often go out before you can ease the lit end carefully toward the stencil. But Western cigarettes are an ideal "correction tool" for stencils. You light one, take a puff, melt the wax and then pinch out the cigarette again. You can repeat this process ten times with a Western cigarette. So I was grateful for the Lucky Strikes. Pocketing them, I headed south down Shohei Street, passing through this single road cutting through the scorched landscape. Sukiyaki—the last time I'd eaten sukiyaki was at Kinuko's wedding on May 4th. And the time before that was the autumn before last.

On that occasion, Gen the tailor had heard the rumor that the Suehiro Restaurant beyond Matsuzakaya in Ginza 6-chome would be serving sukiyaki. We rushed over there, and in spite of the fact that an hour and a half remained before the restaurant opened at 5 P.M., about fifteen people were already waiting in line. In those days, an important part of a man's work was to get out and about at least once a day, even if he had no specific thing to do. If he could find a place to get something to eat and put something in his stomach before returning home, his portion of the food rations would be freed up. In other words, a family's survival could depend on a man's success at eating out. This is no less true today than it was then.

As a matter of fact, things are much more desperate now. Delivery of food rations is much more delayed, and even women can be seen wandering the streets in search of something to eat. At any rate, by 5 P.M. the line behind Suehiro stretched about two hundred meters. There was a scuffle when the restaurant opened. The restaurant staff came out and told us to enter in order from the back of the line. Those in the front of the line shouted angrily that they'd been waiting for nearly two hours. Gen and I were among those shouting. When shouting wasn't enough to appease us and we started pounding and kicking the wall in front of the restaurant, a man in a grimy kitchen apron came out and said: "Are you proud of having waited for two hours? You're not doing any honest work, you're just loafing around, so you can wait that long. The ones who came rushing up just before we opened, on the other hand, have been working hard all day, and they're hungry. They're the kind of people I want to feed. A day without work is a day without food—that's Suehiro's policy."

What he said made sense, and we all calmed down. We gave up on sukiyaki and treated ourselves to a plate of "substitute sushi" at Yoshino Zushi across from the Kabukiza Theater instead. It was sushi made from vegetable pickles on top of rice mixed with wheat noodles, but it turned out to taste better than we expected. The next day we left a little before five and attached ourselves to the end of the line at Suehiro. Things unfolded the same way they had the day before, so Gen and I got our sukiyaki. It was a fairly nasty mess consisting of one slice of nearly spoiled meat, a wedge of tofu and five or six konnyaku noodles twined together; in no way could it have been described as good. We decided to treat ourselves to a 10 yen coffee at Monami to get the taste out of our mouths, but the coffee was just as strange. We paid our 10 yen, were given a coffee cup, and were told to serve ourselves from a bucket at the back of the shop. The bucket contained a liquid that, while it was indeed the color of coffee, tasted like bitter hot water. Nor was there any ladle. When I asked about that, I was told to dip the coffee cup directly into the bucket. Since they didn't even have a ladle, you can bet there was no saccharine or shiso sugar. So we sat there sipping this lukewarm, bitter liquid whose only resemblance to coffee was its hue. And there was a line even for this coffee shop, which tells you how desperate we were then. Things actually are still the same.

Me and Gen really did get around a lot, looking for places to eat and drink. Wherever we went we were met with long lines. The longest were at restaurants selling rice gruel and government-managed bars, and Gen and I often stood in line in front of one of those waiting for it to open. One of our regular spots was the government-managed bar in Ginza, on a back street on the west side of Ginza 5-chome, because while the snack served with drinks at the other places was a pinch of salt, here they placed a smidgen of pickled greens in the palm of your hand. And, perhaps because they had an especially good ration quota, you managed to actually get a drink all the way up to about the four hundredth person in line. At other places, the saké ran out in the early three hundreds. For that reason, we often found ourselves heading over to Ginza 5-chome in the afternoon. The bar opened at 5:30, and it was always a little exciting just before opening. When the door opened, a wave of anticipation ran through the waiting crowd, lined up four abreast. One of the bar's employees would come out and begin counting the people in line. At a certain point he would stop and say, "All right. Up to here," and give that person a placard to hold that said "Up to here." Then he'd turn to the rest of people in line and say, "Today's quota is 150 bottles of beer. I'm sorry, but we'll have to ask you to go somewhere else."

Everyone in the four lines behind the man with the placard would sigh and disperse in all directions. Hoping against hope, they rushed to the nationally managed bars in Kyobashi, Shinbashi, Tsukiji and Hibiya. But then there were always five or six, sometimes ten men who would stride purposefully through the disintegrating crowd and step boldly into the bar. This was the scene every evening. Once I asked a waiter who those men were, who drank two or three bottles of beer when the limit was one per person; the waiter said that they were from the police, as he gave me a large helping of pickled greens—maybe as a bribe to keep quiet.

One day in February of this year, Gen was in the line holding the "Up to here" placard. We'd just made it, and we were very pleased for ourselves. As we were chatting, the man behind me whispered, "I'll give you 10 yen for that placard."

The man, of very distinctive appearance, was pushing a tightly folded 10 yen bill toward Gen. He seemed about the same age as me, and he was wearing a necktie and a warm-looking camel colored coat. The nearly universal dress for men was the khaki national civilian uniform, a military cap and a black coat, so this man stood out like a shining golden eagle among a flock of crows.

"Wow, that's cashmere, isn't it?" said Gen, who was a tailor and more interested in the fabric than the 10 yen bill. "I'd love to be able to work with material like that."

"I really need a drink tonight," the man said. "My son's remains arrived today."

"If that's the case, you have a right to have a drink," said Gen, passing the placard to the man in the cashmere coat. "Put your money away. You shouldn't waste 10 yen just to drink a beer that costs 2 yen 5 sen. Just stand with us."

Grateful, the man in the cashmere overcoat recited a poem written secretly by Roppa Furukawa, called "In Line."

In line
In line
Standing silently in line
at the rice gruel restaurant;
Men, women, and children, all in line
Impossible!
That anyone in this line
should be feeling good.
This is what the war has brought us.
In line.
In line.

The man in the overcoat was the vice president of the Roppa Furukawa Theatrical Troupe, it turned out.

It was Tokiko's single utterance—"Remember, it's sukiyaki tonight"— that triggered this series of memories about eating and drinking over the last year or two, thanks to which I was able to walk all the way to the Metropolitan Police Department without getting bored. But a chance remark of Kobayashi when he came to pick up my work suddenly connected with Sen-*chan*'s saying cavalierly that they always had the soldiers drop them off at Shinobazu Pond, and I was hit by a wave of surprise as thunderous as if a cannon had been fired off next to my ear. Kobayashi had mumbled, "The Imperial Hotel has become a nest of high-class pan-pan girls. The MPs don't like it, but I don't see why they have to take it out on us at the Police Department. The hotel isn't Japan any more, it's like a part of America…"

Suddenly, the countless tiny doubts and questions that had been building in my mind since I got back from the prison coalesced into one great mass.

"The Imperial Hotel a nest of pan-pan girls?"

"That's right."

"But the regular girls working there are still safe, right?

"The waitresses and maids get recruited. Most of the female employees end up as high-class prostitutes."

"But only important people lodge at the Imperial Hotel. In the military, generals and high-ranking officers. And on the civilian side, high-ranking State Department officials and members of investigatory committees sent from the U.S. They're all high-quality people, aren't they?"

"You know how they say, 'Good character stops at the navel.' You know that Roppa Furukawa song—something about in a bath, a lord and his retainer are both naked. The same thing with a general or a common man when they take their pants off."

"You're being cynical. On my part, I have never been with a woman other than my wife since I got married. And the same is true even before I was married. I never played around. Of course there are times when I find myself attracted to another woman, but I've never done anything about it, knowing it would be a mistake. Some say it's hard to control yourself, but it's not really hard at all."

"What is it you're trying to say?" asked Kobayashi, his eyes flashing like they did back when he was a Special Higher Police Officer. "Why are you so determined not to accept the facts?" His eyes narrowed to slits cut by a razor.

"I've always believed that the female employees of the Imperial Hotel, at least, were protected from becoming the playthings of the Americans. I mean, it's Japan's top hotel, and the people staying there aren't hicks from Texas…"

"Well, all I know is what I was told. I was investigating a case at the Imperial Hotel, where I was told that most of the women working there as 'female employees' or 'companions' are actually prostitutes—especially the companions. Really, I'm not making this up. This is what I was told."

"Okay, okay. So what was the case you were investigating?"

"A silly case of battery. A naval lieutenant commander by the name of Hall was staying at the hotel and he wanted to give his companion some onions, so he went and got a case of onions from the kitchen.

The Imperial Hotel manager, First Lieutenant Morris, found them and shoved the companion, accusing her of stealing hotel food. The lieutenant commander was angry to see his companion treated that way, so he punched the manager in the jaw. It turned into a brawl, until the MPs arrived.

"I learned that the lieutenant commander is the Official in Charge of Language and Language Simplification at the GHQ's Civil Information and Education Section. Apparently he's urging that all Japanese writing be outlawed and we switch to *romaji*—which is Japanese written out phonetically in Romanization. But his own Japanese is excellent. When I asked through an interpreter for the name of his Japanese companion, he replied in perfect Japanese without a moment's hesitation: 'That's my personal business. I was the one who tried to steal the onions and who hit the manager. She had nothing to do with it.' That's kind of admirable, in a way."

After Kobayashi left me, I stayed in my chair for a long time. I think I may have remained there motionless for about an hour, until finally I came to a decision. I left the building through the service entrance, walking toward Ginza. If I asked at the office of the Japan Water Company on the fourth floor of Kyobunkan, at least I could find out if Sen-*chan* was lying.

I got home a little after three in the afternoon. No one was there. I immediately went to the house down the street. The sliding wooden shutters were closed. This was done to prevent the smell of meat cooking from wafting outside. When the children at Nezu National Primary School exercised, more than half of them fainted from malnutrition; the family knew that if the neighbors found out that we were eating meat, there would be hell to pay. When I opened the door, the air in the room was a warm miasma of the odors of meat and onions. It angered me, and I found myself holding my breath. Two braziers, a large one and a small one, were set up in the living room, with a large clay pot resting on each. My wife, who was stirring the ingredients of one pot, looked up, greeted me and said, chopsticks in hand: "Ah, we were just starting."

"You should come home when you're supposed to," said Kiyoshi, sitting by the further brazier. "Put yourself in my place, kept waiting like this."

The Furusawas, seated on either side of Kiyoshi, gently reproved him for the way he addressed me. Sho Takahashi, seated across from Kiyoshi, turned toward me and bowed. Those four were at the one brazier, while the others were seated around the one near to me. Tomoe was kneeling on a sheet of newspaper, slicing onions on a chopping board.

"What are you standing there like a post for?" asked Sen-*chan* from her place beside my wife, adding more meat in the pot. "A dragonfly will land on your head."

"There's another brazier for you, Father," said Fumiko, who had her back to me until then, rising and walking into the kitchen. A thick bandage was wrapped around her left hand. The sight of its pristine whiteness cut into me like a knife, and from that moment, I don't clearly remember what happened. I do know that I shouted: "I know that Sen-*chan*, Tokiko, and Tomoe aren't working at the Accounts Department."

I remember that Tokiko burst out crying and ran upstairs, and that Tomoe began to sob, her tears falling on the onions she was slicing.

"Who wants to eat the onions of a man who's trying to force us to write our language in *romaji*? Fumiko! That's your boyfriend, isn't it?" I remember kicking over the brazier that she was carrying in. My right toe still aches.

"Why did you hide it from me?" I demanded, slapping my wife across the face. That set Kiyoshi off, and he leapt on me, shouting: "How dare you strike Mother?" I fell flat on my back, hitting the back of my head on the brazier.

"Who do you and all the rest of the grown-ups think you are? With all that big talk, you start a war, and then you lose it and roll over for MacArthur!" cried Kiyoshi, choking with heavy sobs as he sat astride my chest. That I clearly remember.

"You all try to get out of it, saying you were deceived, but every time you came back from a block group meeting, you'd be all excited about this 'sacred war.' You're irresponsible. You're ridiculous. You're gullible and weak. That's why my sisters have to do what they do."

Though I was consumed with anger when I started writing this, now that I've finished recording the day's events, I'm almost calm.

Perhaps it's the effect of writing, or maybe it's what Kiyoshi said that has had an effect on me, somewhere deep down inside. Whatever the reason, this father's modest hope that his daughters would get married and live happy, ordinary lives is definitely not going to come true. That much is certain.